Praise for the novels of ~~Kate Furnivall~~

Shadows on the Nile

"An enjoyable, page-turning blend of history, mystery, and love that will intrigue readers." —*Booklist*

"Furnivall laces this fast-paced historical adventure with surprisingly poignant interludes that ultimately connect to the family mystery at its heart." —*Publishers Weekly*

"A dazzling and energetic story with historical mystery [and] huge twists . . . The author demonstrates an incredible understanding of the period." —*BestChickLit.com*

The White Pearl

"Furnivall weaves the dramas of her characters into the threads of history, creating an engrossing read on many levels."
—*Publishers Weekly*

"[Furnivall's] ability to strike the perfect mood and evoke a time and place is wonderful." —*RT Book Reviews*

"A wonderfully evocative tale." —*The Sun*

The Jewel of St. Petersburg

"Furnivall skillfully intertwines historical fact with a heartfelt love story . . . A delight for [her] fans and equally a joy for those new to her work." —*Publishers Weekly*

continued . . .

"Gripping, elegant, and fierce, this is a classic war-torn love story, and Furnivall's best yet."
—*Library Journal*

"[Furnivall's] vivid descriptions and the shimmering beauty and treachery of the era combine with a memorable love story that will speak to readers' hearts and minds."
—*RT Book Reviews*

"Furnivall portrays a country in dreadful conflict, with the grinding poverty of the masses fueling rebellion against the privileged classes. A must for readers of *The Russian Concubine* and Furnivall's *The Red Scarf*."
—*Booklist*

The Girl from Junchow

"An engrossing adventure that sweeps readers in lush waves of drama and romance."
—*Library Journal*

"Furnivall deftly evokes the details of a bygone era."
—*Publishers Weekly*

The Red Scarf

"This romantic confection can make a reader shiver with dread for the horrors visited on the two heroines imprisoned in a labor camp, and quiver with anticipation for their happy endings. Furnivall shows she has the narrative skills to deliver a sweeping historical epic."
—*Library Journal*

"Furnivall again pinpoints a little-known historical setting and brings it vividly to life through the emotions and insights of her characters. Beautifully detailed descriptions of the land and the compelling characters who move through a surprisingly upbeat plot make this one of the year's best reads."
—*Booklist*

The Russian Concubine

"I read it in one sitting! Not only a gripping love story, but a novel that captures the sights, smells, hopes, and desires of Russia at the dawn of the twentieth century, and pre-Revolutionary China, so skillfully that readers will feel they are there." —Kate Mosse

"The wonderfully drawn and all-too-human characters struggle to survive in a world of danger and bewildering change . . . caught between cultures, ideologies—and the growing realization that only the frail reed of love is strong enough to withstand the destroying winds of time." —Diana Gabaldon

"This stunning debut brings the atmosphere of 1920s China vividly to life . . . Furnivall draws an excellent portrait of this distant time and place." —*Historical Novels Review*

"The kaleidoscopic intensity of British writer Kate Furnivall's debut novel, *The Russian Concubine*, compellingly transports us back to 1928 and across the globe to the city of Junchow in northern China . . . Furnivall's novel is an admirable work of historical fiction." —*Minneapolis Star Tribune*

"Furnivall vividly evokes Lydia's character and personal struggles against a backdrop of depravity and corruption." —*Publishers Weekly*

BOOKS BY KATE FURNIVALL

The Russian Concubine
The Red Scarf
The Girl from Junchow
The Jewel of St. Petersburg
The White Pearl
Shadows on the Nile
The Far Side of the Sun

The Far Side of the Sun

Kate Furnivall

BERKLEY BOOKS, NEW YORK

THE BERKLEY PUBLISHING GROUP
Published by the Penguin Group
Penguin Group (USA) LLC
375 Hudson Street, New York, New York 10014

USA • Canada • UK • Ireland • Australia • New Zealand • India • South Africa • China

penguin.com

A Penguin Random House Company

This book is an original publication of The Berkley Publishing Group.

Library of Congress Cataloging-in-Publication Data

Furnivall, Kate.
The far side of the sun / Kate Furnivall. —Berkley Trade paperback edition.
p. cm.
ISBN 978-0-425-26509-3 (paperback)
1. Women—Fiction.   2. Diplomats' spouses—Fiction.   3. Bahamas—Nassau—Social life and customs—
20th century Fiction.   4. World War, 1939–1945—Bahamas—Nassau—Fiction.   I. Title.
PR6116.U76F37 2014
823'.92—dc23
2014009050

PUBLISHING HISTORY
Berkley trade paperback edition / October 2014

PRINTED IN THE UNITED STATES OF AMERICA

10 9 8 7 6 5 4 3 2 1

Cover design by Erika Fusari
Cover photos: Back Beads © Todd Holbrook, Dream Theory Studios/Getty Images;
Tropical island surrounded by lagoon © Sakis Papadopoulos/Getty Images
Back cover image courtesy of Shutterstock
Interior text design by Laura K. Corless.

To April
with all my love

ACKNOWLEDGMENTS

I am enormously grateful to my wonderful editor, Jackie Cantor, to the fabulous Pam Barricklow, and the whole team at Berkley. They are superb. And thank you to Martin Karlow for his expert attention to my manuscript.

To my brilliant US and UK agents, Patty Moosebrugger and Teresa Chris, thank you for always being whirlwinds of skill and energy and kindness.

Very special thanks to my twin sister, Carole Furnivall, for coming with me to explore the Bahamas. It was like being ten years old again and on a thrilling adventure together. Unforgettable.

Huge thanks to the gang at Brixham Writers for listening to my woes and making me laugh at them.

Thank you again to Marian Churchward for turning my scrawl into a beautifully typed manuscript and for leaving me some biscuits.

As always, mega thanks to Norman for a constant supply of inspiration and coffee, as well as for his passion for each book I write.

Chapter 1

Dodie

"Help me . . ."

The words slipped out of the darkness, thin and weightless, barely denting the sultry warmth of the night air. In the unlit street at the wrong end of Nassau, Dodie Wyatt halted, nerves tight.

"Who's there?" she called out.

A soft groan. A stifled curse. A rustle of movement. Then stillness settled down in the shadows once more.

"Who's there?" she called again, sharper this time.

Silence. It was the stark kind of silence that only exists after midnight. The smell of the ocean was rolling in over the Bahamas, leaving its salty breath to linger on the beaches and in the humid corners of the city. Dodie knew that if she had a scrap of sense she would march straight to the far end of the street without stopping, but his words—that fragile "Help me"—had snared her. She moved toward the spot from which the groan had risen.

"Say something," Dodie urged, as her eyes scoured the ink-black spaces. Her voice sounded ridiculously calm. "It's too dark for me to see you. Where are you?"

There was no response. Her pulse kicked uneasily.

She was on her way home from her late shift at the Arcadia Hotel, where she worked as a waitress. Her feet ached, the kind of ache that she couldn't ignore anymore because she had been standing for twelve hours straight and the only thing she wanted was to climb into bed and sleep. But now a stranger was asking for her help.

"I'll help you," she said, not sounding quite as calm as before as she moved closer to the wall. "Just show me where you are."

A hand seized her ankle.

* * *

The wind drifted up the street in fits and starts, making a shutter rattle and a dog bark in a nearby yard, and even at this hour of the night the gust of air was warm and scented with tropical flowers. It was just enough to persuade the clouds to shift, so that moonlight spilled into the narrow space between the houses, and for the first time Dodie could make out the figure at her feet.

A big man was slumped against the wall like a rag doll, his chin sunk on his chest, his legs stretched out in front of him in the dirt. Dodie could see a head of bushy brown hair and a pale gray suit that was crumpled and stained. One of his hands scrabbled jerkily on the ground, trying to reconnect with the ankle she had snatched away, but his other hand lay clamped to the front of his white shirt. It didn't look so white anymore because a black stain was spreading rapidly from under his palm. For a moment Dodie hesitated. She knew that if she knelt down beside this man, trouble would enter her life. She had grown up with trouble and could smell it at fifty paces, which was why she had avoided it ever since she first came to the Bahamas six years ago, when she was only sixteen and had no more sense than a hummingbird.

"Please . . . ?" he whispered.

She dropped to her knees. "You're hurt."

"Help me . . . to stand up."

Dodie's hand wrapped itself around his free hand and his fingers clung to hers.

"You're hurt, you must stay still. Don't move. You need an ambulance."

He lifted his chin and looked up at her, his skin silvery and bloodless in the moonlight. His eyes were deep sunken holes in his head and made her uneasy, and though he moved his mouth, no sound was coming out. She couldn't tell how old he was—in his forties perhaps, although there were too many shadows to be sure.

"Don't try to speak," she said gently. "There is a telephone box back up on the main road, so I'll just—"

"Don't."

"But you need a doctor."

"No ambulance." The word came out in bits. "No doctors."

"But you need help."

They both stared down at the hand clamped to his white shirt, just above his waistband, at the black stain that had grown to the size of a dinner plate, feathery streaks reaching out like tentacles across his chest. He raised his eyes to her face and his mouth dragged in a labored breath. Silently he shook his head.

Dodie didn't delay further, she rose quickly. "Don't move. You need to be in hospital, so I'm going to call a—"

His hand seized her ankle again. "No."

"Yes."

"No!"

The word stopped her. She crouched down beside him once more and lifted his hand into hers. It was as cold and clammy as one of the toads that burrowed under her shack at night. "I'm Dodie," she said softly. "What's your name?"

"Morrell."

"Well, Mr. Morrell, we both know you need to be in hospital. You're bleeding badly. Why shouldn't I call an ambulance or at least a doctor?"

He sighed, the life seeming to ebb from him with each of his slow measured breaths. "They will kill me," he murmured.

"What?"

His voice sounded dry and exhausted and she noticed it had an

American drawl from the deep south, perhaps from Alabama or Tennessee. "The person who stuck a knife in me"—she saw his eyes roll in his head so that their whites caught the moonlight—"will be at the hospital. Looking for me."

"Why will they be doing that?"

"To finish what they started." He exhaled heavily and she smelled rum on his breath.

"Were you in a fight?"

"Of sorts."

"We have to get you bandaged quickly."

He grunted agreement, but slowly his chin started to descend toward his chest. It was at that point that Dodie thought about walking away. Back to her quiet routine where nothing disturbed the monotony of her work at the hotel and her walks on the smooth white beach. She knew she should leave this Mr. Morrell to rest here on his own. *They will kill me*, he'd said. And her? Would they kill her too? A lone young female would be nothing to them. Her hand unconsciously sought out the tender section on her own body, the soft spot just below her ribs, and sat here, fingers splayed in protection. But the wounded man started to slip sideways down the wall and Dodie quickly pushed her hands under his armpits to hold him upright, but the weight was more than she'd anticipated.

"Come on now, Mr. Morrell. Time to stand up."

His head lifted.

"I'll help you," she promised.

The empty shadows of his eyes fixed on hers for an age and she could feel his distrust crawl onto her skin, but he nodded. "Yes."

It was going to hurt, they both knew that. She leaned over him, easing his feet toward him, so that his knees were bent. She fixed her arms around his chest, clenching her fingers together behind his back, and inch by inch she dragged him to his feet. He didn't cry out. Didn't moan. But his breathing grew loud, almost a growl, and when he was standing upright, swaying on his feet despite her support, she thought it was the end of him.

⁂

Progress was agonizingly slow. Sometimes the pauses were so long that Dodie feared the man's heart had paused too, but no, just when she thought he was giving up, he would start up again—left foot, right foot. His arm across her shoulders was muscular, an arm that did things, unaccustomed to lying helpless, and the grip of his fingers was tight, snarled up in her cardigan.

Neither spoke. Their steps were slow and labored. Fears were racing through Dodie's head and every sound in the darkness, every movement in the shadows, sent a chill through her. She struggled to work out what to do, where to take him, how best to get him away from here. So when they reached the end of the road she steered him left, ducking down a dim and scruffy street. It was flanked by warehouses where the smell of the ocean was so strong it ousted the smell of blood in Dodie's nostrils, but there would be no one around at this hour.

Why, Mr. Morrell? Why does someone hate you enough to stick a knife in your gut?

She shuddered, her heart racing as she listened for footsteps behind them, but when she glanced nervously over her shoulder, the shadows were empty. As they walked, Morrell muttered sometimes, small incoherent noises that pinned him to her and they drew soothing sounds from her in response, a brief wordless conversation. Her arm tightened its hold around his thick waist and she watched carefully where he put his feet. He was wearing neat white loafers that stood out in the darkness.

"Not far now," she told him.

Dodie's instinct was to hide him, to find somewhere he would be safe. So she chose a little-used path that headed in the direction of the beach, leaving behind the houses and the hazy neon lights of an occasional late-night bar where people might be searching for him. It seemed to take forever but finally they reached the point she was aiming for—a sandy track that branched off and twisted away through a dense fringe of coconut palms edging the shoreline. She breathed in the warm humid air with relief.

"All right, Mr. Morrell?"

"All right," he grunted.

She was killing him. He didn't say it, but she knew it was true. She was killing him. She couldn't go on.

"Enough of this," she announced.

With her heart thumping she edged him over to one of the palm trees that looped drunkenly over the track, its trunk a slender black streak against the velvet of the night sky.

"Sit down."

He needed no second bidding. His knees buckled and he sank to the ground in an untidy sprawl. With care she sat him so that his back was propped against the slope of the trunk, checked that he was still breathing, and hoped that he wouldn't fall over.

"You'll be safe here," she assured him.

There was a silence, a moment when neither breathed, both wanting to believe her words, before he murmured with elaborate southern courtesy, "Thank you kindly for your help, ma'am."

"I'm leaving you now."

He managed a nod. "Good-bye."

"Don't worry, I'll be back."

She removed her cardigan and tied it tightly around his middle. There was a smell to him now, not just the blood or the rum, a smell of something bad. It was the sour stench of terror. She recognized it because she had smelled it on herself the day her father had waded into the wide turquoise waters of a Bahamian beach and announced, "Wait here, poppet. I'm going to swim back to England."

In the lonely darkness under the palm trees, Dodie felt a rush of sorrow for this wounded stranger and wrapped her arms around him, while above their heads palm fronds shuffled in the salty breeze that came exploring off the ocean.

"Trust me," she whispered in his ear.

"There's no need to lie. You've helped me this far and I'm grateful."

She shook her head. "I'm only going to find you some transport, Mr. Morrell. You can't walk anymore." She sat back on her heels and patted his shoulder awkwardly, aware that he didn't believe her. "Just sit tight. I'll be as quick as I can." She even managed a smile of sorts. "Don't go running off anywhere, will you?"

His hand clutched her bare arm.

"It's all right," she said softly. "I promise I'll come back."

A tremor ran through his fingers before he let his hand fall to his side. "Thank you, ma'am. You have been kind." He exhaled a long breath as if he expected it to be his last.

* 　 * 　 *

Dodie ran. She zigzagged through the trees, sprinting along the sandy track. The route was familiar to her feet even in darkness—she took it every day—but panic made her feet clumsy. Twice she crashed into a tree, skinning an elbow and thumping the air from her lungs, while the nightly chorus of cicadas reverberated through the undergrowth. She made herself slow down and concentrate as she headed for old Bob Coster's place. Off to her right beyond the trees came the rumble of the waves as they raced up the narrow beach and the familiar sound of it calmed her.

Oh, Mr. Morrell, what is going on?

She thought of him sitting alone in the dark, believing she had abandoned him. The poor man should be in a hospital, but she had no right to make that decision for him if there really were people lying in wait for him there. *To finish what they started.* The way he'd said it sent a shiver through her because he'd said it as if it were normal. As if any of this were normal.

The moonlight allowed her to quicken her pace and she had no problem locating Bob Coster's house. It was set back in a small clearing, a wooden building with a roof of corrugated iron that rattled in the wind, and a small wooden porch where old Bob liked to laze in his rocking chair and spin a yarn with anyone who cared to split a beer with him.

The windows were dark, no sign of life. Dodie hurried down the side of the house to the back, where Bob boasted a good-size plot of land, cleared and planted up with sweet potato. He had built himself a toolshed. In these parts nobody locked doors—it was regarded as unneighborly—so Dodie lifted the shed latch. She reached in, found what she was searching for, grasped its handles, and backed out. She had her transport.

*   *   *

The wheelbarrow creaked with each turn of its wheel. The noise of it sounded raucous among the softly spoken trees and startled a yellow-crowned night heron into spreading its great wings in flight, silent and ghostly as it skimmed the silvery treetops. There was a brief spatter of rain, big bloated drops that drummed in the well of the barrow, but the clouds passed overhead, allowing Dodie to see more clearly.

Please, be alive.

She hurried through the warm night, bats darting on leathery wings above her head, and as she approached the spot where she'd left him she called out, "Mr. Morrell?"

Shadows stubbornly cloaked the tree where he'd been sitting.

"Mr. Morrell!"

He was gone.

She peered into the black blur of tree trunks. "It's me, Dodie."

Only then did she catch a whisper that drifted to her from farther back among the trees. She abandoned the barrow and, nervous of every rustle, trawled through the prickly undergrowth until she found him. He had buried himself under a carapace of slick wet leaves, and at the sight of him still alive, the depth of her relief took her by surprise. He'd dragged himself here and camouflaged his body—so he wasn't ready to die. Not yet. Slowly he raised his head from the foliage.

"You came back."

"I said I would."

"I didn't believe you."

"I've brought a barrow for you to ride in."

A strange hiccuping sound escaped him and Dodie realized it was a laugh.

"So that's what the noise was," he muttered.

"Yes, your chariot awaits."

His hand grasped hers and didn't let go until she had lowered him into the wheelbarrow, but as she tightened her cardigan around his waist, she could hear an odd rumbling vibration at the back of his throat that scared her.

"Off we go," she said brightly, and took the strain of the handles. It was heavier than she expected.

She gripped the handles tighter but the weight of it was making her shoulder sockets burn. She blinked away sweat from her eyes as mosquitoes honed in for their midnight feast. What frightened her was that when she shook her head to try to clear it, nothing changed. Only her heart thumped harder and the wheelbarrow tilted, as though it wanted to rid itself of Mr. Morrell.

Chapter 2

Ella

"Help me."

The words drifted out of the bedroom. Ella Sanford flicked away the cigarette she was smoking on the balcony, watching the lights of Nassau spring into life one by one as the sky grew dark and the city prepared for another night of partying. Since the war had come to the Bahamas, the city had changed. The military had moved into the island of New Providence like a force of nature with its airfields and its uniforms and its loud laughter. These men knew how to work hard and how to play hard, and the petty colonial atmosphere of idle inbred gossip had been swept aside. With a little smile of anticipation Ella returned to the bedroom.

"What's the matter, Reggie?" she asked.

"Help me do these bally things, will you?" Her husband was holding out a pair of gold cuff links. "They're little bastards."

She laughed and slipped them into his starched white cuffs with ease. She always thought Reggie looked at his best in evening dress. She knew he liked her to do things for him, especially things that meant he could touch her, and as soon as she had finished the small task he rested both hands on her naked upper arms.

"You look lovely tonight," he said.

"Thank you. So do you."

Reginald Sanford had worked for His Majesty's government in

the diplomatic service most of his life and the stamp of it was all over his face. From the polite set of his full features to the cautious expression in his gray eyes and the slightly secretive mouth. He liked order. He liked hierarchy. And he never raised his voice. He was skilled at calming others down and he possessed a remarkable ability to persuade them to see reason. His reason, of course.

It was why he now had the honor of representing His Majesty in the Bahamas as right-hand man to the governor. It was why he lived in a magnificent house and drove around the island in a silver-gray Bentley. And Ella suspected it was why he sometimes tossed and turned at night or wrapped an arm tight around her in bed, nuzzled her neck, and murmured, "Do you ever wonder what our life would have been like if I'd taken my father's advice and become a quiet country solicitor?"

"No. You'd have hated it."

But it wasn't true. Sometimes Ella did wonder. She smiled at him now and tried to smooth away a slight crease at the side of his mouth, but he held her arms firmly.

"You'll be good tonight, won't you?" he said.

"Reggie, I'm not a child. I'm your forty-one-year-old wife."

"You know what I mean. Dance with him if he asks."

"He may not ask this time."

Her husband's gaze traveled from her golden hair which hung in heavy glossy waves over her naked shoulders to her evening gown of chartreuse silk which cast new lights into her blue eyes and seemed to glide like a second skin over her slender hips.

"He'll ask." He nodded.

"Do I have to?"

Reggie gave her one of his serious smiles. "It goes with the job, I'm afraid, my dear. Talk to him about that ghastly music he's so keen on."

"Jazz?"

"Yes. I don't know what on earth he sees in that noisy caterwauling. But he's always so eager to be regarded as modern." He said the last word as if it tasted dirty in his mouth.

Ella laughed. "Maybe its rhythms make him feel young again. We all like to feel young at times."

Reggie frowned. "He's only two years older than I am. Forty-nine's not old."

Unconsciously he touched the spot at his temple where his thinning brown hair had begun to sprout badger-gray tufts. She had one morning caught him dabbing cold tea straight from the teapot onto the telltale patches. He had been acutely embarrassed but she had been tactful, never mentioning the brief moment of vanity.

"He looks older than you," she told her husband truthfully.

To be honest, Reggie ran slightly to fat. Not excessive, but definitely well cushioned despite the hours spent on the golf course. His cheeks were round and smooth as billiard balls and showed no sign of aging. The years of hard toil had manifested themselves only in the two tension furrows across his brow and in the soft sadness that bloomed around his eyes when he was tired.

Ella gave a throaty chuckle. "I could talk to him about something else, I suppose."

His eyes narrowed suspiciously. "Like what?"

"A donation to my auction."

He abruptly released his hold on her arms and headed straight for the whiskey glass on the bedside table. It was still half full. He lifted it to his lips and studied her face with a neutral diplomatic gaze.

"Don't pester him tonight, Ella."

"No?"

"Please don't discuss donations—or any other kind of work—with His Royal Highness, the Duke of Windsor, when he's off duty." Annoyance flickered in the corner of his eyes. She said nothing while he knocked back the scotch in one swig. "Come along, my dear." He picked up her velvet wrap from the bed and draped it over her shoulders. "Best foot forward."

*   *   *

Ella was fond of her house here in Nassau. It wasn't that she hadn't had splendid houses before on other postings. She had. There was the one in Alexandria with the tapering tower that caught the cooling breezes off the sea, and there was the one in Malaya with the lewd mosaics and peculiar drainage system. Both were provided by courtesy of His Majesty, of course.

But this house—Bradenham House—with its long colonial verandas and elegant white pillars where bougainvillea cascaded in abundance, was more than just her house; it was her home. Her first *real* home. She and Reggie had lived here longer than in any other house, eleven years. Where had all that time vanished, all those wasted hours? But she had been young then, just thirty years old when she arrived and still clinging to the hope that they would have a child one day soon. But it didn't happen. The set of lead soldiers that she had bought from Stanhope's Toyshop on Bay Street had been thrown in the bin. Those days were long gone.

Tonight Ella intended to enjoy herself. It was a fund-raising party over at the British Colonial Hotel for the Spitfire Fund and all the usual crowd would be there, but she was quick-footed. She knew how to sidestep the old dullards and make for the young bucks in uniform with their laughter and cocktails and tales of manhandling one of the heavy Liberator bombers up into the air, roaring up into the endless blue skies. But as she descended the wide sweep of the stairs, she saw her black maid, Emerald, hovering by the front door. Reggie's gloves were folded neatly across the palm of her plump hand.

Ella saw the maid's bright gaze fix on Reggie as she lay in wait like a spider, but one in a frilly white cap and with hips as broad as a barn door and a laugh that could crack a brick. Her thumb was slowly stroking the calf-leather fingers of the gloves.

"My oh my, Mr. Sanford, you lookin' mighty fine here this evening."

"Why, thank you, Emerald." Reggie beamed.

"I ironed you the dress shirt real careful. All special."

"I appreciate that. Don't think I don't notice your good handiwork around the place."

"That's real nice to know, sir. Real nice."

Emerald had started shimmying her hips from side to side. Always a bad sign. Ella hurried down the last steps and headed for the door.

"Good night, Emerald," she said pointedly.

"Mr. Sanford, sir," Emerald cooed sweetly as Reggie reached for his gloves, "I been thinkin'."

Reggie took root in front of her, puffing out his rotund stomach, happy to pass the time of day with the one person in the house who thought he could do no wrong.

"What have you been thinking about, Emerald?"

"About you, sir."

"Oh?" He looked pleased as he slid the gloves on with a graceful movement, easing the leather down between his fingers.

"You know I got an aunt up in Bain Town and she got a niece by marriage livin' over in Grant's Town, Mr. Reggie?"

"No, I didn't know that."

"Well, seein' as how all them folks from the Out Islands has come flockin' to Nassau to get themselves jobs with the military and all, there ain't much chance for a girl—even a real smart one— to find herself a job round these parts anymore, and I was wonderin', Mr. Reggie, if you could find her somethin' in your office."

"Ah, well, Emerald." He frowned. "Not sure about that."

"Nothin' much. Just a bitty job?"

Ella paused at the door to see what Reggie would say.

He sighed. "I'll see what I can do, Emerald. But I warn you, there is a strict order to these things."

What he meant was a hierarchy. White men at the top, black

men below, white women somewhere in the middle, and young black girls kicking around at the bottom.

"Thank you, Mr. Reggie. You is a good and kind man."

Ella studied her flushed husband for a minute with fresh eyes. Yes, Emerald, you're right. Reggie is a good and kind man.

*   *   *

Ella entered the magnificent British Colonial Hotel on Reggie's arm and knew at once the evening was going to be a success. She had worked hard to set up this fundraiser event and was relieved to see it so well attended. There was a bright energy in the room that rebounded off the shimmering marble pillars and the gold crystals of the chandeliers, the kind of energy that sweeps through the blood.

It rose in waves from the crowd of young servicemen, flooding the room with a kind of urgency. Once you were up in one of those big silver crates in the sky, God only knew whether tomorrow would ever come, so there was a sense of taking everything today with both hands. The mood was infectious and it made Ella laugh out loud, though she wasn't sure why. Even the stolid inhabitants of Nassau could feel it in the air. The noise level was rising steadily as a band played "By the Light of the Silvery Moon" and all along one wall the row of tall windows stood open on to the terrace, to let the heady scents of a sultry tropical night mingle with the cigar smoke and Dior perfume.

It was obvious that New Providence Island was the paradise these young men had always dreamed of. Rich blue skies, warm turquoise seas to bathe in, and white tropical beaches that dazzled the mind as well as the eye. And its capital, Nassau, was offering the kind of delights a boy from Bermondsey or Brooklyn had never thought within his grasp. Society was changing because of this war and something in Ella wanted to change with it. The old order was passing. She didn't want to be left behind with just a rocking chair and a rum cocktail for company.

"Hello, Reggie, old chap, how are things up in the hallowed halls of Government House? Have you heard the latest?"

Ella turned to find a sunburned man with a vast ginger handlebar moustache greeting her husband.

"Ella, this is Wing Commander Knightley. He's been keeping the duke up-to-date on the new intake at the Operational Training Unit at Oakes Field. They're a group from Czechoslovakia, I hear."

"Good evening, Wing Commander," Ella said.

Beside him stood two men. One was extremely tall and dark, a stylish figure with a pointed little beard, acutely aware of his own attraction. This was Freddie de Marigny, who possessed a swarthy complexion and all the confidence of a man who has recently married the teenage daughter of one of the world's richest men, Sir Harry Oakes. Terms like "fortune hunter" and "cradle snatcher" always trailed in Freddie's wake.

"Hello, Hector," Ella said to the second man, and he kissed her cheek warmly.

"Good evening, Ella. A great turnout. Congratulations."

"We must thank Tilly for that."

Hector Latcham was the husband of Ella's good friend Tilly. She was the one who had persuaded Ella to march into the air base at Oakes Field and suggest that all the men should buy tickets for a chance to dance with the duchess this evening. The fact that the duchess hadn't turned up hadn't disturbed Tilly in the slightest and she stepped into the breach herself.

"So what's the latest?" Reggie asked the wing commander.

"We've had a report that U-boats have been withdrawn from the Atlantic."

"That's great news, if it's true."

"They're being pulled back to counter the possibility of an Allied invasion of Europe. That means we can free up planes from patrolling the ocean for enemy submarines."

"God knows," Reggie said, "those aircraft are badly needed in the Far East."

"About time we had some good news from your lot, Knightley." Freddie de Marigny smiled, flashing his extraordinarily white teeth. He clapped the wing commander on the back. "But I hope it doesn't mean you'll be reducing military numbers on New Providence Island. We need you chaps to keep our economy going."

"On the contrary," Knightley assured him politely, though he clearly didn't care to be touched by the likes of Freddie, "we will be instructing more aircrews than ever."

The RAF had selected the Bahamas as a training air base because of its uninterrupted blue skies. There was no fear that the B-24 Liberator bombers would be shot down by German intruders. Planes were constantly flying into Windsor Field from America before being ferried across the Atlantic to the war in Europe and Africa. It was something the island was proud of, this essential role in the war effort. The sight of RAF uniforms thronging the streets gave the islanders a sense of pride, so that Bahamians queued to sign up on the dotted line to become a part of it.

Ella left the men to their war talk and their cigars, and circulated among the crowd. She greeted friends and stopped to talk with any serviceman who seemed at a loss, but it was only when she reached the dance floor that she managed to track down Tilly. Tilly Latcham was a tall striking woman with dark elaborately waved hair and tonight she was wearing a dramatic burgundy gown with milky pearls gleaming at her throat. But her expression was one of acute misery. She was clutched in the arms of a short pilot officer with two left feet who was singing blithely along with the band and kept bumping into other couples.

"Tilly!"

Tilly rolled her eyes with relief and bolted off the dance floor. "Darling, where have you been? You're late."

"I'm sorry, but Reggie had a flap on up at Government House and was wretchedly late home."

"Then I forgive you."

She kissed Ella's cheek. There was a softness to the edges of her usually crisp words. Tilly had been drinking more than just a cocktail or two.

"Go and sit this one out, Tilly. You've done your duty." She gave her a mock salute. "I'll take over your mission here."

Tilly laughed, her scarlet mouth relaxing. "You are a lifesaver, darling." She gave a shiver and added, "Talking of lifesaving, how is your family back home?"

Ella's parents over in England lived in the Kent countryside under the flight path of the German bombers' nightly run into London and their house had recently been hit. Damn rotten luck. But thank God they—unlike their poor house—escaped with no more than minor injuries.

"Tilly," she said firmly, "go and sit this one out. And that's an order."

"Is the duke here yet?"

"I haven't seen him."

"Oh," Tilly said. "Drat."

"He'll probably drift in later, don't worry. You'll get your dance with him, I'm sure."

Tilly grinned. "Especially as *she* is not here."

"Behave yourself." Ella laughed and turned back to the matter of Tilly's abandoned airman. "Now, Mr. Pilot Officer, here I come."

She scooped him up from where he was hovering uncertainly on the edge of the dancing and twirled him expertly across the floor.

*　*　*

"Had enough?"

Ella turned at the sound of his voice. She was standing at the bottom of the terrace just where it spilled down onto the beach, and was staring out at the vast blackness of the sea in front of her. She liked the nights best. That was when she felt the island cast off its dazzling daytime mask and let its true self emerge under the cloak of darkness. She could sense its quick hot breath on her neck, and hear the pad of its feet as it reclaimed its beaches from its colonial overlords. Only at night could she smell the sweet scent of its ancient hardwood trees that had been stripped from the island for shipbuilding. Pines and palms and the ghostly casuarinas remained in abundance, but the island remembered its hardwoods. The island forgot nothing.

Long ago the Lucayan people had lived peacefully among the seven hundred islands of the Bahamas for hundreds of years, but they were ousted by the Spanish after Christopher Columbus discovered the islands in 1492. From then on, the Spanish, the British, and the freebooting pirates spent years slitting each other's throats over possession of these lush islands with their natural harbors and secret cays. They became a crown colony of Britain in 1717, but even now, at night when the masters of the Empire slept, New Providence Island released its sounds and smells and breathed in the wild scent of the sea.

"Had enough?"

"Good evening, Your Royal Highness. Just taking a breath of air. It's hot in there."

"It's good to see the men enjoying themselves. You are to be congratulated, Ella."

"Thank you."

"A great boost to our Spitfire Fund."

"To the men's morale as well, I hope."

"Yes, you only have to look at their faces. A grand job."

The Duke of Windsor stood beside her in the warm semidarkness, the lights of the elegant terrace and the brightly lit hotel behind them. He was a slight man, no taller than Ella, with soft fair hair and a face that managed to look boyish despite being deeply lined. Ella wondered why he was out here instead of carousing inside. Everyone knew that the duke liked to party. They lapsed into silence while he offered Ella a cigarette and lit one for her and one for himself, inhaling with satisfaction.

"How is the duchess?" Ella asked. The terrace lights caught the edge of the surf on the beach and turned it into lace.

"She is indisposed, I'm afraid."

"I'm sorry. Give her my best wishes for recovery."

"Thank you. I will."

If the duchess was "indisposed," it usually meant her stomach ulcer was playing up, although she had commented to Ella the other day that it had been much better recently. Maybe she just didn't want to dance with airmen. Or just had something better to do. The Duchess of Windsor was a secretive person and there was much that went on behind her intelligent violet-blue eyes that she didn't divulge. Ella thought the duke always looked a little lost without her.

"Is your husband here?"

"Yes, Reggie's inside."

"I might have a word later."

She wanted to say, *Keep your demands away from my husband tonight, let him relax. Isn't it enough that you suck him dry each day at work? Can't you rely on yourself instead of on him?*

But she didn't say it. No one ever said it to him. Except the duchess.

The sound of the breakers on the beach was joined by a sudden roar overhead as a formation of bombers set off to train the new recruits in the skills of nighttime maneuvers.

"Ella, do you like it here?" the duke asked in a sad voice.

"Of course I do. It's beautiful."

The aircraft droned into the distance.

"Don't you?" she asked.

She knew he longed to be governor of Australia, or of Canada at the very least.

"Sometimes," he said, exhaling his frustration into the humid darkness, "I regard these islands as my Elba."

Elba? Napoleon's place of exile. The hubris of his pronouncement took Ella's breath away. Did he think he was that important? She shivered and moved to go back indoors, but with a sudden display of charm he took her arm through his and smiled engagingly.

"Come, Mrs. Sanford, let us have the next dance."

Chapter 3

Dodie

Dodie's house lay farther along the coast in the next cay, tucked under a grove of casuarina trees that drooped their long green fingers over the sand. It was no more than a wooden shack with one room, a roof of thatched fronds that didn't leak too often, and two windows that kept constant watch over the ocean. Summer storms were harsh, dramatic, and frequent here, and their ferocity had shocked her at first when she and her father came to this tiny speck in the ocean six years ago.

She lit the lamp. The oily smell of kerosene rippled through the room and the amber light shuffled the night shadows into dark corners.

"How are you feeling?" she asked.

Morrell was lying on the single bed, curled on his side with his arms wrapped around his stomach.

"All right . . ." His breath came in shallow gasps.

"Good."

Now that she could look at him in the lamplight, she could see that his skin had taken on the same color as the galvanized bucket she had placed beside him, so gray it no longer looked like skin. She didn't know where to start. Where to touch. Where not to touch. She knelt down beside the bed and tucked a folded clean white towel under his hand on his stomach. He shut his eyes.

"I owe you," he muttered.

His face was heavy-featured under a mass of bushy brown hair, and even with his eyes shut, Dodie could see the toughness of him. But that toughness was crumbling as the pain started to eat away at it. She rested her hand on his cheek and a faint smile touched his lips.

"What are we to do?" he whispered.

"You must let me look at the wound."

"Leave it."

"It needs to be bathed and cleaned."

A grunt came in response. His mouth clenched in a tight line.

"Mr. Morrell, there is a woman who lives not far from here who knows about this kind of thing, she's good with illness and—"

"No."

"She's not a doctor or a nurse or anything official. She wouldn't report you to anyone. Her name is Mama Keel and she knows everything there is to know about herbs and healing, so I could—"

"No."

"—fetch her and she would know what to do to help you. She wouldn't breathe a word."

"No."

"I have to, Mr. Morrell, can't you see? Because I don't know what to do."

His eyes opened a slit. "Do nothing."

She started to move but his hand gripped her skirt. "Do you like this woman?" he asked urgently.

"Yes, she's—"

"Do you want her to die?"

"No, of course not."

"Then tell her to stay clear of me."

Dodie felt the hairs rise on the skin of her arms. "Are the people who did this to you so dangerous," she asked in a stunned voice, "that they would hurt people who help you?"

His eyes stayed fixed on hers. He nodded.

She backed away from the bed, fear sharp in her chest. "Very well, Mr. Morrell. No Mama Keel here."

"You are quick to understand," he said with an attempt at a gallant smile, but she could see he was losing strength as fast as the clean towel was losing its whiteness.

"Mr. Morrell." She spoke louder, her voice trying to drag him back to her. "I'm going to run over to Mama Keel's place. To get something for your pain. I will be quick." She smiled at him brightly. "We both need help if we're going to get you through this."

Before he could reply or seize her skirt again, she had kicked off her shoes and was flying up the beach.

Chapter 4

Flynn

She's gone.

To hell with her. She complicated everything.

The dark figure of Flynn Hudson was crouched at the water's edge. He watched her run. She was fast as a jackrabbit. He reckoned she must have cat's eyes in her head, the way she could see in the dark even when the clouds switched off the moonlight.

It was one of the things he hated about this darned island. The dark. It got to him. It was a world away from what he called darkness in Chicago, where he could flit down unlit rat-infested alleyways and still see where he was going. Here the darkness was so intense it felt like being chucked down a well and having the lid slammed shut on top of you. That kind of dark. Solid and unbreakable. It swallowed her now. As he trailed a hand through the water, he questioned where the girl had gone. At this hour? With blood still wet in the barrow?

Don't come back.

He rose to his feet, his limbs eager to be on the move once more. They didn't like to stay still, didn't care to be a sitting target the way Morrell had been. The moon slipped free from the grip of the clouds, making the white sand of the beach glow silver-blue in the moonlight.

Goddammit, what kind of color was that?

A color he'd never seen before in his twenty-four years, but in the weird light he could see the shack up on its little plot of scrub, clear as fresh spit. A minute or two was all he had, he reckoned. The jackrabbit could come skidding back at any moment.

He moved forward, conspicuous on the beach now. His thoughts were leaping ahead of him, unleashed. He could almost see their footprints in the sand.

Chapter 5

Dodie

Mama Keel's cabin was perched alone on a rocky stretch of land and showed no lights, but Dodie could hear the soft crooning of an island song somewhere inside. Everyone knew Mama Keel never slept.

"Mama Keel," she whispered, and tapped on the door.

It shifted on its rusty hinges, in no hurry to get itself open. Behind it stood Mama Keel, a broad smile of welcome on the strong bones of her face before she even knew who it was who had turned up on her doorstep in the dead of night. In her arms lay a sleepy-eyed infant.

"Well now, Dodie, you look mighty het up." She stepped back into the darkened room at once and pulled a box of matches from her dressing gown pocket. "Come in." She lit a lamp, keeping its flame low, and when she turned to look at Dodie a stillness settled on her.

"Oh my Lordy, girl," was all she said.

"Mama Keel, I need help."

"You is covered in blood, child."

"It's not mine."

"I'm real glad to hear that. Whose is it?"

"A stranger's. I found him in the street on my way home."

Mama nodded and half closed her purple-black eyes, as if peering at something only her own gaze could see in the dim light. Her long stringbean of a body in its tattered old dressing gown seemed to grow very still, and Dodie had no idea what she was imagining. The wound maybe? The blood spilling from it? No one knew what went on inside Mama Keel's head under that tangle of wild gray hair.

The main room was plainly furnished—handmade seats, a table, a cupboard—everything strictly functional, except for a colorful decoration of bird feathers suspended on a rattan thread that zig-zagged back and forth across the ceiling. Mama Keel's black skin gleamed in the lamplight and a calmness radiated from her that steadied Dodie's breathing.

"Mama Keel?"

The woman blinked.

"He's been stabbed," Dodie told her. Her voice sounded strange and unfamiliar.

Immediately Mama Keel eased the sleeping child onto a rug that lay in a cardboard box in one corner of the room, scooting a gray cat out of it first with her foot. "Joseph!" she called softly. A door opened and a gangly white youth in his teens emerged from a back room. He was wearing nothing more than a pair of shorts and his fair hair was ruffled into spikes from sleep, but his eyes shot wide open at the sight of Dodie.

"Don't stare, boy, it's bad manners," Mama Keel said briskly. "Just a splash of blood. Here, take Elysia for me."

The boy ducked his head, scooped up the cardboard box, and vanished. Dodie looked down at the scarlet stains embedded thickly under her fingernails and at the streaks of blood over her waitress uniform. What kind of man did this? Pushed a blade into another man's flesh. Cold hard sorrow rose up in her and she opened her mouth to speak, but no sound emerged. She raised her hand to her cheek and found her fingers cold as ice.

"Sit down, Dodie."

"I have to get back. He's waiting for me."

Mama Keel spent a moment resting a warm comforting hand on Dodie's shoulder, then abruptly she was all movement, gathering pots and packets and jars of strange-smelling liquids. She thrust a tin mug into Dodie's hands with the command "Drink it," and Dodie did so, though it tasted bitter and felt as if it stripped enamel from her teeth. When she saw Mama Keel wrap a scarf around her head and tip the herbs and potions into a straw basket, she laid a firm hand on the basket's handle herself.

"You mustn't come, Mama. You must tell me what to do."

"You bein' foolish, darlin' heart. You know nothin'."

"It's too dangerous. There are men who want to silence him."

Mama Keel paused. "You scared?" she asked softly.

"Yes, I'm scared. Of course I am. I'd be crazy not to be. But I'm also scared for you. You are too . . ."—she gestured toward the door from which the boy had emerged—"too precious here. They need you."

Dodie knew that Mama Keel watched over a shifting pack of feral waifs and strays. She had no children of her own but her door was ever open to the island's orphans and runaways, and behind that door there could be anything from ten to twenty young souls who clung to her. Without her, the waves would come for them.

Mama Keel breathed hard through her broad nose.

Dodie opened the basket purposefully. "Just tell me what to do."

* * *

The door of her shack swung open at Dodie's touch. Yet she had latched it, she was sure. Behind her the vast reaches of the Atlantic Ocean sighed, low and insistent, and threads of moonlight floated on the waves. As if nothing had changed. She stepped over the threshold. Wary, but not wary enough. The black muzzle of a gun was pointing straight at her and sent her heart spinning up into her throat.

"Get in here. Quickly."

It was Morrell. He was propped up awkwardly on one elbow, sweat pouring off his face, a tiny pistol dwarfed in his hand.

"Shut the door," he growled, and collapsed back against the pillow, letting the gun fall to his side.

Dodie kicked the door shut and bolted it. "Don't ever do that to me again."

"I didn't know it was you."

She dumped the basket on the table and started unloading it. "Has anyone else been around?"

"No."

"Sure?"

"Yes."

Why would he lie to her? "Have you been out of bed and opened the door?"

He rolled his head to one side and gave her half a smile. "Yes, I've been out for a half-mile swim and a few handstands under the stars."

She tried to smile back at him but didn't quite make it, so she busied herself with the medicines instead, smelling them, tipping ingredients into a cup, putting water from the enamel jug to boil on the kerosene stove. The shack started to fill with aromas.

"What the hell is all that stuff?" Morrell muttered.

"It's native bush medicine."

He grimaced. "Does it work?"

"Of course it does. Bahamians have been using these herbs for hundreds of years." She looked up from the bowl of chopped green cerasee leaves. "Don't worry, Mr. Morrell, they know what they're doing. It's often impossible to get a doctor to the hundreds of Bahamian Out Islands. They had to find alternative medicines that work, so"—she paused and walked over to his side with a small pot of what looked like rabbit pellets—"take three of these." She smiled encouragingly and held out a cup of cerasee infusion for him to wash them down with. "They will help the pain."

He took them and swallowed them down, making no comment

on the bitterness of the infusion. His skin had a slick sheen over it like furniture polish and Dodie could feel the heat radiating from him as she removed the towel.

"Now, Mr. Morrell, let's look at this wound of yours."

*   *   *

He was tough. She'd give him that. He made no sound but watched everything she did, his hands curled into fists at his side. Dodie worked with great care. She did exactly what Mama Keel had told her. She bathed the wound, applied a pungent herbal antiseptic, and holding the raw edges of his flesh tight between her fingers, she drew them together over the slippery innards inside. A coating of stiff antiseptic paste to seal the wound finished the job. And all the time her fingers worked, she murmured to him constantly, to steady him, though she had no idea what words were coming out of her mouth.

Painstakingly she bound him up with strips torn from her best sheet and dosed him with more of the pellets. With a flannel she gently wiped the sweat from his face and smeared cream on his bleeding lip where he had bitten a piece out of it.

"Thank you," he said when she'd finished. "That took courage."

"You'll feel better soon. Close your eyes. Try to sleep now."

"You are kind."

"It's Mama Keel you should be thanking."

Dodie plunged her hands into a bowl of warm water and scrubbed hard at the blood under her nails.

*   *   *

"What are you doing here in the Bahamas?"

Morrell's voice startled Dodie. She thought he was still asleep. She had continued to dose him every hour throughout the night with one of Mama Keel's concoctions, but it was only with the first hint of dawn that the heat at last ebbed from his skin. When he opened his eyes she smiled with relief and asked, "How are you feeling?"

"Better than last night."

"Good."

She rose from her stool at his bedside and unbolted the door. The shack was stifling and she needed to breathe in fresh sea air, so she threw it wide and sat down on the front step. Her toes touched the cool sand and she felt calmer.

"I like it here," she told him.

Her eyes scanned the beach, still wearing its night shadows like a shawl. Off to the right, dawn was starting to paint the slender trunks of the palm trees gold.

"Are you on your own here?" he asked.

"Yes."

"No family?"

"No."

Silence settled while they both listened to the easy roll of the waves, and at the far end of the bay an egret spread its shimmering white wings to catch the first thermals of the morning.

"You're English, aren't you? What brought you here?" Morrell asked.

She turned to look at him. "Why the questions?"

"I'm interested in you." He shook his head weakly from side to side, his hair dark with sweat. "You saved my life."

She could tell him to mind his own business. But she recalled the feel of the hairs of his chest, springy and full of life, when she washed the blood off them, and somehow the intimacy of that simple act linked her to him in a way she couldn't explain.

"I grew up in Chippenham, a rural town in England. My mother died in the influenza epidemic of 1931 when I was nine, and my father struggled after that. He'd had a bad war and my mother always said he came back from the trenches of Ypres with part of him missing. But he grew worse after her death. More of him was missing."

She stopped. Stared bleakly at the sea.

"I'm real sorry about that, Dodie."

She shook her head, quietly moving her thoughts around. "It was the old story, the same as thousands of others before him. He took to the bottle and could never hold down a job after that."

"So," Morrell continued for her, "he brought you out here for a fresh start."

She nodded. "When I was sixteen."

"But it didn't work out?"

"No," she admitted, "it didn't work out."

"So where is your father now?"

"He's dead."

A silence rippled through the shack and it was a long time before either spoke.

"I'm sorry," Morrell said again. He sighed. "Life can be tough on youngsters."

"So, Mr. Morrell, tell me what you are doing here. What business are you in?"

He took his time. "You don't want to know, ma'am."

"I do."

Outside, the sun finally burst over the horizon and set the crests of the waves on fire. Dodie watched her shins glow pink and the sand around her feet glitter like glass, and she shook her thick chestnut hair loose to catch the warmth of it.

"I'm in insurance," Morrell said. "Of a kind."

But something in the way he said it sent a shiver through her. "What does that mean?" she asked. "What do you insure?"

He lifted a hand and gently tapped the side of his head. "I insure what's in here." He made an odd sound that at first concerned her because she thought it was a groan of pain, but she recognized it as a chuckle of amusement. "Information," he explained.

Dodie glanced out at the beach and her eye was caught by the information she could see there. That was the thing about sand, it cradled imprints as efficiently as wet cement, until the waves or the wind came to steal them away. In front of the shack she could clearly make out the jumble of her own hurried footprints from last night and their track off to the left. But off to the right the marks in the sand told a different story. There was another set of footprints, large and intrusive. They led straight as a poker from the water's edge right up to her own front door and then dipped away along the tree line, where they vanished inland.

Insurance.

Well, Mr. Morrell, I've taken out my own insurance. Your dainty gun is lying wrapped in a towel, safe under my cooking pot.

Chapter 6

Dodie

"Don't let him bury my wedding ring with me, Dodie. The undertaker will only steal it."

They were her mother's words. The wedding ring was a thick gold band, bought when times were good. Toward the end of her life the ring fell off her hand, her fingers were so thin.

"And don't let him spend it on one of his crazy schemes. Or," she added darkly, "on his demon."

The demon was whiskey. Silk-smooth or rotgut, it made no difference to her father, it all went down the same slippery way. An ardent Baptist who could not say no to a drink when the devil was riding his shoulder. To be fair to him, he never asked for the ring, not once in the hard years that were to follow. But she would catch him sometimes casting sidelong glances at the band of gold that hung on a black ribbon around her neck, especially when he had the shakes real bad. But he never asked and she never offered. It was all she had left of her mother. That and her sewing machine.

The ring had paid for this beaten-up old shack. Sometimes when the nights were blackest, she thought she could hear her mother humming in the roof timbers but it was only the wind in the thatch. Now the morning was looking better than she'd dared hope last night—the beach had remained empty and acquired no fresh footprints, and Mr. Morrell had slept quietly all morning, his breathing smooth and regular, his skin a better color despite the sweat that glistened on it.

In the clear light of day Dodie could see him more distinctly, but even in sleep the toughness never left the set of his features and she could tell that at some point his nose had been broken. A street fighter, that's what he was, a man who knew how to use his great fists, and yet the gentle drawl of his voice and the manner in which he had clung to her told a different tale. She was sweeping out the sand that had blown into the shack, driving it back on to the beach where it belonged, and working out what her next move should be. She needed to contact Miss Olive at the Arcadia Hotel to explain why she was not at work but she daren't leave Morrell, not even to run to the phone box on the edge of town.

"Young woman."

His voice surprised her. It was far stronger than the whisper of last night and the southern accent was more pronounced.

"I'm Dodie," she reminded him with a smile, pleased to see him awake and looking about him at his surroundings.

"Well, Miss Dodie, what a right pretty home you have here."

It was the last thing she expected. She abandoned the broom and glanced around the room at the abundant cushions, as well as a patchwork quilt that hung on one wall. The colors were bright—kingfisher blues and hummingbird yellows, all shades of green—the colors of the island.

"Thank you," she said. She wasn't used to compliments. "I made them myself."

His gaze fell on the treasured sewing machine in its curved box in one corner. "You made all this stuff?" He stared at the quilt on the wall, at the intricacy of it.

She nodded.

"It sure is beautiful."

"It took a while."

"I bet the hell it did. It's lovely."

"Thank you."

"Where d'you learn all this pretty stitching?"

"My mother taught me."

"That's nice," he murmured. "Real nice." In the same quiet voice he added, "If I die, tell no one. Especially not the police. Just chuck me in a hole somewhere and forget about me."

She sat down on the stool by the bedside. "What happened?" she asked. "Who did this to you?"

Slowly he raised the hand that had been lying across his stomach and pressed his forefinger on Dodie's forehead, right between her eyes.

"You don't want dirt inside that lovely clean and shiny mind of yours."

He withdrew his finger but the imprint of it remained on her skin.

Clean?

Shiny?

You don't want dirt inside.

Too late for that, Mr. Morrell.

* * *

Dodie was picking beans in her vegetable patch when she heard the tin rattle. She dropped them in panic and raced barefoot back to the front of the shack. She snatched up a spade as she ran, wielding it like a club, and lost her battered old straw sun hat, so that the midday sun landed like a blow on top of her head. But when she reached the door it was still locked.

"I'm here," she yelled as she pulled the key from her pocket and kicked open the door. "I'm here."

She had given Mr. Morrell a tin can with a handful of stones inside and told him to shake it like a rattlesnake if he needed her. She was just popping round the back to pick some beans to cook for him for his lunch. She'd locked the door. Taken no chances this time. Now the tin had summoned her. Sweat cut a path down her back as she burst into the shack, but at first glance nothing had changed. Morrell was exactly where she had left him. He was still stretched out on the bed, a single cotton sheet draped over him, an enamel mug of Mama Keel's brew on the stool beside him. But one hand was clutching the tin can and banging it like a death knell.

Dodie saw the blood. Scarlet threads of it creeping from under his hand, through the bandages and twisting into the fibers of the sheet. Thick bile shot up into her mouth. He had talked of her sewing and pointed at her quilt, and was about to eat the beans she'd picked for him. He couldn't be sick again. But she snatched a clean towel and hurried to his side, lifting his hand and sliding the towel beneath it.

"Pressure," she whispered.

But instead his hand grasped her wrist. She could feel the slickness of the blood between their skin, and the smell was back, stifling the room.

"It's all right," she said calmly, "we stopped it before, we can stop it again."

But he was shaking all over, and when she looked into his eyes, there was something different in them, something that she couldn't bear to look at.

"I'll get the medicine," she said quickly.

But still his hand gripped her wrist and she could not bring herself to break the contact in case the tiny spark that was keeping this man alive blew out in the shuffle of air as she moved. She pressed down on the towel to stem the flow.

"Dodie."

"I'm right here."

"Give me . . ." His voice was a thin whisper. "Give me my shoes."

"Your shoes? But you're going nowhere, Mr. Morrell, you're far too weak to—"

"My shoes."

She bent and reached under the bed for the white loafers. Brown speckles of blood marred their surface.

"A knife," he said.

"What?"

"I need a knife."

She didn't argue. She fetched a knife from a drawer but his fingers were trembling so hard he couldn't control the blade and pushed it back into her hand.

"Pull up the insole," he muttered.

She lifted the insole with the tip of the knife and took out a small square of folded paper that lay under it. On it in a bold hand was written a name and an address: *Sanford, Bradenham House, West Bay Street, Nassau.*

"My jacket," he whispered.

"Mr. Morrell, I really think you should lie quietly. This isn't helping you. Please keep still."

He fixed his eyes firmly on her face. "If anything happens to me . . ." A grimace touched his bone-white lips. "In my jacket . . . please."

She picked up the crumpled jacket, stiff with dried blood, and felt something heavy in one corner. This time he didn't even attempt to do the work himself.

"There," he said, "open it."

She did as he asked, opening a cleverly concealed pocket. Onto her lap tumbled two gold coins, gleaming in the muted light within the shack. She stared at them.

"One for you and one for Mrs. Sanford."

"No, Mr. Morrell." Her tone was sharp. "Forget about the money, just get well. I'll boil up more of Mama Keel's herbs to fix a tisane for you to—"

A fragile cough slipped through his lips. That was all.

"Mr. Morrell?" Dodie leaned closer.

Blood spurted from his nose, a trail of scarlet that stained his lips, and his eyes rolled up in his head.

No.

No, no, no.

"Mr. Morrell?" Her fingers touched his cheek. It was slippery with sweat.

Please, no, please no.

"Can you hear me?"

Nothing. Just the echo of her own voice in the sudden emptiness of the room. But she was not willing to sit there in silence and watch him leave. She wrapped her arms around him, drew him up against her chest as she sat on the bed, his head slack on her shoulder. Gently she rocked him back and forth, humming to him, a soft tuneless sound, and her tears fell warm on his cheeks.

Chapter 7

Flynn

Flynn watched her. He didn't help, but his fingers itched to seize a corner of the sheet she was using as a shroud and haul the deadweight of Johnnie Morrell through the trees.

Johnnie, this wasn't meant to happen.

He spat out the gum he was chewing, turned his back on the dazzling emerald sea that rippled quietly behind him, and sank deeper into the shadows of the palms. It was too hot. Sweat dripped off him, though he was scarcely moving, and he could only guess at what she must be feeling, dragging a dead man.

Under the trees the air was trapped, humid and heavy, unable to find its way out. He saw her pause, but she didn't look up from the swathed figure at her feet. She dropped to her knees beside it, laid a hand on its broad chest, and remained there for a long moment with her head bowed, before she resumed the man-hauling once more. The sheet kept snagging on roots, snatched at by branches and glistening tendrils of ivy. Her limbs were skinny and looked to him as though they'd snap if he yanked on them, but she moved with quick decisive intent. The light-greenish dress she was wearing today blended with the undergrowth and he had the odd feeling she might disappear if he took his eyes off her, vanish in the dappled mosaic of light and shade.

Johnnie Morrell's death was a failure. It was a word that didn't sit easy on his tongue. More than anything right now he wanted to get off this island, where the sand was so fine it scratched at his eyes and crept into his ears, where sandflies sucked out his blood and where natives talked with a lilting singsong accent that invaded his head at night.

He could see where the hole had already been dug in the ground, black and empty. She had wrenched it from the sandy soil with her spade, the muscles of her neck jumping, tense with effort. He watched her drag the body to the brink of the hole and prepare to roll it in. Abruptly he could bear no more. He could not watch Johnnie Morrell take his final dive. The scent of the island itself seemed to rise from the hole and suffocate him.

Flynn moved away on silent feet, back through the trees, avoiding the sunlight. What did it matter if she had to live with a body under the soil only fifty yards from where she slept? Why should he care?

She was nothing to him.

Chapter 8

Ella

Letter writing. Two words that struck gloom into Ella's heart. It was the part of her job as a diplomat's wife that she liked least. Once a week Reggie's male secretary arrived at Bradenham House clutching a box file of letters for her attention and a patient smile.

Today was letter day. She took over the large rosewood dining table and summoned a pot of coffee from Emerald. She then arranged the letters in separate piles over its polished surface, shuffled them around a bit to delay the moment of actually starting work on them, and picked up her fountain pen. The first one she dealt with was a simple plea for more benches for the children in a school. The second one was a more complicated request for her to intervene in a dispute over legal fees that were bankrupting the correspondent. The third one was at least amusing. It came in the form of an invitation to support a small museum celebrating the history of the Bahamas and was written as if from Anne Bonny and Mary Reed, the two most infamous female pirates to roam the Caribbean seas. She marked that one down for further attention and continued with the next.

People saw her as a route to Reggie. She didn't resent that. Often they had exhausted other avenues—their Member of Parliament or local police—and she was their last resort. She always tried to do what she could for them but refused to pester poor Reggie. His days were full enough already.

After two hours, with the sun struggling against the shutters and the ceiling fan feeling the strain, Ella pushed back her chair, tracked down her sunglasses, and headed outside. Ella loved her garden with its well-watered lawns and its borders filled with the great splashes of vivid color from the cannas and vibrant allamandas. But her favorite was the overarching flame tree which treated her to a display of extravagant flame-scarlet flowers every spring and folded up its delicate leaves at the onset of dusk each night. She loitered contentedly in its deep shade now, a respite from the glare of the sun.

When Ella arrived in the Bahamas eleven years ago she had been all prepared to find something close to the lush tropical vegetation of Malaya, where the dense jungle stalked the fringes of the towns, just waiting for a chance to march in. But she was wrong. Here on New Providence Island the thick forests had been savagely cleared long ago, first for shipbuilding and then for sugarcane, and never replanted. That had saddened her.

The island now had thin soil and was covered mainly with a dry scrubland of ferns, pines, and palms which the locals called the bush. It wasn't as aggressive or as vigorous as the landscape of Malaya but neither was it as oppressive. It let in the light. Let in the sweet salty air. Allowed you to breathe, and Ella loved it for that. In summer the island grew hot and humid, but most of the year it possessed a balmy climate that beguiled visitors and gave the islanders their easy rhythm of life.

Ella moved purposefully down to the bottom of the garden, where a fence of wire mesh divided off a large section of open ground. She rattled an enamel bowl in her hand, making the sunflower seeds it contained jump, and called out, "Ladies!" Instantly a chattering flock of hens stampeded toward the fence, barging and pecking in a swirl of excitement. Their antics made Ella laugh, especially Josephine, who led the charge, a formidable Rhode Island Red with a penchant for watermelon.

"I don't know why you bother with those damn chickens,"

Reggie complained whenever Ella came in from hosing down their houses or from puffing sweet-smelling louse powder over them.

"I like them."

"Can't you just buy eggs instead?"

"I like the hens," she explained. But Reggie was never going to understand.

A voice behind her startled her.

"Ah, there you are, my dear Ella. I thought I'd find you down here."

"Tilly, good morning."

Her friend was wearing an immaculate blouse and skirt in matching buttermilk linen and a hat broad enough to keep the sun off her face at all times. Her nose was slightly pink but Ella suspected that it wasn't from the sun.

"Everyone is saying how heavenly last night was, my clever darling. A great boost to the funds as well."

"Our boys certainly know how to party. I hope you had a good time too."

Tilly pulled a face. "The duke left early. Seemed horribly out of sorts. I didn't get my dance with him."

Ella threw a handful of seeds to the hens, causing a minor riot. "Buck up, Tilly, there's always next time."

"What are you doing today?"

"Writing letters."

"Don't be a silly ass, darling. I want you to come and watch today's yacht race with me." She prodded impatiently at the wire fence with a lacy parasol. "Hector is competing."

"Well, I really should be—"

"You wantin' somethin', Mrs. Latcham?"

Emerald's rich voice boomed out across the lawn and her bosom advanced down the garden path toward them at a fair pace. Clearly Tilly Latcham had managed to sneak down the side of the house, giving a wide berth to the fearsome maid. Ella chuckled.

"It's all right, Emerald. We're fine."

Emerald halted, her bosom still trembling like a truck with its engine idling, and pursed her large ruby lips in disapproval, giving Tilly the stare. She was adept at the stare. It was one of the weapons she used in a white man's world in which she found herself black and female.

"I spotted you, Mrs. Latcham. You ain't been announced."

Tilly waved a hand airily. "No need. I didn't want to disturb you when you were"—she glanced at the maid's hands, patchy with flour—". . . you were doing things."

"That will be all, thank you, Emerald," Ella said, tipping the last of the sunflower seeds in front of the scavenging posse.

Emerald rolled her black eyes, and with another well-aimed stare in Tilly's direction she headed back the way she'd come, her sandals slapping down on the path with a voice of their own.

"Ella, I swear I don't understand you," Tilly exclaimed. "Get rid of her, for heaven's sake."

Ella watched the broad rear view of her maid in her white uniform, shuffling away toward the house, the sun glistening on her greased curls and throwing her shadow across the lawn. Ella thought about the way Emerald would huddle by the coop all night to nurse a sick hen, recalled the sound of her voice when she launched into a hymn while baking, and she felt again her solid presence at her back when they went delivering eggs in the black shantytowns over the hill.

"No," she told Tilly firmly, "I'll not get rid of her."

"She's so rude."

"True." Ella nodded. "But she's also loyal. And she worships the ground that Reggie walks on."

Tilly laughed and looked Ella over with affection.

"How do you live with it, darling?" she asked. "It would drive me mad."

"Oh, you know me," Ella answered easily, "I can learn to live with most things."

Chapter 9

Dodie

Dodie was searching the sand. The midday sun beat down on her back as she paced the beach under a brilliant blue sky, punishing her skin beneath the thin cotton of her dress and scorching her neck each time she bent her head to examine the sand. She was seeking out Mr. Morrell's footprints.

They were here. Somewhere. Proof beyond doubt that he had once been alive. That he could leave his mark on the world. She didn't want his shoes or his clothes or his filthy gold coins, all inanimate leavings, all objects that meant nothing and possessed no trace of him. Of *him*. Of the man he was under his skin. Useless things. No, she wanted . . .

What did she want?

She sat back on her haunches, shielding her eyes with one hand, and shook back her hair as she scoured the graceful curve of white sand that stretched away from her, glistening like sugar spilled from a bowl. An empty beach. Only the eagerness of the turquoise waves as they wriggled up the slope and the bobbing of the noisy sandpipers disturbed the stillness. The palms along the tree line seemed to snooze, lethargic in the breezeless air.

She needed to find Mr. Morrell again. She didn't want to remember him as the lifeless piece of flesh wrapped in the shroud she had sewn for him, but as the man who had grimly held on to her ankle last night and asked for her help.

Help me.

She had helped him to die.

But now she could not allow herself to bury him with dishonor in a forgotten hole in the ground. She ignored the scrabble of footmarks outside her shack and instead she narrowed her eyes at the fading line of prints that trailed up from the waterline. Large feet in hard-soled shoes belonging to a stranger with a long stride.

"Didn't you trust me, Mr. Morrell?" she asked. "Not enough, it seems."

She tracked back to where she had helped him out of the wheelbarrow last night and found several clear footprints still etched into the sand. She placed her own bare foot in one but the imprint was too big to be one of hers. She knelt beside it and carefully brushed the curve of the sole with a finger.

This was him, this is what she sought. It was his strength that had created this form, this mark of Morrell. She crouched down over it greedily, her hand flattened out inside the indentation, sweat dripping from her forehead and leaving speckles on the sand like tears. A moan slipped through her lips.

Chapter 10

Ella

Ella drove. It was safer. Her friend's pink nose was always a good indicator of her alcohol intake and clearly she had been topping up this morning. Tilly was leaning back in the passenger seat of Ella's navy-blue Rover and dozed discreetly behind her sunglasses. That suited Ella. She had an errand to run before driving over to the yacht club, which lay on East Bay Street over on the far side of Nassau. She wanted to take a quick look at the school that needed more benches, so she headed west along the coast road and then took a left, winding inland up through the sparsely inhabited interior.

As her car kicked up a trail of dust on the dirt road, she relished the heat-laden air buffeting her cheek through the open window, lifting tendrils of her hair off her neck and flooding the car with the rich scent of wildflowers. Above them the sky arched in the kind of kingfisher blue a child would choose to paint a sky and reminded her of her own dreams when she was young. As a child she had wanted to grow up to be an intrepid explorer in darkest Africa and she had endured her brother's daily scorn as she taught herself how to use a compass and to take readings from the sun. She had such grand plans. But they came to nothing.

Instead she met Reggie. He was a shooting star, a bright young Member of Parliament, tagged as one to watch. Front-bench material. A different kind of adventure from hacking her way through virgin jungle or wading crocodile-infested swamps, but exciting nonetheless. As the wife of an MP she would be able to do something positive, influence his policies. She could leave a dent in the world that said, *Ella Sanford was here.*

So what happened?

How did she end up in a backwater like New Providence Island? Right now there was a war on in Europe, tearing countries and lives apart, and part of her hankered after driving an ambulance. Or taking down important radio messages. Delivering packages of secret documents. Anything . . . anything to break the crushing tedium of her life.

She swerved to avoid a rail-thin dog that had chosen to take its nap in the middle of the road in the sun. Tilly opened her eyes but closed them again, and Ella thought she must have a very clear conscience, the way she could fall asleep faster than a lizard. On each side of the road the trees dozed lazily in the heat above an underlay of young palmetto, a fan-shaped palm, whose leaves were used for thatching and weaving. A roadside stall selling yellow melons shot past and the dark-skinned woman behind it waved a hand. Ella waved back.

So what happened? Why wasn't Reggie in the war cabinet?

Everything changed, that's what happened.

"I will of course release you from our engagement, Ella," Reggie had announced stiffly in her mother's drawing room, "if you wish."

"No, darling Reggie." She had walked up to him, taken his face between her hands, and kissed his mouth. "It is not what I wish. Not at all."

His eyes had filled with tears. In the twenty years that she had spent with him, it was the only time she'd seen her husband cry. He didn't offer the details and she didn't ask. They never discussed it again. Some financial misdealing he'd got mixed up in, that was all she knew, but it was bad enough for him to withdraw discreetly from Parliament. Instead he was sidelined into the Colonial Office,

shunted out to postings in far-flung corners of the Empire to keep
him from being snubbed in decent London drawing rooms. So
instead of hacking her way to the source of the Nile, she had hacked
her way through cucumber sandwiches and polite conversation year
after year.

That's just the way it was.

*   *   *

The school, when she found it, was small, only twelve pupils, and
ill-equipped. There was a blackboard in the schoolroom but a
shortage of slates for the children, some of whom were perched on
upturned wooden crates. Ella greeted each child and talked with
the black female schoolteacher about the need for books for them
to read and chalks for them to write with. Maybe even a few stick
pens and inkwells. A notebook and ruler each would make such a
difference.

"I'll see what I can do for you," Ella promised.

"The School Commission ain't goin' to like that I went behind
their backs to you, Mrs. Sanford."

"I expect they're white and male and like their own rules. But
don't worry." Ella smiled with respect at the fresh young face of
the teacher, who was no more than nineteen or twenty herself.
"We won't tell them."

The young woman's eyes were excited. "I appreciate that.
Thank you, Mrs. Sanford."

The children sang "God Save Our Gracious King" to Ella not
once but twice, and as she was leaving, the schoolteacher said,
"Good-bye, Mrs. Sanford. Do take care in town."

Ella halted. "Why? What's happening in town?"

"Nothing much. It's just some construction workers again."

"But the pay dispute and all that trouble was settled last year,"
Ella pointed out. "Aren't they being paid enough now?"

"It depends on what you mean by enough, doesn't it?"

Ella made no comment and climbed into the car. "Wake up, Tilly. We have a race to watch."

It wasn't until she was approaching town once more, motoring along West Bay Street with the sea sprawling away to their left in a dazzling patchwork of emerald and midnight blue, that Ella suddenly sat up straight behind the steering wheel. Alert and watchful.

"Tilly, what exactly did she mean when she said, 'Take care in town'?"

* * *

Downtown Nassau was pretty. No other word for it. Pretty as a picture. All pastel-painted façades and shady canopies to shield shoppers from the inconvenience of sun or rain. Bay Street was the broad tree-lined main thoroughfare of Nassau that ran parallel to the ocean, and Ella was struck yet again by its elegance and its unadulterated prettiness.

Bay Street was where the money was. The Bay Street Boys— that's what they called them—were the greedy men in cool linen suits who ran this island. They smoked their fat Cuban cigars together in the offices above the rows of stylish shops and sometimes Ella caught sight of them gazing down from their upper windows with self-satisfied smiles. They were the men who controlled the economy and the House of Assembly, they were the lawyers and land agents, accountants and merchants, traders who made fortunes and knew exactly where to go for an official government stamp on their contracts.

They were male and white-skinned, and much of their power depended on keeping the blacks in their place and the island's agriculture primitive. Yet Ella had to admit that one of the qualities she loved most about the island was its free spirit. It flaunted its indifference to any kind of rules. Its history was riddled with illegal rum-running and barefaced roguery, all the way back to the time when formidable pirates such as Blackbeard stalked its dirt streets with a pistol strapped to each thigh, or when wreckers lured ships onto rocks to plunder their cargo.

It took the appointment of Woodes Rogers as the first British governor of the Bahamas in 1717 to knock some law and order into the taverns and brothels of Fort Nassau. But the island always remained a magnet for risk takers. For blockade runners to the Confederacy during the American Civil War, and more recently for bootleggers of illegal alcohol making a quick buck out of Prohibition in the United States. Those glory days were gone now— when a boat packed with crates of rum could make more money in one dangerous night spent sailing across to Miami than it could in six months of hard fishing.

But the standard of living for the island's black population continued to be woefully low and Ella could understand all too well why the riot had occurred last year. It was over inequality of pay between black and white construction workers on the new airfield. The physical damage inflicted on Bay Street had been repaired, broken glass and masonry rapidly swept out of sight, but the damage to the islanders' trust in the fairness of the system went beyond the reach of a broom and a bucket of cement. Black Bahamians by nature were easygoing people, always ready with a smile and eager to break out their infectious calypso music over a beer. It took an awful lot to get them riled up, but the unrest was growing, just below the surface.

"Do you know what happened to me yesterday, Tilly?"

"I know you're going to be wearing that surrey's pretty little fringe on your bonnet if you don't slow down, darling."

In front of them was one of the decorated horse-drawn surreys that trotted up and down Nassau's main streets, used as taxis by locals and as sightseeing vehicles by visitors to the island. Ella braked hard. The heat was billowing through the open window and the high wheels of the surrey were churning the road dust into a soup that stuck between her teeth.

"So what happened, Ella?"

"I was in Walker's Haberdashery yesterday. That toffee-nosed wife of his refused to serve a black woman who wanted to buy a pair of gloves."

"Christ!"

"Exactly."

"Did you say anything?"

"Of course. I closed my account there."

"Good for you."

"Gwen Walker is such a damn hypocrite."

Tilly lifted her sun hat from her lap and fanned her face with it. "Did you inform Reggie?"

"Yes, I did."

"I bet he was cross."

"He telephoned Rob Walker immediately."

"What was his—"

A noise like a slap made Ella jump in her seat, and abruptly the world turned bright red. She blinked hard. Still red. She put a hand up to her face and pulled it away at once, her heart hammering.

So much blood.

Chapter 11

Dodie

What was the smell?

Dodie inhaled sharply. A distinct odor of sadness seemed to seep out of the woodwork. It made the hairs prickle on the back of her neck. She had stood, rigid with indecision, outside the pink building with its green shutters and its blue glass lamp. It certainly didn't look like a police station on the outside. In front of it a monstrous cottonwood tree stood in the middle of the buildings that made up Nassau's administrative center in Rawson Square and Parliament Square. With their pink and columned façades arranged as charmingly as a doll's house, the Assembly Hall, the Supreme Court, the fire-brigade HQ, the post office, were all gathered behind a grand statue of Queen Victoria.

But inside the police station it was no doll's house. Dodie walked nervously toward the counter, where the duty sergeant was deep in conversation with a spiky-haired woman who seemed to be relating a complicated account of her dispute with her neighbor.

"Then the bastard chopped down my fig tree," she complained loudly, flapping a handkerchief to her face. "I just loved that tree."

"That doesn't give you the right to let your goats trample all over his . . ."

Dodie stepped back to where a line of hard-backed wooden chairs waited. Three men were seated on them, two black, one white. The white one was old and drunk. The other two were young and silent, their mouths tight, like they had something to hide. Neither even glanced at her. It had not occurred to Dodie that there might be a queue. She wanted this whole thing to be over quickly.

She took a seat and waited. The minutes crawled past. Her hands kept fidgeting, plucking at the material of her skirt, so she sat on them to keep them still. She was supposed to be at work now. Olive Quinn would already be snapping at the other waitresses at the Arcadia Hotel because she was short-staffed. Dodie eyed the telephone on the desk. Maybe she could ask to use it to explain why she was late, but when she glanced at the sergeant she changed her mind. He had the intractable look of someone who enjoyed saying no.

"Can I help you, miss?" A face loomed over Dodie. It belonged to a tall white man with an English accent, in a lightweight suit and tie. She could see *policeman* printed all over him, in the way he stood with feet planted firmly apart as though confident of his claim to this piece of territory. His mouth was polite, friendly even, but his gray eyes were so direct and intrusive that for a split second she looked away.

"I'm Detective Sergeant Calder," he said.

Before she could answer, the entrance door burst open with a crash and two women ran—literally ran—into the station covered in blood.

Everyone stared, but it was the tall policeman in the suit who reacted first.

"Call an ambulance, Sergeant," he ordered as he stretched out a hand to the taller of the two, a dark-haired woman who was clutching a hat in one hand with blood trailing from its wide brim like scarlet ribbons.

She seized his wrist, leaving smears on his sleeve. "This is an outrage," she shouted.

Blood was slashed across one side of her face, over her shoulder and blouse, puddling on her skirt, but the blond woman was worse. Her face was a mask of crimson, glistening on her eyelashes so that the intense blue of her eyes was startling in the midst of it, yet she was the one who remained calm. The top half of her summer dress was plastered against her breasts.

Dodie leaped to her feet. "Can I help?"

"We're not hurt," the blond woman announced. "It's not our blood." Her blue eyes glittered, bright with anger. "Fetch Colonel Lindop at once," she ordered.

The detective gave a quick nod to the desk sergeant, who ran for the stairs, and then he slipped off his jacket and draped it around the scarlet shoulders of the blond woman. She pulled the jacket tight around herself, hiding her humiliated body from public gaze.

"Thank you."

"What happened?" the detective asked. His voice sounded steady and comforting.

"We were attacked in the street." The woman smacked her palms together, as if she would crush the offenders.

Sharp footsteps sounded and an older man with military bearing marched into the room, effortlessly drawing eyes to himself. All over the world men like him were propping up the Empire on their shoulders. He was wearing the khaki uniform of the island's police commissioner with a black gun belt and highly polished boots. Immediately the atmosphere in the room altered.

"My dear ladies! Dear God, what the devil has happened to you?"

He advanced on them with outstretched arms, but Dodie noticed he didn't touch, didn't risk spoiling his crisply ironed uniform. Not like the one who gave up his jacket.

"There were five of them, they threw a bucket of blood over us," the blond woman declared. She had herself under control now.

"Whoever did this, I shall come down on them hard," Lindop assured her.

"Black workers shouting at us, hurling blood at us," the dark-haired woman said angrily. "I'm telling you, Colonel Lindop, that we're lucky to be alive." She had released the detective sergeant and her hands fluttered through the air like crimson butterflies in a panic.

"Tilly," the blonde said, suddenly embarrassed, "don't exaggerate. Other than . . . this"—she gestured at their ruined clothes—"they did us no harm. They ran off immediately."

Colonel Lindop waved a hand toward a door at the far end of the room. "Come, ladies." He glanced around the spectators, his gaze skimming over Dodie before returning to make a quick assessment of the two women. "Blake," he said briskly to the desk sergeant at his elbow, "fetch a doctor. And a photographer. At once."

Abruptly they were gone. The women vanished through the door and Dodie was left in the middle of the room. She turned toward the door that led to the street. She could leave now and no one would notice if she hurried back out on to the street.

"What can I do for you, miss?"

She swung round. Detective Sergeant Calder was leaning over her once more with concern.

"That was quite a shock, wasn't it? Can I get you some water?" He briefly touched his chest as though to slow a galloping heart and Dodie's eyes were drawn to the blood on his sleeve.

"No, thank you." She had to push the next words off the end of her tongue. "I want to report a murder."

* * *

The tiny interview room was full of stillness and heat. Dust motes drifted aimlessly across Dodie's line of vision and she tried to focus on them rather than on the expression in Calder's gray eyes. It made her uneasy, that look of wariness contained between narrowed lids. It wasn't what she expected.

This is what she'd expected: she would tell them about Mr. Morrell. All of it. The policemen would listen attentively, then they would collect the—she could barely think the word—the *body*, and using whatever method it was that detectives used, they would find his killer, drag the culprit before a judge and jury, and then throw him in jail for life. She had even expected a little sympathy, like the two women received.

That was not what she got.

The moment she uttered the word *"murder,"* everything changed in the police station. The smiles vanished. People stepped away from her, as if she were unclean. Even Detective Calder with his bloodstained sleeve moved back, putting a no-man's-land between them, and his shoulders seemed to lock into a rigid line.

He ushered her into an interview room that was windowless and fanless, so that the heat steadily rose. She sat down and told him the story while a young constable in a corner made notes. She kept it simple: I found Mr. Morrell last night wounded in the alleyway, I took him to my home where I nursed him, but he died today. He told me to bury him in a hole somewhere, but I couldn't bear to do it. At the last moment I changed my mind and came here to you. When she'd finished, the length of the silence in the room felt like a rope winding around her neck.

"Miss Wyatt," the detective said in a considerate voice, "that must have been a deeply shocking experience for you. I'm sorry."

Sorry for her? For Morrell? For the reputation of Nassau?

"Yes." Even to her own ears it sounded guarded.

"Why didn't you call the police last night?"

"I told you. Mr. Morrell begged me not to inform anyone, not even the hospital. He said it was too dangerous."

"And you thought that was more important than saving his life?"

"No, of course not."

"So why didn't you contact us?"

"I told you. He was frightened. He believed that whoever did this to him would come to finish the job."

"So you forced a wounded and bleeding man to walk through the streets of Nassau."

"He wanted me to get him away from there. He was frightened. I didn't force him, I helped him."

"At the cost of his life."

"I didn't know he was going to die. I thought that . . ."

That I could save him.

Instead she said, "I thought that he was getting better after I stopped the bleeding. He improved and started to ask me questions about my life and he even admired my quilt on the wall. He was"—she looked directly at the detective seated opposite her—"interested. I didn't think people who were dying would be so interested in others. I liked him."

Calder nodded and glanced at the few notes he had jotted down on a lined pad in front of him. He squared it up with the edge of the table, tapped it thoughtfully with one finger, then pulled out a packet of Players cigarettes from his pocket. He offered her one, but she shook her head. He lit his own and exhaled a string of gray smoke that hung lifelessly in the humid air, and she wondered what was coming next.

"I have some questions," he announced.

"I've told you everything."

The drumbeat of her own blood was loud in her ears.

"Where is the body of Mr. Morrell now?"

"I told you." Why was he doing this? Making her repeat the facts over and over. "It's in my house on the beach." She noticed her use of "*it*" instead of "*he*."

"May we have the key to it, please?"

She slapped her key on the table. "You have my address written down in front of you."

He nodded. The constable in the corner shot to his feet, picked up the key, and took it outside before returning to his gloomy corner. Oddly, during the brief interval in which she and the detective were alone, Calder studied her face and gave her something that was halfway toward a smile. She didn't know what it meant. It turned something ice cold inside her.

"A few more questions," he told her. "What was Mr. Morrell's first name?"

"I don't know."

"You said he was American. Where did he come from?"

"I don't know."

"Was he here on business?"

"I don't know."

"You said he had no wallet or passport. So how did he get to be here on New Providence Island?"

"I don't know."

"What reason did his attacker have to stab him?"

"I don't know."

"Where was he staying?"

"I don't know."

Detective Calder leaned back in his chair, tipping it onto its back legs, and smoke hung on his lips as though reluctant to leave him. He stubbed out his cigarette and gave her a blank stare. "You don't know much, do you, Miss Wyatt?"

Bile slid into her throat. She had made no mention yet of the gold coins or the name Sanford or of Mama Keel's medicine.

"I've told you all I know," she said.

He tucked his hands under his armpits and his eyes focused on hers. "I do hope so."

She didn't look away. She opened her mouth to tell Calder that she needed that glass of water now, but suddenly it dawned on her that he believed she might be the one who stabbed Morrell in that dark alleyway. It had happened before. A girl taking a man home for sex and getting caught thieving from his wallet. A knife in his guts before he could beat her to a pulp.

She snapped her mouth shut. A layer of sweat glistened on her skin. *He thinks I killed Morrell.* She looked down at her hands. *I'm shaking.*

"Now, Miss Wyatt, let's start again," the detective said in a controlled voice. "From the beginning."

Chapter 12

Flynn

How do you tell when a man is lying?

You look at the disconnect at the back of his eyes.

You watch for the telltale twitch at the sides of his mouth.

You listen to the change of pace as his words fall from his mouth.

Sometimes you have to work at it. But today it was easy. Flynn Hudson could tell the Englishman seated opposite him was lying through his pearly whites by the way the tips of his ears turned pink. A fleeting rush of blood. Blink and you'd miss it. It happened each time he said the words "Believe me."

"Believe me, Hudson, Meyer Lansky is incandescent over in Miami. Not at all happy about this outcome. It's a fiasco."

"Believe me, Hudson, I should have listened to Morrell. He didn't want you to participate in this operation in the first place."

Both lies.

Flynn yanked out a pouch of tobacco and took his time rolling himself a smoke. Johnnie Morrell was his friend and now he was dead. You don't have a smoke with a buddy one day and call his death a *fiasco* the next. You just don't do that. Not to friends. So to hell with this guy who spoke with a dainty British accent and talked as if he'd swallowed a dictionary for breakfast. He was calling himself Spencer. Another of his limey lies.

They were in a bar tucked away behind a seedy row of shops

where locals came to drink beer and gripe about the soldiers getting first pick of the girls. The guy was wearing no tie and no jacket, which was clearly his idea of blending in, though the blade-sharp creases in his pants and the curve of distaste on his mouth didn't exactly help with that plan. Half-moons of sweat had flared under his arms. They spoiled the look of his shirt. The light in the bar was dim, which suited Flynn just fine. It came as a relief to the eyes after the glare of the plate-glass sky outside. Around them there was a mix of skin colors, men who paid no heed to Spencer and himself because they had their own cares to drown in their beers. They didn't need trouble from two strangers glaring at each other like a pair of fighting cocks.

Flynn lit the cigarette he'd been rolling and sent a barrage of smoke into the cloud of mosquitoes that had been stalking him. Johnnie Morrell should have been here with them, knocking back the rum and making with his wisecracks, giving this guy a hard time. Not lying in a hole, talking with the worms.

"This is the big one," Morrell had whispered to him in the girl's shack last night. "This will cut us loose."

Yeah. Cut you loose from life, Johnnie.

Flynn felt the sharp point of sorrow in his chest, like some bastard was taking a chisel to the inside of his ribs, and he grabbed a long swig of his beer to rinse it away.

"Listen to me, Hudson." Spencer leaned forward, thought about putting his elbows on the table, but changed his mind fast when he saw the sorry state of it. "I want some answers."

Flynn didn't blink.

"Where's the girl?" Spencer demanded.

Flynn shrugged, as if she were of no importance. "She's headed into town. She works in one of the laundries. She's not a problem. You got anything on her?"

He was careful to keep his eyes rock-steady, his mouth and his voice under tight control. If you're going to lie, do it properly. He'd seen her walk up the steps into the police station.

"No. You're certain she's out of our hair?" Spencer frowned.

"Sure."

"How much does she know? What did Morrell tell her?"

"Nothing."

"What makes you think that?"

His tone was nasty. Like most Englishmen Flynn had met, his teeth were bad and Flynn considered whether it would be a kindness to rearrange them for him.

"I spoke to Morrell," he said instead, "when the girl left the shack. He'd told her nothing."

"Don't let them find her, Flynn. Please." Morrell's face was whiter than the sheet on the bed and he had the glassy look of a dead man in his eyes.

"She's fixing me up, Flynn. I can stay hidden here, they'll never find me. Just a few days. Don't tell anyone about her."

"Sure, Johnnie. You get better and I'll have a boat ready. We'll wait till dark." He'd patted his friend's arm and it was worse than touching seaweed, cold and slimy. "I'll stay, Johnnie. Don't worry. I've got your back covered."

"No, go. She's on the edge. She'll bolt to the police if there are two of us. Too dangerous. Come back tomorrow."

Flynn didn't let himself look at the blood that had soaked into the shirt and dripped on the floorboards in case he stopped believing in a tomorrow.

"Okay. Sleep well, Johnnie. I'll be nearby on the beach." He opened the door. "I'm not going nowhere without you, pal."

A whisper stopped him. "I've told her nothing." Morrell's eyes glittered darkly in the lamplight. "Don't let them hurt her, kid."

Flynn nodded and slid out into the darkness.

The English guy was tense and signaled to the barman for another scotch. He didn't offer Flynn one. His eyes were small but focused, and the smell of success seeped from the gold cuff links that winked at his wrists and from the signet ring on his pinkie when he ran a palm over his smooth brown hair.

"Morrell was a fool to get caught," Spencer said bitterly.

Flynn revealed nothing in his face but indifference.

"Morrell was sent here," Spencer continued, emphasizing each word, "in secret to do a deal. Right?"

"Sure." Flynn gave a single nod.

"And you were sent over from Miami by Meyer Lansky to watch his back. All nice and tidy. It's what you're good at, I'm told. Correct me if I'm missing something here."

"You're not missing anything."

Spencer jabbed a finger at Flynn. "Who did this? While you were sleeping on the job, who got close enough to stick a knife in Morrell's guts?"

Flynn drew in a long silent breath, the stink of stale alcohol clinging to his nostrils. "That's what I intend to find out," he said.

"And the girl? Is she in on it?"

"Forget the girl. She's nobody."

"You'd better be right about that, Hudson," Spencer hissed.

Suddenly Flynn could not stand to breathe the same air with this guy any longer. He abandoned his beer and headed for the door without bothering with the nicety of good-byes.

"Hey!" Spencer called after him. "You had better be right about that girl, Hudson."

Flynn pushed open the door. "Jackass," he muttered under his breath.

Outside a man was trundling past with a barrow stacked high with sponges and treated him to a smile that was warmer than he deserved. Sometimes it was easy to forget that there was a real world out there, where your biggest problem was the price you'd get in the busy sponge market that day.

Chapter 13

Dodie

The sun sat alone in the huge blue sky like a golden eye that refused to blink. It was watching over the systematic ransacking of her home by meticulous men in uniforms and overpolished boots. Dodie retreated into the waves up to her knees, wading the length of the cay, eyes concentrating on the tiny fish that darted between her legs like silver teardrops. When the police had completed whatever it was they had to complete, Detective Calder summoned her back to his patch of sand and reluctantly she left the water.

"We've finished here," he said. His manner was official.

She nodded.

"Thank you," he added, "for your cooperation."

She nodded again. His shadow enveloped her and she stepped to one side to escape its weight.

"Find anything?" she asked.

"Nothing definite."

"Surely it can't be so hard for you to find out when Mr. Morrell came to Nassau and who he's been with. It's only a small island, everyone knows what goes on."

She halted her words, put an end to them by crushing her hand over her mouth.

The detective dragged his shadow back over her.

"Miss Wyatt"—he lowered his head to her height—"are you all right?"

"Yes."

"You don't look all right. A cup of tea might—"

"Detective Sergeant Calder," Dodie said stiffly, "what I want is a killer, not a cup of tea."

"I assure you that we will do all in our power to track down the person who stabbed Mr. Morrell but"—he paused, his gaze flicking back to her shack—"you have given us very little information. Is there anything else you can add?"

Two gold coins. A name on a scrap of paper.

"No," she said. "Nothing."

In the silence that followed, she did not let her eyes drop from his. Over his broad shoulder she could see two more uniformed policemen waiting patiently for him. The cry of a black-headed gull as it stalked the waterline was the only sound, yet when the detective spoke, he lowered his voice to little more than a murmur and she felt a ripple of concern creep across the patch of soft white sand that divided them.

"Miss Wyatt, we are dealing with a dangerous person here, a brutal killer who left his victim to bleed to death in an alleyway. I have a team of men examining that alleyway right now, but if they come up with nothing, it will not be an easy task to trace the person who murdered Mr. Morrell." He drew in a quick frustrated breath. "Unless you can help us further."

"I'm sorry, I can't."

He waited a moment longer, as if he could coax more words from her, and when none came he glanced along the peaceful stretch of beach with a kind of longing on his face, as if peacefulness was not something that intruded often into his busy life. A pair of scarlet macaws swept across his eye line, trailing their long spindly tails, and he gave a smile, but when he turned back to her it was gone, his official face firmly in place.

"I see," he said, "thank you." If he still suspected she was the one who wielded the knife, he was disguising it well. "I suggest," he added, "that you avoid back alleyways in future."

With that comment, Detective Calder walked up the beach and took his shadow with him.

* * *

The Arcadia Hotel had started life as a private mansion. With its columned façade and four embellished turrets, it was constructed to be the grandiose home of Sir Archibald Caroll, who uprooted his family from Scotland and moved them to Nassau in 1787, when his good friend the Earl of Dunmore was appointed governor of the Bahamas.

That was a period when gracious living blossomed on the island, when many fine houses started to line the streets, all served by retinues of slaves who were hidden away at night in the Over-the-Hill shanties. So keen was the earl to acquire more servants that he paid a bounty to slave ships bound for America to bring their cargo to the Bahamas instead. Word spread and Europeans took passage to the islands—attracted not only by the enticing climate and beauty of its beaches, but even more by the prospect of easy living and the fortunes to be made out of cotton plantations.

Olive Quinn had transformed the mansion into one of Nassau's most desirable hotels. She had no time for old stories about the inept Earl of Dunmore, though she did approve of his construction of the two most eccentric forts on the island—Fort Charlotte with its drawbridge and dungeons and Fort Fincastle in the shape of a flatiron—both packed with thirty-two-pounder cannon to blow any marauding pirate or Spanish ships clean out of the water. That was more her style of doing things.

"Wyatt, it's the kitchen for you tonight," she declared, eyebrows swooping, the moment Dodie came through the servants' entrance of the Arcadia. Olive Quinn was an impressive presence. She was solidly built with sallow skin and hair dyed jet black. It was cut into a short, sharp bob, as neat and precise as her hotel.

"I'm sorry, Miss Olive. I was detained."

"By whom?"

"By the police."

"Well, well, that's a new one. So what have you been up to, Wyatt?"

Olive Quinn addressed her employees, all of whom were female, by their surnames. Her rules were rigid. Her punishments harsh. Her kindness unconventional. But she had given Dodie a job when no one else in Nassau would touch her. Dodie knew what was coming next, so she headed straight for the big enamel sink, already pushing up her sleeves, ready to face the next five hours up to her elbows in greasy water, scouring pots and pans with baking soda and vinegar. It was Miss Olive's specialty for tardiness.

"I found a man on my way home last night. He was hurt. I tried to help but he died." She started to shunt the pans around noisily. "I told the police about it today but it took much longer than I expected." Her back was turned toward the others working in the kitchen. "Next time I'll leave him in the alleyway."

She heard a moan from Cook, a joyful Bahamian woman who liked to hum hymns while she made bread. She claimed it filled the dough with God's good grace and made it lighter. Little Minnie, the kitchen dogsbody, uttered a squeak of shock.

"Two hours at the sink and then she can come up," Olive Quinn told Cook.

"Sure thing, Miss Olive," Cook agreed. She liked having Dodie down in her kitchen.

Dodie plunged her hands into the hot water, expecting it to turn bright scarlet as if she hadn't washed Morrell's blood off her skin fifty times already. But to her surprise she found Miss Olive's solid figure standing right behind her.

"Are you all right, Wyatt?"

"Yes, Miss Olive."

There was an awkward pause, during which Dodie's hands started to scrub the pans with a vigor that was intended to show just how all right she was. For a fleeting moment the woman's hand rested on her head, offering comfort, but then the warmth of it vanished and Dodie heard the usual snort of impatience.

"Good." Miss Olive's shoes tapped briskly back to the world of cocktails and glossy smiles that she presented to her guests each evening.

"Good," Dodie echoed under her breath. Life was back to normal.

*   *   *

The only advantage of being a servant was that you heard things. Often things you were not meant to hear. Some people regarded a waitress as a human being as well as a servant, so they were more careful about what they said when you were around. But many saw a waitress as no more than a disembodied hand carrying a tray of glasses, or as a frilly uniform that placed a plate in front of them. Sometimes Dodie wondered if she was made of glass, she was so invisible in the room, but Miss Olive claimed that it proved she was an excellent waitress. It was meant as a compliment but Dodie didn't see it like that.

The party that evening was loud. American voices from the U.S. Army Air Force contingent boomed across the room, bouncing off mirrors and champagne glasses, with many of the men looking handsome in their immaculate dress uniform. With over three thousand service personnel stationed permanently on the island, as well as the numerous aircrews who passed through the base for training each month, there was a constant oversupply of men on the island and always an insufficiency of women, which vexed the young bucks.

Dodie entered with a tray of drinks, her hands pink from kitchen duties, and the bright laughter in the room sliced under her skin like slivers of bamboo. She wanted to shout, *Be quiet. A man has died.* But she pulled the polite meaningless smile of a servant onto her face and circulated with the drinks. The masculine smell of cigars and the talk of war dominated the room, as the men crowded around the women like bees, unable to resist the shimmering satins or the fragrance of their languid perfumes. Dodie stood, invisible, at elbows, lingering longer than strictly necessary when she caught a scrap of conversation that interested her.

"Bomber command is hitting the Ruhr hard in Germany."

"I hear that the U.S. Eighth Air Force sent two hundred B-17 aircraft to bombard the German naval base at Wilhelmshaven. That'll knock the blighters back."

"God, I hope so. Their U-boats have been a blasted plague on our Atlantic shipping. Over six hundred tons of Allied ships lost in March, can you believe that? Lost to those filthy Nazi wolf packs."

Dodie saw the veins in their necks pulse and heard the edge in their voices grow sharper. A woman with diamonds in her hair wept quietly and whispered to her friend, "My sister was killed in the terrible bombing of Plymouth." She looked as if she did not want to be at the party, but seized a glass from the tray and drank it straight down. Elsewhere Dodie learned that the U.S. Marines were island-hopping in the battle against the Japanese in the Pacific and that the 43rd Infantry under General MacArthur was heading for New Guinea. An attractive young blonde had just come back from seeing *Oklahoma!* on Broadway and an earnest man in glasses was trying to impress her by talking about Raymond Chandler's hard-boiled prose, but he was totally unaware of the sidelong glances she was casting at the Leslie Howard type across the room.

"Go get me a bourbon whiskey, girl."

Dodie turned to the American voice that had delivered the abrupt order. It belonged to the burly man in his sixties who had entered not long ago, head thrust forward, the broad muscles of his chest tense, his eyes sharp as he worked out what was on offer in the gathering. He was no stranger to the Arcadia Hotel and Dodie recognized him immediately. Everyone on the island knew

Sir Harry Oakes was the owner of the most productive gold mine in the Western world up in Canada, as well as of the British Colonial Hotel, the impressive seven-story building overlooking its own private beach and tennis courts on the edge of Nassau. Purchased, Dodie had heard, in a moment of pique in 1939, when the maître d' refused him entry because of his usual ragbag of scruffy attire. His first action as the new proprietor was to sack the offending maître d'. A lesson to others.

Nobody crossed Sir Harry and got away with it. Yet in contrast, Dodie heard everywhere of his concern and generosity when it came to his black employees. He was Nassau's most passionate philanthropist, but one who, after twenty years of living with little more than a bucketful of dirt and a pickax for company in his prospecting days, lacked the polished edges of the colonial breed.

"A bourbon."

"Yes, sir."

She fetched it at once and presented it to him, eyes down. Never look them in the eye. It was one of Olive Quinn's rules. It made you instantly visible and they didn't like that. Sir Harry was busy discussing the price of copper with a slight man who had an impatient whine to his voice, but he broke off and addressed Dodie directly as she proffered the drink on her tray.

"So, young lady"—Sir Harry took the drink—"a busy day, I guess."

Dodie wasn't sure what he meant. She flicked her gaze to his face, a high forehead with receding hairline and a belligerent square jaw. His eyes were those of a man who had done more than most in his life and who valued his privacy, one who hoarded his secrets. She could sympathize with that.

"Every day is busy," she answered with a polite-servant smile.

"But not every day do you find a body."

Her throat tightened. "I didn't find a *body*."

"Near as dammit, you did, from what I hear."

"How did you hear?"

He took a satisfied swig of his neat whiskey. "Well, girl, let me tell you, there's not much goes on in this island that I don't get to hear about."

Oh yes, she could believe that. She could feel the force of his will even through the fine fabric of his expensive black evening jacket. She lowered her eyes and started to move away with her tray.

"Did the guy talk to you?"

"Who?"

"The guy you found."

"No."

"Is that so?"

"Yes."

Across the room a hand wreathed in gold rings was beckoning for another cocktail.

"That's not what you told the police, is it?"

She felt heat rising in her chest, but the tray in her hand remained steady, the glasses didn't rattle, and she didn't join in the laughter. *Help me, help me.* Morrell's words hurtled round inside her head. She turned and looked at Sir Harry Oakes once more, and saw that he was studying her intently.

"I'm sorry, that is a private matter," she said.

He rolled a slug of whiskey around his mouth, washing his teeth in it, and nodded. For a moment they both stood staring at each other in silence, indifferent to the wave of noise around them.

What does he want?

"Do you like working here?" he asked somberly.

"Yes."

Don't get me sacked. Please, don't get me sacked. I need this job.

He tapped his expanse of white shirtfront. "Come and work for me."

Dodie's mind stumbled. She realized her mouth was open and she shut it quickly, but the glasses on her tray rattled.

"I've watched you for months," he continued easily. "You're

good at your job. In fact, darn good, I reckon. I'm always on the lookout for top-notch hotel staff and you fit the bill." He glanced across to where Olive Quinn hovered near the door, her sharp eye ready to pounce on trouble in any corner of the room. "She pays you chicken feed I bet. It's what the lady is known for." He moved half a step closer. "Come over to my British Colonial Hotel to work and I'll pay you double her rate. What do you say to that?"

"No, thank you."

"Don't be dumb, young lady. It's a damn good offer."

"I'm happy here."

"Is that a fact?"

"Sir Harry, I am grateful for the offer but"—she shook her head firmly—"no, thank you."

She moved away quickly before he could say anything more. Ignoring the beckoning hands of guests and aiming straight for the door, she shot down the corridor till she reached the kitchen, threw the tray on the table, snatched up her cardigan, and didn't stop. She kept on going, though Minnie called after her. She kept on going right out the back door and kept on going into the night.

Something was wrong.

Chapter 14

Ella

Ella was playing poker. She'd just lost her watch on a pair of tens. Time to leave.

"Don't go, Mrs. Sanford. Watch me one more time."

Ella sat down again. "I'm watching."

The sooty-haired Welsh pilot spun his wheelchair and scooted over to the table-tennis table, where he wielded his bat with an aggression and purpose that she had caught no hint of during their conversation over a beer. His manner had been mild, his voice soft. But put a bat in his hand or a pack of cards on the table and he transformed into a daredevil. Is that how he'd crashed his plane? Skimming its wings too low over the water, drawn to the limits of danger.

"Jonesy, give it a rest!" someone called out.

But Ella clapped when he scored another point, agile in his chair, and he grinned across at her. He'd paid the price for his devilment, only one leg now, but he'd been patched up at the service hospital at Oakes Field. Though he'd been offered a cushy trip home to Blighty, he'd declined it and settled for an RAF office job in Nassau pushing paperwork around.

"At least I'm still here," he'd told her proudly. "Still doing my bit."

It wasn't unusual to see men in uniform being escorted around Nassau's streets in wheelchairs. They were always the ones treated to the widest smiles by shopkeepers or given free beers by bartenders. They were one of the reasons Ella liked to drop in on the Canteen for a couple of hours. After a day like she'd had today, it put things back in perspective.

The Canteen had been set up as a place of entertainment for servicemen, somewhere they could go to blow off steam when they needed a drink or a game of darts, or even just to hit the dance floor for a jitterbug with a pretty girl. The Society of Freemasons had donated part of their magnificent lodge on Bay Street for the Canteen's use and a committee arranged dances and singers or a steel band, and even film shows when they could get the projector to work.

There was a lively atmosphere here and a deep-chested laughter that Ella liked. And she wasn't the only one. She was pleased to see that a handful of local girls had looked in on the boys, sparking off the usual rivalry between the British and American servicemen. All it took was an attractive blonde or a striking redhead to get the flags flying.

"Dance, Mrs. Sanford?"

Ella looked up. A corn-haired flight lieutenant stood in front of her, a hopeful smile on his face. So handsome. So young. Probably barely in his twenties. As bomber crew, the likelihood of him ever seeing his thirties was slim, and she knew this was where the energy in the room came from—that glimpse of death around the next corner.

"I really should be going," she said. "I'm late for something already."

He grinned cheekily. "Is it important?"

Ella glanced around the room. Felt the fast beat of the music. Saw the frightened blue eyes.

"No, not important at all."

*   *   *

"You're late."

"I'm sorry, darling. I got caught up."

Reggie frowned. "You had me worried. After what happened to you and Tilly this morning, I don't like you being out alone."

Ella kissed his cheek and accepted a rum punch from a white-jacketed waiter. "Don't fuss, Reggie, please. Now," she added with a bright smile, "where's Hector?"

They were celebrating the birthday of Tilly's husband, Hector, at the Nassau Yacht Club. It was a rather dull sprawling building with yellow stucco and well-tended gardens on the eastern fringe of the city, near the Fort Montague Hotel and the old fortress, but it was a popular watering hole and the usual crowd had gathered there.

"Happy birthday, Hector!" Ella greeted him.

Hector was a lawyer, one of the pack of Bay Street Boys. They were out in force tonight in their dinner jackets and gold watch chains, but it struck Ella that the mood of the party was less buoyant than she had expected. Or was it that the one she'd just come from at the Canteen was so animated and spirited that this one, by contrast, felt dull?

"Ella, my dear girl, what a delight to see you safe and sound. Bit of a scare you and Tilly gave us all. Damn rioters!"

"It was hardly a riot, Hector." Ella laughed and changed the subject rapidly. "How did the yacht race go this afternoon? Sorry we missed it."

Hector drew down his burly eyebrows but didn't bother to drop his voice. "That johnnie-foreigner won again. You know, the lounge-lizard fellow."

"Freddie de Marigny?"

"Damned right, that's the one. What Sir Harry's little girl Nancy sees in him I don't know. Likes to win, he does."

Ella smiled. "Don't you all?"

He laughed and drifted over to a group of cigar smokers who were deep in discussion about the ten-day Axis bombardment of Pantelleria, a Mediterranean island between Sicily and Tunisia.

"Wiped out those bloody Italians we did," one voice said, gloating.

"Not a single British life lost. Our troops just marched in and they surrendered like sheep. No backbone, you see."

"It'll be Sicily next. And then we'll slice through Italy like a knife through butter." It was Reggie's voice.

"General Montgomery and the Eighth Army will make mince-meat of those gutless Italians, mark my words," Hector asserted.

Ella edged away. She didn't want to picture the young men fighting, maybe even some of the men she'd seen in the Canteen tonight. With bullets slamming into their flesh and their smiles buried in the foreign mud. It made her think unwillingly of Mr. Morrell's sudden death and a shiver passed through her.

She reached for another rum punch and was just lighting a cig-arette, when Reggie appeared at her side and asked crisply, "What happened to your watch?"

* * *

"The island is changing, Tilly. Changing for the better."

"Don't be ridiculous, Ella. Look at what happened to us today. Simply ghastly."

They were standing at the yacht club windows that looked out over the eastern harbor. It was dark outside, but amber lamps picked out the terraced grounds below that ran down to a small marina where yachts bobbed and bustled against their mooring ropes. How many times, Ella wondered, had she stood in this spot? With these same people. Drinking the same rum punch.

"The war has been good for the island," she insisted. "Don't stick your head in the colonial sand, Tilly."

"How can you say that, darling? It's been vile. The streets and cafés are packed with brash young men in uniform who think they own this island. They strip their shirts off in all the wrong places and steal all the girls, so that our own decent young men don't stand a chance." She knocked back her drink in one shot. "Simply vile."

It was true. Ella couldn't deny that there was some friction between the island's men and the newcomers. She exhaled a cloud of cigarette smoke at her own reflection trapped inside the windowpane, blurring the lines of her face.

"But the war has brought prosperity as well, Tilly, you have to admit. Thousands more jobs. Not just at the air bases but in the shops and restaurants, and that means lots more work for black women on the island too, better pay and better—"

"Ella, don't."

"Don't what?"

Tilly sighed. "Don't try to change us. I want things to stay exactly as they are."

Ella stared at her tall graceful friend with her precise dark hair and her finely sculpted mouth, and realized that in an odd way she didn't know her at all. She was not sure what lay behind the carefully cultivated colonial mask. Is that what Tilly thought of her too?

"Don't worry, Tilly," Ella teased. "I'm sure the duke will be staying on as governor until the end of the war, whenever that might be."

Tilly raised a carefully groomed eyebrow along with a languid smile. "Darling, you are such a comfort."

Outside, the muted murmur of the ocean drifted closer.

Chapter 15

Dodie

The warmth of the night wrapped itself around Dodie as she ran from the Arcadia. Shadows brushed against her skin with moist breath that did little to cool the heat in her veins. She stretched her legs and fell into a steady lope as she covered the distance to the shoreline and then swung west along the fringe of tall palm trees that leaned over her with grasping fingers in the dark. Fronds whispered overhead and night creatures chirruped unseen in the undergrowth.

Some instinct was driving her toward home, though she wasn't sure why. There was no reason for it. Just a need to hunker down in her own house, to close the shutters tight, to lock out the world.

Something was wrong.

Badly wrong.

How did Sir Harry Oakes know who she was or what she'd done? Or which words she'd used in the privacy of the police station? And why would he care?

*　*　*

The red glow in the sky behind the trees ahead of Dodie could have passed for the first fingers of sunrise. But she was heading west, not east, and it wasn't even midnight yet. She flew over the ground, drawing closer till she could pick out the shimmers of gold splashed over the trunks of the casuarinas and the slashes of vermilion that flickered and danced along the leaves of the palms.

As she burst on to the beach, it was as if a scarlet hole had been punched into the blackness. A great roar of sound charged across the sand at her and she felt the heat hit before she saw its source. Her house was on fire.

Oblivious to the sparks and embers that swirled through the air, she ran to it, desperate to save her home. A small crowd of people had gathered around the burning shack, their shadows writhing over the sand as the flames clawed up into the night sky. Voices were shouting. But Dodie's ears heard only the crackle and clamor of the fire, her heart hammering as she darted in and out and tried to sneak under the flames to retrieve something—some small shred—of her life. But a hand clamped firmly on her arm and dragged her back. It was Mama Keel.

"Quiet, child, stop your noise."

The sounds coming out of her own mouth were fearful. She jammed her arm across it to shut them off. It was the stink of singed cotton on her sleeve that brought her back to her senses and the realization of how close the flames had come to devouring her, as well as the house. She let Mama Keel lead her away to safety and only then did she notice the string of people working fast with buckets, passing water along a chain of hands from the sea to the shack. In the glow from the blaze she could see sweat gleaming on their faces and she wanted to tell them to stop, to give up, to abandon their task. She could see it was too late. The flames had won. Mama Keel stood beside her, her arm wrapped around Dodie's shoulders, but neither could look away from the fire.

"Thank the Lord you ain't in there, child."

Dodie shivered.

"Think of it this way," Mama Keel said against the roar of the flames. "You just losin' things. You had a life before you got those things and you'll have a life now those things is gone. There ain't no end to our desire or to our greed, but they is just foolish nothings. Believe me, child."

"Mama, tell the men that I am grateful but now they can stop."

"Your spirit is more solid than them there flames. Remember that."

"I will, Mama."

But as Mama Keel moved off to speak to the men with the buckets, a section of the shack caved in with a spectacular shower of sparks. Dodie caught sight of a young man, etched in gold, raking with a long branch into the inferno that used to be her home. He was dragging some of those foolish nothings back to life and was in serious danger of injury to himself. *Stop*, she tried to say, *I want you to stop.*

But she couldn't. She felt herself standing on the edge of a cliff. She didn't look down but she could sense something dark moving below her. Waiting for her to fall.

*   *   *

Dodie woke. The light was muted and grayish, matching the mood behind her eyelids. At first she was still in her dream, with her father selling Bibles door to door around rainy Manchester in England when she was only eight. But she heard the cry of a seagull and opened her eyes and that was when she remembered the fire. A knot of barbed wire seemed to lodge itself in her throat.

She had spent the night at Mama Keel's, curled up on a blanket on the floor. She had not believed she could sleep, but Mama had given her something to drink and she had drifted into a black empty space where there were no dreams. It was scarcely light but the front door stood wide open and Dodie could see the pack of gray clouds hunched low on the horizon, as if peering in, and Mama Keel shelling peas on the doorstep.

Dodie didn't linger. She accepted Mama's offer of an old cotton shift to wear instead of her waitress uniform and headed out into the early-morning wind. She couldn't bring herself to travel along the beach this time but instead she chose the coastal road, snake-gray and deserted at this hour. She cut down through the trees and arrived at the beach from behind.

She had prepared herself. She had promised herself no tears. But she had not thought to prepare herself for the smell of it. That's what reached her first, the stink of charred wood that drifted on the air, and then the sight of her vegetable patch scorched and shriveled behind the remains of the house. The bean plants lay brown and lifeless as dead spiders, and a rat was rummaging among the remains. Just a few pumpkins had survived, still flagrantly orange amid the bleak debris.

Her house was gone. A wasteland of memories. No good to anyone. Only a few scraps of twisted metal reached up like rotten teeth out of the blackened heap. The wind whipped up ash from it and chased it down the beach, but Dodie could not bear to look anymore. She turned away from the grim sight, and anger at whoever had done this tore through her, somehow getting all tangled up with the policeman standing right here on the same beach, pressing her with questions that frightened the life out of her. She moved away, and as she did so, she glimpsed the outline of a lone man sitting under a palm tree, just where the bay curled round into its horseshoe. From this distance it was hard to see his face clearly, but she could make out that the young man was white, with a pale shirt and long rangy limbs.

He was watching her.

She didn't want to be watched, didn't want her grief to be spied upon by a stranger, so she turned her back on the figure and walked down to the ocean.

The sky was heavy with leaden clouds and the waves came charging toward her with fraying white caps, warning of the summer storm that was rolling down to the island from Florida. Trails of coarse kelp had been thrown up on the sand and tiny orange crabs were seeking shelter in its folds. Dodie hitched up the hem of her dress and waded into the water, her toes squeezing the sand into hard humps with each step, the only outward expression of the anger inside her. She prowled the shallows for a long time, back and forth along the cay, thinking about the men who had lain in wait for Morrell at the hospital and asking herself what it was he could have done to drive them to murder.

What kind of people were they? Was the burning of her house a warning from them? A sign to keep her mouth shut? What else would they do to her?

What the hell was going on?

She had come to this island to escape demons, not to find them. Her father had struggled from one dead-end job to another, from one whiskey to the next, and Dodie had tried to help him. She had hidden rum bottles from him, bound up the cuts and grazes from all his drunken falls, and splinted his arm when it broke. But it was like trying to pour sand uphill, and eventually she lost that particular trial of strength.

After his death, she could have retraced her steps back home and started afresh in England, but she didn't. She couldn't bring herself to leave the Bahamas. She had fallen too much in love with this beautiful exotic island. Its soft warm breezes, the vibrant colors of its flowers and birds and its saucer-size butterflies, the deep call of its ugly frogs and the distinctive whisper of its palm fronds in her ear—they had all bewitched her. And the vast blue ocean encircled her mind as completely as it encircled New Providence Island, so that she set about building a new life for herself. It had been tough at times. She learned to be wary of people. At first she was employed at the Stanley Sewing Factory, but when that went wrong and she became an outcast, Olive Quinn gave her the waitressing job at the Arcadia and she'd been there ever since.

But now they were trying to take the island away from her, these people who went round sticking knives in men's guts. They wanted to frighten her. To drive her away. She lifted her head and stared fiercely up at the underbelly of the clouds that hung low over the waves. She was going nowhere.

A solitary Liberator aircraft was forging its way through the sky, buffeted by winds on its course to the new Windsor airfield, and the determined growl of its four engines found an echo inside Dodie's own head. She swung round to head back to rake through the black debris of the shack before the rain came, but she halted. Up ahead the young man was still there in the shade. Still seated with his back molded to the trunk of the tree as though he'd been there a long time. Still watching her.

Who was he? Why was he there? Come to deliver another warning to her?

No, not this time. She wasn't going to sit and wait timidly for his warnings. This time she would get to him first and shake the truth out of him. Without hesitation she ran up the beach toward the stranger in the shadows before he could even think of leaving.

Chapter 16

Flynn

Flynn saw her coming up the beach toward him, her long chestnut hair snatched in all directions by the wind, her footprints chasing behind her in the white sand. But he didn't move. All he did was stub out his cigarette and wish she weren't so angry. He could see her anger in the quick purposeful strides she took and in the sharp set of her elbows as she raced up the slope.

He had been watching her for more than an hour, wondering what was going on in her head as she made her way through the water. She kept throwing up wide arcs of sparkling sea with her hands, stirring up the heavy roll of the waves as if trying to rear-range her world. She carved a course back and forth along the full length of the cay in her faded blue dress, absorbed in her own thoughts. He had always been quick to read a person's mood—from the angle of their neck, from the swing of their hips, from the way they held their hands. It was a skill that had kept him alive more than once. He could see that, despite her obvious anger, this girl's body was caving in on itself, as though someone had taken a hammer to her once too often.

She was not used to death. He could recognize that in her, and the thought of all the blood that spilled on her floor disturbed him more than he cared to admit. It took courage to do what she did for Morrell. Yet she was a shy creature. It showed in the manner in which she looked around her at the world, not quite sure of her place in it. Ready to duck and move away fast. He admired that in her, her alertness.

"*I've told her nothing.*"

Flynn wanted Morrell's words to be true.

"*Don't let them hurt her, kid.*"

The question was—how much could she hurt them?

Dodie.

That's what poor Johnnie Morrell had said that her name was.

Chapter 17

Dodie

"Who are you?" Dodie didn't wait for an answer. "What are you doing here at this hour of the morning?"

She took a good look at the man. He was sitting with his head tipped back, looking up at her, and it struck her that here was someone who wore his city toughness like an overcoat. Under a dense mop of dark hair, his brown eyes were quick and capable.

"Why are you watching me?" An angry pulse jumped at the base of her throat.

"It's a free country, you know," he said quietly.

He uncoiled easily and rose to his feet. His nicotine-stained fingers brushed his hair from his eyes in a gesture she realized was intended to give her a moment to reflect. But all she wanted to reflect on was why he'd been there so long, spying on her.

"My name is Flynn Hudson."

His accent was American, from somewhere up in the cold northern states by the sound of it. His skin was pale, as if it didn't get to see much sun in the normal run of things. Flynn Hudson was in his midtwenties, tall and lean, with a raw uneasy edge to him that was at odds with the calmness in his deep-set eyes and the patience he'd shown in his vigil under the tree.

"Well, Mr. Hudson?"

"I apologize if I've upset you by being here. I didn't mean to.

I was just biding my time under the tree, waiting for you to come back up the beach."

"What is it you want with me?"

"I thought you might need a hand, so—"

"There's nothing I need from you, Mr. Hudson." She regarded him warily. "If you are the one who started the fire or if you are here to give me another warning, I'm telling you—and your friends—to stay away from me. You don't scare me. I'm going nowhere." Her voice sounded loud in the fresh morning air and her heart had slid into her throat, but she stared intently at the brown eyes so that he would understand that she was not a cockroach to be stamped on. "I repeat what I said, Mr. Hudson. There is nothing I need from you." She turned on her heel.

"I think there is."

It made her halt. She waited for more, and when it didn't come she was obliged to look at him again. He was dressed in a long-sleeved shirt, no tie, and he wore brown lace-up shoes that were coated in sand. Respectable enough but the shirt looked cheap and the knees on his trousers were shiny. It appeared that he got by, but only just. He was standing with his hands sunk in his pockets, his gaze scrutinizing her with a fixed attention that unsettled her.

"What exactly do you mean, Mr. Hudson?"

"Nothing much." He shrugged his shoulders. "I wish it was more but I was too late—to help last night, I mean. The blaze was out of control but I did what I could. I'm real sorry."

Dodie stared at him wordlessly.

"About the fire," he added. "I tried to help."

"Look, Mr. Hudson, I apologize if—"

"Come with me," he said, "I'll show you something."

He headed off in his unsuitable shoes across the sand to the far side of where the hut had been but she couldn't bring herself to follow. He must have sensed it, because halfway there he cast a glance back over his shoulder and gave her a smile.

"Don't look so worried. Hell, I'm not going to kidnap you or sell you into white slavery or anything so exotic."

He said it with a laugh that rolled easily out of him and animated his whole face. Dodie felt herself blush right up to her hairline but he seemed not to notice. He knelt down on the beach beside a small heap wrapped up in what was obviously his jacket, its material crumpled and coated in sand, black smears like tide marks across it.

"Look."

She came closer as he withdrew the jacket with the panache of a conjuror. Her mouth fell open and a sound came from her. It didn't form into words.

"I figured you might want it," he said.

It was her mother's sewing machine. Dodie's knees abruptly buckled and she dropped to the sand beside him, reaching out to touch the machine's wheel. Its wooden base was badly charred and the black enamel paint on its metal body was blistered, but amazingly the workings looked to be still intact. Dodie felt a hollowness open up inside her that was the exact shape of the sewing machine.

"Yes, I saw you last night." She remembered him. "With the long stick in your hand raking out objects from the fire. I thought you were stealing. I didn't know that you"—she waved a hand at the damaged machine—". . . that you . . ."

"Worth saving?"

"Yes," she whispered.

"Good."

She gathered the blackened machine into her arms. When she cradled it on her lap her isolation did not feel so complete. But when she finally thought to lift her head to thank Flynn Hudson, he had gone from her side and was striding away through the trees.

* * *

Dodie was on her hands and knees in her vegetable garden, her hair tied back to keep it from whipping into her eyes. She was finding it strange, adjusting to owning nothing. It should be easy and yet it felt hard.

She laid a hand on the edge of the hole she had opened up in the earth in front of her, big enough to hold a modest metal strongbox wrapped in sacking. But now she had enlarged it to take the battered sewing machine as well. Lovingly she had bathed the filth off this one thing she possessed that had been her mother's and she bartered a clutch of potatoes for a towel and strip of oilcloth to wrap it in. Now that it was buried safely alongside the strongbox, she felt better.

She again checked the beach, but Flynn Hudson had not returned. She could see no one near. She listened. There was only the shiver of the wind through the pines and the boom of the waves reverberating up the beach. She could smell the coming storm. Quickly she opened the strongbox and from it removed an envelope that held seven pound notes. She removed two. She wouldn't starve, not yet anyway. This time she didn't allow herself to spend a moment on the yellowing photograph of her parents that lay at the bottom of the strongbox or on the seductive gilt-edged pages of her father's Bible, but snatched out one of the two gold coins tucked in the corner and slammed the lid shut.

Chapter 18

Ella

Ella sliced the top off her boiled egg and glanced up from her breakfast plate to find Reggie watching her.

It was always the same. After a night like last night. As if the strings that controlled his face had turned to elastic and stretched to let his features soften. His lips were parted in a loose smile as he gazed at her without feeling the need to make small talk about his round of golf. She liked him like this. With his guard down and that undisciplined look in his eyes which she knew meant he was thinking of her in bed.

Ella never said no to her husband in bed, not even when she was exhausted or he was drunk. She felt she owed him that. He had given her a nice life—not the one she had expected, but still nice—and he was unfailingly loving and kind to her. They both knew in their heart of hearts that there was a slight tilt in the balance of their marriage, that he loved her more than she loved him. But he never pushed it, never let himself express disappointment when she delivered perfunctory sex in response to his tentative approach each night.

He seemed happy enough. He certainly never complained. They had their little signs, the telling signals that Ella thought of as their mating ritual. She and Reggie nearly always read in bed—she would get stuck into the latest Hemingway or Ngaio Marsh while he studied some office documents, memorizing streams of facts and figures with which to brief the duke the next day. Ella was always impressed by her husband's ability to remember things.

After exactly twenty minutes in bed, timed by his watch, Reggie would carefully shuffle his papers together, clear his throat, stretch out his arms with a yawn, and turn off his bedside lamp. That was the signal. She would put aside her book but didn't turn off her light until afterward. She liked to see what she was doing. Twenty years of marriage and yet Reggie approached her each night as if she might say no. A tentative leg hooked over hers, a hand stroking her waist, a kiss on her neck. Nothing too intrusive. Not until she turned to him and kissed his mouth, her tongue stalking his.

Time and again she wished he would come at her like a lion, claws gripping her tight, snarling and snapping and taking what was his by right. But each time he would stroke and caress her body as though he'd never seen it before and was struck dumb by his good fortune. He'd told her he had never slept with any other woman and she believed him, but more and more often now she found herself wishing that he had. When he thrust inside her, he always watched her face closely, checking that he was not hurting or offending in some way. And she was tempted to tell him that tedium was by far the worst pain—but she never did, of course.

Then, once in a while, she lost patience. She would straddle him fiercely and ravage him till they were both slick with sweat, his skin impregnated with hers and the taste of her breasts on his tongue. No endearments. Just bruises on his lips and scratches on his thighs. When she finally collapsed off him with her lungs heaving and her body still shuddering with release, Reggie would turn his face away from her, a blush seeping up the side of his neck.

"Good night," he would murmur.

"Good night, Reggie."

And then this. This stretching of the strings of his face when she looked at him the next morning, as though she had somehow pulled him out of shape. Neither of them ever voiced any comment or made any reference to the night before. Ella took a bite out of her toast and smiled at her husband in a civilized manner, but this morning Reggie put down his napkin, rose to his feet, and walked over to the French windows. He remained standing there with his back to her.

"What is it, Reggie?"

She saw the slight straightening of his well-padded back. When he turned, she knew she wasn't going to like whatever it was he was working himself up to say.

"I am concerned, Ella."

"What about?"

"The danger that you and Tilly Latcham were put in yesterday. It could have been far worse than a bucketful of pig's blood thrown over you."

"Ah."

Ella did not want to discuss it further. They had talked it to death last night.

"You could have been seriously hurt."

"But we weren't, Reggie darling."

"That's not the point. We saw last year what can happen when a riot runs out of control."

"But yesterday was nothing more than a small disgruntled group of workers who—"

"For heaven's sake, Ella, don't underestimate what that labor dispute last year signaled. Those black workers faced us down and won. Don't forget that there are only ten thousand of us, compared with sixty thousand of them. I tell you this is just the beginning."

"The beginning of what?"

Reggie smoothed his lips, taking the thorns out of his words. "Of the end of the natural order of society in this colony. One day the native blacks will demand to be our equals and then . . ." He smiled sadly.

Ella felt a ripple of alarm. Reggie had never voiced that conviction to her before. Yet she could imagine him closeted behind doors up in Government House with the governor and a few select and powerful Bay Street merchants—all discussing options. *The beginning of the end.* She experienced a sharp pulse of panic.

The riot last summer had come about as an outburst by black workers. Two thousand of them crammed themselves into Parliament Square outside the pink government buildings and demanded fair pay compared with the highly paid American laborers who had been brought in to work on what was known as the Project. This was the construction of the two airfields for the U.S. and RAF forces.

Before the war, the Bahamas was one of the most impoverished colonies in the Empire. The lack of employment on the islands made life hard. Most black inhabitants led a hand-to-mouth existence as both the fishing and sponge industries were in sharp decline. With news of the Project, the whole atmosphere in Nassau changed and Bahamians came flocking from the outlying islands to find work. But the government had miscalculated—Reggie included. They paid Bahamians half what they were paying the American laborers for doing exactly the same job—four shillings a day instead of eight. Ella could not believe that so-called intelligent men would be so stupid. Of course anger flared. Of course it ended in a terrifying riot. The mob exploded in a two-day rampage of violence, smashing shops and looting up and down the length of Bay Street, the very heart of white colonial territory.

Peace was restored only after four men were killed by British troops and over forty injured. Finally a new pay deal was struck. Life in Nassau seemed to stumble back to normal, but underneath the tranquil surface there flowed a dark undercurrent that hadn't been there before.

That's why Ella—and Tilly as well—had reacted so badly yesterday in the car. This time it turned out to be nothing more than a handful of young stonemasons who were angered by a wage cut. Buckets of pig's blood had been their weapon rather than staves. But it was enough to remind everyone of the terrors of last year when white women dared not leave their houses and white men lost their livelihoods when their shops were destroyed.

Ella pushed her plate away. "What are you trying to say to me, Reggie?"

"That I have spoken with the duke and with Colonel Lindop. We have agreed that until we are certain that the current situation presents no threat, the commissioner is assigning a policeman as bodyguard to a number of wives of prominent figures on the island. So—"

"No, Reggie."

"So you will have a bodyguard to accompany you outside at all times until—"

"No, Reggie. No."

"Until we are confident there is no further danger."

"Reggie! You're not listening to me."

"It will probably only be for a week or two."

"I refuse to—"

He came toward her with quick purposeful strides that took her by surprise. He leaned over her where she sat and took her face between his hands. Not with the tentativeness she was used to. His palms were rigid and the force behind them made her teeth ache. His gaze was set on her face and what she saw in his eyes shocked her: it was stark unbridled rage.

"You could have been killed, Ella. Left dead in the street. Isn't there enough of that going on in the towns and cities of Britain at the moment? Aren't you thinking of that? Our families back home are going through hell already, without you putting yourself in danger over here too."

"It wasn't that bad, honestly. And that's not fair, Reggie. You know all of us over here worry all the time about our families and the bombing back home. Look what happened to Tilly's poor uncle in the raid on Bristol."

"You must have a bodyguard, Ella, I insist. I can't risk . . ."

She placed a hand over his on her cheek and gave him a nod.

Instantly a veneer of politeness descended and he went back to being her diplomatic Reggie.

"Good," he said brightly. "I'll go and telephone Lindop. He's the one arranging it all." He smiled at her, nothing but the usual affection in his eyes now. "It's not just you, Ella. There are other wives as well who will be protected, Tilly included."

"But it was your idea, wasn't it?"

He cleared his throat. "I admit it was, but"—he was turning away to the door, so he missed the sudden sag of her shoulders at the prospect of being dogged by a stranger wherever she went—"it's important to prevent any further incidents that would inflame resentments on either side."

"Of course, Reggie."

The moment he departed, Ella fled the room into the garden.

*   *   *

Ella was tightening the restraining string around her abundant growth of passion flowers, which had a habit of unfurling their amethyst star-shaped blooms with outrageous abandon. That was the joy of a garden in the tropics—it never knew when to stop. It was never diplomatic. Ella loved the vitality of her garden and its wildlife. She paused to watch a woodstar hummingbird flash its iridescent violet throat at her, just as the first few drops of rain began to fall.

"Miss Ella!"

"What is it, Emerald?"

"You got yourself a visitor."

Ella straightened up. "I'm not expecting anyone."

"Especially not this anyone."

Emerald's bulky neck was hunched down between her shoulders and Ella wasn't sure if it was against the rain or against her visitor.

"What do you mean, Emerald? Who is it?"

The maid's broad nose wrinkled in distaste. "A skinny white miss who claims she has a private matter to discuss with you."

"What's her name?"

"Miss Dodie Wyatt."

"What does she want?"

"She ain't sayin'."

They started walking up the path together.

"What's wrong with the young lady, Emerald?"

"She ain't no lady."

"Emerald, you are a terrible snob."

Emerald grinned proudly. "Yes, I sure am."

"I hope you were polite to her."

"'Course I was polite. Ain't I always polite?"

"No, you ain't."

They both chuckled.

They were nearing the house, the bougainvillea on the terrace flailing its magenta flowers in the wind. Ella frowned. It would take a battering in the coming storm.

She shook her finger at her maid. "Just because I feed you too much, that's no reason to take against a girl for being skinny. It's hard to find employment on this island."

Emerald smacked her palm on her own broad backside with affection. "That's 'cause us fat black folks will insist on hoggin' all them dirty low-paid jobs ourselves. Can't understand it, myself." She turned wide innocent eyes on Ella. "Can you, Miss Ella?"

"Stop that, Emerald. If you want to argue politics, go and argue with my husband."

"I ain't arguin'. I'm just sayin'."

"Well, go say to Miss Wyatt that I'll be with her in a moment after I've washed my hands. Where did you put her?"

"On the south veranda. It's out of the wind there."

"What's wrong with the drawing room?"

"There's good silver in that room."

"Emerald, you are bad!"

Emerald grinned. "Just lookin' out for you, Miss Ella."

*   *   *

Emerald was right about one thing, Ella had to admit. The girl was thin. As Ella stepped out onto the covered veranda, the girl turned at once from where she was studying the manicured lawn and the towering mango tree swaying in the wind. Her face possessed fine delicate features, but her cheekbones were too prominent and lips too full for conventional attraction. Yet there was something of the little hummingbird about her, an iridescence that made it hard to take your eyes off her. At the moment her mouth was pulled into a tense line and she was assessing Ella from under thick dark lashes. Her pale green eyes looked young and Ella realized she must be little more than half Ella's own age.

"Good morning, Miss Wyatt. What can I do for you?"

"Thank you for seeing me, Mrs. Sanford." Her fingers twitched at one of the folds of her dress. "I need to speak to you about something."

There was a diffidence in her manner that appealed to Ella and a bright awareness in her eyes, but her dark chestnut hair was yanked back by baling twine and her feet were in ragged sandals.

"Let's sit down." Ella gestured to two chairs beside a table and noticed with a smile that Emerald had laid out a jug of fresh lemonade and a plate of her homemade ginger biscuits. Obviously, in Emerald's book, even Miss Wyatt needed feeding if she was skinny. "What is this about?"

"It's about Mr. Morrell."

"I'm sorry?"

"Mr. Morrell. A big American with bushy hair." Her eyes were fixed on Ella. "I think you know him."

"Oh, yes, possibly." Ella hesitated and looked at the girl uneasily. "But I don't exactly know him. I just met him briefly the other evening and we exchanged a few words, that's all."

"May I ask what about?"

"I was collecting donations for the Red Cross and he was generous enough to oblige. But what's your interest in Mr. Morrell?"

The young woman looked down at the biscuits, at a trail of ants marching across the stone flooring, at her own hands wrapped together in her lap, all without saying a word. When finally she raised her eyes, they had changed. Something dark had pushed forward in them.

"He's dead."

A whoof of air rushed out of Ella's lungs and her hand flew to her throat. The young woman picked up the jug, poured lemonade into one of the glasses and placed it in front of Ella.

"Oh no, that's terrible. So sudden. I'm sorry. What happened?"

"He was stabbed. I found him in an alleyway the night before last," she answered. "I tried to save him but . . . he didn't make it." She shook her head.

"Who did it?"

"I don't know. That's why I'm here."

The air was growing cooler as the rain slapped down on the glass roof of the veranda, slithering down it, leaving tracks like snails.

"How did it happen?" Ella asked.

"I don't know. Morrell told me nothing."

"Have the police been informed?"

"Yes. But they know nothing either."

Ella took a sip of lemonade. Her mouth was dry. "How horrible for you."

The chestnut head seemed to sway forward as though about to say more, but instead she picked up a biscuit and regarded Ella in silence.

"Why have you come to me?" Ella asked, baffled.

Dodie Wyatt replaced the biscuit and drew something from inside her pocket and set it down in the middle of the table. It was a gold coin, gleaming even in the dull morning light, an old coin that would be called something like a doubloon or a noble, something equally odd. Ella wanted to touch it.

That's the thing about gold—it is fantastical. It is all-powerful, it corrupts the soul. It hypnotizes the mind. The coin of the devil. Yet it decorates and debases churches across the world.

She recalled the words she'd heard spoken by Sir Harry Oakes the night before last, soft and seductive.

Go on, Morrell, take it. Free your soul.

She remembered Morrell's grunt of gratification as the gold won. Saw the sweat on his neck.

"Mrs. Sanford?"

Ella dragged her eyes from the coin.

"Mr. Morrell asked me to give you this coin."

The girl placed a scrap of paper on the tabletop in front of Ella and stood her glass on the corner of it to prevent it blowing away. On it was Ella's name. At once she recognized the bold handwriting. It belonged to Sir Harry Oakes.

"Why," Dodie Wyatt asked, "would he do that?"

The quiet intensity of her voice scarcely reached across the table because of the buffeting of the trees.

"To be honest, I don't know. Believe me when I tell you I didn't know him. I met him once for no more than five minutes and—"

"When was that?"

"The night before last."

"That's the night he was killed."

Ella glanced out the window at the driving rain that was enclosing her world in a chill gray overcoat. She unhitched her fingers from her glass and rose to her feet.

"Let's go inside."

The drawing room was warmer, but this time neither woman sat down. The inlaid rosewood cabinets with their fine Meissen porcelain, the delicate marquetry tables, and the jade silk curtains felt formal to Ella and she noticed the way they both stood more stiffly, facing each other in the center of the room.

"Why would he send me to you with such a coin?" Dodie Wyatt asked bluntly. "He must have meant something by it."

"I have no idea."

"Have you seen the coin before?"

"No. It doesn't make any sense to me, I'm sorry."

That should have been the end of it. Miss Wyatt should have said her good-byes and left, so Ella was taken by surprise when her visitor stepped closer.

"You're lying," the girl said softly.

"Don't be so rude, Miss Wyatt. Or I will have to ask you to leave my house."

"I'm not being rude. I just want to find out the truth about Mr. Morrell. I owe him that much."

"It strikes me that you owe the man nothing at all if he was a stranger to you."

"Mrs. Sanford, my house was burned down last night and I lost everything I own. I believe it happened because I helped Mr. Morrell, so I need to find out all I can about him."

"How ghastly for you. I'm sorry."

Ella picked up a tortoiseshell cigarette box on a nearby table. She didn't usually smoke till cocktail hour, but she needed one now. She offered a cigarette to Miss Wyatt, and when it was politely declined, she lit one for herself.

"If you are so keen to discover the truth," she said through a skein of smoke, "why didn't you take the gold coin and that piece of paper with my name straight to the police?"

It happened in the blink of an eye. The girl changed. She took a step backward and a flush of crimson flooded up into her cheeks.

Ella became concerned. "What is it?"

"Nothing."

"Tell me."

The girl stared down at her sandals. "It's just that I reported a crime once before. No one believed me, not even the police. They all said I was a troublemaker. I lost my job because of it and no one else would employ me until Miss Olive took pity on me and gave me a chance at the Arcadia Hotel. If I go to the police with a story about Mr. Morrell and it drags you in as well, they might . . ." The words jammed behind her lips.

"They might rake up the past and see you as a troublemaker again?"

A silent nod.

"So why not leave this alone?" Ella urged. "What is Morrell to you? Or to me? We know nothing about him. He is just a ripple on the surface of this island. For heaven's sake, he was only here less than twenty-four hours, so—"

The chestnut head shot up. "How do you know that?"

"He told me."

"So you *do* know something about Morrell."

"I remember that he mentioned that he'd come over that morning and was leaving that night."

"Anything else?" Her eyes were bright once more.

"No, I'm sorry, that was all."

"I wanted to speak to you first," the girl explained. "That's why I came here."

"I'm very glad you did. I'm not connected in any way with Mr. Morrell, I swear to you. All I did was bump into him while out on the stump for the Red Cross."

"So go to the police," Dodie Wyatt said earnestly. "Tell them that. And tell them what you won't tell me—where you met him."

"I'm sorry, I can't do that."

"Why not?"

Ella frowned. "I am married to a diplomat who works every day alongside a lot of powerful people to keep this beautiful little island afloat. He can talk for England on how important it is to keep connections open and the business of government and commerce flowing freely. The murder of a solitary stranger is sad and, yes, it's horrible—I readily admit that—but it's not worth disrupting the system for. The good of the island comes first."

Dodie Wyatt's eyes were looking at her as if she were speaking a foreign language.

"Why would it disrupt the *system*?" she demanded.

"Because . . ." Ella sighed. How do you explain to a young and innocent mind the way things work to maintain the fine balance of diplomacy? "You know what it's like yourself. To be tainted. A troublemaker. People don't let you forget something like that. If I label someone as the person who introduced me to Morrell— someone involved with a murdered man—despite all protestations of innocence, rumors would start. It will do damage to him. I'm not willing to do that."

Dodie Wyatt moved away from Ella toward the door.

"Mrs. Sanford, maybe you've been married to a diplomat too long."

Chapter 19

Ella

Today was Ella's Red Cross day at the hospital. It was her turn in the children's ward to sit with Gus, massaging his small lifeless legs on the bed. He insisted on singing "Onward, Christian Soldiers" to her, because his father was fighting somewhere over in France and his eyes shone with certainty. Only seven years old and recovering from poliomyelitis, he helped Ella buckle the heavy metal calipers on his thin legs and held on to her as she walked him a few fumbling steps up and down the ward.

A burst of laughter erupted at the far end of the ward where Ella saw a familiar neat dark head hard at work. It was the Duchess of Windsor. The duchess liked to laugh and she liked to be active. Forty-seven years old but constantly doing something, as if she didn't dare keep still. Always wrapping bandages, straightening sheets, combing hair. In her crisp Red Cross uniform she drew eyes effortlessly. The nurses were besotted and the doctors scurried about finding excuses to examine patients in whatever ward she happened to be on.

During the last two years, Ella had watched with admiration the way in which Wallis Windsor had thrown herself into the role of the wife of the governor-general, with an energy that would exhaust most women half her age. She visited clinics, schools, hospitals, setting up a canteen for the Bahamian Defence Force and a hostel for survivors of bombed ships. Ella often joined her to go dancing with servicemen to boost morale or at tea parties for them at Government House, and the duchess was just as industrious in looking for ways to improve the lot of black Bahamians as she was for the servicemen.

Ella walked down to her now. That's what happened when the duchess entered a room—people were drawn to her the way a pot of honey draws flies. Ella was willing to admit that Wallis Windsor could be imperious when she wanted to be, sharp-tongued, and certainly capricious at times, but Ella liked and respected her for her passion for life.

The duchess lifted her head at Ella's approach, finishing pinning a nappy in place on one of the infants. "Ah, Ella, just the person I want to see."

"Good afternoon, Your Highness."

"I saw Freddie de Marigny last night and he scared me with a story about you being attacked on the way through town yesterday." Her violet-blue eyes swept over Ella with concern. "Are you all right?"

"Yes, it was just my poor Rover that bore the brunt. Tilly Latcham and I got a bit of a fright, that's all."

"I bet you were scared witless, you poor thing."

"We did make rather a fuss, I'm afraid."

"So you should, my dear Ella. You can't always play the sensible-and-helpful-wife role, not all the time. You're allowed to scream sometimes, you know."

* * *

"They hate me."

They were in a small sluice room, just the two of them, and the duchess was staring moodily out at the rain sheeting down outside. She was smoking a cigarette in an ebony holder, the muscles at the corners of her wide jaw flexing back and forth.

"Who hates you?" Ella asked.

"The British public. But even more, the royal family. They hate me for stealing away their king."

"Oh, you're exaggerating, ma'am. They were disappointed to lose him, of course they were, but they don't hate you."

"Then why do they vilify me in their press? As though I am the devil incarnate." She turned her gaze from the window and raised a finely arched eyebrow at Ella. "Prime Minister Churchill wants to destroy me."

"No, he's probably trying to distract the public eye from the number of tons of shipping sunk in the Atlantic last month. Tucked it away in a bottom corner of the newspapers somewhere, while you are paraded on the front page to attract public attention. See it as doing your bit for keeping up morale."

The duchess laughed, a low sultry sound. Her hand touched her throat, fingered the tendons and the pearls.

"That bitch," she muttered, stubbed out her cigarette in the sink, and lit herself another. "She has everything—the throne, the titles, the jewels, the palaces, the adoration of the gullible public." She shrugged. "I could go on . . ."

"Please, don't, ma'am." Ella smiled and tossed the sodden cigarette butt into a bin. "I might talk in my sleep and what would Reggie think if I murmured your comments?"

Wallis laughed again but her face looked strained and her shoulders tense. She was a small thin woman, not exactly attractive, yet oddly compelling, a strange mix of masculine bone structure with southern belle charm which she had the wit to know when to turn on.

"They've said no again," she told Ella.

"To the title?"

"Yes." She was being denied the title of "Her Royal Highness," the usual form of address for a royal duchess, but she craved it nevertheless. "Your Prime Minister Churchill has just refused my husband's latest request for it."

"I'm sorry, ma'am."

Wallis narrowed her eyes at Ella. "Believe me when I say it all comes from that bitch in Buckingham Palace." Her eyes sparked with annoyance and her southern accent grew more pronounced. "And now that she's queen, she goes around saying that she's glad that Buckingham Palace has been bombed because it means she can look the East End of London in the face when it is ravaged by bombs night after night."

"I suppose it's true."

"Oh, Ella! She lives in a house with six hundred rooms, for Christ's sake. She owns five other houses. Their royal estates pile food as high as a goddamn mountain on their plates while the rest of the nation squabble like cats over a measly pat of butter or an egg. Rationing is vile. And she is a hypocrite."

It might be true. But Ella had heard enough. She was well aware of the whispering campaign against the Windsors and where it emanated from. Reggie told her that Wallis Windsor was right in pointing her finger at the palace. "But the king shirked his duty by abdicating the throne of England. It was unforgivable," Reggie muttered in an uncharacteristically caustic comment. "What did they expect?"

Indeed. What did they expect?

"You know, ma'am," Ella said, "it's not wise to say those things."

"Not even to you, my dear Ella."

"Especially not to me, ma'am. I can hear Reggie swooning to the floor at my elbow."

It teased a smile from Wallis and Ella seized the moment to say, "I've got a question I'd like to ask you."

Instantly the duchess's full attention focused on Ella in that direct way of hers. "Fire away."

"You have people around you who . . . well, who keep you in touch with what's going on here."

The duchess slid her a silent smile. It was a well-known fact that the royals had a tight-knit set of informants.

"So," Ella continued, "I wondered if you'd heard anything about a man who was killed in the street the night before last." Ella tried to keep it casual but failed.

"Aha, Mrs. Sanford. What is this mystery man to you?"

"Nothing. It's just that a young woman came to me about it today, but I hadn't even heard of the tragedy."

The duchess exhaled a swirl of smoke that fogged the air between them. "You are not a good liar, Ella. I am expert at spotting liars"—she laughed softly—"and expert at lying." She waved the smoke away. "But I will forgive you that and answer your question. Yes, they were talking about it this morning up at Government House. Colonel Lindop was there as well. I wasn't really paying attention."

Ella leaned against the door. She didn't want anyone bursting in now. "Do they have any idea who did it?"

"I think they're blaming it on the unrest among the workers. They assume it was an expression of native anger. Like the attack on you and Tilly in the car."

"Really?"

"Yes."

"Are they going to investigate it further?"

"Of course." The duchess approached slowly, her shoes as silent as a leopard's paws on the linoleum floor. "Now, what's it about? This sudden interest of yours."

But at that moment, someone barged against the door and Ella leaped aside, allowing Tilly Latcham in her Red Cross uniform to rush into the room. She grinned at Ella, then saw the duchess and became more muted. She was always less forthcoming around Wallis.

"Good afternoon, Your Highness. Hello, Ella. Guess what I've got."

"What?"

"A bodyguard chauffeur. He's a policeman." Tilly shook her dark hair and let loose a raucous laugh. "One who is fat and old and has a forest of nose hair. Just my luck!" She turned to Ella. "What's yours like?"

"I have no idea," she said. "I haven't met him yet."

"I hope for your sake he's a damn sight more fun than mine."

"I'm certain he will be," the duchess commented.

Tilly eyed her sharply. "And why is that?"

"Isn't it obvious?"

"Not to me, ma'am."

"Nor to me." Ella smiled.

"It's because of your husband, Ella. He's the one making these decisions."

Ella could see that Tilly looked suddenly ill-pleased with an undisguised downturn of her crimson mouth. "Damn Hector," she muttered. "Why doesn't he bother to make sure I get a decent bodyguard?"

"Don't be a dunce, Tilly," Ella said. "Hector cares just as much that you should be safe. I don't even want a bodyguard."

"Come on now, ladies." The duchess laughed. "We all know that Reggie will have requested Colonel Lindop's top man to guard his lovely wife. The quickest, the sharpest, the brightest of the Nassau crop of policemen. So of course he'll be more fun to be around than some fat hick with nasal undergrowth."

Tilly sighed dramatically. "If I were you, darling, I'd scoot home right now and find out."

* * *

Ella drove home through the rain. It lashed down like bullets while sudden streaks of lightning ripped open the low slung clouds. The violence of it snaked across the island, causing Ella to drive faster than she should. She liked storms. As much as dear Reggie loathed them.

Was it true what the duchess said? That the police were pinning the murder of Morrell on a disgruntled black worker? A convenient scapegoat. It sent a jolt of anger through her that the system could be so easily manipulated by those in control, especially when the one in control was Sir Harry Oakes.

Now, my dear, he'd said to her the night Morrell died, *you've seen things this evening that are best forgotten.* He'd leaned close to her, his head thrust forward like a bull's, his prospector boots restless as though they could barely restrain themselves from trampling over her. Sir Harry was a bully. A generous and unpredictable man who devoted millions to Bahamian charities. But still a bully. He would physically knock down anyone fool enough to stand in his way.

No need to mention Mr. Morrell to anyone, he'd growled. *I think you understand me, Ella.*

She understood him all right.

And now the girl had come asking questions. Ella yanked the wheel sharply to take a corner and felt the rear wheels slip and squeal as they struggled for grip on the wet road.

＊　＊　＊

Ella parked the car in the garage and made a run for the house. She dashed through the door into the kitchen, shaking rain from her hair and undoing the buttons of her drenched blouse.

"Emerald, I need a . . ."

She stopped. Emerald was seated at the table with an expression on her face that belonged on a cat that has just found itself a bowl of cream. In front of her sat two of Ella's second-best china teacups and a man in a lightweight suit who was eating one of her biscuits. He stood up as soon as Ella entered the room, put down his biscuit, and stepped forward. He was tall and muscular, with wavy dark hair and the look of a man who would hold open doors with courtesy but also knew how to slam them in the face of anyone who stepped out of line. It was in the calm gray eyes. In the quiet steady gaze he laid on Ella.

"Good afternoon, Mrs. Sanford, I am Detective Sergeant Dan Calder."

She extended her hand. "Good afternoon, Detective Sergeant Calder. I remember you at the police station. I apologize for ruining your jacket. What can I do for you?"

He shook her hand with a firm grip, but there had been a moment's hesitation and it occurred to Ella that maybe people did not shake a policeman's hand often. She saw his eyes travel to her buttons and she quickly did them up again.

"I have been assigned as your bodyguard, Mrs. Sanford."

Her mouth fell open. The duchess was right. This wasn't one like Tilly's, one with nasal hair and a beer gut, this was someone in his early thirties who looked as though he liked to ask too many questions.

"I assume your husband has informed you that you have been assigned a bodyguard," he said.

"He did but . . ."

"But you don't want one?" His mouth smiled, but his eyes remained serious, studying each part of her face as though committing it to memory.

"I don't want a policeman in my house."

"I understand," he replied. "I will wait in the garage and keep a watch on the house." He started to move past her toward the backdoor.

"Miss Ella!" Emerald's palm slapped down on the table with a sound like a steam hammer. "Mind your manners."

"Detective Calder, I didn't mean that. Finish your tea and biscuit. I just meant that I'm not comfortable with having somebody trailing along behind me all day."

He should have nodded respectfully, should have said, *I quite understand, Mrs. Sanford. I will do everything I can to make my presence as unobtrusive as possible.* Isn't that what a bodyguard should say? But he didn't. Instead he looked her directly in the eye and frowned.

"I am here for your convenience, Mrs. Sanford." He used her name like a small wedge, hammering it in place between them. "I am here to protect you, and for no other reason."

"I don't need protection."

"Your husband and Colonel Lindop think you do."

"I am not inclined to agree with them."

"But they are the ones who are making the decisions in this instance."

Color trickled into Ella's cheeks. How dare he be so rude in her own house?

"Decisions for you," he said. "And for me." A sudden smile lit up his eyes, taking her by surprise. "We are both doing the best we can." He ran a hand through his hair, spilling it over his forehead, and the warm intelligence in his eyes brought her back to her senses. She should be grateful to him. Outside, the wind wailed around the veranda, while inside, the only sound came from Emerald crunching on her biscuit.

Ella waved a careless hand. "So much silliness," she said lightly. Meaning Reggie.

"They only want to keep you safe." He leaned forward a fraction, his suit straining across his broad shoulders. "So do I."

"It's your job."

"Yes. It's my job."

Abruptly she sensed it was not a part of his work that he enjoyed, and who could blame him? Hanging around an idle woman all day when he wanted to be off fighting crime. Maybe he had been removed from a case to do this silly work. That thought made her turn away. She touched her sodden hair and realized she was cold inside her wet blouse. She headed for the door.

"Hot tea, please, Emerald."

"Yes, Miss Ella. Right away. Don't want you takin' no chill. Go get out of them wet things."

First her husband. Now her maid. Both telling her what to do. She thought about her childhood plans to become an intrepid explorer and wondered at the person she had become. Sometimes she felt like a stranger to herself.

Chapter 20

Dodie

Storms pass.

That's what Dodie told herself. Storms pass. Like the one today, which had finally rolled its way south, tracking a path toward Cuba. But behind them storms leave damage. It's dealing with the damage that is the hardest part.

It's not worth disrupting the system.

That's what the diplomat's wife said. The words had shaken Dodie. She had liked the woman, liked her warmth, liked her beautiful house and her razor-sharp lawn, liked her orderly desirable life, which she inhabited so effortlessly. Dodie had not expected her to put the *system* above a man's life. It was on her long walk home in the rain that she wished she had told Mrs. Sanford that you only care about the system if you are a cog within it. If you are an outsider, a spare part rejected by the system, then you don't give a damn about it.

"Need a hand with this?"

The question startled Dodie. She was salvaging what she could from her battered vegetable plot and was pushing what was left of her produce into a sack to take over to Mama Keel. She recognized the American voice at once.

"Mr. Hudson, I'm glad you've come back." She straightened up, abandoning her sack, and smiled at him. "I wanted to thank you for rescuing my mother's sewing machine."

"No need."

He stepped forward into the sunlight, wearing a clean blue shirt rolled up at the sleeves. The skin of his forearms was pale city skin, but his face had caught the sun, and when he smiled back at her, his mahogany-brown eyes seemed to catch the sun as well, warming the dark spaces within them. He approached a tree that the storm had felled and that lay broken-backed across one end of her plot, crushing what remained of her melons.

"A bad day for melons, I guess," he said.

A cigarette hung from his fingers and he expelled smoke lazily while he gestured toward her sack. "Can I help?"

She thought about it. She liked the way she didn't feel the need for haste around this man, as though he slowed time to a crawl with his quiet unhurried manner.

"Why not?" she said, and tossed him a spade. "You can gather the potatoes."

He inspected the plot's scorched foliage with a quizzical frown. "Where are the potatoes?"

"You don't know?"

"Nope."

"They're buried under the soil."

"Ah. That explains it."

She laughed, a light ripple of amusement that expelled something tight and jagged in her chest that shouldn't have been there in the first place.

"They're under those mounds of earth over there."

He set to work while she finished collecting some peppers and a few squash plants that had survived the roasting, shoveling them into her sack. When she glanced back at him he was squatting on his heels, examining a cluster of small potatoes as white as bird's eggs on the palm of his hand. As she watched, he proceeded to scrub one on his trousers and then lifted it to his mouth. He took a bite and smiled.

Without looking round at her, he asked, "What are you doing about a house?"

"I'm sleeping on a friend's floor at the moment."

"Sounds rough."

"It's better than under the stars with the mosquitoes."

He laid the potatoes in a pile and moved farther down the row. "What started the fire?" he asked.

"The police think I left the stove on while I was at work."

"Did you?"

"No, of course not. Someone set fire to my house."

His head jerked up and he scrutinized her. "Deliberately?"

"Maybe."

"Or accidentally? A couple of guys fooling around with too many beers inside them?"

Dodie kept her thoughts to herself. First she had to work out whether Flynn Hudson was just making idle conversation or whether there was something more behind his questions. He stood up and brought her the potatoes. She held out her sack and he tipped them in, as pleased as if he'd grown them himself.

"And your shack? Are you ready to clear up that too?"

"I can't bring myself to look at it."

"I'll dig a pit," he offered.

He took the spade and did the heavy work, digging a large pit in the sandy soil up behind the trees while she raked together the last blackened fragments of her life and shoveled them in. He covered it up, and she stamped the earth down on top of it so hard that it felt like a war dance. Then he buried the remaining scorched scar on the beach under a deep layer of sand, and when he'd finished it was as though her life here had never existed. Scavenging seagulls strutted over it in the hope of finding spoils.

"It's better this way," he told her, "better to bury it fast, to rid yourself of the bad memories."

"Come on," she said. "Let's clean up."

She headed down to the water, glad to move away from the spot where her house had been, and kicked off her sandals. She breathed in the heat of the day and sensed the weight of Flynn Hudson's gaze behind her. It seemed to touch the naked skin of her arms and rummage in the loose fall of her hair after she snatched away the string that bound it. Her feet were filthy and her hands caked with earth and ash. She felt she was a mess of dirt and damage inside and out and she wanted to rid herself of it. She plunged into the waves.

*   *   *

They walked the length of the beach. Their bare feet glistened in the sand and Flynn Hudson carried the sack of vegetables over his shoulder, smudging even more dirt onto his clean shirt. She noticed the long tendons in each of his feet and the bloodless color of them, as though they had never seen the light of day before. The bottoms of his trousers were wet from the waves, though he'd gone in no farther than his ankles to rinse his hands in the salt water while she swam out in her dress, losing herself in the clear sparkling ocean. She dripped as she walked.

"My name is Dodie Wyatt."

"Well, Miss Wyatt, where does this Mama Keel of yours keep herself?"

"Inland a way, behind the trees. She was there at the fire last night."

"Lots of people were at the fire last night."

She could feel an undercurrent in his voice but she didn't know what it meant or what to make of it. She cast a glance up at his profile, his high forehead hidden behind the tangle of thick brown hair, the hollow of his cheek in shadow under his deep-set eyes. A dusting of sand etched on one eyebrow.

"Mr. Hudson."

He swung round to look at her. Maybe he heard some undercurrent in her voice too.

"Tell me where you come from."

"From the United States," he said without the usual pride in the statement that most Americans seemed to take in it. "From Chicago."

"It must be cold there in winter."

"Cold enough to freeze the thoughts in your head."

"And are you on holiday here?"

He laughed, a loose easy sound. She liked his laugh. It was the only time he let control slip through his fingers.

"Hell no! Do I look like a guy who comes on vacation to the Bahamas? I'm not in the forces, if you're wondering, because I had tuberculosis as a child and one of my lungs is a mess. No, I'm here working."

Nothing more. No explanation. *What kind of work?* But she didn't ask. She was aware of barriers within him and she didn't push against them. She knew only too well that barriers were what held a person together, the scaffolding of daily life.

"Are you thinking of staying long?"

He looked out at the vast world of blue that was the sea and the sky all rolled into one, and drew a breath through his teeth as if to taste the scent of it.

"I would like to stay longer," he said. "Even if it's just to make sure you're all right after this disaster. You'll need to find another house."

He kept walking, as though his words were slight, unimportant things, but Dodie felt the pull of them, like gravity, drawing her to him.

"Don't stay," she said.

He stopped to look at her and wrapped a fist into the cotton of her sodden dress, holding on to her. "Why not?"

"Because I'm bad luck. Two nights ago I helped a man who was wounded. He died and the next day my house burned down. I think I'm in trouble. I'm warning you that it could be dangerous to be around me, Mr. Hudson."

His eyes locked on hers and the hairs rose on her forearms. "Call me Flynn," he said, and then added with a smile, "I'll stay." A pulse started up in her throat.

* * *

They ate potato-and-squash fritters fried outdoors by Mama Keel under a darkening star-studded sky, along with strips of fresh conch fished out of a rocky cove farther along the coast.

"It won't bite you none." Mama Keel chuckled at Flynn as he regarded the rubbery conch flesh on his plate with caution.

Around them on a scrubby stretch of dirt, children of all colors, shapes, and sizes tumbled like puppies. One small girl called Rosa picked up a garlicky strip of conch from his plate and dropped it into her own wide-open mouth. "See? It's real good."

Flynn regarded the child as if he seriously expected her to drop down dead, and when she didn't, he fed the rest of his shellfish to the thin-ribbed hound that skulked under the house. The way his hand ran soothingly along the animal's flank told Dodie he'd spent more time around dogs than around children.

"You done good, I hear, Mr. Hudson. Clearing up our Dodie's shack like that," Mama Keel commented.

He lit one of his rolled cigarettes and nodded respectfully to the tall black woman. He tipped back his head and stared up at the night sky as if he'd never seen anything like it before. It soared over them, tar black and embedded with what looked like a million chips of glass. Moths and other winged insects were blundering in close, drawn by the light of the fire, and somewhere off in the trees a shrill hissing scream made Flynn jump.

Mama Keel chuckled. "That there's just a bitty old barn owl."

"Is that a fact? We don't get none too many of those round the backstreets of Chicago." He drew on his cigarette, spat out a shred of tobacco, and said, "I hear you done good yourself, Mama Keel, in caring for that wounded man Dodie found."

"I didn't do nothin'. Just gave her some ointments to ease his pain. She done the carin' herself, but got herself in bad with the police over it."

He switched his gaze to Dodie. "How bad?"

"Nothing much."

"Sure?"

"Yes." Dodie jumped to her feet. "I'll put the children to bed, Mama."

She hurried out of reach of the conversation. But with one infant on her hip and little Rosa clinging to her skirt, she paused in the doorway when she heard Mama Keel stretch out in her creaky rocking chair under the stars and say, "How about you hand me one of them smokes of yours, Mr. Hudson, and tell me what in the good Lord's name you doin' in these parts?"

"I was hired to do a job."

"What kinda job?"

"Can't tell you straight out, Mama, but it's a job that means I have to poke my nose in places where people don't want it poked."

Dodie heard Mama exhale smoke from her cigarette and the whine of mosquitoes grew louder.

"You know, Mr. Hudson," the black woman said, "when I meet a smart man like you whose head is just buzzin' with thoughts, sometimes I wonder what they are, but most of the time I just want to smack them out of his head before he does harm with them."

Dodie heard Flynn's chuckle of amusement as the evening's darkness settled around them as warmly as a blanket.

*   *   *

"What house? She don't need no house. She can stay here."

"Mama, she's not a child. She needs a place of her own."

"Don't talk about me as if I'm not here," Dodie told them. "Whose house is it?"

"It belongs to a man who has gone to work in Miami for a spell," Flynn said. They were sitting around the table, the three of them. "I heard of it when I was looking for somewhere for myself."

"So where you livin'?" Mama Keel asked.

"I'm lodging in a room over on the other side of town."

"So it's a shack," Dodie said, "this place you're talking about."

"Yep. It's not much. But it's empty and it's free. You could take a look at it now, if you want."

"Why now?" Mama demanded. "It's dark outside. Tomorrow is time enough."

"Today is my day off, Mama," Dodie pointed out. "I'm working tomorrow." She turned to Flynn. "Where is it?"

"In Bain Town."

Dodie and Mama Keel looked at each other.

"That's a black district," Mama said, shaking her head. "She don't belong in no black district."

"I figured"—Flynn turned toward Dodie—"if you're in trouble, no one is going to come looking for you there."

"Trouble?" Mama Keel snatched her clay pipe from her mouth. "What trouble?"

* * *

The shack had a tin roof and was tiny. But it boasted a lock on the door, curtains over the windows, and the roof looked sound. It was empty except for a stained mattress on the floor and a faded ruby-red armchair whose gray horsehair stuffing was emerging through its skin like an old man's whiskers. The room was spotlessly clean and in one corner stood a brand-new galvanized bucket, clearly the work of Flynn.

Why are you doing this for me?

But the words didn't reach her lips. Whatever his answer might be, she didn't want to hear it. His kindness warmed cold places inside her where shadows fretted against each other and she didn't want to lose that warmth. Whatever his answer, it would change things. She wanted to believe it was just a coincidence that he happened to be passing last night and saw the flames. Nothing more than chance that brought Flynn Hudson into her life.

She knew she would have to ask him questions, of course she did. About his life. About why he was on the island. Maybe even about whether he knew Morrell. She would ask them, she promised herself that. But not yet.

She said simply, "Thank you, Flynn."

In the flickering light of the candle the contours of his face seemed to shift, unwilling to be pinned down, and as if he could read what was in her mind he kept his eyes well guarded. Their expression was polite and warm, but that was as far as it went. Yet when he lifted her hand and placed a heavy old-fashioned iron key on her palm, his fingers lingered against hers, as though reluctant to give back her hand. He inclined his head so close she could smell the sea salt in his hair.

"Sleep well, Miss Wyatt," he said, and left.

From Mama Keel Dodie had brought a pair of clean though threadbare sheets, two candles, and her freshly laundered waitressing uniform. But when she lay down on the mattress she could hear the night's silence breathing within the room and the words "*Sleep well*" humming inside her head. Without the sound of waves she couldn't sleep.

* * *

Dodie opened her eyes. The edge of dawn was nudging its way around the thin curtains and curling up on the floor like a ginger tomcat. For a while she lay there, listening to the unfamiliar noises in the street outside—the creak of a cart, the insolent bray of a donkey, the swish of a broom, and a woman's voice quietly crooning a hymn. Life in Bain Town started early. Most of its residents worked as servants in the city, so had to get their own chores done at the crack of dawn before heading into downtown Nassau to spend their days doing white man's chores.

Quickly she dressed in her uniform and unlocked the door. A standpipe farther down the street had a group of women already gathered around it, but they all stopped and inspected Dodie with round surprised eyes. She smiled at them and raised a hand in greeting but no one responded except a child.

She had to be at work at eleven o'clock for a twelve-hour shift, but first she had something to do. As she hurried down the dusty road, a cockerel crowed to announce that the sun had stopped dragging its feet and had painted the sky blood red.

Chapter 21

Flynn

"Jesus Christ! What the hell are you doing here?" Sir Harry Oakes demanded. "I thought you'd cleared off and left the island."

"No," Flynn answered softly. "I'm still here."

Flynn remained in deep shadow while the early-morning sun came slinking around the side of the villa. By day it was a cheerful place of red tiles, latticework, flawless lawns, and a long balcony draped in the fragrance of bougainvillea, but at this hour, veiled in semidarkness, it exuded a different smell that was masked by the flowers when they opened up. It was the stink of money. Money and secrets. Flynn knew that smell like he knew the smell of his own breath.

Beyond the luxury property's perimeter the green swathes of Cable Beach Country Club and Golf Course had yet to wake up, but the broad-chested man in front of Flynn had already descended the outside staircase of his sprawling white-shuttered home and inhaled the new day with relish. Even in his work boots and khaki shorts, Sir Harry Oakes cut an impressive figure. Heavy-featured and well muscled, he had the look of a man who had wrenched gold from the land with his bare hands and thought nothing of it. He was about to set off on a stroll of inspection of his Westbourne estate before the staff arrived.

"What's on your mind?" Oakes demanded.

"Johnnie Morrell is dead."

"Jesus Christ, Hudson, I know. I heard that already. Poor bastard."

"Is that all you have to say?"

"The dumb jerk should have watched out for himself better."

"He had other things on his mind that night."

"So what do you expect?" Oakes challenged. "You want me to wear sackcloth and ashes or something for the guy?"

Oakes was breathing heavily. Flynn had dealt most of his life with men like Oakes, guys who liked to talk with their fists. The Chicago rackets were full of mobsters with more brawn than brain; that's why they needed him. Thinking was something he was good at. He'd seen men shot through the heart because they believed a bullet or a knife or a broken bottle held all the answers. Hell, they'd forgotten that you have to keep dancing the dance, weaving the web, shuffling the cards, if you want to wake up each day without a hole in your head.

"I want you to know I'm staying around for a bit."

"Not too long, Hudson. You've got to tell that shit Meyer Lansky in Miami that I'm not doing no deals. Tell him to stay out of my way, to keep his boys off my turf. You got that? I'm not having the mob hanging around Nassau." The line of his jaw set firm, his shoulders hunched.

Flynn kept one eye on the fists. You never knew with Oakes. Some days he was like a bull looking for a red rag. "Okay, I'll do that. But he won't like being told, you can bet your next buck on that."

"That's your problem."

"You're the one with a problem, Sir Harry."

"What's that supposed to mean? What's your beef now?"

"Johnnie Morrell is my beef. The small matter of how a knife found its way into his guts."

Oakes didn't flinch. If anything, those fists of his quieted down, but his gaze shifted to somewhere over Flynn's shoulder.

"Morrell was a fool," Oakes said, "to let anyone get so close.

The police are saying it was local unrest, that some resentful guy—probably drunk—waylaid him and—"

"Do the police know that Morrell was here that night?"

Oakes gave a hard smile and didn't even bother to answer the question. Somewhere in the distance a motor throbbed. Sounded like a boat engine.

"When he left here, did you have him followed?" Flynn asked.

"No."

A silence slid onto the damp grass between them. Flynn let it lie there.

"What are you implying?"

"Morrell came to see you that night and immediately afterward he died," Flynn pointed out.

"A coincidence."

"One hell of a coincidence."

He went for Flynn. Not bad speed for a man in his sixties. Must have been good when he was younger, but too much gold in his boots had made him slow. Ten years earlier he might have caught Flynn with the punch he threw, but Flynn swayed back on his heels and the blow thumped nothing but air. Oakes growled and looked around, searching for the two security guards who patrolled his property, but Flynn knew they were sneaking a smoke under the tamarind tree over on the far side of the estate, well out of sight of their employer.

"Get out of here, Hudson," Oakes snapped. "You're annoying me." When Flynn didn't move, he swung back toward the house.

Flynn let him get as far as the door. "The gold is missing."

Oakes froze. At that exact moment a great white egret drifted overhead through the darkness, heading toward the marsh lakes that sprawled over the western end of the island. Flynn glanced up and looked away quickly. Dammit, it felt like a bad omen.

Oakes's gaze locked on Flynn. "Find it."

"I'll find it," Flynn said. "On one condition."

Oakes snorted. "You're not in a position to lay down conditions."

"On condition that you keep the police off the girl's back."

"What girl?"

"You know what girl."

"It's your own fucking people you need to worry about. Meyer Lansky doesn't like loose ends. That girl is a loose end."

"I can take care of that."

Oakes studied him in the dim light while Flynn lit a cigarette. The thing about Oakes was that he was his own man, he didn't play by anybody else's rules. He was a crass individual who possessed a bulldozer mentality, but at the same time he was a generous man. And now he was facing down the mob alone.

Christ, Flynn had to admire the guy. Oakes had guts. That counted for something in his book. But Oakes was getting his nose put out of joint not only by the mob and the likes of Lansky, but by the arrival of the military as well. The war had come to the Bahamas with a vengeance, and Oakes was not top dog anymore. Even he could not control the might of the military. They had swept on to the island and shifted the balance of power in their favor, so that men like Oakes and the Bay Street Boys had to watch their step.

Without another word Flynn started to move away across the lawn, the tip of his cigarette drifting like a firefly in the darkness.

"I'll speak to Colonel Lindop about the girl."

Oakes's words hung in the cool air, and somewhere close by, the boom of the surf could be heard nudging the island awake.

Chapter 22

Dodie

Dodie opened the gates of Bradenham House and walked straight in. No sounds, no lights, just the purr of silence in her ears. She had not expected it to be so easy. No padlock on the wrought-iron gates and no guard to deter her. The Sanfords seemed to believe in the inherent decency of Bahamians rather than in overnight locks.

Dodie closed the gates quietly behind her, but this time she had no intention of knocking on the front door, where the maid could inspect her from head to toe like she was something the cat had sicked up on the doorstep. This time, while the morning light was still hampered by a thin veil of darkness, she slid under the pine trees that lined the property and moved across the grass on silent feet to the rear of the house.

The garden was huge and the air was heavily scented by the blooms that grew in such profusion. Dodie took up a position behind a camellia bush that gave her a good view of the house, and the stillness was only broken by the chirruping call of a pair of bananaquits that flew to a branch of the poinciana tree and flashed their bright yellow bellies at each other.

She sat down to wait.

* * *

Mrs. Sanford and her maid emerged from the back door into the early-morning sunshine, both wearing long brown pinafores, both with a bucket in each hand. A humid breeze was ruffling the trees as they strode over the wet grass past the shrubbery and down to an enclosure at the bottom of the garden. Here they proceeded to release a huddle of bright-eyed hens from their coops. As the birds swirled around their ankles with trills and chatter, Mrs. Sanford scattered grain into troughs and poured water into trays, talking as she did so.

Dodie watched, totally absorbed by the contented scene. One woman so golden and slender, the other black and broad, as different as oil and water. Yet even from where she was hidden under the trees, Dodie could sense the affection that existed between them. For that moment she forgot why she'd come to Bradenham House or why she was loitering in a patch of shadow on her own. That was why she heard nothing behind her. Sensed no movement coming at her.

The hands that seized Dodie's elbows from behind pinned her arms together, disabling her. She screamed with shock and tried to swivel around to catch sight of her attacker, but he knew exactly what he was doing. He yanked up her arms, forcing her forward as she fought in vain to wrench free from his grip.

She lashed out with her heels and connected with bone. Someone was screeching, yelling abuse, threatening to rip her heart out, but it was only when she hit the grass face-first with this man clamped to her back, the weight of him crushing her into the earth, that she realized the abuse and threats were coming from her own mouth.

She couldn't stop them. Out flooded the words that she didn't say when this happened three years ago. When she had fought in silence, too ashamed to scream. The words that had been stored in her head since then cascaded out of her mouth this time in a torrent of curses.

"Leave her!" a woman's voice was shouting. "Let her go!" A pair of grass-stained canvas shoes came into focus inches from her nose, a pair of dainty ankles above them. "Detective, release her right now."

Instantly the weight lifted off her back, but a strong hand still gripped one arm and dragged her to her feet. She was shaking and her cheeks were soaking wet—whether from tears or from the dew on the grass she had no idea. Her heart was grating against her ribs and she tasted blood in her mouth, slimy on her teeth, but the words had stopped. Where they had been inside her head was now an empty dark space.

*   *   *

They sat at the table in the kitchen, the three of them. Emerald stood by the stove, arms folded across her hefty bosom, her face puckered in a frown, her large teeth on show as if thinking of taking a bite out of someone.

"What are you doing here, Miss Wyatt?"

It was Detective Calder speaking, but Dodie didn't look up. She stared at the cup of coffee in front of her and thought about throwing it in his face. The skin of her arms still held the impression of his fingers and her mind still fought against the submission he had forced on her.

"I came to see Mrs. Sanford."

"Hiding under the trees? At seven o'clock in the morning. Trespassing? Spying on her? With a knife in your pocket?"

Put like that, it didn't sound good.

"What," he continued, "did you want to see Mrs. Sanford about?"

"That's between me and Mrs. Sanford."

She heard him exhale. Smelled the coffee on his breath. She was hunched in a ball and knew she looked guilty.

"Why the knife?" he asked.

"It's only an old penknife. It was my father's. I found it in the ashes of my house and just kept it in my pocket. There was no need"—she flicked her long hair forward to curtain her cheeks—"to attack me." Still she didn't look at him.

"Dodie—" Mrs. Sanford said softly.

"Miss Wyatt," the detective interrupted, "I would like to point out that you were the one who did the attacking."

"No."

Again Mrs. Sanford's steady voice. "It's true, Dodie."

"No."

"Yes." Calder's tone was calm and reasonable. "I watched you for some time spying on Mrs. Sanford from under the trees and when I approached you from behind and held your arm, you exploded like a firework in my face."

She shook her head.

"I'm sorry, Miss Wyatt, but I was forced to restrain you."

"Forced by whom?"

"By you. You became dangerous."

"You had my arms pinned behind my back, so how could I be dangerous?"

A coffee-scented silence settled on the table.

"Look at Detective Calder," Mrs. Sanford said.

Dodie forced herself to look. His face was bloodied. A bowl of ice sat at his elbow. On his left cheekbone a bruise was sending out purple tentacles as she looked at it and on the side of his neck was the clear oval outline of a bite. Each tooth had left its mark.

Color flooded Dodie's cheeks. She wondered why he was even being polite to her.

"You done used that head of yours like a batterin' ram," the maid told her. "Don't it hurt you none?"

"I'm sorry," Dodie whispered through her hair.

All she could remember was his body crushing hers and the taste of grass and soil in her mouth. A moan crawled out between her teeth. At the sound of it, Mrs. Sanford abruptly left her chair and opened the back door.

"Miss Wyatt," she said in a matter-of-fact tone, "I think you need some fresh air."

Dodie was on her feet and out the door before the policeman could tie her to the table leg.

*   *   *

"Was that the crime?" Mrs. Sanford asked.

"What crime?"

Dodie didn't want to talk. She was happy admiring the garden. There was a lushness to it and a beauty that slowly reeled her back from the edge. Dense swathes of tropical shrubs encircled the lawn and her gaze was drawn to the vibrant greens of their leaves and the shimmering shades of jade rather than to the bold splashes of scarlet and magenta of the heliconia and the hibiscus blooms. Their colors were almost overwhelming right now.

"The crime you told me that you reported before, but no one believed."

"What about it?" Dodie asked.

"It was rape, wasn't it?"

Dodie's hand was poised over a succulent leaf that was almost purple, its color was so deep. She held her breath. It was the way she dealt with it. Whenever that image of a man tearing at her clothes, ramming her on to his desk, and ripping into her flesh flared up in her head, she held her breath. Starving it of oxygen was the only way she knew to put the flames out. So she held her breath and felt the pain recede.

"Yes," she said bleakly, "it was rape."

"I'm so sorry. But Detective Calder wasn't trying to hurt you."

"I know. But he seized my arm and—"

"I understand. You panicked."

Dodie steadied her breathing and looked at Mrs. Sanford, but her large blue eyes held no pity. No scorn. No fear of being in the presence of the unclean. Just concern and a flicker of sorrow.

"Who was it?" she asked.

"My boss. At the sewing factory where I worked." It brought relief to let the words see daylight. "Afterward he spread it around that I was trouble and made it impossible for me to get a job anywhere. I almost starved."

"And now?"

"I work at the Arcadia."

"That's Olive Quinn's place."

"Yes. She took me on when no one else would touch me."

"Typical Olive. Always running against the tide."

"I am grateful to her."

Mrs. Sanford was standing near a bed of pure white roses. Their delicacy and freshness was such a sharp contrast to the vigorous growth and vivid tropical colors of the rest of the garden that Dodie wondered whether they belonged to Mr. Sanford rather than to his wife. But Mrs. Sanford wasn't looking at the roses, she was staring back at the house, her gaze narrowed on the kitchen window.

"It was shocking," she told Dodie, "to see a man reduce a woman to nothing in my own garden. To strip her of respect the way Detective Calder did to you. He was just doing his job of protecting me, I know that. But it was so ugly."

Dodie was not willing to talk about the ugliness. It felt like dirt in her mouth. "Do you need protecting?"

Mrs. Sanford smiled. "Do I look as if I do?"

"No."

Mrs. Sanford looked once more at the kitchen window behind which they both knew the detective sat and she asked abruptly, "Why are you here, Miss Wyatt?"

"To ask if the person who introduced Morrell to you was Sir Harry Oakes."

The woman's eyes popped wide, her mouth open. "No. Of course not. Why would you think that?"

"Because he offered me a job."

"I don't see the connection."

"Neither did I at first."

"No, you're mistaken. No, no, it wasn't Sir Harry."

Too many no's, Mrs. Sanford. But Dodie liked her, despite her lies. Liked the way she looked at you as if she was really listening. Not many people did that to her.

"Coming in for breakfast, darling?"

Both women jumped. The unexpected request had issued from a man standing beside the rose bed. A solid and confident figure in a beautifully tailored pale suit, his hair combed to perfection with just a touch of macassar oil to keep it in place, and a way of looking at Mrs. Sanford that lit up his smooth face. Dodie had never seen that in a man before.

"Ah, Reggie, I'm just coming. Let me introduce Miss Wyatt." She turned to Dodie. "This is my husband."

"Pleased to meet you, Miss Wyatt. Are you joining us for breakfast?"

"No thank you, I have to go to work."

She saw him glance at her waitress uniform but he smiled kindly and pointed to the chicken enclosure. "At least take some of those blasted eggs with you."

"What do you do with all the eggs?" Dodie asked.

"She gives them away," her husband answered. "She goes to all this trouble and then gives all the wretched things away free."

"Really?"

"Yes." He smiled indulgently at his wife. "Really."

Mrs. Sanford returned the smile, but a flash of color had appeared high on her cheeks.

"I'm starving," her husband announced cheerfully. "Breakfast time. Delighted to meet you, Miss Wyatt." He beamed at her before taking himself off toward the house.

Neither woman spoke. Mrs. Sanford watched her husband's straight back recede across the lawn, growing smaller with each step. An arrow of sunlight squeezed its way through the canopy of the trees and set the kitchen window on fire.

"You're right, Dodie," she said after a full minute. "It was Sir Harry Oakes who introduced me to Morrell."

"Thank you."

"So what next?"

"I have to find out who killed Mr. Morrell and burned down my house. Before they come for me again."

Chapter 23

Ella

Ella sat stiffly in the passenger seat of the car. She was awkward around the policeman now. In the back of the Rover, as noisy as a cricket, Emerald was flirting with Detective Dan Calder. He was busy driving but that didn't stop her. She'd perched her broad backside on the edge of the seat so that she could lean forward and swat his shoulder whenever he made a comment that amused her, and right now all his comments amused her.

Something was the matter. Something was hurting. But Ella didn't know exactly what. Except that everything this morning made her feel as though the top layer of her skin was being scraped off by a blunt knife. Ever since she had spoken with the girl. Ella sat with an arm trailing out of the car window as if trying in her own discreet way to escape. She didn't talk much. It didn't matter because the other two were doing enough of it for all of them, and anyway it was too hot today.

The air hung limp and humid in the car, the sun dazzling on the windscreen and her blouse sticking to the back of the seat, so that it took an effort to move. They left behind the lavish pastel mansions that drowsed behind vivid green swathes of palm trees and pines, and the car slipped over the modest hill that divided white Nassau from black Nassau. Here in Bain Town the houses were really nothing more than small huts cobbled together from wood or corrugated metal, but they burst onto the eye bright and colorful. They were painted brilliant yellows and greens and blues, gaudy colors that seemed to dance in the street.

Dark-skinned ragamuffins were playing a game of hopscotch in the middle of the road, but as soon as they spotted Ella's sleek car purr around the corner, they all swarmed around it and jumped up on its running boards for a ride. Watermelon grins split their young faces and small arms reached in to touch the golden waves of her hair.

"You had better stay in the car," Ella told Calder, "if you don't mind."

"You think I'll scare them off?"

She gave him a half smile. "Police don't go down too well round here. I know you're not in uniform but . . ."

"They'd gobble you up for dinner, Mr. Detective." Emerald chuckled in the back. "And very tasty you'd be too."

"Why, thank you, Emerald."

Ella climbed out of the car and opened the boot. Bright little faces followed her every move as she removed a bag of sweets and handed them around.

"You spoil them kids somethin' rotten, Miss Ella," Emerald muttered as she hoisted a sack of rice out of the boot.

Women came ambling over from the houses, greeting her with smiles.

"How you doin' today, Miss Ella?"

"The dear Lord takin' good care of you?"

She doled out eggs and rice into their bowls and all regarded Calder with undisguised interest, bobbing their heads to inspect him through the car windows.

"You caught yourself a fine fellow there, Miss Ella. Been in a fight, by the look of him."

"Ladies!" Ella laughed.

Bahamian women wore loud colors and possessed loud voices with big rolling laughs that could knock the birds from the trees. They worked hard, growing vegetables to sell in town and weaving their Bahamian bags, hats, and dolls of straw to take to the straw market down by the harbor. But times were hard. The war had put an end to foreign visitors who were the easy-money customers, but the city was busy with the military presence on the island, so many women had abandoned the traditional crafts and taken to employment in the hotels and bars instead.

"Leah, have you got a minute?" Ella called out to a woman in a scarlet dress.

"Sure, Miss Ella."

She ambled over to where Ella was standing by the car. That was the thing about Bahamian women, they never liked to be hurried.

"How's that son of yours?" Ella asked pleasantly.

"My Joshua? He's just fine."

"Still working for Sir Harry?"

"Oh yes, he surely is, thanks be to our dear Lord in heaven."

"At the British Colonial Hotel?"

"Sometimes there or sometimes out on the land beyond Oakes Airfield, drivin' one of Sir Harry's tractors. He likes that."

Leah had ten children and a backside broad enough to carry the lot of them. Her husband was a quiet respectful man but one who unfortunately liked his ganja weed too much.

"Is Joshua still aiming to join the Bahamian police force one of these days?" Ella asked.

Out of the corner of her eye she saw Calder turn in his seat to stare at the woman.

"Sure is," Leah answered. "Got his heart set on it."

"My friend here might be able to help with that."

Leah ducked her head to the open window and took a long look at Calder. "You a cop from England?"

Obligingly he stepped out of the car and stood tall next to her. "I am."

Leah eyed his muscular frame and ran a fat pink tongue over her lips. "Okay, what you wantin', Miss Ella?"

Ella chose her words carefully. "I was just wondering whether Joshua sometimes heard things at work, picked up gossip. That kind of thing."

Leah's eyes grew huge. "Gossip about what?"

"About Sir Harry Oakes."

Leah shuffled her feet. "Well, yes"—she lowered her voice—"sometimes he does." She hesitated and let her eyes roam back to Calder, as though checking whether he was part of the deal. "Joshua says Sir Harry has had a lot of trouble lately."

"What kind of trouble?"

"Rows and arguments." Leah leaned forward, her bosom swaying dangerously. "In the hotel. Behind closed doors." She frowned. "My Joshua takes coffee into Sir H's office of a mornin' and he's heard him a heap of times yelling down the phone line. Real bad, he says."

"Sir Harry can get irate sometimes, I know," Ella encouraged. "Did Joshua hear what any of the rows were about or who was on the receiving end?"

Leah pointed a finger at Calder, almost stabbed him in the chest with it. "You remember this, Mr. Policeman, when my boy comes calling. Just needs a helping hand. His name is Joshua Tuttle. He's a smart kid."

Calder nodded solemnly. "If your son is a good candidate, I will do whatever I can to help his application, I promise."

"You won't get my Joshua into no trouble, will you, Miss Ella?"

"No, of course not."

"Them quarrels were about a contract. And the other man was a Mr. Christie."

"Harold Christie? The land agent? But he and Sir Harry are good friends. They play golf together."

"Not no more, by the sound of it."

"Did he ever mention someone called Morrell?"

"Not that I heard."

"Thanks for your help, Leah, I appreciate it."

"I'm trustin' you, Miss Ella."

Leah hitched her bowl of rice on her hip and, aiming a nod at Calder, she set off walking back down the street, shimmering in the sun. But after twenty paces she turned and her voice rang out clear as a church bell.

"Hey, Miss Ella. You know about the room he keeps there for his own personal use, if you get my meaning?" She jiggled her bosom suggestively, then she meandered away, chuckling to herself.

Ella looked at Dan Calder warily and to her astonishment found that he was laughing. She gave him a wry smile.

"So, Mrs. Sanford, what the hell was all that about?"

*   *   *

The two of them were in her car and it was stifling hot. Flies, drunk on heat, staggered in and out of the open windows and the metal of the car was now too hot to touch. Ella leaned her head back and felt sweat trickle down her neck, pooling in the hollow between her collarbones.

They were waiting for Emerald. As usual when she'd finished her egg work in Bain Town, Emerald waddled off to visit an ancient bedridden aunt who was tucked away somewhere in one of the narrower streets. The maid had been as pleased as punch when Reggie announced that he'd found some kind of work for her aunt's niece by marriage. She'd baked him a steaming-hot jam roly-poly and Ella had looked on with amusement as he devoured the lot with relish.

"Mrs. Sanford?" Dan Calder's voice prodded her out of her stupor.

"Mmm?"

"Do you actually believe you are in any danger?"

It was too hot to move her head. "No."

She heard the rhythm of his breathing change.

"Why?" she asked. "Do *you* think I'm in danger?"

"I'm here to protect you. So no, I think you are safe."

"Like you protected me in my garden this morning, you mean?"

She heard a click, the sound of his teeth snapping together. She rolled her head to look at him.

"I'm sorry," she said. "I didn't mean that to sound rude. You did what you had to."

A muscle below his ear moved back and forth under his skin. "I hope," he said, "that you sorted out the problem that is Miss Wyatt."

"You think she is a problem?"

"Don't you?"

"I think," she said, "that you are taking care of me so well that I have no problems."

With a flick of his head, he looked across at her. But when he saw she was teasing him, his gray eyes relaxed.

"Do you carry a gun?" she asked.

"Ah, that's top-secret information, I'm afraid. If I told you that, I might have to kill you."

Ella burst out laughing, just as Emerald came trundling down the street toward them.

※   ※   ※

The moment Ella reached home, she stripped off her clothes, took a shower, and toweled herself dry.

What did it feel like?

She stretched out on the floor of her bedroom, having made sure that the jalousie blinds were securely drawn. She lay flat on her stomach, her breathing reined back to something close to normal.

What did it feel like? To be facedown on the grass. To have a man treat you like dirt. She clasped her hands behind her back the way she'd seen it done, her cheek pressed to the floor. Nerve ends twitched in her skin. She tried to imagine it. To imagine Calder's knee on her back, his strong hands gripping her wrists. She closed her eyes and felt heat surge through her blood.

The door of the bedroom opened.

"Good God, Ella!" Reggie swept into the room. "Are you ill?"

Ella leaped to her feet. "No, I . . . was dozing." Color burned her cheeks.

"With no clothes on?"

"I was hot. The floor felt cooler."

His gaze raked over her breasts, sank to the glint of the golden triangle of curls between her legs, and without comment he quickly closed the door behind him.

"It was too hot to work in the office. I didn't have too much on today, so I came home early," he explained.

He approached her with the tentative smile and the diffident steps of someone who would die rather than push a woman's face into the grass.

Chapter 24

Dodie

The shop looked respectable enough from the outside. Dodie inspected it from across the street. It was Minnie who had told her about it, the tiny kitchen maid she worked with at the Arcadia who seemed to possess a mental map of every shop in Nassau. It was an area that looked just a mite run-down without actually tipping over into shabby. The tone was raised by a smart dress shop with flower tubs outside and an expensive brass sign that glinted like solid gold in the sun.

But Dodie wasn't looking at dresses. Her gaze was fixed on a jewelry shop with a fancy display of watches and pearl necklaces in its window. She waited just long enough for one of the pretty surreys—the little horse-drawn carriages adorned with bells and fringes—to tinkle past, then she dodged across the road and entered the shop.

Inside the temperature shot up a few degrees. The large brass fan whirred dutifully on the ceiling but didn't stand a chance against the many lights trained on the display cabinets. The air sparkled with flashes of gold and silver and the floor was polished to a mirror sheen, so bright that Dodie had to narrow her eyes against the glare. Behind a bead curtain at the back of the shop stood two figures, a man and a woman. The man had his arm looped around the woman's waist but she detached herself and brushed her way through the curtain when Dodie entered. Her heels tapped their way across the floor to take up position behind the counter.

"May I help you?"

The woman had ginger hair cropped short as a boy's, scarlet-painted nails, and was a walking advertisement for her wares. A ring on every freckled finger. She wore a three-string pearl necklace and milky earrings to match. Three gold bracelets jangled together on each pale wrist. It occurred to Dodie to wonder how the woman dared risk walking down the street even in broad daylight. The smile she gave her customer was friendly.

"I'm told you know about old coins," Dodie started cautiously.

The woman's smile slipped. She turned her head toward the curtain. "Marcus," she called.

The man emerged. He had glossy ebony skin and the slow easy manner of one born and bred to the island's rhythm, a place where the women took charge and the men were content to let them. He went about his own business with quiet dignity and placed himself beside the ginger-haired woman, his hip brushing hers.

"What can I do for you, ma'am?"

"I have a coin. I'd like you to take a look at it, please."

"Certainly. I am always interested in old coins. They have lived a life and they tell a story." He laid out a rectangle of black felt as an invitation for her to reveal what she had.

Dodie felt nervous. She didn't know what was coming. She placed the coin on the felt and stood back. But she saw the way the jeweler's eyes ignited in the light that flashed off the gold surface and the sudden flaring of his broad nostrils.

"I think it's French," she suggested.

He nodded. A magnifying glass sprang from his pocket.

"You're right. It's French." He smiled at the coin affectionately and with a gentle touch picked it up. "A forty-franc napoleon. See its date? *An IZ*. That's French for year twelve. That means it was minted twelve years after the Revolution when the new French government set up a brand-new calendar system." He glanced at the woman at his side. "That was 1803, see?"

"Is it gold?" Dodie asked.

He twirled it under the lights. "Oh yes, ma'am. It's ninety percent pure gold and signed by its engraver. See here? Tiolier. He was the engraver general of the Paris Mint until 1816, a true master artist."

"Is it rare?"

"Rare enough." He turned it over on his palm. "Look at the head of Bonaparte as premier consul, how finely Tiolier crafted it. That's why it's called a napoleon."

"Were many of them made?"

"Yes, over a quarter of a million were minted."

"Oh."

"But not so many survive today. Most were melted down."

"Is there anyone in Nassau who is keen on old coins, do you know?" Dodie kept it casual.

The air in the shop changed. Ice water dripped into it and the temperature dropped. Dodie saw the shopkeepers exchange a look. The man replaced the coin on the felt and leaned his elbows on the counter either side of it, surveying her calmly. He was in a business that liked to keep its secrets under the counter.

"Do you have someone in mind?" he asked mildly.

The name of Sir Harry Oakes teetered on the tip of her tongue but she clung on to it. "Maybe one of the big businessmen on the island has an interest in collecting coins." That was as far as she dared go.

The woman picked up the napoleon and flicked it in the air, catching it again as though tossing Dodie for it. "Where did you get this?" she asked bluntly.

A thief. That's what she thinks I am. A thief selling dirty money.

"It was given to me. A gift. I don't know its history. Would you be interested in it?"

"We only buy items," the woman announced, "when we know

where they have come from." She dropped the coin on the counter and folded her arms. "So no, we—"

"But perhaps"—the man with the kind eyes was gazing benignly at the gold napoleon, as at a favorite son—"we could make an exception in this case."

"Marcus!"

"It's a beautiful coin in fine condition."

The woman sighed. "You are too easily seduced by lovely things."

They looked at each other and smiled. But when the woman turned back to Dodie, the smile had gone and in its place lay suspicion.

"What's your name?" she asked.

But Dodie was not caught out so easily. She said, "Oh, I've just thought of someone. What about Sir Harry Oakes?" An innocent afterthought, nothing more. "Does he collect coins by any chance? I've heard he's a man who likes gold."

The woman rippled her rings in the rays of the nearest lamp, skimming flashes of brilliance as fleet as shooting stars across the ceiling. "My dear girl," she said with a look of disdain, "everybody likes gold."

❊　❊　❊

"Is Detective Sergeant Calder here, please?"

"No, he's not."

The police station smelled sickly sweet. Dodie glanced behind her at a bench where a man and his wife were fanning themselves and biting into overripe peaches, juice running down their dark fingers onto the linoleum floor as they waited for their turn at the counter. Flies, glossy and fat, droned around their heads, pestering their lips and settling on their hands like dried scabs.

The desk sergeant was regarding Dodie with undue interest. "Who's asking?" he said.

"My name is Dodie Wyatt."

"Oh right, I thought I recognized you. You're the little lady who reported the murder."

She could feel the two people on the bench against the wall switch their attention from the peaches to her.

"Will he be in later?" she asked.

"No, Detective Sergeant Calder is not on duty today, I'm afraid. What can I do for you?"

"I was wondering"—she lowered her voice—"if your inquiries have discovered anything further about Mr. Morrell."

"Well, Miss Wyatt, from what I'm told, it seems that he's proving to be something of a mystery, I can tell you that much. No trace of him arriving on the island. Not easy to find out where he came from, but it is under investigation, I assure you."

"So you haven't found any of his family?"

"Not yet."

"He'll need a funeral."

"That's true."

Dodie was acutely aware of the fruit eaters' gazes watching the back of her head; nevertheless, she placed a bundle of pound notes on the counter.

"What's that for?" the desk sergeant asked uneasily.

"For Mr. Morrell's funeral. I don't want him buried in an unmarked pauper's grave."

He picked up a pencil on the desk and sank his teeth thoughtfully into its end. "As I understand it, you don't know this man."

"I don't."

"So why are you paying for his funeral?"

"I want him to have a proper grave with a headstone. A decent Christian burial."

"Why? What's he to you?"

"Nothing. Except that I was with him when he died."

"That doesn't mean you have to pay for his funeral, you know."

"I know." But it was her way of saying sorry to him for letting him die.

The desk sergeant was a good-looking man with a solid dependable manner, but his features were now spoiled as they twisted into a sneer. "Paid you good money, did he?"

He thought she'd had sex with Morrell. For money. Dodie felt a rush of shame crawling up the skin of her neck.

"I think you'd better have a word with one of our other detectives, Miss Wyatt," he added sternly.

Dodie fled from the flies and the peach juice and the money lying on the counter, out into the street.

*   *   *

Money for sex.

No, Mr. Desk Sergeant, that wasn't what this was about. But whichever way she turned, tracking down Mr. Morrell's trail seemed to be leading her to places where she ended with her face in the dirt.

Under the hard blue sky, Dodie wove her way along pavements bustling with RAF uniforms and with women in colorful dresses carrying children on their hips and baskets on their head, till she reached the Arcadia Hotel. But the gloom that clung to her thoughts was swept away at the sight of a figure standing on the steps of the rear entrance. It was Flynn Hudson. He held a cigarette in his hand and a lazy smile sat on his lips as if it had been waiting there for her. He stepped toward her and she saw a strip of pink sunburn above his collar where the sun had run its fingers.

"Good morning, Miss Wyatt, I looked for you," he said, "first thing this morning. In Bain Town. But you'd left already."

"Oh."

She'd missed him. She would have stayed. Stayed till he came. Why didn't he tell her? Why didn't she realize he might come?

"I had some errands to run," she explained, "before I went to work."

"And now more errands in your break?"

"Yes."

"You're busy today."

"Yes, I am."

His smile widened. "I brought you breakfast."

"Breakfast?"

"Yes. To Bain Town this morning."

"No one has ever brought me breakfast before."

"I arrived too late," he said. "I'm sorry."

"Or I left too early."

He laughed, a warm sound.

"What was in it?" she asked. "In the breakfast?"

One of his dark eyebrows swooped upward, surprised. But he held up his fingers and started to tick them off with the cigarette. "Bread rolls fresh from the bakery, boiled eggs, a papaya, banana . . ." He paused for thought and Dodie was aware of his mouth becoming unguarded in that moment, as if recalling the pleasure he had in choosing food for her. "And a pot of crab and—"

"Crab?"

"Yes. Just cooked on the harborside. I thought you might like it."

"I would."

"And milk for tea," he finished with a flourish. "That's all."

He inhaled on the cigarette, his eyes observing her with amusement, waiting for a comment. But how could she tell him that if she could turn back the clock, rewind it through the sneers in the police station, through the ginger-haired woman's suspicion, and through her face full of dirt in Mrs. Sanford's garden, she would. Wipe out every minute of today and start it again with him and his breakfast. She would.

"What happened," she asked, "to this breakfast fit for a queen?"

"I had to eat it on my own."

"Oh. Lucky you."

Flynn was smiling at her, the kind of smile that came from somewhere deep enough to banish the shadows that usually haunted his face, but Dodie looked away. A cart carrying crates rattled past and a bicycle bell bleated at a reckless pedestrian, but she saw them only dimly. She had to look away because if she didn't, she would cry.

But he mistook her intention. He thought she was leaving to enter the hotel and his hand grasped her wrist. "Don't go," he said. "Not yet, Miss Wyatt."

"Please call me Dodie. Anyone who brings me breakfast is allowed to call me Dodie."

She stared at his fingers. Not the big strong knuckles of the other man who had laid hands on her today. These were finely boned, threads of blue vein under the skin, as pale as the rest of him, with well-shaped fingernails and a sense of purpose in their grip. It could mean so many different things when a man's hand was fastened like a shackle around your wrist. The image of Mr. Morrell clinging on to her for dear life rose unbidden to her mind and she shook her head to dislodge it. Immediately Flynn released his grip.

"No," she said. "I didn't mean . . ."

A clock somewhere struck four. Dodie's hour-long break was over. Today her work shift was eleven in the morning till three, then four till eleven at night, and she had taken enough liberties with Miss Olive's patience recently. It was time to walk away from him. But her feet wouldn't move.

"Flynn," she started.

She meant to say: *Tomorrow bring me breakfast and I will eat papaya and crab with you with pleasure. Bring me your smile to banish the dreams that stalk my sleep each night. Bring me your certainty that lies in everything you do—in the way you hold your head while you're listening to me or in your long pale fingers when you roll one of your cigarettes. Bring me all those things tomorrow, Flynn Hudson, when the sun comes up.* But the wrong words slipped out instead.

"Flynn, when you were on the beach the night before last, did you see anyone else? Anyone who might have started the fire that burned down my house?"

The memory of laughter that still hung on the edges of his mouth faded completely. Dodie was tempted to go down on her knees and snatch her words off the ground and cram them back into her throat.

"No," he said quietly, "I'd have told you if I did. I was drawn there by the flames, like everyone else. I didn't set fire to your house."

"Of course not."

But the laughter had vanished. The damage was done.

"Thank you," she said. She reached out and lightly touched his hand. "For the breakfast."

He nodded and his dark eyes watched her every step as she entered the hotel.

* * *

"Dodie, take care of table twenty, will you?"

Dodie looked up from the tray of teacups she was arranging, surprised. "But that's one of Angela's tables."

Olive Quinn waved a dismissive hand. "He has asked for you to serve him. Don't keep him waiting. It's Harold Christie."

Dodie glanced across. She knew the name. Everyone on the island knew the name. She was standing on the colonnaded terrace of the hotel, overlooking the fragrant garden and manicured lawn. Harold Christie was seated at one of the bamboo tables, and Dodie took note of a short but muscular man of about fifty. Bald as a turtle and with the air of one who is pleased with his life, he was jotting something down in a small notebook while he inhaled thoughtfully on a cigarette. His fingers bore the egg-yolk stain of a dedicated smoker. As she approached his table, he looked up and smiled, an affable, lined face with a bulbous, unshapely nose.

"May I help you, sir?" Dodie asked politely.

"Ah, excellent, my dear." He folded away his notebook and fountain pen, and his alert green eyes inspected her at his leisure.

"Yes." He smiled. "I rather think you can. A pot of Assam tea." He tapped his waistline and chuckled. "And a plate of Miss Quinn's irresistible cakes as well, if you please."

"Certainly, sir."

Dodie did as he asked. It didn't take her long. Customers were scarce this afternoon. She wasn't sure why. Maybe it was the heat, or maybe it was just the latest mood swing in the city. The atmosphere was very dependent upon the war news from home. When it was good—like the recent successful air raids on more German factories in the Ruhr—the inhabitants of Nassau were buoyant and eager to celebrate. But some days, when the wireless reported severe loss of life, especially among the heavy bombers, the mood grew somber and fewer people were willing to fritter away their time aimlessly. Nevertheless Dodie had noticed this summer that more and more American servicemen were turning up on Miss Quinn's terrace, adopting the British ritual of afternoon tea.

She could hear them now at the other end of the terrace as she brought Harold Christie his tray of tea and fancy cakes, which she laid out before him. As she poured his tea she wanted to demand, *Why did you ask me to serve you?* She saw the pleasure he took in his first mouthful of dainty éclair. This was a man who knew what he liked.

"Sit down, my dear." His manner was avuncular as he gestured to the chair opposite him.

Dodie was startled. "Thank you, but no. It's not allowed. I'll stand, if you don't mind."

"Miss Quinn will make an exception in this case, I am quite certain. Please do sit down. You're giving me a crick in my neck." He chuckled again to show he meant it kindly.

She glanced around awkwardly and then sat on the chair opposite him.

"Well now," he said, and lit himself another cigarette, "you are Miss Dodie Wyatt, I believe."

"That's right."

"Excellent. That's a good start." He took another bite out of his éclair. Cream spilled over his lips.

"A start to what?" Dodie asked quietly. She was uncomfortable and wary of what this man wanted from her.

"To getting to know each other."

"Is that what we're doing? I think you probably just want to ask me something."

There was a silence between them, the kind of silence that made her hear her own heartbeat in her ears. She noticed that his jacket was creased, as if he'd taken a nap in it, and she wanted to ask how such a crumpled person could become one of the most important men on New Providence Island. Because that's what he was. His name was on sale boards all over the island, the main real-estate agent in Nassau and the boss of the Bay Street Boys, the wealthy traders who ran the city.

"I like that, Miss Wyatt," he said. "A young woman who gets right to the point."

But she didn't think he did like it. Not much.

"What is it you need to know, Mr. Christie?"

"I need to know whether you like living in this island paradise."

"Of course I do. It's beautiful."

"So do I. That's my point. I was born and bred here." He spread his arms theatrically to encompass the whole of New Providence Island. "It's my home."

"It's mine too now," she pointed out.

"How long have you lived here?"

"Six years."

"Well, Miss Wyatt, I've got a good forty years on that."

"So you trump me, Mr. Christie. Where does that get us?"

"Ah, back to the point again. Yes, I like that." But his eyes narrowed and grew careful. "Most of New Providence Island is covered in just wild uncultivated bush and pine trees. The city of Nassau is all we've got on this island of ours. And our beaches, of course."

Dodie glanced away, uncertain of the path this conversation was taking. There were five other couples taking tea on the terrace but they were all at the far end, where the trickling of a fountain gave the illusion of coolness. Harold Christie had chosen his table well, tucked against a wall and fringed with potted palms for seclusion. She fanned herself with her order pad.

"Why are you telling me this, Mr. Christie?"

"When this wretched war is over, the world is going to change. The ordinary man in the street has had a taste of travel and he's going to want more. So where do you think would be a good place for them to come?"

"The Bahamas?"

"Exactly."

The excitement in his face worried her. She wanted to know where it was coming from.

"So after the war, I assume your land-sales business will boom, Mr. Christie. That's very nice for you, but why are you telling me?"

He sat back in his chair, stubbed out his cigarette, lit another, and sipped his tea. He took his time composing his face.

"Because, Miss Wyatt, I want you to understand how important it is that this island remains a paradise in the full heat of the sun. No dark sides."

"That's how you refer to Mr. Morrell, is it? A dark side?"

He hung on to his smile, but only just. He ran a hand over the tanned surface of his bald head, massaging its mottled skin before taking another cake between his fingers.

"Now," he announced, "we get to the point. The Duke of Windsor is our governor."

Dodie nodded.

"Because of this," he continued, "we have the world's media keeping a watchful eye on our every move, despite the fact that we are a tiny insignificant island."

Ah. So that was the point. She felt a dull throb of anger.

"Mr. Morrell's death is being investigated by the police," he said in a low undertone. "What they do not need is *you* getting in their way."

"Who was Mr. Morrell?" she asked flatly.

"I thought you were the one with the answers to that. Nobody else seems to know."

He jabbed his cigarette into the ashtray and seemed about to say something more, but stopped himself by taking a bite out of a creamy meringue. Dodie stood up. He was tapping a finger impatiently on his silver cigarette case, making it rattle on the table. The conversation clearly had not gone as he'd expected.

"Mr. Christie, you are friends with Sir Harry Oakes, aren't you?"

The smile returned with full force. "Indeed I am."

Dodie could see in him the self-belief that invades a man who has made his fortune himself and could sense the arrogance that fails to recognize where the boundaries lie.

"I thought so," she murmured.

A flicker of a frown crossed his brow without dislodging the smile. "Don't get involved, that's my strong advice to you."

"Mr. Christie, why on earth should you care enough to come down here today and have me sit at a table with you?"

The smile widened and nearly reached his eyes this time. "I care about everyone in the Bahamas," he said kindly. "Even you, Miss Wyatt."

Dodie turned away and returned to her work. But as she continued to jot down orders on her notepad, to carry trays, and to offer her best servant smiles to her customers, one thought kept beating a path inside her head. Why were these powerful men so nervous about what Mr. Morrell knew? What was it that they feared he'd said to her in her shack?

Chapter 25

Ella

"I want to give you something, Ella. Something special."

"Reggie, how lovely of you."

"It's our anniversary next week."

"Clever of you to remember, darling."

"Of course I remember. I always remember."

It was true. He was better at remembering the date than she was, but this time she had already booked them a table for two at the Greycliff and had told Reggie's secretary to keep that evening free in his diary.

"Twenty years," he said.

"Twenty good years, Reggie."

His round cheeks flushed with pleasure and Ella wished she said it more often. They were taking a stroll through the garden, a moment of calm that she knew Reggie needed. His work was demanding and some days she spotted tiny burst blood vessels in the whites of his eyes that worried her.

"What would you like? As an anniversary gift, I mean," he asked.

She was drawn as usual toward the vibrant colors of the abundant heliconias and put out a hand to polish one of their big glossy banana leaves. She loved the sensuous feel of them. The bright scarlet flowers were bold and flashy, always attention seeking.

"I think, Reggie, that just a cake with twenty candles would be lovely."

He gave a snort of disgust. "It's china, you know."

"What's china?"

"A twentieth anniversary. The gift is supposed to be china—like a dinner service or something of porcelain."

"Really? Reggie, what a lot you know."

He laughed and steered her away from the brash heliconias to a more delicate white oleander bush. The fact that every part of the plant was toxic had always made her wary of it and she moved off to inspect a flash of a black-and-white bird in the buttonwood tree.

"I really don't think we need any more china," she said, but turned and smiled at him to show she appreciated the offer. "We have so much already."

"Something special, Ella. To mark the occasion. What about something gold, then? Because that's what you are, my darling, pure gold."

Ella had to keep watching the mangrove cuckoo or she would have cried.

* * *

Ella was quiet in the car. Dan Calder made no attempt to disturb her but respectfully left her to her own thoughts as he drove her to the Belmont Hotel. It was where a number of the American servicemen were billeted and both Allied flags—the Stars and Stripes and the Union Jack—fluttered their patriotic colors over the entrance. The building was painted a rather unpleasant shade of green and had a wide veranda that ran along its frontage, where pilots and aircrew in khaki lazed in the shade on bamboo chairs, the big brown shoes propped up against the wooden railing as if they didn't have a care in the world.

Ella entered the hotel and headed straight for what used to be the old billiards room, but was now the office of Major Leigh.

"Mrs. Sanford, good day to you, ma'am."

He gave her a broad Texan smile and ushered her to an upright chair in front of his desk. He was a man with kind eyes and a loud voice, who was prone to sneezing fits at all the wrong moments. Pinned to the walls around them was a colorful display of maps of the Atlantic, and two large gray metal filing cabinets stood where the smoking armchairs used to be before the war.

"Thank you for finding time in your busy schedule, Major."

"The pleasure is all mine, ma'am. Though I must say I didn't expect to see you again quite so soon."

Ella smiled prettily and crossed her legs, ignoring the oppressive heat in the room and the fact that a large, rather pungent black retriever had just lain across her foot.

"Hello, Ike," she said to the dog, and its tail lurched into action. "I hope your boys enjoyed the party, Major."

"Indeed they did. A real shindig, and the duke was there as well to put the frosting on the cake for them. Damn me if this isn't an assignment like no other." He settled into his chair and Ella saw his glance skim toward a tall pile of buff-colored files on the desk.

"I won't keep you long, Major, I know how many demands you have on your time." She patted the dog's head. "I have a favor to ask."

Major Leigh uttered a deep belly laugh. "Holy smokes, Mrs. Sanford, don't you ever give up?"

Ella shook her head and her fair hair swung loose, allowing a welcome breath of air to ripple through it. "No, Major, I'm afraid I don't. But don't worry, I know you'll really approve of this cause." She smiled at the photograph of his two young sons on his desk. "It's for a school out in the bush. They badly need new equipment. Seats and writing pens."

"Black kids?"

"That's right. They really need your squadron's help, Major."

"Mrs. Sanford, you sure are a powerful persuader with those

beautiful blue eyes of yours." He laughed once more, happy to have a pretty woman in his office, and opened a drawer.

"How much this time?"

*   *   *

"Thank you, Mrs. Sanford."

The chorus of young voices made Ella smile as the row of pupils lined up outside the schoolhouse with huge grins on their faces to wave her good-bye.

"They are all eager to write to Major Leigh to thank him for his kindness," the schoolteacher said as she walked Ella to her car. "We can buy paper and pens for each one of them now, as well as books and benches." She regarded the bright expressions of her flock proudly. "They are hungry to learn."

"It is the way forward," Ella said. "It's people like you who are the future of the Bahamas." She waved again to the children. "Thank you for my picture."

The twelve pupils had made a drawing of their schoolhouse under the spreading branches of a cottonwood tree and included themselves waving with toothy moon-shaped grins for Ella. She laid it carefully on the backseat of the car and climbed in beside Dan Calder.

"It's hot," she sighed, even though the car had been parked in the shade. She fanned herself with her hat as he drove back through the rough bush land, without being conscious of the fact that she was still smiling broadly at the images in her head of the children. When Dan Calder spoke, she wasn't prepared for it.

"Tell me, Mrs. Sanford, all this handing out of eggs to villagers and checks to schoolteachers and arranging entertainment for the airmen before they enter battle, does it make you feel good about yourself at the end of the day when you get home? Or is it just a job?"

Ella was stung by the question. She stared out at the spiky vegetation instead of at the man in the seat next to her and retorted, "Tell me, Detective Calder, at the end of another day of protecting the life of Mrs. Sanford or saving Nassau from breaking out into lawlessness, does it make you feel good about yourself or is it just a job?"

His head turned sharply to look at her and he braked hard, bringing the car to a sudden halt in a cloud of beige dust that swirled in through the open windows.

"I apologize, Mrs. Sanford. It was a thoughtless thing to say."

"Yes, it was." She brushed dust from her hair. "But your apology is accepted."

She expected him to start the car again, but he let it sit there, throbbing in the heat, the sun drumming on the roof.

"I asked only because I wanted to know you better. To understand what drives you to work so hard for others. I didn't mean to be rude."

He wasn't looking at her anymore. His eyes remained focused on the dirt road ahead and the patch of shade where a goat was tethered. Ella wanted to thank him. To say no one else had ever asked her that question, not even Reggie, and that she was deeply touched that he cared enough to think of doing so. But the solid sunbaked earth seemed to be shifting under the car and she had a strange sense of being unsafe. Not unsafe because of Dan Calder. But unsafe because of herself.

So instead she said lightly, "Don't worry about it. Let's go into town. I have a present to buy."

*   *   *

The shop was not exactly what Ella expected. It was in a street that Detective Calder suggested.

"It's our twentieth wedding anniversary next week," she'd told him as they drove into town. "My husband wants me to buy myself something. Something gold."

He didn't comment on the twenty years or on the generosity of the gift, but only asked with a wry smile, "Why doesn't he choose it himself?"

Ella had no answer to that. So she said briskly, "He's a busy man."

Instead of heading for the stylish but expensive jewelry shops on Bay Street where she would usually go looking, he took her to one she'd never heard of in a street she didn't know. At first sight it didn't look as promising as she'd hoped. The street was slightly run-down, not somewhere you'd come to choose a special anniversary present, but when he pointed out the jewelry shop to her, even from the outside she could see that the interior was lit up like a Christmas tree.

"How exciting." She laughed and gave Calder a teasing look. "Is this where you always come to buy jewelry?"

But he was slow to join in her laughter. "No, but I have been inside a number of times when trying to trace stolen goods and I was impressed. I found the owners helpful as well. I'm sure you will too." His tone was scrupulously polite. "I'll wait in the car."

For a moment she'd hoped he might come in with her, but knew that was foolish. She left the car and entered the shop alone. It was small inside but felt larger because of all the mirrors and the array of bright light reflected in them. The heat hit her, as did the smell of coffee, and she noticed an exquisite Royal Crown Derby cup sitting on one corner of a counter with steam rising from it.

"May I help you, madam?"

At first glance Ella thought it was a man, the ginger hair was so short and the voice so deep, but she realized her mistake when she saw the nail varnish and the pearls. The woman bobbed up from a low seat behind the counter, abandoning a copy of *Moby-Dick* beside her coffee.

"I hope so," Ella said. "I'm looking for something special, an anniversary gift from my husband. I was thinking of maybe a gold ring."

The woman smiled. "Certainly, madam. We have a good selection." Within seconds she had spread out on the counter a variety of high-quality gold rings and was watching her customer try them on. "That's a beautiful emerald you are wearing, may I say," she commented silkily.

Ella glanced down at the engagement ring on her finger, a large square emerald set in a cradle of diamonds, a showy ring that Reggie had a goldsmith design especially for her. She hadn't chosen that one herself.

"Thank you," she said.

The woman was scrutinizing Ella carefully, taking her time and unconsciously rippling her fingers, so that her numerous rings brushed against each other, singing a soft metallic chorus that she clearly enjoyed.

"I think," she said with no preamble, "that I have exactly what you want."

She disappeared, and Ella thought of Detective Calder outside in the car, waiting for her. It unsettled her, though she wasn't sure why, and she pushed the rings away impatiently. He was right about the shop and he was right about Reggie. Why on earth shouldn't her husband choose her anniversary gift himself? Just because he hated setting foot inside a shop of any sort, it was no excuse. She had grown too accustomed to doing his shopping for him.

With a little huff of annoyance she turned to leave, just when the woman reappeared with an object on a black velvet cushion. It was a bracelet.

"Here we are, madam. This is perfect for you."

"It's beautiful."

"It's eighteen-karat rose gold, a gate bracelet design from the end of the last century." She smiled at it, almost purring. "It's Russian."

At its center gleamed a vibrant sapphire and two diamonds. Ella knew instantly that it was the right choice. Reggie would love it on her.

"I'll take it."

"Don't you want to try it on?"

"No need."

"I'll wrap it for you, then."

"Thank you."

You see Reggie. It's not hard.

The woman vanished behind a bead curtain at the back of the shop. There was a murmur of voices, then a black man emerged and smiled warmly.

"Good day to you, madam."

"Good day. You have a lovely shop here."

"Thank you. We like it."

He ambled over, holding something on the palm of his hand, and as he came closer Ella saw that it was a coin.

"May I see that?"

He closed his hand immediately, unwilling to give it up. "It's just a coin."

"May I see? It looks similar to one that I have."

Reluctantly his fingers unfolded and he handed it over. "It's gold," he told her. "French."

"What is it called?"

"A napoleon."

"Is it for sale?"

He started to shake his head, but the ginger-haired woman breezed through the bead curtain and said, "Of course it's for sale."

"I'll take it." Ella closed her hand over it before the man could snatch it back.

*   *   *

"Happy?"

Ella slid back into her seat in the car, surprised by the question.

"Yes."

"Did you find what you wanted?"

"Yes, I did."

"I'm glad."

"Thank you for bringing me to this shop."

"It's my pleasure."

Something in the way he said it made her turn to look at him. He was smiling at her, a smile with real warmth, not his polite bodyguard one.

"Why is it your pleasure?" she asked.

"I was rude earlier and I regret it because I hurt you. I would never mean to do that. So I'm glad to make up for my mistake by finding this shop for you now."

"Thank you."

"Happy?"

"Yes."

Chapter 26

Dodie

Ten o'clock. Darkness had swallowed the city as Dodie walked out of the Arcadia. Her shift wasn't due to finish until eleven, but business was still sluggish and Olive Quinn had sent her off early. She inhaled the night air, full of rich and exotic scents, and decided she needed a detour to the ocean.

She felt tired. Harold Christie had set up too many vibrations in her head. But she walked quickly through the deserted streets, keeping to the well-lit thoroughfares, her footsteps echoing, and headed in the direction of the beach. She ached to see the ocean, to hear its voice, to feel its cool breeze on her skin, and when she finally stepped onto the sand, the noises in her head at last ceased.

She gazed out over the ocean that lay like a shining sheet of steel in front of her. The moon hung bloated and overbright in the black sky, its tissue-thin light spilling onto the surface of the waves. Dodie could feel its pale fingers reaching inside her, drawing her forward the way it drew the tides.

*   *   *

Dodie kicked off her shoes, tucked up her dress, and waded out into the water. Even at this hour it was warm and exhilarating. The inky waves billowed around her, buffing her edges as smooth as the sand. Somewhere close she could hear the call of a nightjar and the stirrings of a sultry breeze in the trees, and gradually the tensions of the day started to fade in her mind, so that when she finally emerged from the ocean she could feel her thoughts clean and refreshed. She had a clearer sense of what needed to be done. She knew that there were questions she had to ask, and the first person she needed to question was Flynn.

Would he arrive with breakfast tomorrow? She wanted to believe it. With shirtsleeves rolled up, his long legs striding up the dusty street, a string bag full of crabmeat and bananas swinging at his side, and a look in his eyes that told her he didn't intend to miss her this time. Dodie smiled as she walked back up the beach in the moonlight and it was only when she reached the spot where she had left her shoes that she experienced the first trickle of unease. Her black shoes were gone.

Her eyes scanned the dark dips and hollows of the beach. No sign of them. Her unease shifted to alarm. Twenty feet away rose the black line of palm trees and in front of them stood two male figures, indistinct in the darkness. But one held his arm stretched out toward her, something dangling from his hand before he let it fall to become a black stain on the sand. She had no doubt what it was. Her shoes.

Fear, sharp as an ice pick, pricked at her throat. She heard a low laugh that rolled toward her under the cover of darkness.

With the last dregs of moisture in her mouth, she spat on the sand. Not this. Not again. She fought down panic and tried to think lucidly. She could run. Her lungs started to pump in readiness. The men would give chase through the shadows but there was a chance she might be faster than they were.

"Just leave my shoes and go."

Her words sounded angry in the silence of the empty night. Only the sea whispered encouragement and heaved itself closer. The men moved a pace or two away from the shoes and the moon spiked a gleam on the spectacles of the shorter, stockier one. She could feel their gaze raking over her.

"Come over here and get them," one shouted out, and the two men laughed.

They backed off another few steps to tempt her.

"We won't hurt you," the other called.

Like a cat won't tear the wings off a bird.

"We just lookin', that's all. No harm in that, is there? You a good-lookin' lady in this moonlight."

His accent was Bahamian.

The short one laughed. "Be nice, lady."

"You be nice," she answered back. "Throw me my shoes and get the hell away from me."

"That ain't no way to talk."

The Bahamian bent down to the sand, a slow deliberate movement, and scooped up the shoes. He tossed them in a loop toward her and they settled on the sand like a pair of blackbirds. They now lay midway between her and them. Dodie's only thought was escape. She glanced off to the side. The sand up the slope was soft and slithery and would suck at her feet like wet cement. They would easily catch her there. Behind her lay the solid slab of darkness that was the sea.

She spun around and started racing toward the water, her knees as unsteady as rubber under her. Both men came tearing after her, yelling and shouting, frightened of losing her, and the tall Bahamian was fast. Too fast. His gasps snaked behind her and moonlight skidded under her feet as she plowed into the sea up to her knees. She forced herself to pause. To think. To glance behind. Both men were at the water's edge, stepping back from the surf, hesitating. Shouting to each other.

"Come on," she jeered, kicking out at the waves and sending spray leaping toward the two men. She was tempting them in, using herself as bait. "Don't be shy. The water too cold for you?"

With a curse the Bahamian yanked off his shoes and lurched forward into the sea. She stood her ground. Waited with her heart burrowing into her ribs until both men had their legs partially immersed, and when they hesitated, uncomfortable and wet, she laughed at them.

"Scared?" she jeered.

That did it. They launched themselves forward, charging straight for her, but she didn't wait around. She was off, darting to her left, knees lifted high above the water like a hurdler. She skimmed over the waves and looped around the men to the shore. Too late they realized their mistake. But by then Dodie was haring up the beach to the trees. Frantic, she snatched up her shoes and vanished into the black shadows where even moonlight failed to find her.

She could still hear them. Their shouts. Their curses. Their threats. She kept weaving stealthily through the trees, keeping ahead of them, but only just. They scoured the area, poking into shadows, calling out and tramping through the undergrowth. It was when they fell silent that Dodie's legs almost failed her.

* * *

Dodie was in her shoes and running up the hill, heading toward Bain Town. Not far now, she kept telling herself. She should be able to make it there easily. Don't panic now. They're far behind you, but still she shook.

Never before had this happened to her on a beach. So why now? What was going on? Her life seemed to have been slit open from top to bottom ever since that night she helped Morrell. What were you up to, Mr. Morrell? For heaven's sake, give me a clue, make it easy for me. Her lungs were pumping, sweat under her dress. She was running past a row of down-at-heel houses and a huge tamarind tree loomed out of the night sky. No street lamps here. Just moonlight and rats.

Yet she didn't hear them. They came at her from behind, the same two men. How had they found her? One hand seized her hair, wrenching back her head, the other caught the belt of her dress and lifted her off her feet.

"Bitch."

She tumbled to her knees and opened her mouth to scream but a blow to the back of her head shut it for her and her teeth clamped down on her tongue. She tasted blood and saw splinters of light streak across the tamarind branches.

"Did you think you'd got away from us?" A grip like a vise twisted her hair. "Did you?" Ripping it out. "Did you, Miss Wyatt? You thought you'd lost us?"

Dodie lashed out. With her feet and fists she fought them, terror giving her strength. It was the short one, the white one, the bastard one, who was tearing her head off. How they'd trailed her from the beach she had no idea, she'd been so careful. She tried to shout, to scream for help, but a hand clamped over her mouth. She bit it hard, right to the bone.

A screech. Then a fist landed hard in her throat and she couldn't breathe. She kicked out, stabbed fingers at eyes and raked nails down a cheek, but the big Bahamian turned her like a toy, flung her facedown in the road.

"No!"

His heavy hands held her down. Her mouth pinned to the gravel.

"No!"

They started to beat her back with their fists, pounding and thumping, pain scouring through her body until, with no warning at all, her mind abandoned her. It stepped away. Abandoned her to the beating. It looked down at her from somewhere high up in the tamarind tree and watched two thugs knock the hell out of her to their heart's content and it told her again and again that she was a fool.

Fool.

To think you could have it your way. Look what they did to Morrell.

But a shout of anger suddenly exploded in her ears in a voice she recognized.

"Get your fucking hands off her!"

There was a crack, followed by a scream, and the hands released her. Just like that. No argument. She was free.

Her head instantly rolled to one side. She grabbed air into her lungs and spotted the small man, the vicious white one, rolling in the gutter. He was clutching his leg, which seemed to belong to someone else because it was sticking out at an odd angle. And the big man with blood cascading from his nose was rearing up like a great bear to attack a tall slender figure in front of him.

But the newcomer didn't wait for the attack. There was a flash of movement, a hard leather shoe connected with the big man's groin. He doubled over with a grunt that took the air out of him, and the slender figure moved behind him, drilling punch after punch into his kidneys. Then an elbow to the side of the head sent the Bahamian toppling to the ground.

The tamarind tree seemed to shake and Dodie could feel the vibration of it under her as she struggled to sit up. A dog barked and a light flared in a nearby house. Voices sounded in the street. The figure who had saved her was bending over her, saying something, touching her face, lifting her to her feet. Yet all she could see was the concern in his eyes and all she could hear was the rage hammering in her ears.

Chapter 27

Flynn

"Tell me."

"Tell you what?" Flynn asked. As if he didn't know. As if he couldn't see.

"Tell me what's going on."

"You should rest."

They were sitting on the mattress in the shack in Bain Town. It was thin and lumpy on the floor and smelled of other people's bodies. He had carried her here from the street where she was attacked and was carefully bathing dried blood from her chin. He wished he could bathe the memory of the beating from her mind and it worried him that her skin was cold despite the oppressive heat in the shack. She wasn't shaking anymore but the delicate bones of her face were looking flimsy, brittle as eggshell, as if they might break at his touch. In the halfhearted glow of the candle her eyes had taken on the color of tiger's eye with small fires burning fiercely within them. They were fixed on his face, not letting him go.

"It's not my blood," she told him. "It's from the bite."

"Bite? You bit him?"

"Yes. His hand."

He looked at her jaw. At the amount of blood. "That must have been some bite."

Gently she wrapped her fingers around his hand that held the cloth and pulled it down on to her lap. "With luck he'll get rabies."

He laughed. He wouldn't have thought it possible right then, but it burst up from somewhere and seemed to startle them both.

"Tell me what's going on?" she said.

Flynn knew only too well what it was that he was looking at. It was a controlled calmness. The kind that disguises acute fear. She had every right to be fearful. Every right to demand the truth. Every right to know. But the truth was buried so deep down in him that the words were hard to reach even when he *wanted* to give them to her. So he deliberately misinterpreted her question.

"I came to find you," he said. "I came to the Arcadia tonight at eleven o'clock to walk you back to Bain Town after work."

"Why?"

"I don't like the way you wander the streets alone at night."

She made a sound. Then she lifted his hand and placed a kiss on the back of it. It was a thank-you, open and honest, one that shocked him profoundly. He hadn't expected it. That kind of trust. He was too used to a world of deceit and lies. He wanted to touch her, to smooth her hair, which was wild and disordered, as though by doing so he could quiet the wild-eyed creature within her.

"Thank you," she murmured.

Something had changed in her since the beating. As if the blows she received had broken open the shell behind which she'd sheltered for so long and now there was a frankness in her eyes that hadn't been there before. It put its hand down his throat and started to drag the words up from the dark places where they were hiding.

"At the hotel they said you'd checked out of work early, so I came up here to Bain Town. But"—he shrugged as if it were nothing—"you weren't here either."

He didn't tell her. About the dread when he saw the shack dark and empty at that hour of the night. How he had slipped a metal spike into the lock to click it open and checked that her body was not lying there, a rag doll on the floor. He didn't tell her that.

"I went to the beach."

He wanted to shout at her. But all he said was, "You should take more care."

She nodded.

"I was coming back down the hill into town," he continued, "when I saw you . . ."

"Having fun with my two friends?"

There was a razor edge to her words and she rubbed her hand hard across his, chafing their skin together. "Thank you, Flynn. For your help." Her eyes were huge as she stared at him. "You fight hard."

"I've had practice."

"I imagine so."

"How bad is your back?"

"I'll live."

He reached out and his fingertips brushed her throat where even by the muted candlelight he could see a livid bruise. "Yes," he said, "you'll live."

I'll make sure you live.

"I'd be dead—or worse—by now, Flynn, if you hadn't come."

"I don't think so."

He saw her eyes flicker.

"What do you mean by that?"

"I mean . . ."

"Tell me." Her hand slid up his forearm inside his sleeve, as if he were concealing the answers from her under his shirt.

"I mean"—he spared her nothing—"look at Morrell. If they wanted you dead, you'd be dead. They intended to make you suffer."

*   *   *

He made her tea on an old oil stove he'd brought for her. He laid her down on her side on the mattress, careful not to touch her back. Her Arcadia dress was covered in dirt and her skin went from chill to hot, as though someone had lit a fire under it. He sat beside her on the mattress and fanned her with a palm frond to cool her and to keep the greedy mosquitoes at bay. She lay with her eyes closed but he knew she wasn't asleep as he listened to her breath whisper in and out of her lungs, a shallow snatched version of breathing to spare her bruised ribs.

Outside, as the night hours trickled past, a wind had blown in off the sea and rattled the tin roof, a sneak thief trying to squeeze in. Flynn was growing used to the way the island seemed to shake itself loose and come to life at night, full of sounds and smells that drenched the air. Here the blackness was blacker, so black you could dive into it, and the stars brighter. A far cry from the hard gray streets of Chicago. It had unnerved him at first, set his teeth on edge, the strangeness of this island, but he was becoming accustomed to it now. He found he was even smoking less, so that he could smell its scents more.

He sat in the humid darkness, one hand clenched firmly between Dodie's. It was how he knew she was awake. He could feel her grip on him become more persistent as the moon sauntered through the window and lay on the bed with her. Not just her grip on his hand. It was her grip on his heart that was growing tighter.

Chapter 28

Dodie

Dodie woke. Listening to strange noises in her head. She didn't move. If she moved, everything would hurt. But she risked raising her eyelids and found Flynn there, sitting with his back against the door, barring entry. Watching her. Smiling at her. She smiled back at him and for a long moment that was all that filled the overheated space of the shack. The air felt grimy and smelled of tallow from the burned-out candle. Early-morning light filtered in, gray as a cobweb, but it brought with it the stark memory of the night before with its humiliation on the beach and its thrashing in the street.

"Feeling any better?" Flynn inquired softly.

"Much."

A small sound escaped him that she realized was a stifled laugh.

"Good," he said. "Ready for breakfast?"

She nodded and regretted it.

"Flynn, who were those men? They knew my name."

His limbs lost their looseness and he moved forward. "They got away. That big bastard must own a skull of granite. I was sure he was out cold, but when I finished fixing you up, they were both gone. The white guy had a busted leg, so the big one must have carried him out of there."

"Did anyone see where they went?" She could hear her fear inch its way into her voice.

"No, not that they were saying. Do you want me to call the cops?"

"Police? No, thank you. You can keep them."

It came out more vehemently than she intended and she saw him wonder what Nassau's police force had done to make her so wary of them.

"The citizens of Bain Town are a tight-lipped lot," she pointed out. "They'll have no interest in getting the police here. Anyway, what would be the point? The police would get nowhere and just blame me for enticing the men by wandering a beach at night and . . ." She shivered.

"Don't, Dodie."

"Who were those men?" she asked angrily. "What is going on? What are you doing here in Nassau? Or here in this hut? Tell me."

But he didn't answer her questions. Instead he drew near to the mattress where she was lying.

"It's because of that wounded guy you helped. You know that, don't you?"

"Morrell?"

"Yes."

"I have a theory about him."

Flynn sat up straighter. "What's that?"

"I think he was blackmailing Sir Harry Oakes."

"What?"

"It fits." A pulse was throbbing at the base of her skull.

"Fits with what?"

"It fits with the fact that Morrell was secretive about what he was up to here and frightened that someone wanted to hurt him. And it fits with the gold coins he had in his possession."

"He had gold coins?"

"Yes."

"Did you see them?"

"Yes."

"How many?"

"Two. Apparently Sir Harry Oakes collects gold coins. I suspect he must have paid Morrell off with them."

"Jeez, Dodie, where on earth did all this come from?"

But she had thought it through carefully.

"There's a woman on the island called Ella Sanford. She was with Morrell and Sir Harry that night."

"How do you know?"

"She admitted it to me. But she's lying about what went on, I'm sure."

"Oh, Dodie, come on, even if you're right about her—which you may not be—that's still one hell of a jump to assume blackmail."

"What if they were having an affair?"

"Morrell? And this woman?"

Dodie shook her head. "No, of course not." Her head seemed to be floating around the room. "Sir Harry and Ella Sanford. It's possible." Flynn's face drifted back into focus. "Maybe Morrell found out somehow and was blackmailing them. At the end, when he knew he wasn't going to make it, he asked me to take a gold napoleon to her. As a warning, I think. He knew Oakes had hired thugs to kill him and he was warning her to stay clear of such a man."

Flynn was staring at her, eyes dark with disbelief. "That's quite some story you've concocted there."

"It fits."

In the street a dog barked, startling them both. They had forgotten the world outside.

"As soon as Sir Harry knew," she continued, "that I had nursed Morrell, he offered me a job. To shut me up. He's a dangerous man, Flynn, this respectable knight of the realm."

"So you think he's the one who got those bastards to beat you up last night?"

"Yes." She paused, conscious of something going on in the room that her head was too fogged to reach for. "Don't you?"

He was silent for a long time. She expected him to light a cigarette, but he didn't. Instead he kept his eyes fixed on her.

"There's something I want to tell you," he said.

Dodie waited for more. She struggled to sit up but only made it onto one elbow.

"Johnnie Morrell was my friend." His voice was bleak.

She felt something dark enter the room, something cold and suffocating. It took her a full minute to recognize it as grief.

"He and I came here together to fix up a business deal. I was watching his back but . . . he died."

"Flynn," she whispered. "Don't."

"I might as well have stuck the knife in him myself."

Chapter 29

Flynn

Dodie looked all wrong. The pain was visible on her pale face and the sight of it did something bad to Flynn. Yet somehow she got herself upright and sat on the floor directly in front of him, taking both his hands in her own.

"Don't," she said again. "I was the one who let him die. Not you."

"Is that what you think?"

"Yes."

He drew a breath and held it a long time because he knew he was going to trust her. Knew it was his life at stake, as well as hers.

"Dodie, you've got it all wrong. Johnnie Morrell wasn't blackmailing anyone. I'll tell you what happened that night."

Her hands gripped his firmly.

"We came in after dark," he told her. "A boat ferried us in from the plane to the far end of the island up near Lyford Cay. It was rough water. Morrell was sick as a dog, poor guy. But we got here and went together to settle the sale of a tract of land with someone, and—"

"Are *you* buying land here?"

"Hell no, I don't have that kind of dough. Morrell and I work . . ." He corrected himself. "Morrell and I *worked* for an organization in America that wants to invest heavily in the Bahamas."

"Why did you come at night? Why so clandestine?"

"Everything is under wraps at the moment. No questions asked. Safer that way."

"Oh."

"So when the meeting was over and we'd knocked back a few whiskeys with the guy, Morrell decided he wouldn't hang around any—"

"Who was the meeting with?"

"Shit, Dodie, you don't want to know."

She regarded him fiercely. "I do. If I knew who your meeting was with and what it was about, I'd have a better idea why I was beaten to a pulp and my house burned down. You owe me that much, surely?"

He turned her hands over and rubbed a thumb over her cold palms. "Sure," he said. "I owe you that much."

But still he hesitated. Whatever he told her could not be untold.

"It was with Sir Harry Oakes, wasn't it?" she prompted.

He nodded. He wasn't going to lie to her this time. "It's not hard to guess. He's the one with the big bucks on this island."

"So tell me what happened."

"After the meeting, Johnnie Morrell was too fired up and in too much of a goddamn hurry. He wouldn't wait around any longer while Oakes and I sorted out some details. He set off to walk in the dark the few miles from Cable Beach—that's where Oakes's Westbourne home is—into town. He told me to catch up with him when I was all done."

"But?"

"But this is where the whole damn plan went haywire. I finished up with Oakes and"—he shrugged uneasily—"downed a final whiskey for the road, then left. I wasn't more than a stone's throw behind Morrell when a dark sedan sidled past me on the empty street. I could see him up ahead in the beam of its headlamps. I saw the car stop beside him, and he ducked his head to talk to whoever was inside it."

Flynn was back there. The car's brake lights winking at him out of the blackness. A shout leaving his throat, his legs pumping, fear for his friend burning holes in him as he ran.

"Morrell got into the back of the car, the stupid jackass, and it drove off toward town." Flynn tapped a spot at the center of his forehead. "What was he thinking in there? What would make him do such a dumb thing? He was too smart to accept a lift from a stranger. He was always careful, that's why he was chosen for this job. So what the hell was going through that thick skull of his?"

She was stroking his wrist, calming him.

"Maybe," she suggested quietly, "it was the drink. Too many whiskeys with Sir Harry blurring his judgment? Or he was too woozy to walk any further."

Flynn gave a sharp shake of his head. "No, Johnnie knew how to handle his booze okay."

"Maybe he knew the driver."

"No." He brushed aside a thick wave of her dark hair that had sprung across her cheek when she leaned forward, and he felt the chill that still clung to her skin. "Johnnie knew no one here. He told me so himself." A spasm of sorrow spiked through him. "He'd never been here before."

He put both hands on her shoulders to prevent her toppling forward, but her gleaming dark eyes fixed on his.

"So where did the gold coins come from?" she whispered.

Chapter 30

Dodie

"So where did the gold coins come from?" Dodie whispered.

But her voice came out so thinly that she scarcely heard it herself. "Where, Flynn? Where did Morrell get them?"

If his face had not been so close to hers she would not have seen the tightening of his pupils or the fraction of a second when the edges of his mouth froze, before he smiled at her gently and slipped one of his hands under her chin, cupping it in his palm. Until that moment she had no idea that her head was falling forward. His hand felt warm. Or was it her chin that was cold? She struggled to focus her eyes on his face but it kept shifting position. Behind his head the walls seemed to be moving.

"Dodie," he said. The word reached her ears a slow beat after it left his lips. "Let's put you to bed, you need sleep."

But she put out a hand and gripped his shirtfront. "Flynn, did he show you the coins? The two napoleons."

"Time to rest, Dodie."

"Did he?"

"Yes, he did."

"Did he say where he got them from?"

"No. He told me nothing about them."

"Oh." She didn't want it to be a lie.

He wrapped both arms around her, holding her still, and only then did she realize that she was the one swaying, not the walls.

He drew her against him and kissed her tangled hair. It was comforting.

"Listen, Dodie, this is all I know about the coins. You said Morrell asked you to take one to a Mrs. Sanford and you believed it was a warning to her not to trust Sir Harry Oakes. Right?"

She thought she said yes, but all that came out was a grunt. Her cheek lay against his shirt.

"Well, Dodie, I think you've got that wrong. I think it was a warning, yes. But to trust Oakes and to keep quiet about bumping into Morrell at Westbourne. Because whoever killed Morrell will come after her next if they find out she was there."

Dodie felt something trembling. She tried to ignore it but it kept on, so she sat up and touched his face to see what was the matter. In the dim light she was shocked to see her hand shaking. Flynn was fading in and out of focus and she had no idea whether the tenderness of his expression was real or a figment of her imagination.

"Flynn," she murmured, "you are a kind man."

He let out a laugh that had no laughter in it.

"Is that so?" he said.

"But why do you turn up in my life bringing violence and destruction with you? Who are you?"

Flynn rose to his feet and lifted her into his arms before she toppled flat on her face. He laid her on the mattress and wrapped the sheet around her shivering body to keep her warm. He bent again and kissed her hair but she draped an arm around his neck and drew his mouth to hers. His lips were warm and tasted of the island, but they withdrew quickly. Instead he stroked her damaged throat with the back of his fingers.

"I'm your guardian angel," he whispered. And this time when he laughed softly under his breath, his laughter wove itself into the weft of the sheet and lay in wait for her each time she turned her head.

Chapter 31

Flynn

Flynn moved through the shadows, barely causing a ripple in them. To the west of Nassau lay a silky blackness that still shone with stars, but in the east the sky was a dove gray, shot through with feathery streaks of blood.

Flynn was careful to choose the dark side of the sprawling bungalow. He slid a stiletto blade between the shutters, then under the window catch, easing the sash up just enough before slipping over the sill and into the room. It was a library of sorts, shelves of books blurred in the gloom. Flynn moved quickly to the door and opened it a crack. Silence, heavy as the gun in his pocket. Ahead lay the wide hallway. He listened. Not a quiver of sound.

This was his world, a world of stealth and violence, a place where people hurt and got hurt. He had learned to silence his breath and slow his heart, to climb fast and not to break sweat when a gun was pushed in his face. He'd learned it well. It wasn't a world he liked but it was the one he lived in. Except now, he wanted out.

*   *   *

"Don't make a sound."

Flynn's hand was clamped over the damp mouth of the man in the bed. In his other hand the stiletto point was puncturing a pinhole in the man's throat. His feet spasmed briefly under the sheet and then he was still as stone, eyes wide with terror and staring up at Flynn as if he'd never seen him before.

"Mr. Spencer," Flynn whispered, so close he could smell his breath, "time for an exchange of views. Get up."

He eased back the knife from Spencer's throat and felt him shudder. The bedroom lay in darkness, the shutters closed, but dimly he could make out the black shape of a head on the next pillow and hear its slow regular breathing, undisturbed by the silent presence of an intruder. He flicked the sheet off and Spencer rolled out of bed obediently. But now the arrogance and disdain that he'd displayed when Flynn met him in the bar the other day lay in tatters.

He was wearing only pajama bottoms and Flynn kept a hand on his shoulder, guiding him out of the bedroom and into the room next to it. Spencer switched on the light. It was a small dressing room that stank of hair oil and narrow enough to mean they couldn't get away from each other.

"What the blazes are you doing in my house?" Spencer hissed at him, cheeks flaming as he struggled to take control of the situation. "Get out of—"

Flynn thudded him back against the wall of closets, his hand jammed on his bare chest.

"Don't," Flynn growled in his face, "ever lay a finger on Dodie Wyatt again."

"Good God, that's ridiculous. I haven't been anywhere near her."

"You set your filthy dogs on her, you bastard."

"No."

"One of them now has a broken leg."

"Fuck you, Hudson. It was you, wasn't it? I should have guessed. What the hell do you think you're doing? Now get your hands off me."

Flynn withdrew the few steps to the opposite wall to stop himself from snapping the guy's neck.

"Have you gone mad?" Spencer demanded. "Coming here like

this. This is not what you were sent here to do. You're supposed to be reporting back to Lansky in Miami and explaining exactly what went wrong here and why you messed up the job you were meant to—"

"Shut up."

"Don't you speak to me like—"

"Shut. Up."

Flynn didn't raise his voice. He stared across the room at the man until the small space seemed to fill up with the unspoken threat that lay between them.

"Leave Dodie Wyatt alone."

"You fool," Spencer responded, his voice more under control. "She will implicate you in the murder."

"No."

"She's been warned. That should be enough. You should be thanking me. You can skip Nassau now and—"

"I'll be thanking you." Flynn said it softly.

Spencer folded his arms tight across his bare chest. The look of panic in his eyes right now told Flynn what kind of man Spencer was. Flynn had seen it happen before. When you kick a guy's props away, it dawns on him how much he has to lose.

"Listen good," Flynn told Spencer now that he had his full attention. "I'll skip Nassau. But only when I'm done here. Don't get it into your head that I don't have"—he paused and he saw sweat on Spencer's upper lip glistening between the stubble—"leeway. Because I have all the leeway I need."

"You're bluffing."

They both knew what "leeway" meant when it came to the mob. It meant elbow room. Room to elbow guys out, even one of your own.

He *was* bluffing. But Spencer didn't know that. Yet there was something about the guy that was dangerous, Flynn could sense it. He was the kind of person only a fool would turn his back on.

"So," Flynn said, "now that's clear, I'll leave you to climb back in bed with your wife." He took a step toward the door. "It *is* your wife, I take it?"

"Of course she is."

"Tell her from me she lives in a nice house."

"Are you threatening me?"

"Just being polite."

Spencer untied his arms and balled his hands into fists at his sides. Flynn saw his glance flick to the top drawer of a fancy tallboy and away again.

"You know, don't you, Hudson, that the Wyatt girl is a common slut. Wags it in your face given half a chance."

Flynn grew very still.

"Don't look like that, Hudson, it's true. Ask anybody. She's well known for it. Used to work up at one of the factories until she set her cap at the son of the owner. Pestered him worse than a damn mosquito. He's a happily married man and wanted none of it, so she ran around screaming rape. Bloody menace the girl is. Not to be trusted. Probably finished off Morrell herself and then went crying to the police to—"

Flynn's hand was around his throat.

The panicked eyes bulged but there was no fight in them. Flynn was fiercely tempted to lean on the pressure just a fraction more until he heard the click that brought silence, and Nassau would be rid of one more of its rats. But the image of the dark head still asleep on the pillow in the next room flickered through his mind and abruptly he released his grip and stepped back.

Spencer clutched at his throat, doubled over, fighting for air as Flynn calmly reached into the top drawer of the tallboy and unearthed the Colt revolver that lay under the neatly folded socks. He slid it into his waistband. From the top of the tallboy he removed a man's tortoiseshell-backed hairbrush and put it in his pocket. He waited patiently till Spencer got himself upright again, eyes and nose streaming, his cheeks vermilion.

"Don't," Flynn said, "think for one minute that this is over.

When the mob's business with Sir Harry Oakes is settled, you and I will finish this."

"I'll report this," Spencer croaked angrily, "to Lansky in America."

"Report what you like."

"The mob doesn't treat turncoats well."

Flynn gave him a thin, cold smile. "So remember not to turn your coat, unless you want its pockets filled with concrete."

He strode out of the room and this time made no secret of his footsteps down the stairs.

*   *   *

"Well now, Mr. Hudson, I'm lookin' at you and wonderin' what on earth you doin' here." Mama Keel peered over Flynn's shoulder, as if expecting Dodie to materialize out of the strands of dawn mist. "Where's that Dodie child?"

"She's up in Bain Town. She's been hurt."

The woman's lovely face tumbled into a multitude of creases and her fingers seized his forearm.

"Is it bad?"

"Bad enough."

Without releasing her hold, she dragged him into the house and set him down on a chair. The simplicity of the place pleased him and reminded him of his childhood when bare boards were the norm and running water a luxury. One scant room for his parents and himself. A freezing attic in the slums of Chicago where the slope of the low ceiling would deposit spiders and cockroaches in his hair that his mother would pick out with an easy laugh, telling him not to be so squeamish. Well, he sure learned not to be squeamish. His father made certain of that.

"Mama Keel, she needs something to shift the pain."

They spoke in soft tones so as not to disturb the sleeping infant in the cardboard box.

"What happened?" Mama asked.

"She got jumped last night. Knocked down and hammered with fists. Two guys."

"Dear Lord in heaven, poor child. How bad?"

"I don't think anything is broken, but can't tell for sure. She doesn't want to check into the hospital."

"And where were you?"

"Looking for her. I was searching Nassau, Mama, like a dumb hound dog."

"And the men who attacked her? Who were they?"

"I don't rightly know. But they're not in one piece anymore."

The tall woman nodded. She leaned down over him so that her large black eyes with their shimmering purple lights could peer right into him, and it felt like she was opening him up with a can opener.

"Listen to me, Mr. Hudson, I got stuff I want to say to you and you ain't goin' to appreciate a bunch of it."

He sat back in the chair. "That's fine by me, Mama. Shoot."

She started gathering together pots and ointments, giving him instructions and grinding seeds with a pestle made of coconut wood. "You know what I think, Mr. Hudson? I think you are livin' in a world that's whirling in a state of chaos."

He couldn't argue with that.

"Some days, Mr. Hudson, you wake in the mornin' and see nothin' but an ocean of black oil and dead things around you. It's true, I see it in your shadows. You been with people whose greed is more real and more solid than rocks or stones, and their desires know no limits. You seen it, Mr. Hudson. How they fornicate with pretty young things and they crush life with no more thought than a cat chewing wings off a butterfly." She lifted her head and stared at him. "Ain't that so, Mr. Hudson?"

"Yes, it's so."

Her hands were placing packages into a straw basket.

"You got dark shadows," she commented, "real dark. But you got white lights too, so bright they hurt my eyes." She grinned at him, taking him by surprise, and he grinned back like a fool.

"Mama Keel, you got eyes like a hawk."

"And I'm watchin' you, Mr. Hudson."

"Dodie won't let go of this Morrell business," he said. "She has sunk her teeth into it. Now she's been hurt, Mama, and I don't want it to happen again."

"No." She put the basket on his lap so that he couldn't rise from the chair. A white kitten crawled out from the cardboard box and mountaineered up his trouser leg, needle claws working overtime. "Neither of us wants Dodie hurt again." Her tall fleshless figure was clothed in a shapeless khaki wrap that looked as though it had been scavenged from one of the military bases, and she rested one hand over her heart. "Bad things happened to her on our island and her heart closed down. Nailed tighter than a coffin."

He stroked the kitten's fluff as if it were Dodie.

"But the other night, Mr. Hudson, when you came here together like a couple of strays, the pair of you, she was lookin' a whole lot different that night."

"Why was that, Mama?"

"You tell me, Mr. Hudson. That was a girl who had just watched a man die and just seen her house burn down, but there was no darkness in her that night." She stepped back. "You take good care of her, mind, young man."

"I'm trying." He stood up and placed the kitten on the seat.

"Mama, I have something to ask you."

"What might that be?"

An early ray of sunlight nipped through the window and shuffled round the room, as though looking for something.

"Dodie told me you are gifted with the powers of *obeah*."

Mama Keel folded her long arms and stared at him, nostrils flared. "And what does a white body like you know about Bahamian *obeah*?"

"Not much. But I know it's like Cuba's voodoo. A way of connecting to the universe that gives people like you a power to influence things . . . or people."

"And you believe in this?"

"Sure, ma'am, I do." His mouth curved into a warm smile. "If you do."

Mama frowned. "This ain't a subject to be taken lightly, Mr. Hudson."

"I understand that. But it might help Dodie, Mama. It might."

She exhaled heavily. "What you want from me?"

"There's a guy who lives here in Nassau. He plans harm to Dodie. I'm keeping him away from her as best I can, but . . ." He shrugged.

"But you want me to interfere?" She looked angry.

From his pocket he drew the hairbrush he had taken from Spencer's dressing room, threads of brown hair caught in its bristles. He placed it carefully on the table before her.

"You decide, Mama."

He picked up the basket and set off up to Bain Town, the island's sun warming his back.

Chapter 32

Dodie

Dodie was somewhere dark. She didn't know where. Lights came and went like shooting stars.

"Dodie."

Instantly her eyes opened. She was lying facedown on the mattress, Flynn's hand touching her shoulder. She noticed his knuckles were skinned and abruptly she recalled the fight in the street.

"You were moaning," Flynn said.

Moaning? She tried to move. "I have to go to work," she whispered, but she made no attempt to sit up. Every part of her was sore and throbbing.

"No," Flynn said firmly. "I've told Miss Quinn you won't be in today."

Relief rolled through her. "Thank you."

"Dodie, I have ointments from Mama Keel for your back and something for you to drink. It will help. But I need to lift your dress over your head so that I can rub it on."

Her body jerked. The painful spasm shocked her. Each muscle was hoarding its own memory of what a man had done to her, so that even if she forgot, they would not. Flynn must have seen it because he added quickly, "Or shall I get one of the women from further down the street to do it for you?"

"No."

"Are you sure?"

"Yes."

She was sure. Even if her muscles were not.

The dress slid off easily as she lay on her stomach, naked under the sheet, but still she didn't turn her head to look at him. If she looked at him, she might say, *No, don't touch me*. Or she might see on his face something she dreaded to see, an awareness that she was dirty. Not the clean and decent person he thought her to be. It might show on her skin like Minnie's acne. He rolled the sheet down to her waist.

The ointment was warm and his hands were warmer. They spread out over her bruised back and she felt her skin tingle, smelled the pineapple aroma of bromelain drench the small room. Slowly. Gently. Flynn massaged her back. His strong fingers worked across her shoulder blades, thumbs weaving down her spine until her flesh seemed to break free from the pain in her body.

Blood pumped under her skin. Shameless and unbidden. It flowed to his fingers and was carried to other parts of her, so that she could feel the heat building in her body. He murmured words to her, but the sounds of them joined together, wrapping around each other, rippling through her brain the way the rumble of the sea did at night in her beach shack.

She closed her eyes and let the whisper of his voice wash over her.

Chapter 33

Ella

Ella lay in bed awake. It was the moment before dawn when the day seemed to hold its breath. A window stood open in the bedroom and she could feel the sultry night air on her skin.

Ella was listening to her husband beside her in the bed. The night was hot and they were both naked with just a sheet over them, though whatever the temperature Reggie always slept in the buff. It was one of the things that had surprised her about him. He was a noisy sleeper. A flurry of grunts and murmurs and subdued snores issued from him all night, but just before daylight his feet would start to rub against the sheets, slight at first but growing stronger. Like a cat scratching at a door. Often she wondered whether he was trying to get in or get out.

But far louder was the sound in her head. Just days ago she would have scoffed at it, laughed out loud at the very thought that in her head she would be listening to such a sound. But it was loud and clear, the sound of Detective Dan Calder expelling air from his lungs.

It was the way he did it. A sharp gust of air. A brief unguarded moment. It happened sometimes when he was smoking a cigarette and she said something that he disagreed with but was too polite to correct, or sometimes when she laughed, though she had no idea what it meant then. And there were other sounds. The click of his tongue when he was impatient with the traffic. The tapping of his fingers on the table. Of his shoes on the pavement. A piercing whistle through his fingers that nearly tore her eardrums out of her head.

He was a symphony of sounds. She tried to block them out but failed, and she was shocked by the failure. The problem was, she decided, that she was seeing him each day out of context—he had no setting of his own because he had been transplanted into hers. She knew nothing about him. Was he married? He wore no ring. How old was he? Easily ten years younger than she was. Where did he live? How long had he been in the Bahamas? What were his aims?

She imagined him in bed. Right now. This moment. Stretched out on a plain white sheet, the hard muscles of his body naked in the darkness. Was someone with him? Touching him? With a moan of self-disgust she turned over in bed, turning away from the images in her head. But almost immediately Reggie felt the loss of her even in his sleep and hunched up close behind her, molding himself to the contours of her back. He draped a sleep-heavy arm across her over the sheet, pinning her to him and his bed.

* * *

Ella breezed into the kitchen, where her maid was picking seeds out of a pomegranate with a pin and popping them into her mouth.

"Emerald, have you seen Detective Calder yet this morning?"

"No, Miss Ella, I ain't. But he's here all right."

"What do you mean?"

"He's in the garage. I seen his smoke. That man smokes too much."

"Oh. Right. I'll take him a coffee."

Emerald paused, pin halfway to the cavern of her open mouth. "Now why you wantin' to do that? That's my job."

"I'm going to get Dryden to make a start on the new fencing today and thought he might like to help us."

Dryden was the gardener and general odd-job man around the place. A section of the chicken enclosure needed to be replaced.

"You thinkin' a policeman wants to fix fencin'? You is out of your mind."

"It would be more fun than polishing the car again."

Emerald rolled her black eyes and stabbed her pin deep into the heart of the pomegranate. "More fun for who, Miss Ella?"

*   *   *

Detective Dan Calder had jumped at the chance when she invited him to help.

"Don't feel obliged," she'd said.

"I'm happy to. Always feel free to ask," he'd responded, but in a way that made her wonder if they were talking about the same thing.

He'd been hammering in posts for the last couple of hours, much to the delight of Dryden, who relished the unexpected bonus of bossing around a minion who was twice his size. Dan Calder's blue shirt was patched with dark sweat and Ella wondered whether he would remove it, but he didn't. When Emerald waddled down with a tray of iced lime juice for them all, he drank his in the shade with Dryden, and when the fence was finished, Ella admired his handiwork and thanked him for his help.

"This afternoon I'd like to go to the library, if that's all right with you, Detective Calder."

"Of course. Wherever you wish." He caught her eyes flicking to the sweat marks on his shirt and he shrugged self-consciously. "Don't worry, I'll go and wash, and borrow another shirt from Dryden."

"I wasn't worried," she said, but by then he was striding off toward the tap outside the garage.

When she looked back at the fence, she saw that Emerald was standing there staring at her, hands on her buffalo hips, mouth pursed.

"What is it now, Emerald?" Ella sighed.

"You done went to the library last week. Got yourself four fat books."

"Two of them are dreadfully dull. I want to change them." Ella started up the path.

Behind her she heard Emerald mutter, "That's not the only thing you aimin' to change."

*   *   *

Nassau Library in Shirley Street was unique. No other library came close. Ella loved to go there, if only because its building was so quaint it made her smile each time she trotted up its front steps. Octagonal in shape and four stories high with a circular balcony around the upper floor and a dome on top, it looked more like a lighthouse that someone had mistakenly stuck in the middle of town rather than a sedate library.

It dated back to 1798, when it was built as a much-needed jail for the lawless inhabitants who roamed the city at that time. Its dungeons were now bursting with books instead of buccaneers, and normally Ella liked to linger, but not today. Today she smiled at Mrs. Faircourt behind the desk, snatched *A Tree Grows in Brooklyn* and *The Body in the Library* off the shelves, had them date-stamped, and hurried back out into the blazing sunlight. Palm fronds hung limply in the grassy square, exhausted by the heat. For two minutes she stood in the patch of shade under one of them and gave herself a serious talking-to, the way she did to Emerald when she was getting out of hand.

"Get in the car. Have him drive you straight home. No small talk about anything other than the fund-raising party coming up and its good cause—the widows of servicemen killed in action."

Right.

"No personal questions. No laughing or tipping the brim of your hat at him."

Right.

"And no staring at his hands on the steering wheel."

Right.

But the last *Right* caused a wrench. Like one of her ribs had been yanked out.

She strode across the square and around the corner to where the Rover was parked in the shade, face stern, books brandished in front of her.

"Where now?" he asked.

"To the Berryhead Bar, I think. I need a cold drink. You too, I'm sure."

*　*　*

They drove to the bar with its terrace of beach umbrellas overlooking the sea and its array of young men and women strolling on the sand that had been swept to a dazzling pristine whiteness. A smiling black waiter in a red waistcoat brought Ella a cool rum and lime and a grapefruit juice for Dan. She was thinking of him as Dan now, no longer Detective Calder. He never drank on duty, he told her. She may have messed up the going-straight-home part of her plan but she stuck scrupulously to the rest of it. She talked about the fund-raiser that was to be held at the Cockatoo Club and the way she had to flutter her eyelashes at the local businessmen to get them to donate luxurious raffle prizes for the cause. She talked about her Red Cross work, she talked about the Duchess of Windsor and her dedication to the children's clinic, she talked about Reggie's scheme to get clean water into more homes.

He listened attentively. She couldn't tell whether he was just being polite or was genuinely interested. She left gaps in the conversation for him to fill and was surprised when he did so with snippets of the history of the island. He told her a story about the slave ships that the Royal Navy emptied onto New Providence Island. It happened when slave trading was declared illegal in 1807, a time when Britain was by far the biggest transporter of slaves from Africa to the Americas. Altogether, he informed her, about three million slaves were transported.

"And many freed slaves traveled here from the southern states of America after the Civil War was over too," he told her, and the pupils of his gray eyes were wide with enthusiasm. She recognized that he really cared about this island. "It changed the population of the islands and formed the basis of today's Bahamians."

"Fascinating."

He smiled. "You knew it already."

"That doesn't make it any the less fascinating."

When they left the bar, Ella was pleased with herself. She hadn't asked a single personal question and she told him briskly, "Home now." But as they were about to climb into the car, he wiped a speck of sweat from his temple and said, "It's a real scorcher today. Do you mind if I take off my jacket?"

"Of course not."

But she did mind. She minded a lot. Because seeing his bare forearm right next to her in the car, with its dense muscle and wide strong bones and curls of unruly dark brown hair, undid her resolve, so that before they had even pulled away from the curb she asked, "Where do you live?"

He glanced at her, surprised. "Albert Street. On the east side of town."

"Will you show it to me?"

"Now, why on earth would you want to see my house?"

"Because I need a context for you."

He seemed to understand. Without further comment he turned the car and headed east. They kept the windows down to catch any breeze, but the sky was relentless in its blueness and its brightness as they took the picturesque East Bay Road running alongside the shoreline, rockier here, more rugged. The sea was glinting a deep jade that faded into rich purple off to their left. This was where magnificent wealthy mansions slept quietly behind high pastel walls draped in bougainvillea and banks of tall pine trees, but soon after they passed the yacht club on their left, they swung right, twisting inland. Here the houses were smaller and the streets no longer had a policeman in a white jacket, white gloves, and white topee directing traffic at junctions.

In a sleepy residential street he pulled up outside one of the houses. They both studied it. It was more modest than Ella had expected but she had no idea how much a policeman was paid. The house was pleasing enough. A two-story place that was painted white with a dark red front door and shutters. There was a tiny parched garden in front in which a spiky yucca was the solitary occupant. Clearly Detective Calder was no gardener.

"How long have you lived in Nassau?" she asked.

"Twelve years."

"Really? You must like it here."

"It's my idea of paradise."

He smiled and something new came into his face that she hadn't seen before. Something hopeful and earnest, a sudden enthusiasm in him beyond his control.

"I joined the police force," he told her, "in Swindon in England as a young lad and loved the work. My father was a policeman in the same town, and his father before him. In the blood, I guess."

Ella was touched. By this family that devoted itself to public service through generations but with none of the rewards that Reggie received.

"So how did you end up here?"

"Oh, I grew restless, I suppose. I was young and wanted to widen my horizons. Britain was in a miserable state during the Depression after the Wall Street crash, and I was lucky. I saw an advertisement in the *Police Gazette* for recruits to police postings here in Nassau and I reckoned this was my chance of adventure." He shrugged self-consciously, as if she might laugh at the idea of adventure. "I passed the interview and arrived in time to miss the dismal British winter. But now"—he glanced out of the window at a pair of aircraft droning across the blue sky—"I'm wondering if I made the right decision not to swap this job for a military uniform."

He sounded unsure. It was the first time she'd heard any hint of uncertainty in his voice.

"Someone has to stay here to keep the island safe," she said brightly. "Clearly you're the man for it."

He smiled at her. "I love it here. Who wouldn't?"

"Lots of people wouldn't. It would scare them. Somewhere so different. But I don't suppose you're easily scared, Detective Calder."

He laughed. "Are you married?" she asked.

Ella glanced away out the window and could feel her blouse sticking to the back of the seat. Not until she turned to face him again did he answer.

"No, I'm not married."

She changed the subject, but awkwardly. "Is there much crime in Nassau?"

She saw him relax. "No, not normally. Mainly a few robberies on a Friday night and the usual clutch of drunken fights on a Saturday. But with so many servicemen on the island now, as well as the present unrest among the black Bahamians, the mood has changed. We have to be far more watchful."

"What about the murder of the man who died on the beach?" She was aware of his frown. "Everyone is talking about it."

"So I hear."

"Have they found out anything about Morrell?"

"No." He shook his head. "No, not yet. With no passport and no wallet, he's difficult to trace, but . . ." He stopped. He clearly felt he'd said enough.

"Any ideas on who the killer might be?" She made it sound like idle curiosity.

"Not yet."

Neither giving anything away.

"As a matter of interest," she said, "I heard gossip about a robbery the other day."

"Oh?"

"Of gold coins. Have you heard anything?"

She wondered if he could see the word "liar" branded on her forehead.

"No, nothing has been reported."

"Just idle gossip, I expect." She flicked a hand through the air to dismiss it and just caught the edge of his shoulder. She swore to herself it was an accident.

He swiveled in his seat so that his whole body was turned to face her. "Mrs. Sanford, it's too hot to sit like this any longer. Would you care to come inside my house for a cool drink?" He smiled easily, a lighthearted curve of his lips, as though he was happy either way. It was up to her.

Ella turned her head. Away from him. Away from his house. For a full thirty seconds she didn't speak. When she finally turned back to him, her smile and her voice were too bright.

"Not today, I'm afraid. I have things to do. Maybe some other time."

"Of course," he said.

He started the car, and the purr of its engine was the only sound inside the car. They drove home in silence.

Chapter 34

Dodie

For two hot days and two stormy nights Flynn scarcely left Dodie's side. He brought her breakfasts of mango and corn bread, in the evening fried up chicken and rice on a tiny temperamental stove. She hardly strayed from the mattress despite the sweltering heat in the shack and gradually she felt her battered muscles start to heal.

Mama Keel came to call and looked her over, pronouncing her a tough young goose, and after that visit the women up the street drifted in through the open door with a dish of scallops and a heap of banana fritters. Flynn sat on the front step with them in the shade of a squat pine, rolling cigarettes and passing round a beer while she dozed.

Each morning and each evening he massaged her back. Her head was hot and her thoughts seemed to wade through wet sand, leaving strange unrecognizable shapes behind them, but when his fingers touched her skin and Mama's ointment glided over the curves and ridges of her back, her mind cleared. They didn't talk, not while he worked on her. Sometimes he hummed softly to himself, something from Dixie or an old hoedown tune, nothing that she would have expected from him.

She closed her eyes and learned about him quietly through his fingers. Discovering the strength and kindness in him, the patience and the understanding. She wondered about his history and what world of danger and violence he had descended from. Sometimes she slept and his hands accompanied her into her dreams, as though a part of him had burrowed under her skin and would not let go.

Once, just once, when he lifted the weight of her tangled hair off her neck, smoothing its knots out with his fingers, he leaned down and she could feel his breath warm on her shoulder blade as he brushed his lips over the nape of her neck. Not a kiss, nothing so brash. But a blending of his skin with hers.

She wanted to thank him. But her tongue lay too heavy in her mouth.

*   *   *

When Dodie woke, it was night. The kind of night that was so warm and silky that she could touch the dense blackness with her fingertips. She had no idea what the time was, but she could feel that her body had turned some kind of corner. The throbbing in her head was down to little more than a discontented murmur and she could flex her back without too much pain. Carefully she sat up, wearing a loose cotton nightshirt that was one of Mama's.

Faintly she could hear Flynn's breathing. It dawned on her that he must be sleeping on the earthen floor, a place not suited to human bones. She eased her feet off the mattress and sat like that while she waited for the moon to rise. An hour, maybe two, during which her mind picked its way through the maze of events that had occurred since the night she found Mr. Morrell bleeding in the dirt.

When the floor turned white in the gleam of moonlight, Dodie abandoned the mattress and moved over to the figure of Flynn. He was stretched out on his side, one arm flung out in front of him as though fending something off and his head resting on a folded towel. His skin possessed a metallic sheen and a sudden fear that he might be dead made her fingers seek out his cheek.

Instantly Flynn's hand snapped around her wrist.

"Flynn, it's me."

"Dodie?" He blinked himself awake.

"Shhh," she whispered.

"I didn't mean to harm you."

"I know."

She lay down on the floor beside him, her head sharing his towel. Her hand lay on his bare chest and she could feel the force of his heartbeat. What was it like, she wondered, to be this man? One who must watch his every breath. One who hugged God knows what secrets to himself. One who possessed the bravery to launch himself into a fight against two hard-bitten hoodlums for her sake, and who could reduce them to gutter trash, as he called it, and seem to think nothing of it. Yet at the same time he was a man who would lay his hands on her naked back with the gentle touch of a nurse and not once make her feel that it was inappropriate.

She wrapped an arm around his waist and he pulled her to him.

"When it's light," she said quietly, "I need to speak to Sir Harry Oakes."

He didn't reply. She waited a long time, but eventually she slept.

*   *   *

"Don't let him bully you."

"I don't intend to," Dodie said firmly.

"Good."

Dodie and Flynn were standing together outside an impressive mahogany door. They were on a gallery that overlooked a sumptuous foyer. She had never been inside the British Colonial Hotel before. She had heard tales about its splendor but nothing quite prepared her. The building was a huge construction that had replaced the original wooden hotel burned down in 1922, and it struck her that it was as arrogant and bombastic as its owner, Sir Harry Oakes. Its central tower dominated the façade, its walls a flushed sandy color and its roof a swathe of bold red tiles. But inside, the extravagant foyer, with its coral-and-white marble and wide stairs, was magnificent. The whole place intimidated her. Flynn had vanished from the Bain Town shack early that morning and returned an hour later to say Sir Harry had agreed to see her.

"Why?" she'd asked.

"Because he's curious."

"About me?"

"Yes."

"A week ago, if you'd told me a multimillionaire was curious about me, I'd have crawled under a stone; now I take it in my stride. Things have changed."

She was tearing strips off a triggerfish for their breakfast.

"I don't want you to change," he said.

She laughed. "Too late for that."

"Be careful," he said. "Of the changes coming."

*   *   *

"What can I do for you, Miss Wyatt?"

He was bigger than she remembered. Or was it the office that made him bigger? From the vast map of the world on one wall to the aerial photograph of New Providence Island on the other, Sir Harry Oakes was a man who did everything on a large scale. Even his philanthropy. His generosity to Bahamian good causes existed on a million-dollar scale. On a shelf sat an array of bulky chunks of rock glittering with quartzite and malachite, as reminders of his prospecting past and indicators to others of their owner's ability to succeed, to wrest from this world whatever he wanted.

She extended her hand and it was swallowed up by his thick fingers, his grip fierce.

"I'd like to ask you a few questions," she said.

"Sit down, Miss Wyatt."

She sat in a finely carved chair in front of his grand oak desk. He took his seat opposite, rested his elbows on the leather surface of the desk, and inspected her closely. She could see he didn't trust her.

But she didn't trust him either.

"And what do these questions concern, Miss Wyatt? I thought you were here to accept my offer of a job."

It was a lie. They both knew that.

"Our mutual associate, Mr. Hudson, did not say what you wanted to discuss with me. I agreed to see you because he thought I would be interested in what you have to say. So, come on, young lady, spit it out."

"I'm sure you know that I am the person who found Mr. Morrell after he'd been stabbed."

"Yes, of course I do, Miss Wyatt. What is your point?"

"I believe he came to see you that night."

"Is that what Mr. Morrell told you?"

She didn't hesitate. "Yes."

"That's not what you told the police."

"No."

The hard line of his mouth shifted a fraction into what might have been a smile. "A wise move." He picked up a pen and tapped it sharply against a metal inkwell like a bell tolling. "Because it's not true and you would have found yourself in court before you could even pick your nose, young lady."

"Sir Harry, I'm not interested in your business dealings with Mr. Morrell."

"So what is it you are so damned keen to stick your nose in, then?"

"I want to know who killed him. Any suggestions?"

Oakes gave a snort. "You've got a damned nerve."

"Between us, Sir Harry. That's all. No police or lawyers."

He had insisted on seeing her alone. Not even Flynn present. She wasn't sure why, unless it was to threaten her. She had prepared herself for that, holding on to the words "Don't let him bully you" and to the certainty that Flynn was prowling on the other side of that door.

"All I'm after," she said reasonably, "is the name of anyone you

think may have wanted to attack Morrell and"—she paused, a
pulse starting up as she saw anger in Sir Harry's eyes—". . . and a
reason why they would want to do so."

He rose to his feet, his bulk towering over her and the desk.
"Get out of here. I don't know what the fuck this man Morrell told
you but it's not true. Do you hear? He didn't come to see me that
night. So get out of here and don't come back."

Dodie immediately walked to the door. She felt powerless in the
face of his denials. She wasn't good at calling a person a liar to their
face. At the door she turned and said, "I shall take my story to the
police, then."

"You're bluffing." He sneered. "I have checked you out. Don't
think I haven't. You are already known to them as a filthy troublemaker who makes false accusations against men who cross you."

"That's not true." But she felt the sting of shame. "They may
take more note when I tell them about the gold coin Mr. Morrell
gave me."

It was stalemate. They both recognized it. Slowly Dodie walked
back to her chair and sat down.

"Now, Sir Harry, let us talk amicably."

The big fist swept a glass ashtray off the desk. "So it's blackmail you're after," he growled. "I should have known." He yanked
a checkbook from a drawer and waved it at her.

"No!" Dodie heard her voice rise. "I don't want your money.
What I want is for whoever killed him to pay for it."

Whatever it was he heard in her voice, he put down the checkbook and in silence he started to pace the room, to roam its corners. Dodie watched him warily, but she caught a sense of his
frustration, of how the confines of an office were galling to an
outdoorsman who had lived and breathed in wide-open spaces for
so many years. He was wearing a well-worn khaki short-sleeved
shirt and trousers and old open sandals, bringing his past with
him for all to see, whereas most people, herself included, kept their
past firmly tucked away in closed cupboards.

Finally he came to a halt in front of her. The bluster had gone and in its place there was a sadness to him. "Why should you care?" he asked. "Morrell was nothing to you."

"You're wrong. When you clasp a man's hand while he fights for his life, when you hold him in your arms as he takes his last breath, he becomes more to you than nothing. Much more. I failed him then. Now I want to do right by him. I *will* find his killer. With or without your help."

Sir Harry nodded slowly. "It's revenge you want. Not justice." A faint smile loosened his lips. "I don't blame you. Revenge I understand. I have taken my fair share of it in my life. I've been known to ruin guys who have crossed me."

"Did Morrell cross you?"

"Good God, no. He and I go way back. To the days when I had no dough and was scouring the wastelands of the world for gold. Johnnie Morrell was a good friend to me at a time when friends were damned hard to come by."

That came as a shock. "I didn't know."

He leaned down over her, his face hard. "There's a lot you don't know, Miss Wyatt."

"Is that why you gave him the two gold napoleons? As a mark of friendship?"

"What I want to know is where the hell the rest of them are."

"The rest of them?"

"Yeah. Those two had a load of shiny buddies, a whole boxful of old coins, real beauties." He reached out and gripped Dodie's chin, keeping her from retreating as his large arrogant face jumped closer, filling her vision. His skin bore the damage of a life spent in harsh sun and harsher cold, etched with lines of distrust. "Know anything about that, little lady?"

"No."

"You sure?"

"Yes."

"Morrell didn't mention anything about them to you?"

"No, nothing."

"He didn't drop the box in the alleyway and you picked it up, but just happen to have forgotten about it right now?"

She jerked her chin free of his hand and stood up, catching him by surprise, so that he was forced backward.

"No, Sir Harry. That is not what happened. I am not a thief."

"And I am not a fool."

She headed for the door.

"Hang on there, Miss Wyatt."

She didn't stop.

"Wait!"

Her hand was on the hefty brass handle.

"You and I, we want the same thing, Miss Wyatt, so let's—"

She swung around. "You don't care who murdered your friend, you just want your gold back and the police kept out of it."

"Well, well, Miss Wyatt, quite a little firecracker, aren't you? But you're wrong about Morrell. I do care. About him, not just about the gold. But you're right about the cops. I sure don't want them around, sticking their noses into my business, asking damn-fool questions that I don't want to answer." His hand was swiping through the air, knocking the questions away.

Dodie said, "You've heard from the police my version of that night's events. Now tell me yours."

For a moment it seemed that he was going to refuse, but she saw him think better of it.

"It's straightforward really. Morrell came to my home, we conducted our business, knocked back a few drinks, and spun a tale or two about the bad old days, then he left."

"With the box of coins?"

"With the box of coins."

"And Flynn Hudson? He was there too?"

"Yes, the Hudson guy was there too. But most of the time he was keeping watch on the outside, making sure we weren't disturbed." He hesitated, uneasy all of a sudden. "Except for when he checked out the rest of the house to be sure that there was nobody eavesdropping."

"Is that when Mrs. Sanford walked in?" she asked.

His eyes widened. A dark vermilion flooded his cheeks and Dodie braced herself for his rage to break loose again, but instead he started to laugh. A big booming sound that racketed off his rocks and shook the glass in the windows.

"Damn you, Miss Wyatt." Sir Harry Oakes laughed. "Damn you to hell."

*   *   *

They rode in one of the horse-drawn surreys, the horse ambling along in a jaunty straw hat under the sun's unblinking gaze. Flynn took Dodie to a bar in the old part of town. It wasn't much of a bar but it was quiet and peddled a decent local beer. They opted for a table outside in a dusty patch of shade and Flynn sat silent while Dodie reeled off what had gone on between Sir Harry and herself.

He grew restless, lighting too many cigarettes and taking impatient mouthfuls of his beer while she described the exchange when she was ordered out of the office, when Oakes hadn't yet realized she was not there to make trouble for him but to glean information. When she finished, Flynn sat quiet, pondering what she'd told him.

"Better satisfied now?" he asked at last. "Now that Oakes has told you what he knows."

"But you didn't."

"Didn't what?"

"Tell me what you know."

Flynn stubbed out his cigarette. He plucked a stray spotted beetle from the front of his white shirt and placed it on the table, where it proceeded to chase around in circles. Right now Dodie felt like that's what she was doing, chasing around in circles, unable to step back and see the whole table.

"You didn't tell me what you know," she said again.

"About what?"

"The box of gold coins."

"Ah, that."

"Yes, that."

"There was a reason."

She waited.

He placed his hand next to hers on the table, so that they lay side by side on the wooden surface, touching but not crowding each other. His was long-boned like the rest of him, with dark scabs healing on his knuckles, the remnants of his fight with the hoodlum.

"Some things are better not told. It is safer for you. Not to know certain things."

She made herself remove her hand and wrap it around her beer. "What else don't I know?"

He laughed. "Sure are persistent, aren't you?"

"You should know that by now." She kept her expression stern. "What happened to the box of coins?"

"Dodie, I have no idea." He frowned. His dark eyebrows hunched together and she was certain he was seeing Morrell on the starlit night moving off with the hoard of gold like an old-time pirate who had struck lucky. "Johnnie Morrell went off with it while I stayed behind, like I told you. To speak to Oakes."

"Morrell didn't have it with him when I found him."

"So either he was robbed or . . ."

"He hid it somewhere."

"I've been over the route. Goddammit, I've hunted everywhere." He smacked the table with annoyance.

"No success?"

"No."

"But it does mean he might have been killed for the coins. Not because he was involved in"—she rolled her eyes at him—"whatever it is you and he were involved in."

"If it's just plain robbery, you realize what that leaves us with,

Dodie? Anyone on this whole damned island could be the murderer."

"That's true. Except for one thing." She picked up her glass.

He watched her drink her beer. "What's that?"

"He told me he was too frightened to go to the hospital because
there would be people waiting for him there, and . . ." The image
of Morrell bleeding strings of crimson on to her floor reared up in
her head. ". . . and he—like you—said it would be better for me if
he told me nothing." She shook her head. "Don't you men realize
how bloody annoying that is?"

He smiled at her. "That's the first time I've heard you cuss,
Miss Wyatt."

"Well, there's plenty more where that came from if you don't
tell me more about what's going on." She abandoned her beer and
let her hand push up against his on the table. "Be honest with me,
Flynn. Please. If Morrell was too frightened to go to hospital, it
wasn't just some chancy robber he was afraid of, was it? It was . . .
what? Your 'organization,' as you call it? Why would they want to
kill him? Who are they?"

Flynn sat back in his chair. He removed his hand from the table
and his face changed. The angles hardened and he regarded her
with a flat stare.

"I work for the mob. The American Mafia, call it what you
will. In Chicago. So did Morrell."

Dodie's fingertips became ice cold.

"A mobster?" Her voice came out hollow. The words seemed to
bleed in her mouth. "You do all that we hear about the mob? With
drugs and alcohol. And gambling. Murder and protection rackets.
You do all that?"

"Yes." He seemed to recede deeper into the shadow until she
didn't know who he was.

Chapter 35

Dodie

Dodie asked Flynn to take her to his room. She knew it was somewhere near because he'd mentioned it earlier.

"It's two streets away," he told her. "Can you walk that far? Is your back up to it?" He was polite.

"Yes."

What she needed was to be alone with him, away from the curious ears and eyes of passing strangers. He walked her to a street that was so narrow it cradled the heat and wouldn't let go, and Flynn moved along it at her pace, for which she was grateful. His arm under hers felt solid and dependable. But it was an illusion. Flynn Hudson was anything but solid and dependable. He was a criminal. And now the gap between them seemed to have stretched into an ocean. No boat. No bridge. Nothing to get her across it.

Flynn unlocked the purple-painted front door of one of the scruffier houses and helped Dodie upstairs to a tiny room. She was glad of the help. Her back was throbbing and her feet seemed to have developed a mind of their own. The room buzzed with heat and he threw open the window, but it made no difference, just let the hot air outside move inside. Two flies crawled listlessly on the sill.

"It's not much," he acknowledged. "But it's enough."

It consisted of a narrow bed with spotless sheets and pillow.

A hard chair, a chest of drawers, and two hangers on a hook on the door. A mirror with scurvy was nailed to one wall. Dodie wanted to go to the chest and open its drawers, to stir her hands through their contents. To look under his pillow. Beneath his bed. In the pockets of the jacket hanging on the back of the door. To find him again.

"Would you like me to fetch you a glass of water?" he asked.

She shook her head. She didn't want him to leave.

"Please sit down, Dodie."

She perched on the edge of the bed, took off her straw hat, and fanned herself with it. He leaned his long frame against the door, observing her for a full minute before he came over.

"Lie down. Rest your back."

"No, I'm fine, thank you."

He raised one dark brow. "Really?"

"Yes."

But her body was no better than her feet. It had a will of its own and caved in with a sigh of relief as it sank backward and stretched itself out on Flynn's pristine bed. Dodie was appalled.

"Better?" he asked.

"Yes, thank you. I'll only stay a moment."

"Stay as long as you like."

She closed her eyes. Outside, children were squabbling somewhere in the dust, making a racket that only stopped when a man bellowed at them. In the silence that followed, she could pinpoint Flynn's breathing.

"So," he said. That was all.

"So," she said, opening her eyes. "Tell me about it."

"How much do you want to know?"

"All of it."

In the quiet of the stifling room she could hear him considering which words to choose.

"Do you know what I wanted to be when I was a kid?"

"What?"

"A pianist." He laughed at himself. "Dumb kid. Didn't know better. But I was born in the Bronx in New York and back in those days there were over sixty piano factories in the borough. They employed five thousand workers and I was hell-bent on becoming one of them. As a kid, I used to mooch around those places after school doing odd jobs, sweeping up stuff, and one of the guys taught me to play. I was nothing special but I could hold a tune okay by the age of nine."

Dodie rolled onto her side and propped her head on one elbow. She could see it in his eyes. Those pianos still eating him up, the music playing in his head.

"What happened?"

He shrugged. "When I was ten I went to work for my pa after school instead."

"Doing what?"

He gave her a slow smile. "I became a runner."

"What does a runner do?"

"Delivers packages. Takes messages. Checks out if streets are clear. Keeps tabs on the cop patrols. That kind of thing."

She frowned. She didn't mean to. Didn't want him to think she was judging him. To have a father who messed up your childhood dreams was sickeningly familiar. She was frowning *for* him, not *at* him.

"What was it your father did?"

"He ran bootleg liquor."

"Oh, I see."

"No, Dodie. I don't think you do. It was Prohibition. Thirteen violent years when President Woodrow Wilson intended us Americans to be dry and abstinent and God-fearing. It didn't work, of course it didn't. It just made the bootleg gangs rich and got too many people shot."

"Your father was a member of one of those gangs?"

"You bet he was. He was thick with Lucky Luciano and Meyer Lansky on Manhattan's Lower East Side. Then got caught up in the Five Points Gang for a time. He and Luciano shifted over to Joe Masseria's organization, the Brooklyn gang boss, just before I started running for him. My pa helped Luciano run his bootlegging racket for him, not that Pa ever got rich, mind you. He drank too much of the merchandise."

He laughed. As if he'd made a joke, but his eyes had darkened and retreated into his head. His fingers were rolling strands of sweet-smelling tobacco into a cigarette with perfect precision, but Dodie could tell he was no longer seeing what was in front of him. He took his time lighting the cigarette and inhaled deeply, sucking the memories back in.

"Anyway . . ." He spoke rapidly. "When I was twelve my parents were gunned down in the street in front of me. A revenge killing. Sicilians are good at revenge."

"Flynn, I'm so sorry. How—"

But he kept going. The need to spit it out was too strong. "Luciano sent me to Chicago, in case they came for me too. That's where I met up with Johnnie Morrell. He was in with Al Capone by then. I went to work for them." He exhaled a long stream of smoke toward the open window. "The rest, as they say, is history."

He stood up, flexed his shoulders as though something was gripping them and he had to wrench them free. He moved over to the window, staring out at the sun-bleached street, where a wind was sneaking up through the sea grape, no more than a furtive ripple of air, but it made life easier for a moment in the hot little room.

"By the time I was fourteen, I walked out on them. I'd had a gutful. Four of my good friends had been shot dead in those two years. Rubbed out. So I hit the road. Needed to breathe clean air. Morrell put me on to Harry Oakes over the border in Canada, a buddy of his from his old prospecting days. I worked for him for a few months but I couldn't keep my feet still now that I was loose. Canada is one hell of a big country, so I took to drifting. Stopping awhile in lonesome faceless towns but always moving on."

The words ran out. He tossed his cigarette into the street but remained at the window, staring out.

"Flynn," she called softly.

He didn't hear.

"Flynn, come here."

He turned his head to her. The hardness had gone from his eyes and in its place lay a sadness that set up an ache inside Dodie.

"Sit down," she said.

He sat beside her, limbs stiff. "How's your back?"

"Forget my back." She lay on the clean white pillow and didn't let her hands touch him. "Tell me the rest."

"There's not much more to tell. Eventually I went back. That's the thing about the Mafia. They're like the Catholic Church. Once they've got their hooks in you, they've got you for life. I did a fair bit of work with Meyer Lansky in Florida and he sent me over here with Morrell to close out this land deal with Oakes. They chose us because we both knew him before he was *Sir.*"

"So who," she asked, "is on the island hiring thugs to beat me up?"

"Lansky has another guy here to do his bidding. Goes by the name of Spencer." He picked up her hand off the sheet and held it flat between his own. "That's why we have to keep you safe."

"What is it they think I know?"

"They are scared that Johnnie Morrell may have spilled too many beans on his deathbed. The only reason they haven't done worse to you before now is that they don't want to attract more police interest, and also I've sworn to them that"—he shrugged apologetically—"you're a dumb little waitress who knows nothing."

"Thanks for that, Mr. Hudson."

He smiled. She frowned at him.

"One more question," she said.

Still he held her hand as though fearing it would move away.

"Go ahead."

"Why did Sir Harry give Mr. Morrell the gold?"

Flynn slowly shook his head. "There you've got me. I don't know, I wasn't there. I was outside. All I know is that Morrell left with it."

"Have you asked Sir Harry?"

"No."

"Why not? It might be significant."

"Because Sir Harry wouldn't tell me. That's why."

She nodded. It sounded right. "One final question."

"Go ahead."

"What was your business alone with Sir Harry? After Morrell had left."

She saw him considering his answer. Didn't he know yet that he could trust her?

He sighed faintly. "Oakes wanted to talk to me about his son-in-law, Freddie de Marigny. The cradle snatcher. He sends Oakes into a fury. Nothing to do with Morrell."

That surprised her. If it was true.

"One more question."

He laughed but it wasn't a happy sound. "Ask away."

"Who do you think killed Johnnie Morrell?"

He didn't hesitate. Didn't stop to think of a lie. "Sir Harry Oakes."

* * *

"You should leave while you still have the chance," Flynn told her.

Dodie was breathing hard, as though she'd been running somewhere where the air was thin. She sat up, touched the pale city skin of his throat, placed a kiss firmly on his mouth, and lay back down on the pillow again.

"I'm not going anywhere, Flynn. Don't imagine that I will run because of what you've told me."

He remained seated on the bed, staring down at her face, memorizing each feature in minute detail as if he expected her to vanish in a puff of smoke. When he leaned closer, his face just above hers, the scent of him swept into her nostrils. His kiss was not gentle. It was fierce and hungry. She could taste the sharpness of his desire. She could feel it in the way his lips took possession of her mouth and caressed the curve of her cheek. It set up a need in her, a need that pulsed through her body.

The strength of it startled Dodie. She had no idea it would be like this, how a few kisses could destroy her body's defenses that had been so carefully erected. Sounds escaped her. Small sighs and moans and faint mews that she did not know existed within her, as Flynn slid the strap of her dress off one shoulder. It lay naked and exposed.

"Dodie," he murmured, "this isn't what you came here for."

Isn't it? Isn't this what she came for?

With an effort he rolled away from her and was about to leave the bed.

"Stay," she whispered.

One by one she undid the buttons of his shirt, peeled it from his shoulders, and ran both hands over the paleness of him. Over the dark glinting line of hairs. She bent her head and pressed her lips to his chest. His heartbeat was hammering through his ribs, vibrating against her tongue as she savored the salty tang of his skin.

Tenderly he stroked her hair and lifted its long chestnut tangle, baring her neck to his kisses, and without shame she lifted her shift over her head. She felt his gaze on her naked breasts, but instead of being self-conscious and shy, instead of being the awkward and inexperienced lover she knew herself to be, she wanted him not only to gaze but to touch. She hadn't wanted any man to lay a finger on her since the incident with her boss at the sewing factory, and she had sworn she would never let any man—however kind or gentle—anywhere near her again.

But she had not bargained for this. For this roaring. This pounding of her blood in her veins. This heat. Suffocating and consuming. She wanted to feel ashamed but couldn't, she wanted to speak but couldn't, she wanted to say: *Look what you've done to me.* But couldn't. His mouth was on hers, his hands touching her, caressing her breasts, her thighs. She stripped his clothes from him and could no longer tell which limbs were his and which were hers, the ache inside her was so fierce as they effortlessly wove themselves into the fabric of each other.

And then he was above her with his eyes looking down at her with such naked concern that she realized that he knew. Knew about the sewing factory. She had no idea how, but he did. He knew all about the dirt in her. A flush of shame burned her cheeks, but he kissed her hard and whispered against her lips, "My love, this is a new beginning. Us together. Forget the rest. This is you and me."

My love.

He knew her dirt, had smelled the filth on her body, yet still he called her *my love.*

Greedily, she wrapped her legs around his hips, and when he entered her she cried out. Not with pain this time. Not with rage and humiliation at having her body ripped open like a butcher's carcass. But with shock. That it could be so gentle, so loving, so exhilarating. She couldn't breathe. Couldn't think. Couldn't be. There existed only their flesh bound together. That was her reality in the small secretive room that was now her world.

⁂ ⁂ ⁂

The light outside grew softer. Shadows edged into the room. Dodie had lost track of time, but it didn't matter. As if time belonged in an unknown world and meant nothing here. She was propped on one elbow, studying Flynn's face while he slept.

Mobster or miller or major in the army?

Did it make any difference to her?

No. The answer banged into her head. No. Not a scrap. Whatever he was, he was part of her now. She smiled down at him, relishing the intimacy in the narrow bed, and she leaned over until her lips were half an inch from his and it took all her willpower not to kiss his mouth. As if it were hers now to claim whenever the urge took her.

"What are you grinning at like a loon?" Flynn murmured, his voice still heavy with sleep. "How's your back?"

"What back?"

He rolled her over and pressed her onto the pillow, where he trailed strands of her hair gently through his fingers and kissed her nipple, sending a bolt of heat to join the ache between her legs.

"So the sore back and purple bruises were . . ."

"A device to get you into bed."

He laughed, delightedly, but heard her sigh.

"What is it?" he asked.

She tucked an arm around his body, anchoring herself to him. "There is someone else we need to speak to."

He laid a finger lightly on her lips, unwilling to hear more, but she kissed it and removed it.

"Who?" he asked.

"Mr. Harold Christie."

"The real-estate guy?"

She nodded. "He came to see me. Now it's my turn to see him. I'm sure he is involved in what went on with Morrell, and it's time we asked him some questions."

Chapter 36

Ella

"Reggie, should we invite Detective Calder to join the party tomorrow night?" Ella asked.

Her husband paused. He was in the middle of undoing his shirt buttons, preparing for bed. "Why on earth should we do that?"

"Oh, I don't know. It just seems the decent thing to do." She leaned over to unpeel her stocking. "The poor man has spent so many hours waiting in the car for me." She walked over to her husband and draped her stocking around his neck, its silk surface sliding against his skin. "It's not as if he's just a chauffeur. He's a proper police officer. Anyway he'll just be one of the crowd there. It doesn't seem fair to him to make him wait outside all evening, does it?"

Reggie thought about it. She could see the moment of doubt perch at the back of his eyes. His fingers fondled the stocking.

"Tilly and Hector won't invite their bodyguard to the party, I'm certain," she pointed out, and kissed his cheek. "But you're a much nicer man than Hector."

She retreated to the dressing table and picked up the dark amber bottle of perfume. Delicately she dabbed a touch of Guerlain's Vol de Nuit at the base of her throat. She knew that Reggie adored the woody scent of it. Sometimes to please him, it was all she wore to bed. Lightly dotted along her thighs. He came over to her now, drawn by its fragrance, and ran his thumb thoughtfully over the raised design on the front of the bottle. It depicted an aircraft propeller because the perfume was named after Antoine de Saint-Exupéry's second novel, *Vol de Nuit*, and Reggie's eyelids half lowered, his lips parted loosely. She could imagine all too well what was going on in his head, so she didn't disturb him. When he finally looked at her, his eyes were faintly out of focus.

"Of course, my dear, whatever you think is right," he said.

She gave him a warm smile. "Oh, Reggie, you are such a dear man."

He stood straighter, his cheeks pink. As if it were all his idea to invite Detective Dan Calder to the party.

✳   ✳   ✳

Ella stared sleeplessly at the black hillock that was Reggie.

It was wrong. Of course it was wrong.

What was she thinking of?

So foolish. So mistaken. So utterly, utterly wrong.

The remedy was simple: she would issue no invitation. Detective Calder could wait outside in the car along with all the other chauffeurs. Why on earth should she care? Reggie wouldn't even notice.

She drew a long breath and released it silently into the night. The darkness of the bedroom wrapped itself effortlessly around her secrets, hiding them away even from herself, and she experienced an overwhelming sense of relief. It made her feel as if she had just climbed up a cliff face. She had made the decision.

Tomorrow morning without fail she would rise early and march straight down to the garage and tell Detective Calder he was no longer required by the Sanford household. He would be pleased. She would be pleased.

Everyone would be happy.

She tucked herself closer to her husband and inhaled his soapy smell. The sex hadn't been good. But neither had it been bad. Not really.

*   *   *

The Cockatoo Club was Ella's favorite. More like the risqué ones Reggie had taken her to on their trips to New York, all gold and glitz and glamour. Huge petal-pink chandeliers cast a sunset glow over the dancers and diners, flattering bare shoulders and setting fire to diamonds and to gold necklaces, so that the place flashed and sparkled. Wide shiny steps swept up to a semicircular stage where a black swing band in glossy white jackets was in full flow. Their silky smoothness made it a delight to dance, while a husky-voiced singer in a startling beaded dress crooned at the microphone.

Tonight everyone was here. Ella was pleased with ticket sales for this fund-raiser, and the duchess was particularly satisfied with the turnout, elegant in her midnight blue Schiaparelli gown and her trademark panther bracelet as she passed from table to table. Ella was on the crowded dance floor. She kept turning her head unobtrusively as she scoured the swirling crush of noisy revelers.

Where was Dan? Had he slunk off somewhere?

He'd said yes. He would come. She was holding on to that. Yes, he'd said, he'd be happy to attend the event, and yes, he did possess an evening suit. She had blushed at the look he gave her when she asked the question. It told her she had gone too far. So now she was ignoring him, unaware of where he was at the club, but she couldn't stop her eyes straying. Betraying her.

There was a vitality to the movements of her fellow dancers tonight. As if a spark flared from one to the other, setting them alight. It was the reports of fatalities that caused it, all that violent and tragic death. For those who had to stand on the sidelines and watch, their only weapon was to fight back with gritted determination to make life go on as normal. To show that the music and dancing proved they would live forever.

"Looking for someone, Ella?"

It was the Duke of Windsor.

"No, not at all." Ella gave the ex-King of England a bright

smile as she danced with him. "Just thinking too much about the aircrews here."

They both glanced around at the uniforms surrounding them, wrapping girls in their arms as if for the last time.

"Well, my dear, you've done them proud again. A pat on the back for you is well deserved." With a laugh he patted her back.

"Thank you."

The band broke out into "Chattanooga Choo Choo" and the tempo on the floor picked up. The duke was a fine dancer, moving well despite his small stature, a smooth slight man who prided himself on his charm. Immensely vain, in Ella's opinion. He lavished no end of care and expense on his personal appearance, his suits all top-quality Savile Row, the waist of his jackets set especially high to elongate his silhouette.

She'd admit that at forty-nine, tanned and trim, he was still good-looking in a boyish sort of way with his soft blond hair swept back. But there was a petulance around his mouth, a pettiness. And a sadness in his large blue eyes that was sometimes so intense that she could scarcely bear to look at him. Yet he had everything—an attentive wife, wealth, status, an important job, good health—the whole works, for heaven's sake. Yet he regarded himself as hard done by. Always greedy for more. Poor Reggie would rather sew his lips together than breathe a disloyal word against a member of the royal family, but when he returned home tense and frustrated some evenings, Ella knew exactly who to blame. But she was being good. Dancing. Smiling. Asking no favors. Reggie would be pleased with her.

"Is Sir Harry not here tonight?" she inquired casually.

Sir Harry Oakes and the duke were frequent golfing partners.

"No, he's a touch under the weather, or so he claims." The duke chuckled to himself, deep lines sprouting around his eyes. "More a case of the cat's away, so the mouse will play. If you take my meaning."

"Really?"

"Oh yes. His wife and daughter are over in America."

The thing about the duke was that as governor, he was remarkably well informed and liked to keep up with all the latest gossip. Ella arranged her face into a sympathetic smile.

"You must have had a busy week, sir. A bit of a headache, what with the murder and the labor unrest."

"Ah, don't remind me, my dear."

He spun Ella around the dance floor, as if to demonstrate the giddiness of his week. She passed close to a set of broad shoulders that towered over the duke and for a second her breath hitched in her throat. But they were the wrong shoulders.

"Anything new on the ghastly murder?" Ella asked.

"It's a damnable business. Such a ballyhoo, but they have turned up nothing on the unfortunate fellow yet."

Unfortunate. Was that the word for him?

"The police are searching high and low," the duke continued, "for his wallet. They are convinced he must have had one. Colonel Lindop tells me that he believes someone stole it on the night of the murder and that they will find it eventually. He's a good chap, I'm sure he's right."

"He usually is."

"So they're going to drag the young woman who found him in for questioning again."

Ella's heart tightened. "I heard that she was in the clear."

"No, not yet. But I'm afraid, my dear Ella, it's time for you to lose your bodyguard. We've made the decision that the situation with the labor bosses is stable now, thank God, and presents no further threat to our women. Anyway, Lindop is pulling his men back from other duties to concentrate on the murder inquiry. Quite a relief for you, what? It can be damned annoying to have one of those chaps hanging around all the time, don't you think?"

He didn't notice that her eyes had frozen wide open, that her jaw had grown slack as she sought for words.

The band started up with "That Old Black Magic" and that

was when she saw him. A gap in the crowd of dancing couples opened up, a narrow ravine leading straight from him to her across the dance floor. Ella stared at him greedily. At the way his muscular frame was barely comfortable within the ill-fitting evening jacket as he bent his attention on the woman laughing in his arms.

He was dancing with Tilly Latcham.

* * *

"Enjoy your dance with HRH?" Freddie de Marigny asked. Sir Harry's son-in-law was plowing through yet another cocktail.

"Yes, thank you."

Reggie treated her to an approving smile.

"He looked very earnest," said Hector.

Tilly's husband was seated at their table with Reggie and Freddie, wreathed in cigar smoke and brandy glasses. Ella sat down and reached for a glass of wine.

"Not boring you, was he?" Hector asked jovially. "With a stroke-by-stroke account of his golf this afternoon?"

He laughed good-naturedly. Hector was rather good at the sport, whereas it was common knowledge that the duke was something of a duffer at it. She accepted a top-up to her glass and drank it down quickly.

"You okay, old girl?" Hector murmured. "You don't look too good."

She nodded. "I'm fine."

She was fond of Hector. He was one of those men who kept life simple. He believed in black and white, had no time for Reggie's grays, yet oddly the two men hit it off well together.

"Where's Tilly got to?" he asked.

"I'll find her."

Ella rose to her feet and pushed her way through the crowded club, scrambling to get as far away from the dance floor as she could.

* * *

How can you look in a mirror and see the eyes of a stranger? A person you have never seen before. How can that happen?

Ella leaned over the washbasin in the powder room and splashed water on her cheeks, but it made no difference. Her face was so hot she thought it would melt. It was shock. She knew that. Not shock at seeing Tilly Latcham laughing in Dan Calder's arms or at knowing his hand rested snugly in the center of her back with nothing but a shimmer of silk between their two bodies.

No. Not that shock. Though even that was enough to knock holes in her.

Worse, far worse, was the shock of how much she cared. How much it hurt. How much she'd lost control of who she was.

She shuddered.

* * *

"Ella, I've been looking everywhere for you, darling. What are you doing hiding in here?"

Tilly had breezed into the powder room on a wave of perfume and cocktails. Her mouth was bright red, as though someone had been kissing it.

"I'm just taking a breather, Tilly. It's so hot on the dance floor."

Tilly inspected her quizzically. "You do look a bit flushed."

Ella rinsed her hands again and took a towel to dry them. She refused—absolutely refused—to ask her friend about the dance with Dan Calder. Instead she combed her hair a little too roughly and pinned back a blond lock that had escaped its pearl grip.

"Hector is on good form tonight," she commented.

"He's been in an odd mood all day. I think he's planning a surprise of some kind, silly chap."

"A trip to New York?"

"Maybe. Who knows? I'm always happy to go shopping for a

new gown. Have you taken a good look at the duchess's Schiaparelli? Must have cost a fortune but she hasn't got the figure for it."

"It looks stunning. But she does seem awfully out of sorts tonight."

Tilly patted her own dark waves and trailed one curl artfully over her freshly powdered cheek. "What do you mean?"

"She looks"—Ella sought for the right word—". . . hungry." Wolfish, she thought, but didn't say.

Is that what I look like now? Hungry. Wolfish. Prowling after what I cannot have.

"Well, darling, that's hardly surprising, is it?" Tilly shrugged. "She's always wanting what she hasn't got."

Tilly was not a fan of the duchess and regarded as inexcusable her habit of issuing blatant reprimands to the duke in public.

"It's not easy for her," Ella pointed out.

Both Ella and Tilly were aware that it was whispered behind closed doors that the duke had a sexual problem, that he was premature when it came to the delights of the bedroom, and only with the duchess had this handicap been contained somewhat. How true the rumor was, Ella had no idea. But it would explain some things about the relationship—his total dependence on his wife, the neediness in his eyes whenever he looked at her, his unwillingness to renounce Wallis Simpson even for the throne of Britain. And it was common knowledge that Wallis had spent time in Shanghai, where—so the rumors went—she had learned certain sexual techniques, including the extraordinary Shanghai Grip.

All tosh, probably. But sometimes Ella was conscious of an unsteadiness about her as though she was wound too tight. Exactly as Ella felt now.

Reggie, take me home, take me home now.

Tilly looped her arm through Ella's and started to march her to the door. "Come along, my angel, I want to dance with His Royal Highness . . . and there's someone who wants to dance with you."

* * *

How could she dance with him and not devour him?

Wolfish. On the prowl. Teeth glistening with saliva.

Ella shut her mouth and kept a respectable distance between their bodies so that she could not reach out and take a bite. A sliver of decency remained to her and she clung to it so that he would have no inkling of the workings of her mind, of the slippery slope down which her thoughts were falling headfirst.

"So, Dan," she said in a voice that grated on her nerve ends, the tone of a colonial matron patronizing her pet servant, "I hear I am to lose you. What a shame."

Gray eyes. Streaked with the palest of blues. They stared at her as if she were a stranger he had never met before, one he didn't particularly like. "I have heard nothing about that, but I wouldn't be surprised. The station is very overworked right now."

Her hand lay lightly in his. No clinging. No sliding up his arm to touch the clean sharp edge of his jawbone.

"Because of the Morrell murder, I suppose," she said.

"Exactly."

And then they ran out of conversation. It just stopped. Something that in all their hours spent together in the car had never happened. She didn't look away at the other dancers or at the band swaying to the music on the stage, but stared at Dan Calder's face mutely, until he abruptly released his hold on her and stopped dancing in the middle of the floor. The crowd surged and swirled around them and the singer crooned, *"Don't go walking down lovers' lane with anyone else but me . . ."*

"This is no good," he said softly. She barely heard it above the music.

"No."

"Better to stop now."

He turned on his heel and walked away from her, wrenching

something out of her. How had this happened? How had she been reduced to this so fast that she didn't see it coming? How? She watched him swerve between tables and disappear through the exit doors.

"Ella? Are you all right?"

She had no idea who spoke. She started to move and then she was running, pushing through the doors and calling his name. When his arm seized her and pulled her into a dark corner behind the cloakroom, she knew it was wrong. When his hand caressed her face and the lean hard length of his body crushed against hers, she knew it was insane. That it was what cheap and nasty girls did behind their husbands' backs.

But her body was out of her control. It was doing things that shocked her—touching the warm full flesh of his mouth with her fingertips and pressing her thigh tight against his, until suddenly his lips were on hers, his tongue driving into her mouth.

*   *   *

"Reggie?"

"Mmm?"

"Are you awake?"

"I am now." His voice was thick with sleep.

"Reggie, we're all right, aren't we?"

"What do you mean?"

"I mean we're happy, aren't we?"

He rolled over in bed to face her, though in the darkness they were nothing more than vague shapes, featureless and anonymous.

"Of course we're happy," he said, but she could hear a ripple of alarm in his voice. "What's got into you?"

She ran a hand over his naked chest, feeling the familiar baby softness of the well-padded waist, coming to rest just short of the dense bush of hairs at his groin. "There is so much unhappiness out there, I could feel it tonight at the club, as if it was dripping from the ceiling, all those young lives at risk. I want us to be always happy. I want us to be always . . ." Her throat was so full of tears she couldn't finish the words.

"My own sweet Ella." He scooped an arm around her, drawing her close. "What's the matter?"

"Nothing."

He kissed her forehead. A gentle reassuring kiss that made her feel worse. She pulled his mouth to hers, desperate to have his stamp on her, his ownership marked plain for her to see, and he obliged. He lifted himself on top of her and carefully, considerately inserted himself inside her. She listened to his muted grunts, felt the warmth, inside and out, of his desire to please her and she told herself it was enough. She didn't need more.

When it was over, the dull restless ache between her legs was still there, unsatisfied and unforgiving. Reggie fell asleep with his face tucked in the crook of her neck, his breath warm and relentless on her breast. She lifted the sheet and pressed it down on her mouth to silence her cry.

*   *   *

"Emerald, I want you to prepare a picnic for me today, please," Ella said breezily.

Emerald looked up from her baking, floury hands flapping. "I'm busy. Bakin' a tart for Mr. Reggie. All them blueberries goin' to waste. Mr. Reggie likes a nice tart."

Ella was feeling self-conscious, which was unreasonable really. She'd let Dan kiss her last night, but that was all. What was a kiss? Nothing. A moment of fun. Over in a heartbeat. So now they could get on with their lives. It was absurd to contemplate otherwise. She was just going out for a lazy day away from the bustle of Nassau, somewhere quieter and cooler, where she could get her thoughts in order.

"What you want in this picnic of yours?"

"Just a few simple sandwiches and a flask of tea," Ella said, offhand because it really was an unimportant little jaunt. A picnic. "Oh, and maybe some cake for Detective Calder."

"Detective Calder goin' to drive you on this here picnic?"

"Yes, of course."

"There ain't no 'of course' about it. You want blueberry pie for Mr. Reggie or a picnic for you?" Emerald stood with her floury hands on her hips, her broad face all screwed up.

Ella smiled sweetly at her. "Oh, Emmie dear, you know I want both."

"Don't you *Emmie dear* me." She sniffed loudly. "You is just plain greedy, Miss Ella."

"Greedy?"

"Yep. You want what you cannot have."

Ella found a smile from some distant cupboard and stuck it on her face. "Just make the blasted picnic."

*   *   *

Dan Calder opened the door of the Rover for her with his usual exquisite politeness, last night's kiss safely in a locked drawer somewhere. He slid in beside her, his expression friendly and professional. He smelled nice in the confined space of the car, some kind of aftershave or hair oil, something with sandalwood in it. She tried to breathe deeply without letting it show.

"Where today?"

"Let's go inland," she suggested.

He slid the big vehicle into motion, and to keep her eyes from staring at his hands on the wheel, Ella turned her head and glanced out. They were driving past the front of the house. Emerald's face was at the dining room window, scowling fiercely. Her bosom was pressed like a giant white cushion against the glass, her heavy lips moving.

In her head Ella could hear the sound of her maid's words. "You is just plain greedy, Miss Ella."

Chapter 37

Flynn

Flynn wanted a drink, a real drink, though it was scarcely midafternoon by the old grandfather clock leaning against the wall. The office fan was efficient, ensuring that the warm air rippled over his skin. They had been welcomed, seated, and offered tea. Tea? In this heat? What was it with the British and tea? As though it ran in their veins or something.

"Or can I offer you something stronger, Mr. Hudson?" Harold Christie asked amiably.

"A beer would do."

Christie produced a beer. It was warm.

Flynn didn't take to this man. His smile was too sincere, his charm was too easy, his manner was too damn relaxed. Any more relaxed and the guy would be splayed out on his own floor with his face on his fancy Persian rug. And what made him think that Dodie was a fool?

Because that's how he was treating her. From the moment they walked into the room, Christie had her marked down as someone he could bamboozle, and she just sat there, reeling him in with her soft-spoken words and her sweet smile. That smile of hers. Flynn wanted to tell her to put it away, to roll it in a ball and tuck it out of sight in her pocket. It distracted him.

She had introduced him. "This is my friend Mr. Hudson."

Christie had accepted Flynn's presence because he had no choice, but that didn't mean he had to like it. His handshake was wary and the accompanying smile barely made it past the corners of his mouth.

Flynn had tried to dissuade her from this meeting. He didn't think it was a good idea, but she had insisted and he was learning that he was no good at saying no when she was saying yes. Not when her lips were brushing his lips and her fingers were twisting his hair as easily as she twisted his heart. Better that he was here on one of Christie's big comfortable chairs than that she came alone and had the land dealer thinking she was fair game. It was significant that just the mention of her name gained them admittance to this inner sanctum upstairs on Bay Street. Her fame marched before her among these guys of wealth and position in Bahamian society, and that scared Flynn. They all wanted to know what exactly was inside that pretty head of hers.

"Well, Miss Wyatt, what can I do for you?"

Dodie hadn't touched her cup. Flynn watched Christie observing her the way a magpie eyes a fledgling that has tumbled from a nest. Flynn exhaled a string of smoke across the desk.

"Thank you for seeing me, Mr. Christie," Dodie said, giving him a smile. "Your reputation in Nassau is well known and you are greatly respected. You took me by surprise when you turned up at the Arcadia the other day, but I've thought about what you said and you were right. We must all take care of the good name of the Bahamas."

Christie smiled, caught off guard. He hadn't expected that, but he recovered easily. "That's pleasing to hear, young lady." He drew hard on his cigarette. "I was sure you'd see it my way."

"I do indeed. That's why I think we can work together."

"Work together?"

"Yes. I've come to you—with my friend Mr. Hudson—to learn more."

"Learn more about what?"

"You know everything there is to know about land on New Providence Island." She shook the loose waves of her hair and they rippled like silk around her shoulders, catching the light, drawing

Christie's gaze. Flynn had an urge to prize his eyeballs out. "I thought," she continued, "you could tell us something about it."

"Something like what? Are you interested in buying land?" His green eyes brightened at even the faintest prospect of a sale. He turned to Flynn with expectation. "Or you, Mr. Hudson?"

"No," Flynn said firmly.

"Mr. Morrell mentioned," Dodie explained, "that he was here in Nassau to do a land deal. We thought you might know about it."

A pause. It vibrated in the room. Like beans in a tin. That loud.

Christie moved his stare to Flynn. "Mr. Hudson, what exactly is your role in this conversation?"

"My role is simple, Mr. Christie." Flynn stabbed his cigarette into an onyx ashtray.

"There has been a murder, Mr. Christie, as you are aware. I am a friend of Miss Wyatt's and it is my business to make certain she doesn't trip over any more dead bodies."

"In my office?"

Flynn gave an easy chuckle. "Most people have a skeleton or two rattling in their cupboards."

It could have sounded like a threat, a civilized one, but still a threat. He wanted Christie focused on him, not on Dodie. What the hell was she up to? Using herself as bait? She hadn't warned him.

"So," Flynn said, "we are on the hunt for something about the sale of land that might have caused Mr. Morrell's downfall."

"Really? Found anything?"

"Nothing definite."

"Have you mentioned this theory to the police?"

"Not yet."

"I know nothing about any deal."

Christie's eyes flicked to the somber portrait of King George VI in full regalia that hung on the wall, as though seeking reassurance that order and justice still prevailed. "But, Miss Wyatt"—he smiled, spreading his charm a little thicker—"I do think you're barking up the wrong tree here, my dear."

"What makes you say that?"

"I can understand your interest in Morrell, indeed I can. But it's time that you were aware of this fact: a black woman came to see me here two days after the murder. She wouldn't give her name, refused point-blank. But she told me about Mirabelle."

Dodie sat straight. "Who is Mirabelle?"

"She's a prostitute. A friend of the woman."

"What is her connection with Morrell?"

"What do you think?"

Flynn didn't allow a flicker of his anger to show. "What did this woman say?"

"Mirabelle came to her the night of the murder, covered in blood."

Dodie gasped.

"I'm sorry, Miss Wyatt, but Mirabelle told her that she had 'entertained' an American gentleman in an alleyway that night and he'd got rough. He'd been drinking. He carried a knife and threatened her with it. They struggled and"—Christie paused to make sure he had their full attention—"she ended up stabbing him."

Dodie's hand went to her mouth. Flynn gave her the faintest shake of his head.

Christie released a fog of smoke into the room. "Mirabelle apparently snatched his wallet and ran. The next morning she left the island, refusing to say where she was going."

"Are you telling us"—Flynn gave weight to each word—"that Morrell was killed by a prostitute who has since disappeared? And you were told this story by a woman you don't know who refused to give her name?"

"Yes, that's correct."

For the first time Christie looked uncomfortable, aware of the thinness of his tale.

"And you haven't informed the police?" Dodie asked.

"On the contrary. I have done so already."

"But why did she come to *you*?"

"Ah, Miss Wyatt, you have to remember that I am well known in this community. I have a reputation for helping Bahamians, though I say it myself. This woman is not the kind of person who would go to the police, but she needed to tell someone in authority—someone who cares about the people here—so she came to me." He spread his arms, as though to wrap them around all Bahamians.

Flynn rose to his feet, pushing back his chair. "It sounds plausible, Mr. Christie. It's a good story and a damned convenient one for everybody. It's true that Morrell carried a knife. It's true he hooked up with prostitutes sometimes." He exhaled a long hard gust and stared down at the man on the other side of the desk. "But you've got one thing wrong. Morrell would never get rough with a woman, not in a million years."

Dodie looked across at him, but there was a tightness to her face; she was holding something back.

"Thank you, Mr. Christie, for your time," she said.

They walked to the door and went through the shaking-hands ritual in a cursory manner. Just as they were leaving the office, Christie said in an unruffled tone, "Mr. Hudson, no man knows what another man fantasizes about when it comes to sex. Any man—or woman—can release his inner monster when there is no one else to see. Think about that."

The words hung in the corridor and Flynn wanted to put his fist through them. Dodie took his arm and steered him out of the building.

*   *   *

In the street, rain was striking the pavement and hissing under tires.

"You could be wrong," she said.

"Dodie, don't believe him."

"What if it's true? He has told the police."

They were standing under a billowing awning on Bay Street, cars hooting at each other on the crowded road, pedestrians darting between the traffic to escape the sudden downpour. The air felt damp and solid, swirling in off the ocean with sudden force. Flynn had an arm wound around Dodie's waist, holding her close.

"Listen to me, Dodie. Morrell was not that man."

She narrowed her eyes, cutting out all else but him. The shock of what Christie had told them still lingered on her face, but Flynn could see there was a desire in her to believe the land agent's words and it made him fear for her. It made him mute. She pressed her face against his neck and his nostrils caught the scent of her wet hair.

"Don't, Flynn," she whispered.

"Don't what?"

"Don't be fierce. Don't be silent. Not with me."

"Morrell was not that man," he said again. "He would not threaten a woman with a knife."

"Not even if he caught her trying to steal his wallet? Maybe that was the truth."

"And his fear of being bumped off if he went to the hospital? What about that? Where does it fit into this convenient story Christie has concocted for you and the police?"

She tilted her head back to look at him. "Morrell was a member of the mob. I know he carried a gun and I assume he used it. You say he wouldn't threaten a woman." She shook her head sadly. "But he was a killer."

Her words lay between them. She couldn't remove them. When a surrey plodded past, the horse gleaming like a seal in the rain, Flynn hailed it and bundled them both inside. They sat side by side, unspeaking, and the knowledge that Dodie regarded Morrell as a killer filled every inch of space under the small vehicle's canopy. Because if she thought that of Morrell, then she thought it of him too.

Flynn took her hand in his. It was cold. But she did not snatch it away.

＊　＊　＊

Dodie was tough. The way she walked upright, denying the pain the slightest outward sign of its grip on her body. In the tiny shack in Bain

Town Flynn eased her down on to the lumpy mattress, stripped off her dress, and massaged more of Mama Keel's ointment onto her back.

"Looking better?" she asked, facedown on the sheet.

"Much."

Her back looked as though someone had thrown an ill-mixed pot of paint over it, a wild canvas of blues and blacks and purples.

"Stop growling," Dodie murmured.

"Growling?"

"Yes. You sound like one of Mama Keel's stray dogs, all stiff legs and hackles raised."

Did he? He knew how to wear a blank mask, how to give nothing away by even the twitch of an eyelid. Often his life had depended on it. But with her he was transparent and it unnerved him. Yet in an odd way it gave him a sense of release. The freedom to let go of everything else and just love her. He lowered his head and kissed her shoulder. It tasted of strange herbs.

"You must rest now and let your back heal." He headed for the door.

"Where are you going?"

"To see a man."

"What man?"

"Dodie," he said calmly so that she wouldn't know what it cost him, "I want you to leave this island."

"No."

"Please, Dodie. I'm going to arrange a boat."

"No."

"It'll be safer."

"Safer for me. Not for you."

"You must go. I'll stay. I gave my word to find Johnnie Morrell's killer and I don't go back on my word."

"Neither do I, Flynn."

He knew she would never leave till this was over.

"Together," she told him. "We do this together. And then we leave."

* * *

The rain had stopped. The sky was a sullen gunmetal gray that robbed the dingy bar of what little light it possessed. But Flynn knew that the sun would put in an appearance in an hour or two. He was growing used to the rhythms here, to the heat and the brilliance of life on the island, very different from Chicago with its air so gray and so brittle it broke in his mouth.

Spencer was there in the bar waiting for him, his narrow face tense, a well-used glass of scotch in front of him. He had been curt on the phone when Flynn rang his office. Neither had mentioned Flynn's intrusion into his bedroom or his removal of Spencer's gun at knife point.

"What the hell are you still doing here?"

"Real nice to see you too, Spencer." Flynn grimaced as he sat down and signaled for a beer. "I told you before, I will leave when I'm ready, and not before. And until then, I could use some answers from you."

"Go to hell." Spencer stood up. "Or more to the point, go to Miami. I only came to deliver this message: Lansky wants to speak to you." He relished the threat implied in those words. Meyer Lansky too often did his speaking with a snub-nosed .38 Special.

Flynn took a long drag on his cigarette and knew Spencer was not going to walk away. The beer arrived and he clinked his glass against the abandoned whiskey tumbler.

"Happy days," he said.

He'd knocked back his beer and followed it with what was left of the scotch before Spencer put both his hands on the greasy table and leaned over it.

"What the fuck are you playing at, Hudson?"

"This isn't a game." Flynn tipped his chair back. "Don't for one minute think I'm playing. I intend to find whoever killed Morrell."

"Don't be a bloody fool. Forget Morrell. Get out of Nassau before . . ."

"Before what?"

"Before things get worse."

"Is that a threat?"

Spencer sat down. "Just stay away from me. I don't want scum like you anywhere near my house and don't even think of breathing the same air as my wife again."

Flynn recalled the dark-haired woman asleep in the bed and wondered how wised up she was on what her husband was up to with the mob. This was a guy who didn't like to get his nice clean cuffs dirty and sorted out his problems by using muscle like the two meatheads who had attacked Dodie. For that alone Spencer was lucky not to find his arms bending in the wrong directions, but right now Flynn needed this guy. He was the bridge. One foot in with the mob and one foot in the limey colonial camp in Nassau. So Flynn let his chair drop back to all four feet on the floor with a clatter that made Spencer jump back and his eyes widen warily.

"I went to see Harold Christie today," he said in a tone that implied more. "We chewed the fat awhile."

Spencer reacted by becoming very still. Not a muscle moved.

"He peddled me a story about a prostitute putting the knife in Morrell," Flynn informed him. "Know anything about that?"

"It's a rumor going around. It could be true."

"It could just as likely be true that one of your hoods did the job for you."

"No, Hudson, don't be a bloody idiot. Whether we like it or not, you and I work for the same side."

"Okay, Spencer, so tell me who is on the other side. Who is it who had something to gain from Morrell's death? You?"

"No."

"Sir Harry Oakes?"

"Christ alive, you are poking a stick into a snake pit if you go about saying that."

Flynn mentally sharpened his stick. "What's so special about this deal? Everyone knows Oakes owns half the island. So what the hell is it that is getting everyone so riled up about this . . . ?"

Spencer went for his glass and pushed it aside with annoyance when he found it empty. "Go back to Miami, Hudson. Keep your nose out of Lansky's business."

A shout came from across the bar where two black guys in dungarees were bickering over a game of cards and it drew Spencer's attention. He turned his head and in that unguarded moment Flynn saw the pulse in his neck below his jaw. It was racing like a cat out of hell. This man was scared. But of what? Of Oakes? Or Lansky? Or of something in his own shadow?

Flynn lit himself another cigarette and drew the smoke deep into his lungs to smother the questions he wanted to hurl on the table. Instead he asked only one. "What happened to the money on Morrell? The police are looking for a wallet."

The mention of the police got a reaction.

Spencer bared his bad teeth at Flynn. "How the fuck do I know what happened to the wallet? For all I know you pocketed it yourself."

Flynn flicked his cigarette to the floor and stamped on it. The other guys in the bar were keeping their eyes to themselves as they talked to each other in their deep voices and slipped a fold of ganja weed from one hand to another. They avoided the two white men in their midst as if they were invisible. Flynn reached across the table, seized the front of Spencer's sweaty shirt, and yanked him forward hard against the table.

"Last question, buddy. What's the name of the factory where the girl used to work?"

Spencer's narrow eyes doubled in size. His hand gripped Flynn's wrist, trying to release his shirt. But suddenly understanding hit him, and with a great whoop of breath, he started to laugh.

Chapter 38

Ella

As a picnic, it was a failure. As a moment of fracturing Ella's life, it was a resounding success.

So much so that she became convinced someone else had crawled under her skin when her head was turned. What else could explain the stranger she found inside her bones who did things and uttered words that would make any happily married woman blush?

Her hand slid into his waistband. "Let me touch you," she'd whispered in his ear.

Shameful, shameful things.

It had started well. Ella was happy and talkative, relaxing in the car with the windows down as Dan drove inland. There were only narrow dust-laden roads that wound like coral ribbons between the overhanging trees, empty except for an occasional donkey cart or a couple of women sashaying along in bright dresses with boxes of limes or melons perched on their heads. No habitations. Just the wild bush with its vivid green scrubland punctuated by dense coppices of pine trees and strong flamboyant palms of all shapes and sizes that fanned out their fronds against sapphire-blue skies.

It felt private. Away from all houses, far from the people of Nassau and their relentless wagging tongues. Was that what did it? Was that what gave her such a sense of freedom and release? Or was it Dan? The way he seemed unfettered. His elbow on the window ledge, the wind clutching at his hair. He must have been to the barber's early that morning because there were tiny snippets of hair on the white collar of his open-necked shirt and the skin behind his ear gleamed pink in the sunlight.

Today there seemed to be no barrier between them and he made her laugh when he sang back to a mockingbird that seemed to be serenading them. She liked to laugh with him. They sang all the words of "London Pride" together, his strong bass voice rolling alongside hers, and it felt good.

Dan knew the tracks and trails well, which ones he could squeeze a car down and which ones he couldn't. The bushland stretched out around them, dense and secretive, full of sounds and smells that were unfamiliar to Ella, as she had never ventured this deep before. It felt wild to her. Trees spread their heavy branches farther, bushes were speckled with red berries that glittered like jewels in the sun, and the undergrowth of ferns and prickly vegetation rustled with the sounds of small unseen animals.

"Are there snakes here?" Ella asked suddenly.

He laughed at her expression. "Yes, but no poisonous ones."

When finally he selected a shaded spot under a grove of pine trees to lay out their picnic rug and spread Emerald's array of fancy cakes and sandwiches around them, Ella felt as though she had a champagne bubble of happiness caught in her throat.

She couldn't eat. Not with that bubble lodged in her throat. She was frightened that if she did it would burst, so she just drank the wine and smoked one of Dan's cigarettes, warm from his pocket. But she watched him. Her eyes feasted on the relish with which he sank his teeth into Emerald's blueberry pie, the purple juice trickling onto his chin, and she was shocked by the strength of her desire to lick it off.

So she lay back on the rug, forcing her eyes to stare at the sky instead of at him, seeing the clouds start to roll in from the west, feeling the lightness in her limbs and the slow contented beat of her heart. When a black ball of mosquitoes chose to hover over her face, she couldn't even rouse herself to swat them away, but Dan's large hand swept back and forth, defeating them.

"You don't want them biting you," he said, smiling.

Was it her imagination or did he put an emphasis on "them"? As if she might want something else biting her. Or someone else. But a sudden sense of stepping too far over the line of what was decent made her close her eyes. Denying them the pleasure of gazing at him, at the way his hair sprang from his temples, at the large collarbones that edged into view above his shirt. She could sit a peach on his collarbones. Above all she denied her eyes their desire to watch his hands. To imagine what they could do.

"Are you asleep?"

She smiled and rolled her head languidly from side to side. "Not yet."

She heard his teeth bite into an apple. Quietly he started to tell her about his work. About the black women who slunk into the police station with swollen faces and cut lips on a Friday night, which was payday. Payday meant rum swilling. He told her about the lost dogs, the drunks, the petty thefts, the spats between neighbors, the traffic accidents, about the fair but disciplined attitude of his boss, Colonel Lindop, but at no time did he mention the murder. The large numbers of military personnel now on the island had brought an inevitable increase in his work, but he spoke about it with a sense of commitment that pleased her.

At one point he rested a hand on her leg, on her bare shin. Casually, as though he scarcely noticed. She made herself breathe quietly. And when he removed his hand to flick away another mosquito invasion, she kept her eyes firmly closed, so that he would not see what that did to her. That was why she didn't catch sight of the clouds turning gray or notice when the horizon flattened to a dull backdrop where the trees around her rose in black-edged silhouettes. When the rain hit, it was like pennies hurled at her face.

"Ella!" Dan shouted, and pulled her to her feet. "Run!"

Ella. He called her *Ella*. She started to laugh as she dashed through the rain.

He darted to the shelter of the nearest tree, dragging her with him, because the car stood fifty yards away up a track. But already they were soaked to the skin. Lightning forked through the sky, slashing it apart, and they huddled against the slick trunk, where Dan held her close, as if he feared the horizontal force of the rain would wash her away.

She wasn't sure which came first. Afterward she tried to remember but couldn't. Her fingers sliding between the buttons of his sodden shirt or his hand cradling the back of her head and drawing her to him. It didn't matter. His lips came down fiercely on hers, his breath hot on her wet face, and something streaked through her that felt like red-hot wires. Burning her flesh, scorching the soft skin of her thighs until the throbbing between them was relentless.

"Hush," he murmured, and kissed the rain off her eyelids. He ran his palm over her lips, reshaping them. "Hush," he said again, and only then did she realize she was hauling air in and out of her lungs with the sound of bellows, stoking the fire that was raging inside her. He stripped off her blouse and licked the rain off her nipples until she slid her hand inside his waistband and whispered, "Let me touch you."

She undid his button flies and touched him, held him, caressed him in ways she had never caressed Reggie. Dan peeled off their clothes until they were both naked in the stinging rain and he took her, standing up against the tree, her back raked by the bark as he thrust inside her. It wasn't gentle. She didn't want it gentle. It was a rough ravenous seizing of her body. He opened her up and filled all the cold and empty spaces inside her with a heat that burned right through her.

As he drove into her, her fingers tore at the hard muscles of his back, and when the final explosion of release came, she screamed. Screamed her heart out, startling a pair of pigeons from the shelter of their branch. Dan's head jerked back for a moment, alarmed, but when he saw her expression he laughed, a soft affectionate sound that she held on to.

Afterward they sat on the sodden earth, his back against the tree, Ella between his legs, her back against his chest. She could feel his lungs rise and fall, and she matched hers to his. He bent to kiss the nape of her neck and cradled her naked breast in his hand, protecting it from the rain. Time passed. She had no idea how much or how quickly. All that mattered was that she could feel his body against hers, sense the weight of his head resting against hers. She did not think of Reggie. Or Bradenham House. Or how she would live after this moment. Instead she continued the conversation about his work, as if it had not been interrupted.

"So Colonel Lindop has a lot of trouble on his hands at the moment."

"Yes. Everyone at the station is extremely busy."

"I bet you can't wait to get back there."

He didn't respond at first but his arm tightened around her. "There's work to be done on the murder case."

"What is happening about it? Has it been written off as a crime of social unrest?"

"We're investigating all possibilities."

He liked talking about his work. She could hear it in his voice.

"What does that mean?"

"It means we are looking at it as a possible robbery because his wallet is missing, unless the girl is lying about it and stole it herself. Or it could be a racial attack, or even the work of a panicked prostitute, it seems."

"What do you think?"

"I have a gut feeling that this involves far more than a small-time thief."

"Really. Why is that?"

"Because someone is trying to shut it down too quickly."

"Who do you think that someone is?"

She was sure he would say Sir Harry Oates, but she was wrong. His answer sent a shiver through her.

"Our governor," he said quietly, as though even out here in the green wilderness his words were only for her.

"The Duke of Windsor?"

"Yes."

"Why on earth do you think that?"

"He wants no trouble here. In case it reflects badly on his governorship."

"Well, you can see his point. Tidy the whole messy business away without much fuss. It's not as if Morrell was a Bahamian, so maybe it would be better to tuck it under a convenient carpet to stop bad publicity for the island."

His legs squeezed her tight between them and she knew she had annoyed him.

"We are policemen, Ella. Colonel Lindop has to face up to all sorts of unpleasant political pressures, but first and foremost he is a policeman. He wants to see the law enforced and justice done."

She stroked the wet curls on his thigh to soothe him. "That's good to know."

She meant it. She didn't want the Reggies of this world to win with their distorted logic and their bending of straight lines.

"What we need," Dan continued, "is to find out where Morrell spent that evening. What he did and who spoke to him. You've not heard anything, have you?"

"Me?" Ella fixed her eyes on a large black beetle that was scurrying through the layers of rotting leaf mold. Raindrops exploded like bombs on its black shiny back, knocking it off course, but it wouldn't give up. "No, of course not. Why should I?"

"Those parties you go to are a hotbed of rumors, aren't they?" He shrugged. "We've put out requests for information with Morrell's photograph in the press, but no one has come forward yet."

"Why do you think that is?"

He took her earlobe between his teeth and bit gently. "People are frightened to get involved."

"Is that what we are, Dan? Involved."

In answer he wrapped his fist in the wet strands of her hair and pulled her head backward, so that he could see her face. His own was flushed, his brows drawn down over his gray eyes as he studied her features intently.

"Ella, I am involved." He shook his head, spraying water, and brought his face down to hers. "Are you?"

"Yes."

His mouth closed on her lips and trailed down her throat, his hand still tight in her hair. And then Ella did something she never thought she would ever do to a man. She begged. Her hand slid between their bodies to nestle at his groin among the dense hairs, and as her fingers found him hard and hot, she begged, "Please, Dan, please." As the words tumbled out of her mouth she was disgusted with herself, but still they kept coming. "Please, please, please."

This time he set her on all fours, her knees sinking into the sodden soil, the rain drumming on her back, and he entered her from behind. Like a bitch. A dirty bitch, Reggie would say. Her husband would never dream of degrading a woman that way, but it didn't seem to her like degradation. Ella could feel Dan inside her, deep and demanding, and suddenly she never wanted to be parted from this moment. Because nothing that was waiting for her in the future could ever come close to this. This overwhelming sense of being alive.

*   *   *

Ella thought Dan would drive her straight home but he didn't.

"You need to wash away the dirt and dry off before you let Emerald catch sight of you."

He smiled when he said it, his eyes lingering with amusement on her mud-streaked cheeks and hands. She had dragged on her wet clothes in the teeming rain but knew she looked a total wreck. She couldn't understand why she would be mortified if Reggie ever saw her looking so slovenly, yet didn't mind a scrap that Dan should gaze at her and laugh.

He drove her to his house. By the time they reached the city the clouds had finished venting their spleen. The rain had stopped and the sky brightened, so that when he parked outside his house the sun put in an appearance once more, and steam came rising from the bonnet of the car and drifting up from the pavements. A mangrove cuckoo flew overhead, flashing its long black-and-white tail with all the bravado of a pirate's flag. There was something so normal and reassuring about it all that it was hard to believe that what had taken place on the picnic was real. Yet Ella climbed out of the car in a hurry, followed at Dan's heel up the front path, and stepped into his house.

It was a narrow hallway with strongly masculine striped wallpaper and a staircase ahead that was covered in a red stair carpet. It took her completely by surprise, it was so vivid. It set the hallway on fire. The moment Dan closed the door behind them he took her in his arms and kissed her, then carried her upstairs to the bathroom, where he ran a bath and sponged her all over. He took his time, gently soaping and rinsing the dirt off each part of her.

"Wait here," he ordered, when he had dried her and wrapped her in his dressing gown. He went to hang her wet clothes in the sun.

Here. She was in his bedroom. More stylish than in her nocturnal imaginings. She moved slowly around it while he was gone, tracking her fingertips along the walnut dressing table and his ivory clothes brush, peering into his wardrobe at the neat and orderly row of shirts and suits. She leaned into its musky darkness and breathed in the smell of him in there. By the time Dan returned to the bedroom she had brushed her hair with his hairbrush, lit a cigarette from the pack in his bedside drawer, inhaled the scent of his pillow, and perched herself cross-legged in the middle of his single bed. It was more years than she cared to remember since she had been in a single bed. It felt small and intimate. Her heart was kicking in anticipation. The inside of her mouth felt dry and prickly.

But when he entered the room, something was different. She could see the change in him the moment she looked up at his tall figure. He had his policeman face on. His mouth had lost the looseness that she loved when he was looking at her, and had taken on a determined firmness that was unfamiliar. This is how he must be at the police station but she didn't want him to be like that with her. Not here. Not now.

"Ella," he said, refraining from sitting on the bed, "will you tell me what you know about Sir Harry Oakes?"

"Dan"—she lowered her lashes—"do you have your police handcuffs nearby?"

Chapter 39

Dodie

"I have to go back to work tomorrow," Dodie announced.

"Too soon."

"If I stay away any longer I'll lose my job."

Flynn skimmed a shell into the surf and watched a wave devour it. They were waiting till dark on a beach and their gaze followed the delicate sandpipers bobbing along the shoreline like ingenious clockwork toys. A warship was steaming out of the harbor with young men bound for battle, its gray menace looming over the peaceful scene, changing the mood on the beach. The war seemed to permeate everything. But out to sea a fishing boat was chugging eastward to the wharf, a cloud of seagulls pursuing it with shrill cries, and a pleasure boat sliced through the waves, showing off its speed with a carefree ease that made Dodie wonder how anyone could live like that. Carefree. Weightless. Racing with the wind. It was a life she could only guess at.

"Dodie, stay here." Flynn's bare foot touched hers in the sand. "I'm asking you. Please, stay here. I'll come back for you. I'll always come back for you."

She leaned her body against his and felt his muscles respond the way they always did when she touched him, with small vibrations. As if she created an electric shock within him, one he had no power to control. They were seated on the sand, Flynn's arm around her, forcing her to rest rather than swim. She was content to sit here with him, waiting for darkness to fall and watching the vast blue canvas of the sky turn vermilion and bleed into the sea, so that it looked as if a thousand men had died in it.

"I can't, Flynn."

"You will be no good to me."

She smiled and leaned her cheek on his shoulder. "You'll have to put up with that."

"Stay here."

"Only if you do."

He turned suddenly and cradled her face between his hands. "Goddammit, Dodie, I have to go."

"Then goddammit, Flynn, so do I."

*　　*　　*

"This is the one."

Dodie didn't ask how Flynn knew. The hairs on her neck rose as he took from his pocket what looked like a set of small metal spikes and inserted first one and then another in the lock. She heard a click. Her tongue was so dry it stuck to her teeth.

The building was pitch dark. They had approached it from the direction of the wharf, where the wind rattled the masts of the boats at anchor, covering the sound of their footsteps. Bay Street was too well lit to risk entering through the front door and there were restaurants where laughter spilled out into the night from the open windows, too much chance of being seen.

So they had made their way along the parallel road that skirted the dockside and ducked down one of the numerous alleyways that connected it to Bay Street. Somewhere behind a shutter a piano was playing. Halfway up the alley Flynn had halted in front of a door set into a high wall. Dodie felt like a thief. Knew she looked like a thief. She was constantly casting glances over her shoulder in every direction. She couldn't stop herself, despite the fact that there was no moon yet and the darkness was as solid as a coal face.

The door opened into a small yard. Flynn headed straight across to a set of wooden stairs that Dodie couldn't see until she cracked her shin on them, and she knew then that he'd been here before. Of course. This was his world. Stealth. Darkness. Sliding spikes into doors. Knowing what lay around each corner. She touched his hand and immediately felt steadier. He led her in silence up to the next story, where he performed his magic on another locked door and suddenly they were inside the building. It smelled of floor polish. She hadn't noticed that when they were here before, but now her senses were heightened. She could taste the blackness, see the threads of the night.

"Dodie," Flynn said in a whisper, "stay close."

She didn't need telling. They crossed the reception area, where desks and old-fashioned armchairs loomed at them out of the blackness, and Flynn guided her with an unerring sense of direction to an office door that was locked. Dodie heard a jangle of the spikes once more, a click, and a faint grunt of satisfaction from Flynn.

They were in.

*   *   *

Dodie went through the desk drawers. She had no scruples about doing so and that shocked her. She was beginning to understand how effortless it could be to step into a world where right and wrong were just empty words with no meaning and no relevance. What she was doing was illegal and yet she carried right on doing it. As she lifted Harold Christie's desk diary from his drawer, she was horrified by the brazenness of the act, but it didn't stop her laying it out flat in front of her and sifting through its pages to the day of Morrell's murder.

Light from the streetlamps on Bay Street flounced into the office, sliced into slats of mustard yellow by the jalousie blinds, just enough for Dodie to read the black scrawl: *9 a.m. Tennis with Duke. 12:30 lunch Yacht Club.* The afternoon was taken up with meetings with three different banks but his evening sounded more entertaining: *8 p.m. Cinema—In Which We Serve.* Dodie felt a kick of frustration. She'd hoped for more.

"Anything?" Flynn asked in an undertone.

"Not yet."

He was standing in front of the portrait of George VI. He seemed more of a stranger to her in these shadowy surroundings, focused on the job he was here to do. He was running fingers around the frame of the picture.

"It could be wired," he had explained earlier.

It was why they were here.

"Did you see Christie's eyes?" he'd asked as soon as Christie had ushered them out of his office. "He couldn't keep them off your king." He chuckled at her baffled expression. "He's either a crazy royalist or"—he'd touched her chin to reassure her—". . . or he has something hidden behind that fancy picture."

Now he carefully lifted it down to the floor. He was right. Behind it was a safe set in the wall. He worked fast and in total silence. He put his ear to the safe and with infinite patience commenced turning the dial, listening intently for the tumblers. Dodie didn't move, didn't breathe, didn't turn a page. But she listened hard. A sudden beam of light in the room made her jump. It came from the headlamps of a late-night car on Bay Street and swept over Flynn, but he didn't flinch.

Ten minutes. That's all, by the luminous clock on the desk. It felt like ten hours. Dodie's teeth hurt, she'd clenched them so tight. She knew when the click came by the sudden release of tension in Flynn's body. He looked round at her, slats of light across his face, and grinned at her.

"Geronimo!"

He worked quickly. He swung open the safe door, for a split second shone a flashlight into its interior, and leaving three cash boxes behind, he scooped out a bundle of folders. He gave half to Dodie and they crouched on the floor away from the window, riffling through their contents by the light of the torch. Most proved to be contracts for the sale of private houses, a couple of factories, a hotel, change of ownership on an inherited orchard.

"Nothing," Dodie hissed.

"Patience."

It was right at the bottom. A contract for the sale of a large tract of land and shoreline called Portman Cay at the western end of New Providence Island. They scoured through its legal terminology, extracted the map which pinpointed its position, and hunted out the names of the vendor and purchaser. A Mr. Michael Ryan and Mr. Alan Leggaty.

"Do you know the names?" he whispered.

Dodie shook her head. "New to me. To you too?"

He nodded, glanced one last time at the map, and flicked off his flashlight. The sudden darkness felt threatening. Dodie quickly put the folders back in order and had just turned to ask Flynn whether there were any more of them in the safe when an abrupt noise made her freeze. Fear sucked the air out of her. It was the door.

Flynn's hand touched her shoulder. "Don't move."

He was across the room and flattened against the wall behind the locked door, invisible in the darkness, though one of his shoes was cut in half by a stray slat of light. The noise came again. It was the rattle of a doorknob, a man's tuneless whistle, and then again, yet another doorknob. A shuffle of feet. Then silence.

"The night watchman," Flynn breathed.

Checking the offices. Clearly not a man to pocket his earnings and laze the night away on a bench under a tree with a pack of Woodbines, this one was conscientious. For another five minutes neither moved. Eventually the whistle vanished and reappeared below them in the street, as the man took his time ambling off to the next building.

"He'll be back," Flynn murmured, his voice urgent. "Time to go."

Together they replaced the files exactly as they'd found them, and while Flynn relocked the safe Dodie returned the diary to its drawer. They left the room in a hurry, locked it once more, and were halfway across the unlit area that was the reception hall for Harold Christie's land agency company, when a rough voice shouted at them from the far corner, "Stop where you are. Put your hands up. Don't move."

Dodie's heart shot into her throat. "No," she whispered. To Flynn more than to the hidden stranger. "Don't do *anything*."

"Are you hungry?" the voice demanded.

Relief tore through Dodie and she seized Flynn's arm. "It's a parrot. Christie keeps a bloody parrot in here."

Flynn gave a laugh. A brief burst of exhilarating sound before he silenced it. Dodie loved him for it.

*   *   *

The smell of wood fires still drifted on the night air in Bain Town, reminding Dodie that she was hungry. Somewhere the staccato bark of a dog pricked the silence of her small hut, and she could hear the murmur of deep male voices. They were swapping late-night stories on their front stoops and drowning the day's troubles in home-brewed beer. It was comforting, that sound. It reminded her of nights lying awake after her mother died and listening to her father and his friends drinking in the next room and arguing over what Prime Minister MacDonald should be doing to sort out the mess left by the Wall Street crash.

She was waiting for Flynn to return. She didn't know where he had gone but could tell by the way he'd set his shoulders and moved on light feet that he was preparing himself for something. She asked what for, but in reply he kissed her mouth and made her lie down so that he could massage her back once more with Mama Keel's ointment. She didn't tell him how much it hurt because she wanted his hands on her. She was happy to trade a little pain for that, and loved the way while he was doing it he teased her about turning into a cat burglar, a shadow's shadow, he called her.

"Nerves of steel," he'd said with respect.

He'd left his jacket behind and she put it on, sliding her arms into its sleeves, rubbing her cheek against its collar like a cat. She prowled the tiny hut, worrying, sliding her hands into his pockets and finding them empty except for a tin containing three of his hand-rolled cigarettes. She smoked them. She made deals with God. *Please let him come back to me unharmed in the next ten minutes and I will never again be a shadow's shadow.* She promised.

But minutes ticked past. She couldn't hold them back.

Let him come back to me in the next half hour and I will tell the police about the gold coins. I will make a fool of myself.

But the minutes became hours.

Let him come back to me. Please. I will give You Morrell's gun hidden in my safe box underground at the beach. I will give You my job. I will give You my father's Bible. Please.

Please.

*   *   *

Flynn slid back into the house, silent as a thought. He stripped off his clothes, the skin on his flanks gleaming white in the faint veil of moonlight that drifted through the window. He crossed to the mattress that lay in darkness and Dodie saw his head whip around when he found she wasn't there.

"Where have you been?"

His eyes struggled to find her in the blackest corner where she was sitting.

"Dodie." She heard him inhale with relief.

"Where have you been?"

He came toward her voice and knelt down in front of her, but something in her voice told him not to touch her.

"Dodie, don't ask me, please. It is better for you not to know." His voice sounded bone-tired.

"It is not better for me not to know."

"It is safer. Believe me, it is—"

"No, Flynn. I'm not going to believe you. I am already in danger just because I nursed Morrell. So don't tell me that."

She saw the dark shadow of his head shake back and forth.

"Listen to me, Dodie. I would never forgive myself if anything happened to you because I—"

"Enough! Enough! I can't go on not knowing. I can't sit alone here night after night not knowing where you are and fearing I will find you in a filthy alleyway with a knife in your guts." She steadied her voice and asked again, "Where have you been?"

The darkness in her corner was hot and airless. Flynn exhaled a hard breath, and after a long silence he drew her face to him, holding it against his cheek.

"I'll tell you," he said.

✳   ✳   ✳

He brewed them one of Mama Keel's herbal teas. It calmed them. Dodie remained in her dark corner, but Flynn lit a candle and examined her face with an intensity that left her nowhere to hide. She was wearing the blue dress, her hair loose and uncombed, her eyes fiercer than she meant them to be, and the world shrank to no more than the circle of light from the candle. It threw pools of color into the shadowy fringes of the tiny room, deep purples and rich magentas that crawled closer each time the candle flickered. They were seated on the floor, face-to-face, Dodie's knees drawn up under her chin as if they knew she would need protection from his words. Flynn was wrapped in the sheet.

"I went to see Sir Harry Oates," he said bluntly.

She felt a layer of sweat spiral to the surface of her skin, but she said nothing.

"I go often. Usually around midnight." His mahogany eyes were gentle. "Aren't you going to ask me why?"

Still she said nothing.

He gave a small sigh. "It's because I work for him."

Outside, a tree branch groaned and cracked. Or was it inside herself? She could no longer tell.

"What do you do?" she asked.

"You're smart, Dodie, too smart. You were bound to figure out that something else is going on. Everything I told you before is the truth, but because I love you, I left some parts out."

I love you. His words moved in the room, rustling around her.

"Explain to me exactly what it is you do for Sir Harry Oakes."

"After I quit Chicago, I ended up with Johnnie Morrell in Niagara Falls. That's where Oakes was living. He was a multimillionaire by then because of the Lake Shores Gold Mine near Kirkland Lake." A smile tilted Flynn's mouth. "Oakes discovered it in 1912 and he was a generous guy with his bounty. The Niagara Falls community struck it rich."

"How did you get involved?"

"Like I said before, Oakes and Morrell were prospecting buddies from way back and so—through Morrell—I ended up working for Oakes."

"Doing what?"

"Anything and everything. Prohibition had only just been knocked on the head. I was only sixteen but Oakes took a shine to me. He said I had guts and persistence, two things he sets high store by. The Canadian government was taxing him into a fury— milking him for eighty-five percent tax—so he shifted himself and his family to the Bahamas, where there is almost no tax. He's no fool."

Flynn rose to his feet, fetched a cigarette, and lit it, but he only took one drag and instantly stubbed it out. He took a prowl around the room before sitting down again in front of Dodie. She hadn't moved.

"You've got to remember, Dodie, that it's all about money with men like Oakes. It's what they eat and breathe, it's their life. He's real clever, you know. He went to medical school before he took himself off prospecting in the Klondike."

"Medical school?" Dodie couldn't imagine Sir Harry as a doctor. He'd scare his patients to death. She put out a hand and touched Flynn's sheet-swaddled knee. "What then?"

"The mob got after him, always on his back."

"Why?"

"They aim to set up casinos here and Oakes won't have any of it."

"I thought gambling was against Bahamian law."

"Darn right it is. But laws can be changed, if the right people decide to change them."

She could hear a bitterness in his voice. "And you?" she asked softly. "What happened to you?"

"Oakes put me back to work with the Chicago Mafia and Capone." He wiped a hand across his forehead as though dragging away the memory of it from his mind. "I was a kid. Too young and too stupid. Did I want to please and impress Harry Oakes, one of the richest men on the planet? You bet I did. So I became his eyes and ears within the mob. I report to him. Through me Oakes knows what's going on and this way he keeps one step ahead of them."

She bridged the gap between them by resting both hands on his knees. "What happened tonight?"

The light from the candle flickered across his tense face. "I asked him straight out if he'd arranged for thugs to kill Morrell on his way back into town. To get back his gold. He said no. We had a row. It wasn't pretty but no one rows with Oakes and finds it pretty."

"I'm sorry."

"He claimed he didn't have anything to do with Morrell's death. And he told me he doesn't own Portman Cay."

"So it has to be Christie."

"Morrell would have known."

Dodie edged forward and slipped her arms around Flynn's waist, drawing them together. "Why don't you leave the mob? Just abandon them."

He laughed and it was a harsh sound.

"You don't walk away from the mob, Dodie. If you do—or if they find out you have betrayed them—they come after you like a pack of hyenas and tear you limb from limb."

Dodie rested her cheek against his and found it ice cold. Everything had changed.

Chapter 40

Dodie

The day dawned gray and morose. Dodie and Flynn took one of the horse-drawn surreys out as far as Cable Beach past the golf club, and walked from there, enjoying the change in the air, the scents of faraway spices carried on the morning wind. Coral-pink tracks twisted away through the wild and wooded landscape, where lizards basked hopeful of sunshine on rocky slabs. Hummingbirds whirred and darted to the last late blossoms of the jacaranda trees, faster than ants to jam.

Dodie didn't talk much. Her mind was still caught up in the night before. But Flynn was determined to repair her mood and whistled with a cheerfulness that made her smile as they walked. He'd brought along a breakfast of fresh-baked rolls, goat's cheese, and mango, and they sat eating it on the gleaming white sands of Portman Cay. The gray sea blurred into the sky and its surface shifted like sheets of polished steel. It looked threatening. As though it wanted to play rough.

"A storm tonight," Dodie commented.

He took a bite of cheese. "You love this island," he said. "You know its moods and its colors."

The remark caught Dodie by surprise. It was true but she hadn't realized he understood quite how much the island meant to her.

"We could leave," she said quietly.

"Leave the island?"

"Yes."

"I thought we agreed we owed it to Johnnie Morrell to find his killer."

"That was before."

He didn't ask before what? They both knew she meant before she learned about the mob. He folded an arm around her shoulders and they sat in silence, gazing out at the relentless roll of the waves. She was utterly aware of every part of his body next to hers. The bone of his ankle where he'd rolled his trousers back. The muscle of his shoulder. The clean scent of him. And she knew she would give up this island that she loved for him if it would save him. But most of all she wanted to charge over to Sir Harry Oakes and tear his eyes out for what he'd done to Flynn, for the way he'd used him. But she didn't tell Flynn that. She let it lie unspoken.

When she lifted her head, she caught him regarding her with a warm smile.

"Why did you leave England, Dodie? You've told me nothing of your past."

She thought twice about raking it over. It was behind her. She wanted it to stay there.

"Beats me," he said, "why anyone would want to leave England. With men like your Mr. Churchill running the place."

She tilted her head back to rest on his arm.

"It's a short story. My father was a kind man but the fighting in the trenches in the Great War destroyed him. He took to the bottle." Two small words—"the bottle"—that hold so much power. "My mother died. In an influenza epidemic when I was nine and that was the end of him. And of me. Things got a whole lot worse. He couldn't work for long periods and I scratched around for odd jobs." The surf was playing tag with the sandpipers and for a long time Dodie didn't speak, while Flynn kept his arm around her.

"Anyway," she said with a shake of her head, "we came out here eventually to start a new life but he hated it. Hated himself.

Three times he tried to kill himself. He would drive us to a beach, kiss me good-bye, and set off to swim back to England."

"England! That's one hell of a swim."

"Three times he came back. But the fourth time he didn't. The next day his body was washed up further down the coast."

Flynn lifted his fingers to her lips, as if to wipe away the sting of her words. "I'm sorry, Dodie. You had it tough."

"Everyone has it tough." She rose to her feet. "Come on, let's walk."

They fell into step together, soft-footed along the beach. It was a long horseshoe cay with a dense fringe of palms and pines, and a slope down to the water with a patchwork of rock pools at one end where crabs congregated like churchgoers.

"What is it," Dodie asked, looking around her, "about this Portman Cay beach that makes somebody want it so much? It is nothing special. No different from all the other beaches."

Flynn glanced along the sand thoughtfully and then back to her. "Tell me about your sewing. You're good at it, I know."

"Oh, that was at the factory." The word "factory" tasted sour on her tongue. "I was a dress designer."

"Really?"

She laughed at him. "Doll's dresses. There were thirty of us. The dolls used to arrive in huge cardboard boxes, a gross at a time, all pink and shiny and crying out for clothes. I must have sewn thousands of tiny dresses, before they were exported back to America. I enjoyed that work. It was . . ." She stopped abruptly, frowning at him. "How do you know I'm good at it?"

"I saw your quilt."

"In my hut?"

"Yes."

"When?"

"When I spoke to Morrell. I went into your hut to see him when you ran off to Mama Keel's."

Dodie stared. "I had no idea."

"He told me how grateful he was to you. Asked me to keep you safe."

Her mind suddenly filled with images of Morrell. Of his big bearlike hands and the mulberry stain on his shirtfront. Of the toughness that he wore like a second skin and yet the southern courtesy in his voice when he addressed her. So absorbed was she in these images that when a bullet slammed into the sand at her feet, she didn't even realize what was happening until she heard the crack of the rifle a split second later.

"What the . . . ?"

She stared at the spot stupidly, her brain refusing to acknowledge that she was being shot at. But Flynn seized her arm and had her racing for the cover of the trees, zigzagging as they went. The sand was soft. The slope was steep. Her feet slid and stumbled. Her back jarred and it sounded as though there was a buzz saw inside her head, so she couldn't hear what Flynn was shouting, though she could see his mouth moving.

Flynn drew her into the trees. Jinking and darting. Dodging patches of sunlight, heads low, feet leaping over the sprawling undergrowth. A bullet thudded into a palm off to their left, splintering the bark, and the crack of it sent a flock of finches scrambling into the sky. Flynn yanked her behind a thick trunk, still gripping her arm hard.

"Go," he ordered. "Keep running. I'll hold him here. Go!"

She was shaking. *Calm down.* She had never been shot at before and wasn't prepared for her body's reaction.

"No," she said.

"Go!"

She focused her gaze on his face. It was composed and intent. His voice urgent, but no trace of panic. No sign of the terror in her own chest. Whatever he was feeling was under control. When another bullet whistled through the branches above their heads, Flynn didn't even flinch, and her respect for him grew.

"No," she said again.

In Flynn's other hand was a gun. She stared at it, trying to make sense of how it got there. Black and blunt-nosed. Where had it suddenly come from? She clamped both her hands around its muzzle and held on tight.

"No, Flynn," she hissed. "Put it away."

"I'll stop him."

"You'll get us killed."

"In case you haven't noticed, that's exactly what the guy is trying to do right now."

They talked fast. "Listen, Flynn. You've forgotten how an innocent person would behave. We should talk to him, not shoot."

"Which would you prefer to be? Innocent and dead? Or guilty and alive?"

For answer, she turned her head to one side and shouted, "You out there with the rifle, what are you doing? We're just here for a walk. Nothing more. There's no reason to shoot at us."

"You're trespassing." His voice was big and rolled through the trees like a bulldozer.

Flynn opened his mouth to respond but Dodie flattened her palm over it.

"I'm sorry," she shouted out to the trees. "We didn't know it was private. We meant no harm. No reason to shoot at us."

"Show yourselves."

"How do I know you won't shoot us?"

"If I wanted to shoot you, you'd be dead by now, missy. I was just warning you to clear off."

There was a rustle of bushes and the harsh alarm cry of a parrot.

"He's circling us," Flynn whispered.

"Stay here."

She stepped out into a bright patch of sunlight that had fallen through the canopy of trees. She listened hard but heard nothing more, and before she could open her mouth to shout again, Flynn was at her side, his body shielding hers. The gun had vanished.

"You see?" Dodie shouted to the man.

Flynn said nothing but held out empty hands.

A figure stepped into view from behind a pine tree, a heavily built man of mixed race with curly hair greased back from his face, and a dark shirt and tie. His hands were great knots of muscle wrapped around the rifle, the tip of its barrel aimed purposefully at Flynn's chest.

"What you doing here?" he demanded.

"I told you," Dodie answered. "Just walking."

"It's a long way to walk."

"We like getting away from everybody to quiet places."

The man laughed, a dirty raucous sound that in other circumstances would have fanned a blush to Dodie's cheeks. "I bet you do."

Flynn smiled amiably. "Know any other quiet places that don't have guards?"

"You want to go down to the south coast, man, where it's real quiet. Plenty places down there and no one to bother you. Just you and the mangroves and the mosquitoes." He chuckled to himself.

"So why shoot at us?"

The man dropped the smile. "I got my orders."

"What's here that needs guarding?"

"Nothing. Just sand and scrub. But it belongs to someone and that someone don't want nobody trespassing on it."

"Who owns it?"

The rifle, which had been drifting downward, jerked abruptly back to Flynn's chest. "Man, you ask too many questions."

"We're curious," Dodie said. "Wouldn't you be if you'd been shot at? Scared us half to death, you did."

The man scrutinized them in silence for a moment, trying to decide what to do next, and then he waved the rifle in the direction of the road.

"Go on, beat it." He scowled at them, as though suddenly remembering how a guard was supposed to behave. "And don't let me see you round here again or next time I'll put a bullet in you."

Dodie could feel Flynn beside her, eager to get his hands on the man and extract every last scrap of information out of him. But it was unlikely that he knew anything at all about the people who paid his wages and in the process someone would get hurt. She couldn't bear it to be Flynn.

"We're going," she said quickly, took a grip on Flynn's wrist, and marched him away.

Chapter 41

Ella

"You'll be hot in that blouse."

Ella glanced up. She was seated at her dressing table and in its large oval mirror the elegant bedroom was reflected with its pale bird's-eye maple modern furniture and its soft feminine colors. All of which she had chosen. All of which were tasteful. But for the first time they struck her as grossly pallid. She felt a gut-deep yearning for bold stripes and vivid colors.

Is that what Reggie thinks but never says?

He was lying in bed, hands behind his head, hair tousled, regarding her in the mirror with curious eyes.

"You're up early," he commented.

"I was restless. Couldn't sleep."

"I noticed. Why is that?"

"Oh, I don't know." She gave a light laugh and shrugged her shoulders. "The time of the month, fretting over the children at the hospital or when to get my hair cut and what to wear tonight. You know, the usual things."

He smiled at her, an indulgent contented smile that normally would have pleased her but today felt like a sliver of glass in her skin.

"You should wear something else. You'll be too hot."

She looked at her reflection in the mirror, at the blouse she was wearing. Purchased at Macy's in New York, a subtle shade of eau de nile that flattered her skin, with long sleeves buttoned tight at her wrists.

"You're probably right."

She picked up her silver-backed hairbrush and was just lifting it to her head when her husband said, "Sir Harry has invited us over for lunch today."

Her hand froze. She looked round at him sharply. "Both of us?"

"Yes."

"Oh, Reggie, I can't make it, I'm afraid. I'm working with Tilly at the clinic." She was speaking too fast. *Slow down.*

He pulled a face. "He won't like it. He made a point of asking for you to be there. I think he likes you . . . and who can blame him?"

"I don't think he does." She turned back to the mirror and brushed the nighttime knots out of her hair with hard punishing strokes, forcing her long blond waves to behave themselves. "I'm sorry, Reggie."

"That's all right, my dear. Another time will do. At least you'll be able to drive yourself today, now that Detective Calder has been recalled to normal duties."

The brush didn't stop despite the fact that her fingers had become numb.

"You'll like that, won't you, Ella? To have him out from under your feet."

"Yes."

The word felt as dead as a stone in her mouth.

* * *

Ella hung up the telephone in the ward sister's small office in the hospital. She looked at her hand. It was no longer shaking. She was back in control, but it frightened her how easily she had lost it. She had dialed the police station.

"I wish to speak to Detective Calder, please."

"Who's calling?"

"Mrs. Sanford. It's urgent."

"One moment, please."

A click. A silence. Then his voice.

"Good morning, Mrs. Sanford."

She hated what it did to her. That something melted inside her. That muscles she had no control of clenched with need.

"Good morning, Detective. I wish to speak to you. About the Morrell case."

She was acutely aware that a telephonist could be listening.

"Can you come into the station?"

"I would prefer not to."

"I am busy all day but I could see you this evening."

"No, this evening is not suitable."

She heard him shuffling papers. Imagined his hands flicking through a diary.

"I can see you at two o'clock, Mrs. Sanford, if that is convenient."

"Thank you."

"Good day to you, Mrs. Sanford."

He hung up. Neither had mentioned where they would meet. They didn't need to. Slowly, as if the telephone receiver would shatter and destroy the arrangement if handled roughly, she replaced it and a current of happiness rippled through her. That's all it took. She looked at her hands. Rock steady.

The door opened and Tilly breezed in. "Have you seen this place?" She was smiling broadly in her Red Cross uniform as she peered over a gigantic bundle of freshly laundered toweling nappies that were clutched in her arms. "My darling, it is positively swarming with Yanks out there. They've come over from the airfield, pockets bulging with sweets for the kids. And"—her grin widened—"delicious nylon stockings galore for the rest of us." She dumped the haphazard pile of nappies on the desk and flashed a pack at Ella. "You'd better go and claim your American booty before it all disappears. You know what gannets nurses are when . . ." She broke off abruptly and stared at Ella. "Are you okay?"

"Yes, of course."

"You look"—Tilly pursed her crimson lips, trying to pinpoint what it was about her friend that had caught her attention—"different."

"Really?"

"Definitely."

How could it show? So fast. As if love changed the structure of your face.

"I've just been gardening too much. Caught the sun."

Tilly prided herself on her bone-white complexion and scowled at Ella. "You'll turn into a pickaninny if you're not more careful."

"I'll be careful."

Very careful.

Ella walked over to the nappies and started folding them into neat white squares. With studied casualness she asked, "How's Hector?"

"Oh, don't ask. He's being a frightful bore today. He planned to go sailing this morning but has the most beastly headache, so is stuck doing paperwork at the office instead, which makes him so grouchy he could spit."

Ella couldn't imagine Hector grouchy. "Has he heard anything more about that ghastly murder case?"

"The stabbing?" Tilly shuddered. "Not much. He did mention last night that he thinks they will arrest the girl. Apparently she has a reputation for trouble. Some little trollop on the make, I expect. Overstepped the mark this time, though."

"What? Surely not. I thought they were laying it at the door of black workers taking their spite out on the white colonials."

"It seems they've dropped that idea. Hector thinks it's for the best."

"As a lawyer, he should know."

"Oh heavens, no." Tilly gave a hoot of laughter. "Hector's only really interested in boats. Anyway, my darling, I must dash." She started to pat her dark waves and primp her fringe. "I'm off to the docks."

"Not another parade."

"The very same."

"Tilly, you are a glutton for punishment."

Tilly took out her compact and powdered her nose. "It's the least I can do for our boys. New recruits this time."

"Poor chaps. Give them a wave from me."

Raw recruits would be disembarking from a troop ship and parading in front of the Duke of Windsor as governor of the Bahamas. But Ella wasn't fooled. She knew that the real reason Tilly went to all the parades was to have the chance to see His Royal Highness in action in full dress uniform. She'd once confessed to Ella it gave her goose bumps each time. Ella couldn't understand it herself. But who was she of all people to lay down rules?

"Go on." She smiled. "Go and . . ."

At that moment the Duchess of Windsor walked in, brisk as ever in her movements, her central hair parting straight and precise.

"Good morning, ladies."

"Good morning, Your Highness," Tilly responded, but excused herself quickly, closing the door behind her. She had a habit of doing that.

The duchess's strong-boned face took on a crease of irritation, but she shook it off and turned to Ella with a smile.

"Ella, my dear girl, you're looking mighty happy about something."

Ella reacted with an expression of innocence. "I heard today that little Gussie will be going home to his mother next week. It's wonderful news for him."

"He's the polio boy you've been doing all the exercises with, isn't he?"

"That's right."

The duchess nodded, fitted a cigarette into her ebony holder, and drew in a lungful of smoke before tipping her head back slightly, as though wanting a better view as she regarded Ella through narrow eyes.

"I'm not a fool, Ella. The one thing I'm good at is people."

Ella returned to folding the pile of nappies.

But the duchess was not a woman to be sidetracked. "You don't shine like someone has stuck a lightbulb inside you just because some kid you're fond of is going to get out of this antiseptic cage."

Ella stopped folding.

The duchess laughed, an amused affectionate sound. "There's only one thing that does that. And we both know what it is, don't we, Mrs. Sanford."

Mrs. Sanford. A reminder.

"Don't," Ella murmured. "Don't spoil it."

"We are all in this colonial cage together, myself included." Her thin neck tightened, tendons suddenly showing the strain. "We all like to be let out now and again. To see what freedom tastes like." She waved her cigarette through the air, as though indicating the way out of the cage, but suddenly paused, strode across to Ella's side, and took hold of her arm. For a small woman she had large hands and a man's grip.

"What's this?"

Ella glanced down at the marks pecking out beneath her own sleeve, at the raw scrapes across the pale skin of her wrist. "It's nothing. I scratched it while winding wire around a fence post for my hens."

The duchess nodded as if she knew exactly what made such marks, but she passed no comment and moved away to sit down on the desk, smoking hard. "I regard everyone in the Bahamas as my business, Ella, and I want the best for each of them. But don't worry." Her angular face seemed to grow older, her eyes sadder, and there was a loneliness inside them that suddenly spilled over into the room. "We each have a right to choose our own life. I wouldn't dream of denying you yours."

"Thank you. You can be certain I won't ever disgrace Reggie."

The duchess smiled softly. "Any more than I would disgrace the duke."

For a long moment their eyes remained fixed on each other, then the duchess headed for the door, her pin-thin shoulders tense as she stepped out to greet the hospital troops.

Chapter 42

Dodie

Dodie had not realized. What it means to be in love.

She hadn't realized that it is like a beach when the tide comes in. What before was still and static, motionless while the world tramped over it, is suddenly full of movement. That's what it felt like. Everything in motion within her, a swirling, tumbling, trembling motion.

She hadn't realized. It would be like this.

Her skin prickled and smarted, burning one moment, freezing the next. Her eyes were permanently wide open as if they couldn't get enough of the world, yet at times her eyelashes felt so heavy they could crush her. Her eyes gained a brilliance, her hands a softness. And inside she felt strong.

She hadn't realized. That love makes you strong.

So when Flynn slid out of her bed just before midnight in a raging storm, she didn't put her hand out. Didn't hold him back, didn't pin him to her mattress. She didn't even open her eyes or break the rhythm of her night breathing or ask for one last kiss. One last kiss. That was her fear. That he would not come back. But she let him go without adding even a feather's weight to whatever burden he was carrying on his back, and all the time she could feel the strong steady beat of his heart inside her own.

*   *   *

He didn't return. Hour after hour, Dodie willed Flynn to burst through the door, wet and windblown, battered by the violence of the storm, but in one piece. She imagined herself peeling off his drenched clothes, stretching him out on her bed, and toweling his body dry. Warming it with hers.

The rain beat down like hammers hell-bent on destroying the roof, which leaked in so many places that Dodie had to keep moving the mattress. For long periods she stood in front of the door in darkness, gripping it fiercely, listening to the wind as it howled outside, threatening to wrench it off its hinges. But she was ready to throw the door open the moment his hand touched it.

Just before dawn he came. Except he wasn't the same Flynn Hudson who had made love to her earlier that night with such wildness of spirit. The Flynn Hudson who returned was damaged. He staggered through the door straight into her arms, clinging to her while the wind sought to tear him apart. She slammed and bolted the door, sat him on the mattress, and lit a candle that leaped and guttered in the damp air but cast enough light on Flynn.

"I'm all right," he said. His voice was thick.

"You're not."

"Just sit with me."

She sat and wrapped her arms around him. He was drenched and the side of his head was bleeding, but she just held him close, her cheek pressed against his wet one. She could hear the sounds of him—his breath coming fast, his teeth clenched hard, the crack opening up somewhere deep in his chest.

*   *   *

"What happened?"

"Sir Harry Oakes is dead."

Shock made Dodie's fingers falter. She was bathing the wound on his head, a gash that was spilling blood faster than she could stem it, and she had removed his clothes. He was draped in the sheet and staring at the door, but not for a moment did she think he was seeing it.

"Tell me," she said. When she touched the wound he seemed not to notice.

"I went to Westbourne House to speak with Oakes. I hung around in the grounds as usual, waiting for him to appear down the outside stairs around midnight, and when he didn't come I figured it was because of the storm." Flynn rubbed a hand across his eyes. "After a while I searched the grounds of the estate. Just past the swimming pool I found him."

Dodie sat still. "Was he dead?"

"Dead as a mackerel."

"Are you certain?"

He turned to her, his eyes glassy. "I've seen my fill of dead bodies, Dodie. I found his flashlight lying on the grass, switched off. I checked him over. Just four small-caliber bullet holes in the side of his head. Probably a Colt .22. Someone got real close to him."

The words ran out. He dropped his head into his hands and a tremor passed through him. Dodie realized that Oakes had become a father figure to Flynn, watching over him, using him, needing him, to the point where he had replaced his true father. And now Flynn had lost both fathers to gunshots. She rested her shoulder against his, letting her warmth flow into him, and could not stop herself hating Oakes. Hating what he'd done to Flynn. She was glad he was dead. She embedded her fingers in Flynn's wet hair and felt like a traitor for wishing Flynn would be glad too.

* * *

The blow had come out of the night, Flynn told her. It lifted him off his feet as he was standing up from crouching at Oakes's side. He'd woken to find his head in pieces and that he'd lost four hours, as well as his gun. Worse, he was stranded on the far side of the island. Somehow—aided by a farmer's horse and cart going to market—he got himself back to Westbourne House before dawn. Nothing had changed. Except for one thing. Oakes was gone. No trace, no blood, the grass sodden from the storm. The windows in the house were dark as boot polish. He scouted the grounds. No sound. No movement. Finally he stumbled back to Bain Town.

"Here, drink this."

Dodie placed an enamel mug of scalding tea in Flynn's hands and propped him up on the mattress against the wall. The place felt damp and unhealthy but he didn't seem to care. She offered to move him to his own room in town, which would be more comfortable and certainly drier, but he declined with the faintest shake of his head. She'd dosed him with Mama Keel's herbs, but after that he would suffer no more fuss.

"What now?" she asked softly.

His eyes were half closed, thin gleams of light in the shadows. "Now," he told her, "all hell will break loose."

*   *   *

By nine o'clock that morning Bain Town was humming with the news. Dodie could hear them outside, the women calling across the street to each other, the men muttering in low voices over their smokes, all aware of what it meant. There was a sense of despair that slunk up and down the road, of genuine mourning that was accompanied by white handkerchiefs and soft rhythmic crooning of hymns in the street.

Dodie left the hut. Inside, Flynn slept at last, thanks to Mama Keel's infusions, but it was a sleep that was restless and spiked with bad dreams. She didn't like to abandon him, even for a few minutes, but she picked up the enamel jug and headed for the communal water tap farther up the street. Overhead, slate-gray clouds were the scrappy remnants of the night's storm and the road was strewn with palm fronds embedded in the mud.

Dodie offered a greeting to the black faces gathered around the tap. Their expressions were solemn, one was crying.

"Good morning."

"Nothin' good about it, child," responded a white-haired woman with earlobes that were stretched by round wooden reels. "Nothin' at all."

"Why, what has happened?"

"You ain't heard?"

"Girl, it's movin' like a summer bushfire. They be tryin' to keep a lid on it, but the good Lord knows we gotta be told too."

"God bless the poor man's soul."

"Amen to that."

Another hymn broke out and the white-haired woman dabbed at her eyes. "May his kind, generous soul rest in everlasting peace and salvation in the bosom of our Lord."

Dodie took her turn at the tap with her jug. "Whose soul?" she asked. "Who has died?"

"Sir Harry Oakes. Ain't you heard?"

Dodie shook her head.

A woman with braided hair and a child on each hip uttered a loud ululation of sorrow. "Sweet Jesus preserve us. These islands are goin' to suffer real bad without the kindness of Sir Harry, bless his soul. You white folk don't know how much he did for us."

"It's not just us," another, gentler voice offered. "My Jake swears the whole of the Bahamas will suffer now, you white folks as well, because it needs Sir Harry's millions to keep everythin' turnin' sweet as honey."

Dodie set down her jug. "What happened? How did he die?"

All the voices started up at once. Eyes rolled, hands slapped at broad bosoms until they quivered, tears slid down cheeks, in an outpouring of grief that made Dodie feel heartless in comparison. None of these women knew personally the man whose death they were sorrowing over and yet they cared for him as if he were one of their own. Dodie could not imagine the white community of

Nassau caring half so much. Or blessing his soul with even a fraction of the fervor.

"What happened?" she asked again.

"He was burned alive in his bed."

"What?"

"No." It was a male voice. It belonged to a tall man with a square head and an eye for the pretty woman with braided hair. He waited until he had everyone's attention. "Don't go spreading bad rumors, Josie. Sir Harry was bludgeoned to death."

"I heard he was shot," a skinny girl chewing gum piped up.

"Then you heard wrong. Take my word for it. But whatever happened, the killer will be found." He flashed perfect teeth at the bevy of women. "If not"—he looked speculatively at Dodie— "heads will roll. I am a policeman, so I know how these things work."

Dodie squeezed out a smile of thanks. Her unsteady hands gathered up the jug of water to her chest, but how she made her feet walk slowly back to the hut without spilling a drop, she'd never know.

                    *   *   *

The one thing the Bahamas was good at was rumors. By midday they had spread like wildfire: Sir Harry was murdered in his own bed, he was shot, he was battered to death, he was beheaded, he was drowned in his bath. He fell into a bonfire and burned all the skin off him. His house was set on fire. A masked killer slit his throat and drank his blood. He shot himself.

Dodie heard them all and shuddered.

"That's a ritual killin', that is."

That was the opinion of the driver of the surrey that Dodie and Flynn were taking into town. Flynn was pale and quiet, but at that he lifted his head.

"A ritual?"

"Yep, no doubt about it, man. Feathers and blood all over him,

I heard. For sure I'm tellin' you, it's *obeah*. That's what you white folk call voodoo." He glanced quickly behind him, the whites of his eyes showing, and clipped the tired old horse with the reins to urge her on.

"It's powerful, you can be sure of that," he added. "You don't mess with that stuff, man."

Dodie put a hand in Flynn's.

"Goddammit, Dodie, let's hope he's right. Because anything else is worse. Far worse."

*   *   *

Dodie felt it the moment she walked into the house where Flynn had his lodgings, a kind of low-pitched buzzing. As though a fly were caught in the net curtain, frantic to free its wings. She had no idea where the sound was coming from. Only when she climbed the shabby stairs and the noise moved with her did it dawn on her that it might be inside her own head. Yet she could hear it clearly, as distinctly as she could hear their footsteps on the boards. It felt like a warning.

Flynn unlocked the door to his room and checked the bed, the cupboard, the window, the walls, even behind the door. Only then did he allow her to enter. Oddly the buzzing grew worse inside and Dodie looked intently at Flynn to see if he was hearing it too, but his face had shut down. He appeared to be far away. The smell of cooked fish was seeping up from downstairs and the plink-plonk music of a steel drum jangled farther down the street, but Flynn paid them no attention. There was a change in him. Dodie could see it, but didn't know what it meant. His movements were sharper, his body on edge, a quickness in the turn of his head. Yet his mouth was slack, as if it had received a blow.

"Flynn, sit down. Sit with me." She perched on the edge of the bed, but instead of sitting, he knelt on the floor in front of her and she could see the gash on his head oozing blood. She had the sense not to mention it.

"Be ready," he told her, "for the world to crash down on this place like a ton of bricks. You and I got to be smart enough not to get caught under them."

She frowned. "Why would the world bother with us?"

"Because whoever did this will be looking for scapegoats and we're both in the firing line."

Her heart kicked against her ribs. "I know the police have got my name on their suspect murderer list because I found Morrell, but why you?"

"This is Sir Harry Oakes we're talking about. This murder will bring every damn newshound in the business down on our necks from all over the globe. Sniffing out every secret on the island, including ours, you can bet your sweet life on it."

"Don't scare me."

For the first time he smiled. "I want to scare you, Dodie, my love. I want you to be so scared you'll leave."

"No." She seized his chin and shook it. "Not without you."

"Listen to me, Dodie. Oakes's death changes everything." He stood up, lifting her to her feet. "If it was the mob who got to him because he wouldn't play ball—wouldn't put pressure on the governor to change the gambling laws—then there's every chance they'll come after me too, if they've found out I was working for Oakes. We just don't know what's going on. That's why I have to go out on the street and pick up the rumors real fast."

"Who else?"

"Who else might have murdered him?"

"Yes."

"Someone who needs land that Oakes was unwilling to sell." He shrugged. "I'm guessing, Dodie, but it kind of figures."

"So, Christie?"

"Who knows? It's a possibility, sure."

"You have to get out of here, Flynn. Please. It's too dangerous now." She was astonished that her voice could be so calm when everything in her was falling to pieces. "Quickly."

She could see the mobsters coming for him with their slick double-breasted suits, their guns and shark smiles.

"Quickly," she urged again.

He pulled a soft bag from under the bed. "We go together," he declared, and started pushing things into the bag.

She felt a bolt of excitement and he laughed at her expression, his head twisted around to look at her, his eyes bright with amusement. Or was it love? She didn't know. But that was how she remembered him afterward, that was the image she carried in her head of him. His hair falling across his forehead as he bent over the bag. His lips curved in a bold smile that told her clearly that he had made his choice. He would not be going to the police with information about what he stumbled over last night at Westbourne House.

The front door downstairs slammed.

Dimly Dodie recalled hearing a car's engine in the quiet street. The moment froze, dragged its feet in the dust, then sprinted ahead of her, so fast that she felt left behind. Flynn reacted with lightning speed, as heavy footsteps crashed up the stairs, so that by the time the knock rattled the door on its hinges, he was holding a gun in his hand. He had pushed Dodie down in a far corner and was waiting behind the door, flattened against the wall.

"Who's there?" he snapped.

Only then did it occur to Dodie to question the knock. Did mobsters knock? When they've come to murder you.

"Flynn," she whispered.

His eyes found hers and she knew in that second that he believed they were about to die. He lowered the gun and took two rapid strides toward her.

"Open up! This is the police."

* * *

The three policemen tore the room apart with the precise brutality of a child tearing the legs off a spider. They emptied drawers, inspected the backs of them, the underside, and stripped the bed, lifted the mattress. Their big fingers rummaged through the pockets of the clothes, over the top of the curtains, gouged into shaving soap, and unscrewed the metal balls on the corners of the bed. They peeled back the cracked linoleum on the floor and tested the boards underneath for hiding holes.

Dodie couldn't watch. She stood at the window beside Flynn, her arm against his, and stared out at the street, at a dog chewing on half a coconut and a woman rolling a barrel along the middle of the road. But all the time Dodie could feel tension in Flynn.

"It's okay," he said. "They won't find anything, because there's nothing here to find."

His gun was in his waistband under his shirt. But his eyes narrowed sharply when the black sergeant in charge of the search took out a knife and sliced open a row of rough stitches in the side of the mattress. He thrust his hand into the horsehair stuffing and smiled grimly. Dodie heard Flynn's intake of breath and turned in time to see the sergeant withdraw his hand. In it lay a tan leather wallet. It was streaked with dried blood. He flipped it open and read the name inside.

Dodie looked at Flynn and her only thought was to drag him through the open window. Run and never look back. At least that way he stood a chance. His face had drained of color and his hand gripped her wrist.

"Flynn Hudson, you are under arrest for the murder of—"

"Sergeant!" the excited voice of one of his officers interrupted him.

The sergeant's stolid face puckered with annoyance. "What is it?"

"Lookee here, sarge, at what I found."

He had extracted something from inside the hem of Flynn's jacket that was hanging on the back of the door. He opened his hand to show his boss. Gleaming on his black palm were four gold coins.

* * *

Dodie ran through the streets of Nassau. The pavements were crowded and people were gathering in huddles to talk and point at the strangers who were flying in on every plane from Miami, cameras around their necks and notepads in hand. An ebony-skinned woman selling sponges shouted out to one of the strangers, "He was one of us, Sir Harry was, God bless his soul. A God-fearing man. Don't you go writin' nothin' bad about him, you hear me now."

Dodie raced across Rawson Square and pushed her way through the doors of the police station. It was just the same as before. The same fan in the ceiling churning up the humid air, the same flies loitering with intent, the same row of chairs occupied by troubled faces, but this time Dodie was different. She didn't politely wait her turn. She hurried to the counter, where the young desk clerk was filling out a form for an elderly man reporting a lost dog.

"Excuse me," Dodie interrupted, "I need to see Detective Calder. It's urgent."

"I'm sorry, miss, but I'm just dealin' with this gentleman. If you would like to take a seat, I—"

"I would not like to take a seat. Didn't you hear me? It's urgent. I need to speak to him right now." Her knuckles came down on the counter. It sounded loud in the sudden silence of the room.

The young constable hesitated. He had the look of a new recruit, and glanced uneasily up the corridor to his right. "I'm sorry, miss, but Detective Calder is busy right now. If you would just wait a—"

"I can't wait. Don't you understand?"

The constable's natural urge to help had not yet been blunted by years on the beat. "Excuse me, sir," he said to the old man, "I'll just be a minute." He set off down the corridor. "Wait here," he told Dodie. He disappeared into Interview Room 3 and bobbed back out five seconds later. "He'll see you in a short while if you wait in the—"

Dodie strode straight past him and into Room 3. She expected to see the detective interrogating someone or maybe several policemen in discussion of Sir Harry Oakes's case. But what she found when she barged in without knocking was Detective Calder standing in the center of the room talking softly with a woman. She had her back to the door and his hand rested on her shoulder. The woman had thick blond hair and slender hips in a pleated fawn skirt. She turned quickly, stepping away from the detective, and looked directly at Dodie.

"Miss Wyatt!"

"Mrs. Sanford." Dodie nodded, but turned instantly to Detective Calder, who appeared to be embarrassed rather than annoyed at the interruption.

"Detective Calder, I need your help."

He seemed to gather himself, instantly more formal.

"What can I do for you, Miss Wyatt?"

"There's been a terrible mistake. Flynn Hudson has been arrested for murder but he's innocent. You must do something, you must make them understand that he had no idea the wallet was there, that someone else planted it in his mattress to incriminate him, you must . . ." Her voice was shaking. Her hands were shaking. "Flynn Hudson has been arrested for murder," she said more coherently. "It's a mistake. He's innocent."

I didn't do it, Dodie. Don't let them tell you I did. His last words to her as they hauled him away in handcuffs in the police car.

"Arrested for Morrell's murder?" Calder frowned.

"Yes, of course. Who else would it . . . ?" And then she realized. She shook her head sharply. "No, no . . ."

Ella Sanford stepped forward. "It's all right, Dodie, we'll sort this out. If your friend is innocent, I'm sure Detective Calder will clear up the mistake. Dan," she added in a low voice, "do you know about this arrest?"

"No. Trench has been handling the case while I was busy on other duties."

"Can you see if you can find out anything?"

For a moment Dodie thought he was going to refuse, but he glanced at Mrs. Sanford and seemed to change his mind.

"Very well. But everyone is in an almighty flap today. Colonel Lindop is in a storming temper. This Sir Harry business is . . ." He stopped himself, unwilling, she realized, to say more in front of her. He headed for the door.

"Thank you," Dodie said.

"And for God's sake, please get someone to bring her a cup of tea before she passes out," Mrs. Sanford called after him.

She sat Dodie down on one of the hard chairs. "You're white as a sheet," she murmured.

Dodie knew she should be grateful, but right now all she could feel was fear. She clasped the woman's hand. Not for comfort. But to make sure she listened.

"I need to know if he's here. If they brought Flynn Hudson to the police station or if he's in jail." She heard her voice struggling, but reminded herself not to frighten this woman away. She needed her. "Please, Mrs. Sanford, they will listen to you. They will give you answers."

The hand in hers did not try to escape. The blue eyes were full of concern.

"Do you care for this Flynn Hudson so much?" Ella Sanford asked in a quiet voice. "So much that his arrest means you can scarcely speak."

Dodie nodded and Mrs. Sanford's face softened, then she shook her head and exclaimed, "For heaven's sake, where's that blasted tea?"

A young black constable scuttled in with a tray and treated them to a respectful nod before scuttling out again. Dodie knew it wasn't for her. On her own she would not receive such treatment. She turned to the woman who was offering such generous help and warmth, and opened her mouth to say, *Thank you. You are kind and I am grateful, even if I don't look it because I can think of nothing but the danger Flynn is in.*

But before the words were formed in her mouth, Ella Sanford thrust a cup and saucer into her hand and asked, "So what is your Mr. Hudson's connection with Morrell?"

It nearly tumbled out. So nearly burst out of her in a torrent. The words ready to leap from her lips to the first person who thought to ask. It was only the memory of Flynn's face trapped behind the glass of the police-car window that stopped them.

"I don't know. But someone planted Morrell's missing wallet in Flynn's room." She sipped her tea to prevent any more words coming out.

"Really? Why would someone do that?"

Dodie was saved from another lie by the arrival of Detective Calder. One look at his face and her heart plummeted.

"All right, Miss Wyatt, this is the situation. Flynn Hudson is here. I've seen him and he is being interrogated at this moment."

Interrogated.

"So, he's not hurt?"

"Hurt? Of course he's not hurt. He's just being questioned. If he's innocent, I'm sure that will be established."

"When will I be able to see him?"

"Not for a while, I'm afraid."

"Why exactly did the arresting officers go to his place?" Ella Sanford asked. "What made them suspect him?"

Dodie expected Calder to refuse to answer such a question, but he didn't.

"They had a tip-off. A telephone call."

"From whom?"

"It was anonymous. Not usually the way we like to work but Sergeant Trench was short of leads, so he followed up this one." He glanced back at Dodie, his gaze shrewd as he inspected her.

"You will of course be questioned too, Miss Wyatt, as a witness to the finding of the wallet. And the coins."

"They're lying," she said firmly. "Whoever made that phone call is lying."

Ella Sanford suddenly swooped down on Dodie's teacup, removed it with distaste to the desk, and headed toward the door.

"Come along, Dodie. I know a good lawyer."

Chapter 43

Ella

Hector Latcham's office was designed to impress. Walnut-paneled walls and an antique leather-topped desk that could have doubled as a polo field it was so vast. But Ella could see it was wasted on Dodie. The girl had a knack of focusing totally on what was important and ignoring the periphery. Ella envied her that ability to see one thing at a time.

Hector was explaining the procedures to her, spelling out that after questioning, if the police charged Flynn, he would be unlikely to be granted bail because of the severity of the crime and would remain in custody till the first court hearing. Dodie was quick, asking questions, pushing for explanations, and Hector was gracious and courteous.

"It's no use just saying he is innocent, Miss Wyatt," he said sympathetically. "It has to be proven. And at the moment I'm afraid the evidence is very much against him."

"I understand that. But the wallet was hidden in his room by someone else." Dodie had become quiet and rational. "I know he didn't do it."

"Unfortunately, knowing it does not count as proof." Hector flicked a professional smile at Ella. "I have spoken to Detective Sergeant Trench on the telephone and I dispatched young Gordon Parfury down there to be present at the interviews." He nodded with pride at the mention of the young black member of his team. "Parfury is top notch, I assure you. You can rely on him."

"Thank you, Hector," Ella said. "I appreciate it."

Hector was every inch a lawyer. There was a smoothness and a solidity to him that was reassuring. His brown hair was combed neatly back from his face, which emphasized the impression of honesty and openness that his clients liked. He wasn't exactly good-looking, eyes and face too narrow for that, but he cultivated an aura of success that was attractive and he possessed the healthy complexion of a dedicated sailor.

"So when can I see Flynn?" the girl asked.

Hector came from behind his desk with the air of a man who would change places with her if he could. "Miss Wyatt," he said, taking both her hands between his own, "this Morrell murder is a terrible business, and the horror of a second murder of a great man like Sir Harry has thrown everyone into a state of shock. But I promise I will do everything I can to prove your friend's innocence if what you say is true. You can rely on me."

Dodie stared at his hands. Ella could see she wanted him to let go. "What happens if he is tried and found guilty?" Dodie asked.

It was a brutal question. They all knew the answer.

"I'm afraid he would suffer the death penalty. But my dear Miss Wyatt, if he's innocent I won't let that happen, rest assured."

Dodie remained silent and Ella tried to imagine what it must be like to have the person you love die.

*   *   *

"Dodie."

Ella had dropped Dodie on the pavement outside Flynn Hudson's lodgings and the girl ducked down to lean in the car's window.

"Yes?" The sun caught her hair and veins of fire glinted among its dark waves.

"Are you sure you don't want me to come in with you?"

"No, thank you." An attempt at a smile softened the stiffness of her face. "You'd frighten her."

Ella didn't argue. This was a poor district and she knew she didn't fit in. "Dodie, what do you know about the gold coins that were found inside his jacket?"

"Flynn didn't put them there." It was sharp. Defensive.

Ella had been startled when she heard Hector discuss the four gold coins found by the police. It was as though something darker walked into the room and squatted in the corner. It was hard not to keep looking at it.

"But, Dodie, they make a connection."

"A connection with Morrell, I know. Did you mention it to the police?" Her fingers were gripping hard on to the sill of the open car window. "About the coin he gave me for you?"

"No, I didn't. But the connection I mean is to Sir Harry Oakes. He was a gold collector, and the police will quickly establish that. And now Morrell and Sir Harry are both dead. One of the connections between them has to be Flynn Hudson." She leaned closer, aware of a faint pulse by the girl's eye. "Where was Flynn last night?"

The girl's face didn't alter but a flame of color flared up on one cheek as if she'd been slapped.

"He was with me all night," Dodie said.

"You'll have to lie better than that, my dear Dodie."

"What do you mean?"

"I mean that when the police get round to questioning you—and we both know they will—you will have to be a damn sight more convincing than that." She rested her fingertips on the back of the girl's hand on the sill. "Come now, Miss Wyatt." She imitated a policeman's deep voice. "Where did Mr. Hudson spend last night?"

Dodie hitched back her slender shoulders and looked Ella directly in the eyes. "He spent it with me."

"All night?"

She gave Ella a slight twitch of a smile as if recalling the hours of darkness in the hut. "He was in no hurry to leave," she said, and lowered her eyelashes with sudden shyness.

Ella smiled. "I am convinced."

Dodie looked at their hands together. "Thank you. You are kind," she murmured. "But why are you doing this?" There was a pause while a man ambled past with a bamboo cage full of crabs and a boy at his heels with a pole of fish heads. "Why are you helping me?"

"Perhaps I see something in you that's in myself."

Dodie studied her face. Ella expected her to ask what that something was, but she didn't. Instead Dodie said, "Whoever put the wallet in Flynn's mattress and the coins in his jacket must be the killer."

The word sounded harsh in the quiet backstreet. A gust of wind, left over from last night's storm, snatched at the girl's long hair to drag her away from the car but her grip on the warm metal remained firm.

"Mrs. Sanford . . ."

"Call me Ella."

"Ella, he didn't do it."

"Are you so certain?"

"Yes."

"Then I believe you. But be careful when you question these people about what went on in the house."

"I will, I promise." She paused. "Your detective friend will know more about Sir Harry's death."

It wasn't said as a question but Ella could hear the question implicit within it. She nodded. "That's true. I'll see what I can find out, if you like."

"Thank you."

Ella slipped the car into gear. Now she had a reason to see Dan again.

Chapter 44

Dodie

The man and the woman of the house with the purple door regarded Dodie with wary eyes. They were both black, both holding back anger behind a solid wall of silence. They had placed their chairs side by side in front of their kitchen stove and sat with arms folded. Dodie wanted to shake them out of their refusal to offer more than a single word at a time.

"Mr. Hudson has been using your upstairs room?"

"Yes."

"Do you have any other lodgers?"

"No."

"Does anyone else live here apart from you and Mr. Hudson?"

"No."

"Did the police question you?"

"Yes."

"What did you tell them?"

"Nothing."

"Did Mr. Hudson have any visitors while he was here?"

"Yes."

Dodie leaned forward in her chair. "Who?"

"You."

An impatient rush of air escaped from her lungs. "Anybody else?"

"No."

"Are you certain?"

"Yes."

"Could anyone have gone up to his room while you were out?"

"No."

"Do you lock the front door?"

"Yes."

It didn't sound like a lie, but it felt like one. Most Bahamians didn't lock their doors. She glanced around the small room. Pots and pans. A log basket. A photograph of a young black man in army uniform pinned to a cupboard door. Nothing to steal.

"May I take a look at Mr. Hudson's room, please?"

A hard stare. "No."

Dodie reached into her pocket, took a pound note from it, and laid it smoothly on the table. "May I take a look at Mr. Hudson's room, please?"

The man shrugged. The woman glared at him.

"Go ahead," he said. Two words. Dodie was making progress.

She took the stairs two at a time in case he changed his mind before she reached the top, and hurried into the room. It wasn't locked, but there was no need. Except for the bed, the chest of drawers, and the chair, it was empty. Clearly the police had taken possession of Flynn's belongings because the drawers were empty and the hook on the back of the door was bare. The mattress had gone too. Perhaps that's why the landlady was so ill-tempered— she couldn't let the room again until she had her mattress back. Dodie sat on the naked metal springs, her back aching, and carefully inspected every inch of the room, the walls and the floor, the ceiling and the window frame.

She looked at them through *his* eyes. Not through police eyes.

She noticed that the skirting board possessed scarcely any paint and in places was toppling forward drunkenly, releasing its hold on the wall. Dodie went down on her knees and pulled at a length that looked secure. As she expected, it didn't budge. She moved farther along and tugged at a loose piece that crumbled in her hand, so that a black hole opened up at the base of the wall. She inserted her arm and wriggled it along.

"Help me, Flynn."

The sound of a step on the stair drifted through the open doorway. Dodie yanked out her hand. Cobwebs wreathed it and a speckled spider sat motionless on her wrist, but her fingers were clutching a small canvas bag. Roughly she propped up the broken section of board, closed the door, and stood with her back jammed against it before she opened the drawstring neck of the bag.

"Flynn," she whispered, "talk to me."

Inside lay two items, which she removed one by one. First came a compact roll of American dollar bills. Dodie didn't stop to count them but pushed them into her pocket. The second item was folded small, but when she opened it up it proved to be a flimsy airmail envelope, its pale blue surface blank. Inside lay two sheets of airmail paper written on both sides. She looked at the signature at the bottom, a bold and aggressive scrawl—*Oakes*. His cold dead finger seemed to touch her neck. Quickly she began to read.

Flynn, you are the only one I trust. You may hate me, I don't know, you keep so much close to your chest, but you've always been straight with me.

Gold rots a man's soul. Not the man who owns the gold but the souls of those who watch and drool and yearn for the gold clippings from his fucking toenails. Don't ever get rich, Flynn. Everyone hates a rich man. Especially his sons. Many men have hated me and I have trampled on them, but I am putting these words down on paper so that you will know where to look. I can smell the danger coming closer, the way I could smell gold underwater.

Your mobster boss, Meyer Lansky, is prime suspect. He hates my guts. For all I know, you will be the one carrying the gun when my time comes. Is that why you came here with Morrell? But I have a hunch that you would put a bullet in Lansky's brain before mine. Correct me if I'm wrong, Flynn, but I'm good at hunches.

On this island I have two friends who would like to dance a fucking jig on my grave. One is Harold Christie. A great guy. Really, I mean it. A rich man, but one who is still hungry for more and more gold. His guts gnaw at him when he sees my ugly mug and thinks about how much more I have than he has. Now he wants to do things to this island that I am blocking. I will destroy him if I have to.

My second golfing friend who would crow on my grave—like the rooster he isn't—is the duke. Our sad little governor. Don't miss his slyness. His title means nothing. He has water in his weak veins instead of royal-blue blood. He would blow over in the wind if it weren't for his wife. But he is hungry. For gold. For power. For love. Like a snake he slides unseen toward the nest. I have every goddamned thing he lacks and I will NOT let him destroy MY island. But he possesses powerful friends, so beware that man.

Don't fail me, Flynn. Kill the man who murders me. Take what you can of mine and leave. But before you go, avenge me. Avenge me, Flynn. What a team we would have made.

Oakes

"You!"

The voice came from the other side of the door, the handle was rattling.

"Out!"

Dodie was trying to imagine the emotions that drove Flynn to conceal this letter from prying eyes rather than destroy it. What does it do to you to have a man like Oakes say, *What a team we would have made?* No wonder he kept it rather than burn it.

"Lady!" The handle rattled. "What you doin'?"

Dodie stepped away from the door and it swung open with a bang, rebounding off the wall. The landlord barged in, his eyes swiveling around the room, hunting for what mischief she had been up to. He was wearing loud checked trousers and a dusky orange shirt, his limbs as restless as a boxer in the ring.

"What's goin' on here?" he growled.

"That's what I want to know," she said, hissing it quietly in his face. "I want you to tell me how that wallet got into Mr. Hudson's mattress."

"That no-good Mr. Hudson put it there hisself, lady."

Dodie's fingers slid to the tight roll of dollars in her pocket. "Whatever they're paying you," she told him, "I'll pay you more."

*   *   *

The police questioned her. Of course they did, Ella was right about that. They hauled her into the police station and politely but firmly put her through her paces, but this time she was ready for them.

"Where did Mr. Hudson spend last night?"

"With me."

"All night?"

"Yes." She lowered her eyes in a good imitation of embarrassment. "He was with me all night. Until six o'clock this morning."

"Are you sure he didn't sneak off while you were asleep?"

She touched her throat and watched their gaze follow her hand. She covered one cheek with her palm, awkward and uncomfortable.

"I'm sure. I'd have known immediately." Scarcely more than a whisper. "It's a very narrow bed."

It was the big detective, Calder, asking the questions. She made herself look straight back at him so that he wouldn't think she was lying or avoiding his sharp inspection, but how do you look at a man who hurled you to the earth and pinned you there? How do you look at him and not spit in his face?

The questions went round and round in circles until her tongue started to stumble and her words wouldn't come out straight anymore.

"How did you meet Hudson, Miss Wyatt?"

"What do you know about him?"

"Why did he find a house for you after the fire?"

"Was he looking for somewhere to hide?"

"Did he ever talk of Sir Harry Oakes?"

"Did you know about the gold coins?"

"Has he ever mentioned Morrell?"

Then back to the beginning. All over again.

"How did you meet Hudson?"

"Do you know he carries a gun?"

A young officer sat beside Calder taking notes and wearing a pin-sharp suit that shouted his ambitions and made Calder's look as though he'd slept in it. But it was Calder whose questions felt like sticks poked into her flesh. She kept the lies to a minimum. Stay with the truth, as near as possible. Remember each lie. But her mind was splintering. The room grew hot and his eyes felt like pokers. He offered no water, no respite, no time to regroup her thoughts.

"Hudson said that you know more about Morrell than you are telling us," Calder said suddenly.

She froze. Flynn wouldn't. He couldn't.

"He told us that he believes you stitched the wallet into his mattress. You were the only one, he said, who had the opportunity."

She banged the flat of her hand on the table. "You are lying to me."

Calder didn't flinch. His gray eyes were steady on hers and he sighed dispiritedly, which was worse than the lie.

It had to be a lie. Had to be.

"Please, Detective Calder, may I visit him now in his cell?"

Slowly he shook his head and in a brief flash she saw him again with Ella Sanford, when she caught them together, his broad hand claiming her shoulder.

"No, Miss Wyatt, not yet."

"When?"

"When I say so. For the moment he sees nobody but his lawyer."

Dodie lowered her face into her hands. Flynn was alone in a police cell, unable to help himself. His lockpicks and gun stripped from him, along with his stubborn pride in his own strength. He had nothing now. Except what was in his head. In his heart. In the intricate depths of him. Staring legal execution in the face for a crime he didn't commit. What did that do to you? A single sob escaped her lips, but when she heard the detective push back his chair she lifted her head warily.

Hold on, Flynn. Hold on to me.

Calder was standing at her side, a tall presence right next to her, but his eyes had changed. They were the silvery-gray eyes she had seen in Ella Sanford's kitchen, a real person's eyes instead of the ones that seemed to be standard issue to policemen along with their uniforms.

"Go home now, Miss Wyatt." His tone matched his eyes. "I will let you know when you can visit Mr. Hudson."

She turned her head away from him and stared at a poster on the wall. It had a picture of an airman with the words KEEP US FLYING. BUY WAR BONDS.

"The landlord is lying," she stated. He had refused her offer of money point-blank but she had seen the fear in his eyes. He had been threatened. "Question him again."

"You should not be talking to witnesses."

"If I don't, who will?"

"It's our job to do so," the young officer said pompously. "Leave it to the police. You don't know what you're doing."

"No, I don't." Dodie swung round to him. "But at least I'm doing something, which is more than—"

"Miss Wyatt," Detective Calder interrupted, "you are free to go."

Without a word, she rose to her feet and left.

Chapter 45

Ella

"You're not eating. I'm worried about you, my dear."

Ella looked up from pushing food around her plate. It was a mushroom omelet, one of her favorite dishes. It was something Emerald always cooked for her when she thought Ella was ill. Immediately her fork froze midpush. How long had she been not eating?

"Oh, Reggie, don't be silly. I'm fine. Just not peckish, that's all."

"You didn't eat anything yesterday either." His gaze lingered on her cheekbones. "Not sickening, are you, old thing?"

"No, of course not. No appetite, that's all."

That wasn't strictly true. Now that she thought about it, she was ravenous. But she couldn't bring herself to put food in her mouth because . . . Abruptly she put down her fork and sipped her glass of water. A shiver ran up her spine. She was punishing herself, that's why she wasn't eating, she was punishing herself for being so shameful. So sinful. So disloyal. There were other words for it. Depraved, immoral, scandalous. She felt color creep into her cheeks at the images in her head of the things she had done.

Her hands fastened to the brass bedstead. Flat on her back on the crisp white sheet, Dan's face between her legs, his tongue hot, making her hips buck. Her lips open in a groan that rose to a shriek as she cried out for more. Her whole body shaking with need for him.

"You're looking flushed, Ella. Are you sure you don't have a temperature?"

"No, Reggie, honestly, I'm perfectly well. Just shaken by this terrible tragedy. Poor Eleanor."

Eleanor was the Australian widow of Sir Harry Oakes, half his age when he married her, and at the moment she was still at their house in Maine.

"She's flying in with Nancy." Nancy was the Oakeses' eighteen-year-old daughter, married to Freddie de Marigny.

Ella tried to reach deep within herself to imagine what Eleanor was feeling. She conjured up a picture of Reggie with a bullet wound in his head, a small trickle of blood dripping down on to his clean white collar, and to her horror she started to cry. Instantly Reggie was out of his chair and at her side, just as Emerald sailed into the room with a tray of coffee.

"My dearest," Reggie crooned, wrapping his arms around Ella, "don't cry." He kissed her hair. "Go to bed and rest. You are generous-hearted to a fault and have taken too much on yourself."

"Mr. Reggie is right, Miss Ella. You gone all queer. I'll make you some broth and bring it to you in bed."

Gently but firmly Ella extricated herself from her husband's embrace. "Thank you both, but no. I'll have that coffee, Emerald."

"Are you sure?"

"Yes, Reggie. Now sit down and tell me what is going on. The duke is bound to be out of his mind with concern. You must be inundated with work and worry. Forget about my silliness." She smiled at him reassuringly and watched him resume his seat, but she felt guilty that she had not noticed earlier the slump of his shoulders and the lines of tension that had crept on to his usually smooth skin while she had been looking elsewhere.

"Freddie de Marigny has been arrested."

"What?"

"For the murder of his father-in-law."

"I don't believe it."

"It's true."

"Freddie may be a bit of a wastrel but he's no murderer. Surely Colonel Lindop knows better than—"

"The duke has removed the case from Lindop's hands."

Ella's jaw dropped open. "He what?"

Reggie ran a tired hand across his forehead. "The duke has taken complete control of the investigation himself. He tried to enforce press censorship but was too late, the news of Sir Harry's murder was already out. So he has flown in two American detectives from the Miami Police Department to deal with the case, a Captain Melchen and a Captain Barker."

"Why in heaven's name would he do that?"

"He says that our local police lack the necessary expertise to investigate such a crime. Normally detectives would come over from London's Scotland Yard in a case like this but"—he sighed discreetly—"it's impossible for anything to be normal with this wretched war on."

Ella pushed her coffee aside. "Oh, Reggie, I'm so sorry."

"Everything has gone haywire because of the duke's stubbornness, just when we are in the glare of the world's media. I don't understand what's got into him."

Ella heard Emerald beside her and looked up quickly. The maid stood with a small triangle of buttered toast on a plate in her hand, her wide lips pulled back in a hopeful smile.

"Please, Miss Ella, eat somethin'." She offered Ella the plate. "Just a little somethin', just to please old Emmie, huh?"

Ella hesitated. But she saw her husband's eyes brighten at the prospect, so made herself lift the toast and take a small bite. Both Reggie and Emerald smiled approvingly.

"Isn't it odd," she said without chewing, "that the duke would do such a thing—take control of such an important investigation?"

The dull fatigue returned to Reggie's eyes but he put on his diplomat's polite smile. "Very odd indeed, but royalty does not play by the same rules as us mere mortals." He even managed a light laugh.

* * *

It had been forty-eight hours since the murder of Sir Harry Oakes and Ella knew she could put off no longer what she had to do. She picked up her gloves and car keys, and was walking out of the house when the telephone rang. For one foolish moment she thought it might be Dan.

"Hello? Mrs. Sanford speaking."

"Ella, you sound very down in the dumps this morning."

"Tilly! Oh, everything is horrible today. I'm worried about Reggie and what on earth the duke is up to that is making my poor husband's life hell."

"Oh heavens, come and have coffee with me and tell all."

"I can't, I have an errand to run. But I'll meet you for a drink at the yacht club at noon."

"Suits me. Oh, Ella, one other thing."

"I must dash, Tilly. Be quick."

"I just wanted to ask if you're still pally with that detective chappie of yours?"

Ella replayed the sentence in her head. She could hear no undercurrent, no innuendo in the tone.

"Not pally exactly," she answered breezily. "Why?"

"Everyone is being so damn cagey about what exactly went on with this Oakes murder. I wondered whether you could squeeze some information out of him." She laughed, but it didn't sound exactly happy. "Use your charms on him."

"Why are you so interested? You never liked Sir Harry. You were always complaining about him."

"So were a lot of other people, Ella. You included, sometimes. I'm just wondering whether some extra legal work will be coming Hector's way. See what you can get out of Mr. Detective."

"I'll try. Must go."

Ella hung up. In her pocket she twisted her fingers around the gold coin Dodie had given her from Morrell. It was burning a hole there.

* * *

"I'm not in the mood, Ella."

"I think we need to have a talk, ma'am."

"Not now."

"I think the sooner the better."

"Ella, I'm not used to being railroaded in my own house."

They were in the duchess's small sitting room. It was every bit as ornate and extravagant as the rest of the refit that the Duke and Duchess of Windsor had lavished on the old Government House at taxpayers' expense, but here the colors were softer, the gilt-framed mirrors not quite so immense. For the last three years the Windsors had been marooned in the Bahamas, hidden away from all that the duke held dear. It was a decision imposed on them by Prime Minister Winston Churchill and King George VI, backed up by his determined wife. The aim was to keep the Windsors as far away from their Nazi friends in Berlin as decorum would allow, but both had set their sights on somewhere more glamorous in the future.

Ella stood at a respectful distance and asked, "How are you feeling, ma'am?"

"I am well." The duchess's eyes were red-rimmed and a vein stood out at her temple. "Please go, Ella. I know you mean well."

"I saw you, ma'am."

Wallis frowned. "Where?"

"At Sir Harry's house. At Westbourne. The night I dropped in to collect funds for the Red Cross. He had a guest there already— Mr. Morrell, the man who was stabbed—but I also saw you there."

"You are mistaken."

Ella didn't argue. "I thought maybe you could use a friend right now. Sir Harry's death must have come as a blow."

The duchess sat down heavily on a silk-covered chaise longue. She placed a hand over her eyes, held it there for a moment, and when she took it away they were moist.

"Don't be too nice to me, Ella, or you'll have me in tears."

"It might do you good."

"No, I can't afford that."

"I hear they've arrested his son-in-law."

"Yes, poor Freddie. He must be terrified. Especially as the prosecution has secured the services of our best barrister, Sir Alfred Adderley, so Freddie is using Higgs to lead his defense team."

"Higgs is very good, ma'am."

"Good enough to get him off?"

Ella sat down in an armchair that gave her a sweeping view out over the roofs of Nassau to the wharf below, where two destroyers rode at anchor. "I hear talk of Harold Christie being involved that night."

"Ah yes, Sir Harry's good friend." The duchess gave a laugh that seemed to drain the sunlight from the room. "Christie had dinner at Westbourne with Sir Harry that evening and spent the night there in a room only two doors away from Sir Harry's bedroom." Her voice was brittle. "Yet he heard nothing. Nothing all night."

"There was a bad storm," Ella pointed out. "The wind was howling."

The duchess gave a sharp shake of her head. "Don't. Don't defend him."

"I'm not defending him. But no one knows enough to decide who is guilty, and Sir Harry could be . . ." She hesitated.

"Difficult? Yes, of course he could." Wallis surprised Ella with a strong smile. "Of course he could. Harry Oakes had many enemies because he was a powerful man who spoke his mind and chose his own path, and people hated him for that. But he didn't give a damn." Her eyes shone pale indigo as she repeated, "He didn't give a damn."

"I know. I came here to make sure you're all right."

"Oh, Ella! How much exactly did you see at Westbourne," the duchess asked briskly, "the night you came rattling your Red Cross tin?"

"Nothing really." But Wallis's fine eyebrow was raised in a quizzical arch and so she added with a shrug, "Enough."

Ella had arrived at Westbourne in the evening. She'd decided to call in on the off chance as she was driving past—to beg further funds for the Red Cross. It was for a project to purchase a couple of houses next to the hospital to provide a room for relatives of patients from the Out Islands.

There was no watchman on the gate. She'd parked and walked up the crescent-shaped drive to the house, but a light was on in one of the downstairs rooms which had French windows open on to the terrace. Ella hadn't bothered with the front door and headed straight toward the French windows instead. But as she passed one of the other rooms her attention was drawn to it by a desk lamp inside. It gave enough light for her to make out two figures in the doorway. One was the familiar bulky outline of Sir Harry, and the other was a woman. Unmistakably the Duchess of Windsor.

He was kissing her. Touching her. His hand was gripping her tiny buttocks with a familiarity that spoke of habit. The figures drew apart and the duchess moved away in one direction while Sir Harry turned in another. Ella started to withdraw silently back across the damp grass, but she caught the sound of Sir Harry's bold laugh now issuing from the open French windows and the low rumble of another man's voice.

Still hopeful of extracting a check, she'd tiptoed forward again, but outside the French windows she hesitated and peered into the room. Inside, Sir Harry and another big man were talking, standing on either side of an inlaid table. Between them lay a small ivory-and-pearl casket open on the table, gleaming in the lamplight. But what the casket contained glowed with a fiery life of its own. It was gold coins.

"Well, Morrell, can I tempt you?" Sir Harry was saying.

She saw the man reach out his hand and touch the casket. "It's dangerous."

"Life is dangerous," Oakes told him.

Morrell didn't take his gaze from the casket.

"Sometimes," Sir Harry murmured, "a man gets one chance in life. This could be yours."

"They'll kill me."

"Don't be a fool. This could buy you a whole new life."

Ella could sense the man's reluctance. He withdrew his hand. But Sir Harry was not one to be thwarted. He slotted an arm around his brawny shoulders, a friendly gesture but one that pinned him there, close to the gold. Ella could smell the greed rippling out through the window.

"Look at it, Morrell. That's the thing about gold, it's fantastical." Oakes trailed his fingers through the coins. "It corrupts the soul. It hypnotizes the mind." He flashed a coin into the air and caught it on his palm. "The coin of the devil. Yet it decorates churches right across the world."

He tossed the coin to Morrell, who took it and tested it between his teeth. Oakes laughed.

"I promise you this, Morrell, I won't make a deal with your bosses, but I'll make a deal with you."

Ella decided it was time to withdraw, but she caught her ankle on an unseen lounge chair on the terrace and heard it scrape across the stone. Immediately she had the sense to call out.

"Good evening, Sir Harry, are you there?"

He came to the open window, while Morrell pulled off his jacket and dropped it over the casket.

"Mrs. Sanford," Oakes said, "how kind of you to call." But his eyes were dark with suspicion.

"Forgive the intrusion," she apologized brightly. "I'm just here to empty your pockets again." She laughed. "But I see you have a guest. I'll come back another time."

"No intrusion, I assure you. Do come in, dear lady." He took hold of her arm and drew her in. "I'm just finishing a spot of business here with my associate." He avoided giving a name.

She'd stayed no more than ten minutes and left with a generous check from Sir Harry and a handful of dollar bills from Morrell's wallet. She refused a drink and was just departing through the French windows when Sir Harry laid a heavy hand on her shoulder. "Ella, it's been a pleasure to see you, but"—his fingers tightened imperceptibly—"sometimes a little knowledge is a dangerous thing." He drew out the word "dangerous" till it stretched into the future. "Sometimes it is better to forget what you think you've seen or heard. Safer for everyone."

Ella slipped her shoulder out of his grasp. "Good night, Sir Harry."

She strode away at a rapid pace into the night without looking back.

Yes, she'd seen enough.

"The island will miss him," she said truthfully to Wallis.

"Not just the island."

It was a sad statement. A lonely expression of grief.

"Did you ever see Sir Harry's gold coins?"

Wallis smiled softly. "Yes, he liked to show them off to me."

"Do you think he would ever have given them away?"

"Hell no." The southern smile deepened. "Not unless he was planning to get them back by some devious means." She glanced across at the French ormolu clock on the mantelpiece. "I know it's early, Ella, but the yardarm has shifted for me today. Go pour me a martini and one for yourself." She gestured toward a cabinet and lit herself a cigarette.

When Ella had mixed the drinks and handed one to her, the duchess rose to her feet, raised her glass, and said with a flourish, "To Sir Harry Oakes! God rest his pirate soul."

"To Sir Harry."

Chapter 46

Dodie

Nassau Jail was designed to rob anyone of hope. It was a grim stone fortress set on a street called Prison Lane on the southern edge of town, with high walls that kept out the sun. Gordon Parfury—Flynn's lawyer appointed by Hector—had prepared Dodie. He had warned her about the dank air inside, about the gloomy corridors and the smell, about the harsh lights in the cells that were never extinguished. She had nodded. Yes, all she wanted was to get there. But when the heavy metal door to the cell swung open, she was not prepared for the sense of isolation that hit her, the despair that coated the walls like slime.

The moment she crossed the threshold Dodie stepped straight into Flynn's arms. She had not expected that. She'd thought a warder would keep them apart, but no. As soon as she and Parfury were in the cell, the door slammed shut and locked behind them, and for the first time since the police came for him in the house with the purple front door, she was able to breathe.

"So," Parfury said with cheerful concern, "how are you today, Mr. Hudson?"

"Couldn't be better."

Parfury gave a wry smile. Dodie wanted him to stand in a corner and say nothing.

"I've brought you cigarettes," she said. She held out a pack of Lucky Strike to Flynn.

"Thank you. Won't you sit down?"

"Don't be polite, Flynn. Not with me."

But she sat down on the narrow bed against the wall and looked around because if she looked at Flynn too long she might forget there was someone else in the room. The cell was about twelve foot by eight, larger than she thought it might be, and was redeemed by the open barred window set high in the wall opposite the door, which let in an ocean breeze that cooled her cheeks. The contents were basic—a bed, a stool, an enamel basin, and a galvanized bucket that stank.

Flynn settled himself on the bed a foot away from her. He didn't touch her, not after that first moment when he had kissed her, held her hard against his chest, and inhaled the scent of her hair.

"I knew you'd come," he said quietly. "But you shouldn't. You should leave now."

"I've only just arrived."

"I mean you should leave the island."

"No, Flynn."

His gaze remained on her face and the only sound in the cell was Parfury perching on the stool and rustling through his papers. Dodie wanted to tell Flynn what leaving would do to her but not in front of the lawyer, so she shook her head at him instead and saw his eyes follow the movement of her hair over her shoulders. She wanted to ask him how he was, to look at the gash on his head to see that it was healing, to touch him, to take his hand between hers. But she did none of these things.

He moved closer to her. "Okay, tell me what you know."

"I've spoken to your landlord."

"And?" She caught the faintest hint of hope.

"He and his wife are saying nothing. He claims that the house is locked and that no one came in. That's what he told the police."

Flynn looked away toward the small window too high to see out of. "He's lying," he said.

"Of course. The question is, Flynn, who paid him to lie? Who wants you dead but with no blood on their hands? Someone made an anonymous telephone call to the police to tell them where to look."

He nodded but made no comment.

"Tell me who would do that? Who should I go after?"

He stared blankly at the wall opposite. "You should go after no one."

"Flynn . . ."

She touched his hand on the rough blanket, but he removed it and took his time lighting a cigarette from the new pack. Neither looked at the lawyer.

Dodie sat on her hands. Made her voice businesslike. "Let me tell you what I've discovered so far about Sir Harry's death."

She didn't say the word *killing*. It was too big for this tiny cell.

Instantly he swung to face her.

"Sir Harry's body was found in his own bed," she told him. "They're saying he was shot in the head. Christie found him. He had dinner with Sir Harry the evening before and stayed at Westbourne overnight. He heard nothing all night because of the storm and found him at seven o'clock in the morning when he went into his bedroom to wake him."

Flynn was listening intently, watching her mouth. She had no idea how much Parfury had already told him, but she could see the color of his eyes turn drab when she mentioned Sir Harry's name.

She lowered her voice. "His body and the room were set on fire."

That hit him hard. His eyes leaped to hers. "Burned?" he whispered.

"I'm sorry, Flynn."

She glanced in the direction of the lawyer, who had his head bent over papers and was pretending not to listen.

"Burned?" Flynn repeated.

Dodie placed her hand silently over his mouth. She was frightened that in his despair he would say too much.

"There's more."

"Tell me."

"Someone slit his pillow and threw its feathers all over him before setting fire to it."

His eyes widened. *"Obeah?"*

Dodie nodded.

"Someone is trying to make it look like an *obeah* ritual killing." He uttered a sharp bark of scorn that made the lawyer lift his head. "That is just dumb. Everyone knows the Bahamians love him."

"That same someone is working hard to confuse the police and cover his tracks."

Flynn's face looked pale and exhausted. "What now?"

"They've arrested his son-in-law, Count de Marigny."

Anger sparked in his eyes. "An easy target," he jeered. "Convenient too."

"He's here. In this prison."

"Poor bastard. He doesn't have a chance in hell. Any more than I do. The big boys are throwing us into the lion's den."

In the corner Parfury cleared his throat. "Mr. Hudson, I will be doing everything I can for your defense and Count de Marigny is being defended ably by Mr. Higgs. You will both receive a fair trial, I assure you of that."

Flynn laughed, a harsh sound. "You are betting on a fair trial for this Marigny guy, Mr. Parfury, even though a more likely suspect was in the next-door room and is supposed to have slept through a murder, a fire, and a storm?" He tipped two fingers in a salute to the lawyer. "Hell, Mr. Parfury, you're a braver man than I am."

Flynn stood up abruptly, walked over to the door, and banged his fist on it. With a jolt Dodie realized what he was doing. She leaped to her feet and seized his sleeve.

"No, Flynn, please."

He turned and took both her hands in his own. "Dodie," he said fiercely, "I am headed straight for the noose."

"No! What about the four coins in your jacket? Where could they have come from? I'll try—"

"Forget the coins." He released her hands and stepped back. "Forget me."

"No, Flynn, you are—"

"Leave now, Dodie." His eyes were implacable. "I want you to leave."

*   *   *

Dodie walked hard and fast. Above her the blue sky stretched pure and clean and limitless after the dank confines of the prison and she drew in lungfuls of the crystal-clear air. She realized why Flynn did what he did, of course she did, but it didn't make it any easier. Didn't he know it was too late? That she was there in that grimy cell with him, whether he wanted it or not.

Her body ached and she was glad of the ache. It distracted her mind from the real pain. She knew she had to work out a plan of attack. To formulate her strategy, her tactics, her maneuvers. All military terms. That was how she thought of it now, because make no mistake: This was her war. Not in Europe. Not in Guadalcanal. But right here in Nassau, her own battle for the truth.

First she had to speak to the detective. She needed to find out more about the telephone call to the police and about Morrell's wallet. She wanted to know what kind of coins the ones found in his jacket were—whether they were napoleons too.

She set off back toward the Arcadia. But she knew she was going to have to go out to Bradenham House again because her best way to get to Detective Calder was through Ella Sanford. But she was conscious of a change in Ella, a new element in her that was unsettling. Dodie saw it every time the name Detective Calder passed her lips. A wildness. A glimpse of a storm. Is that what Ella meant? Is that what she saw in her too, that "something" of herself?

A car door slammed somewhere behind her and she looked around. She was in Silver Street with its quaint little curio shops that the colonials loved so much. It was lazing in the sun, its shutters bleached, its narrow pavement almost empty at this time of day when people took to their midday meals or their noon siestas. A woman riding a donkey plodded past and then it was quiet again.

"Miss Wyatt!"

The man's voice came from behind her. Dodie didn't even turn. Her heart thumped but her legs bounded forward in immediate panic. She knew that voice, knew whose fists it belonged to. Before her mind worked out what was happening, she was running, but she could hear right behind her the heavy feet that had kicked her before, the ones that belonged to the person who liked to use her back as a punching bag.

This time he was ready for her and he was fast. He grasped her hair and yanked her back. She screamed and lashed out at his face but a black sedan swerved to a halt beside her. Its rear door burst open and she was thrown inside, her attacker jammed tight beside her, twisting an arm painfully behind her back and chuckling to himself as though he were playing with a puppy.

It was broad daylight. No one was kidnapped in broad daylight on a pleasant Nassau street. No one.

As the car drove on, pedestrians were going about their business, cars were passing. This was not possible. She screamed at the window. The driver turned casually in his seat and slapped her across the face so hard that she felt part of a tooth break loose.

"Shut it, lady."

A knife appeared in the meaty hand of her companion on the backseat, and before she could start to reason with him, its blade had slid along the underside of her arm from her wrist all the way to her elbow. She watched in horror as a snake of crimson leaped into life and rippled down her pale flesh. It wasn't deep, little more than a scratch, just a warning, but she had to fight back the anger that was absurdly for the fact that the blood was ruining her Arcadia Hotel dress.

"Let me out."

"Shut up, bitch." One hand gripped her while the other held the knife.

"Let me out or I'll—"

"Or you'll what, you bloody whore?"

"Fuck you, girl," the driver shouted, and glanced over his shoulder.

She tried for the door handle with her free hand but was smacked in the middle of her back by a fist. She crumpled, terror gripping her lungs, but she found the strength to scream and curse at them, throwing them off balance, filling the car with noise, and she wiped her hand in her own blood, then smeared it on the window.

"Shut the bitch up!"

The driver lost concentration. The car swerved and its brakes squealed. It bounced off the front wing of a pale convertible that was turning out of a side street, and in one brief second the shocked eyes of its woman driver saw what was going on behind the bloody window.

Before Dodie could draw breath, she was hurled out of the car onto the road.

*   *   *

The woman picked Dodie up off the tarmac.

She drove her to the police station, stayed with her through the pointless questioning by a young officer—pointless because they all knew the men would never be found. They would fade from sight. Disappear to one of the hundreds of Out Islands.

"Can't you at least look for a dented black Plymouth sedan?" the woman demanded.

"We will make inquiries, madam, and put out a description. But we are hard-pressed for manpower right now."

Two murders.

An attempted kidnapping.

The world's press breathing down their necks.

The Bahamas was out of its depth.

Chapter 47

Dodie

It wasn't until Dodie walked into the police station alongside the woman in the elegant linen suit that she recalled seeing her before. In the same police station. That first time when she came to report the murder of Johnnie Morrell, Ella Sanford had burst in through the door, drenched in scarlet, and been fussed over first by Detective Calder and then by Colonel Lindop. There had been a dark-haired woman with her, the one who had left bloody handprints over Detective Calder's sleeve. The one whose voice had been loud and panicked.

Dodie recognized her now. This was that woman, but groomed and sleek and happy to scold a policeman for spelling her name wrong.

Matilda Latcham.

Hector Latcham's wife.

What a small town Nassau could be when it tried.

* * *

"Dearest girl, you can't possibly go back to work today in your state. Just look at you."

"I'm better now. Really I am." Dodie put down her glass. "I have to get back to work at the Arcadia."

Tilly waved her painted nails in the air, as though flicking away a mosquito. "Forget about that, Dodie. I'll telephone Olive and explain what happened and that you are in a state of shock." She shook her dark head in the manner of one well accustomed to making decisions for others. "Don't be foolish. You were nearly killed. Those awful hoodlums!" She gave a shudder. "I'm furious that the police are doing so little. They are such dunces."

"I'm sorry about your car. Is the damage bad?"

"No, just a dent. Don't worry about that, it wasn't your fault. Here, have another drink." Tilly had already drained her own glass and advanced on Dodie's.

"No, thank you, Mrs. Latcham. I am really grateful for all your help—without you I could be dead now."

They looked at each other and Dodie felt an odd connection to this bright brittle woman who hid behind her flagrant disdain for the banality of her days. Was it always like this? If someone saves your life, how much do you owe them? How big a part of you do they own?

Dodie rose to her feet and it took her by surprise when the room briefly danced around her. It was a pleasant enough room but nowhere near as stylish as Ella's, with heavy mahogany pieces that were somewhat the worse for wear.

"If you would let me have my dress back . . ."

"Oh, Dodie, don't rush off. Stay for another drink."

"No, thank you. You've been so kind but I really must go."

"Then stay and watch me drink mine." She had refilled her glass from the cocktail shaker and took a neat bite out of an olive. "I want to hear the gory details about your dead man."

Dodie felt her stomach lurch. What had this woman's husband been telling her? Surely lawyer confidentiality was as strict as doctor confidentiality?

Nevertheless she smiled at Tilly Latcham. "Another time. I have to go to Bradenham House to see Mrs. Sanford."

"Oh, that's easy," Tilly said cheerfully. She knocked back the rest of her drink, ran a hand over her precise silky waves, and added, "I'll drive you over."

"No, really, that's not necessary."

"I insist." She patted Dodie's cheek and gave her a bright red smile, but behind the careful powder and mascara Dodie caught a glimpse of a loneliness that tugged at something in her. "It will be a pleasure."

* * *

"How's your young man?"

"He's in prison."

"So I hear."

Tilly Latcham was driving the dented Plymouth too fast. Her wide sun hat obscured much of her face, but Dodie saw the grimace she pulled.

"Hideous place." Tilly switched her gaze from the sun-drenched road ahead of them to Dodie's face. She frowned, spoiling the neatness of her smooth skin. "I'm worried about Ella."

"Mrs. Sanford?"

"Yes. How well do you know her?"

"Not well at all."

"She and I have been good friends for years."

"What's wrong with Mrs. Sanford?"

"She's scaring me."

Dodie's mouth went dry. "Why's that?"

"Because something bad is going on inside her, I'm sure of it."

* * *

The doorbell of Bradenham House rang and rang. No one answered.

"Mrs. Sanford must be out." Dodie frowned.

"So where is Emerald?"

As Dodie stood on the wide, pillared porch, squinting at the sunlight on the windows, the air seemed to vibrate with the faintest of noises. She took a step back from the house and quickly scanned its elegant colonial frontage but nothing seemed out of place.

"What is it, Dodie?"

"I don't know. Something . . ."

She stopped. Listened hard. The faint sound was high-pitched and made the skin of her arms prickle. She started to run to the back of the house, toward the garden. The sound was growing steadily louder and turning into a kind of keening, when an arm smacked into her chest.

"Get out!" a woman's voice boomed at her. "Leave her alone."

"I heard—"

"Leave her! She don't need you."

Dodie saw before her the big maid who worked for Ella Sanford. Her huge angry eyes glared at Dodie. Tears were careening down her cheeks.

Tilly Latcham's sharp voice demanded, "Emerald, what has happened?"

All Emerald could do was sway from side to side. "Leave her be," she growled. "This is private."

"Nonsense, Emerald." Tilly started to march past her. "What is that hellish sound?"

Dodie hurried forward, aware now that the sound was a woman's voice.

*   *   *

Dodie didn't know which was worse. The terrible keening that tore something loose within her or the numbing silence when Ella Sanford suddenly ceased the noise. She stood frozen inside the chicken pen, staring around her with a stricken, bemused expression on her face.

The gate to the pen stood wide open. There was no need to shut it. Not now. Dodie counted the hens. More than a hundred of them, sprawled dead on the tufted grass like small mounds of autumn leaves. Golds and browns, warm russets and vibrant butter yellows. Some with their necks wrenched over at odd angles, others with their heads sliced clean off and discarded on the ground. Flies were thick, gathering into black shrouds that glistened in the sun.

Dodie went to Ella, but the maid was already there, standing shoulder to shoulder with her mistress, her hand hitched into the back of Ella's collar as though holding her up on her feet. Ella didn't shake, didn't cry. Her face wasn't white or even gray, it was a strange blue color that frightened Dodie, with one small speck of crimson on each cheek.

"Whoever did this," Ella hissed through her teeth, "deserves to be boiled in oil."

It was an oddly biblical pronouncement.

This was the start, Dodie could sense it. The start of something worse.

* * *

They dug a large pit, Dodie and the gardener, and when it was finished, the mass grave was sealed up. Ella stood beside it, bareheaded under the sun. Tilly had drifted up to the house in search of a drink, while Emerald started stripping out the henhouses with loud bursts of "Oh Lordy, oh Lordy, this world ain't fit for decent souls to live in." So they were standing alone by the grave when Ella said, "Who would do this, Dodie?"

"It's a warning, Ella."

"A warning? Against what?"

"Against going to tell the police what went on that evening you called in at Westbourne collecting for the Red Cross. Now that Sir Harry is dead, they think you might be tempted."

Ella shook her head. "But I saw very little."

"You saw Morrell."

"Yes. And I saw a box of gold coins."

They looked at each other in silence.

"Is that enough," Ella said in a low voice, "to cause"—her gaze swept over the empty enclosure—". . . this?"

"I believe it's enough to cause far worse than this."

Ella's attention snapped back to her. "Your Mr. Hudson arrested on a trumped-up murder charge, you mean?"

Dodie nodded. "Ella, we need to know whether the box of coins is back in Sir Harry's house somewhere."

The crimson smudges on Ella's cheeks contracted. "I know the man to ask."

Chapter 48

Ella

Dan smelled of ink. A good sensible down-to-earth smell. It made Ella think of school. Sometimes when she was with him she had to remind herself that he wasn't even born when she was at school and already playing lacrosse. When they lay panting, exhausted and finally sated on his bed, he would often study her face, tenderly touching parts of it, and she would wonder what he was seeing. Today, out in the harsh and unforgiving glare of sunlight, she didn't want him to look at her and see the ravages that she knew had made her face suddenly older in the last hour.

"Oh, my poor Ella, I'm sorry."

She stepped back, detaching herself from him, and looked up into his face. "I don't want your sympathy, Dan, I want your help."

"Of course, let's fill out an incident form at the police station and—"

"No. That's not what I mean."

"What then?"

They were standing on the wharf in the shade of a stack of crates that was waiting to be loaded on board one of the military ships that nudged into the harbor each day. Ahead of them lay the Sponge Exchange building and off to one side the fishing boats bobbed like noisy children alongside the quay, with Hog Island lying just offshore behind them in the shape of a great beached whale. Gulls shrieked and men hauled ropes and shouted to one another. There were five heavy bombers losing height as they came in to land. A seemingly normal day in the busy life of the harbor of New Providence Island. But today was anything but normal.

"Dan, how much of you is Dan Calder and how much is Detective Sergeant Calder?"

He was surprised by the question. "I don't divide myself up, Ella. If you have something to tell me, go ahead."

"Can I trust you?"

He marched her deeper into an L-shaped corner of shade among the crates and she could feel heat rising off him the same way it did in his bed. But she realized that she had offended him. He was waiting for more from her, and so she told him.

Everything. Ella held nothing back. Because she wanted everything he had. So she gave him herself, everything inside her, until there was nothing left to give and she felt purged of a poison deep in her bowels that had stemmed from the day that Sir Harry had waved the smell of gold under Morrell's nose. "It corrupts the soul," he'd said. And from that day something had gone bad inside her. She gave him everything, so that he would know how much she needed his help.

She took him, step-by-step, through the fund-raising visit to Westbourne and the arrival of Dodie Wyatt on her doorstep with a gold coin from Morrell. Was it a warning not to trust Oakes? Or a sign that she needed his help because she was in danger? She told him of her fears for Dodie and of her suspicions about the duchess having an affair with Oakes.

Dan leaned his head back against the tall stack of crates at that. "The Duchess of Windsor and Sir Harry Oakes? You've got that wrong, surely?"

He ran the palm of his hand along his jaw and she heard the sandpaper scratch of his stubble. She had to tie her fingers together in knots to stop herself touching him. Nearby a crane started to hoist a military lorry and swing it through the air toward a transport ship's hold, but they didn't even notice. Their patch of shade had swallowed them. She told him how she had asked discreet questions. Plied a banker with drinks at a party. Coaxed whispers and rumors out of people who should know better than to spread them.

"And what did you discover?" he asked. He lit two cigarettes and handed her one.

"That Sir Harry was moving money around. Large amounts of it, millions into foreign accounts in neutral countries."

"That's illegal."

"Of course."

Since the start of the war, financial restrictions were in place to prevent funds being transferred out of the country's coffers at a time when it needed every penny it could lay its hands on.

"Sir Harry would know that," Dan said, drawing hard on his cigarette, "yet he took the risk. If it's true." He had his policeman's eyes in place now. Had she got it wrong? If she scratched him with her nails now, would he bleed policeman's ink? Yet she didn't stop.

"That's not all."

"Go on, Ella. I'm listening."

She wondered, as she stared at his shrewd gray eyes. *Are you, Dan? Are you really listening to me?*

"He's not the only one moving money around," she told him. "The duke owes him two million pounds."

Dan exhaled a perfect smoke ring. It popped out with no sound but it was like a small explosion between them. He reached for her without a word and for one inappropriate moment she thought he was going to take her here hidden among the crates, and a pulse kicked into life at her groin. But he pulled her close against his chest, so tight that she had to tip back her head to look up at his face when he finally spoke softly.

"Ella, I'm going to tell you things that will get me fired if they ever come out."

She felt her ribs fuse with his under the dampness of his shirt. He was listening.

* * *

"The duke is destroying the investigation into Sir Harry Oakes's death."

They had moved away from the crates. A group of Bahamian dockers had sauntered over, laughing and slapping their thighs to a calypso rhythm, to man-haul the boxes onto the back of a truck, but they eyed Dan warily. They could smell police on him. Instead Ella and Dan found an open warehouse stacked with crates of slatted wood containing lemons and limes. The air was fragrant with the warm scent of them and the tang of citrus caught at the back of Ella's throat, but here they could be private. A balmy Bahamian breeze rustled up from the water's edge and slipped into the warehouse, chasing cobwebs into the corners.

"Colonel Erskine Lindop, our commissioner of police, has been removed from his position and is to be posted to Trinidad."

Ella rocked back on her heels.

"It's true," Dan assured her. "Not only that, the prison doctor, Dr. Oberwarth, who examined Marigny for singed hairs on the day of the arrest—and didn't find any—has been relieved of his duties at the prison. And the two American detectives the duke brought in from Miami are either incompetent or deliberately destructive because they are sabotaging the scene of the crime, washing away evidence such as the bloody handprints on Sir Harry's bedroom wall, and . . ."

His voice trailed away when he saw her face.

"Are you sure of this?" she asked aghast.

"Yes."

"Do others know?"

"Of course. Including"—he hesitated over the word—"your husband."

It was inconceivable.

"What's going on, Dan?"

"You tell me."

A chill passed over Ella's skin and she shivered. She reached out and laid her fingertips on his shirtfront.

"The question is," she said intently, "is the duke covering for himself or for someone else?"

"Or for the island?"

"What do you mean?"

"As governor of the Bahamas, he doesn't want the island's name dragged through the mud, all its secrets raked over, all its bank accounts sifted through. It's well known that Oakes and his son-in-law didn't get on, so Marigny's arrest provides a quick and easy answer to the problem."

"Dan, we're talking about a man's life here. If Marigny is innocent, the duke—"

"It will be up to a jury, Ella, not the duke."

"I know." She shook her head. "I know." She twitched a hand through her hair, as if she could tear out the thoughts inside. "Tell me what happened. To Sir Harry."

He cupped his hand behind her neck and drew her closer.

"It's not pleasant, I warn you. Harold Christie discovered Oakes's body at seven o'clock in the morning, though we believe the murder took place around midnight. The bed had been doused with an inflammable mosquito spray that was in the room and set alight. It was a terrible sight. The bedding, mosquito net, and Oakes's pajamas were incinerated and his body badly burned and blackened, his eyes gone. Feathers from the pillow were strewn over him, though God only knows why. It appears that whoever did it intended to torch the whole house to destroy evidence, but the storm came at the wrong time. Oakes had left his window open, so the wind and rain put out the flames."

"And Christie slept through this in a nearby bedroom?"

"So he claims. But . . ."

"What?"

"He was seen in a car in town. At one o'clock in the morning. He denies it, of course."

"Oh God, Dan, it just gets worse."

With no warning he released her and strode out of the warehouse into the brilliant sunshine outside, drawing in great lungfuls of the sparkling air. Ella didn't follow. She let him have his moment alone. To flush out the images of the crime scene from his head and the squalid taste of corruption from his mouth. A warehouseman in uniform approached him to move him on, but backtracked rapidly when the police badge was flashed. Dan had told her he loved his work, but how do you deal with something like this? How do you stop it eating into you?

She waited in the stillness of the warehouse with the lemons and eventually Dan turned, a tall and imposing figure silhouetted against the blue waters of the harbor. She couldn't see a difference in his walk as he came toward her or in the line of his shoulders, but she had a sense of a decision being made.

"Ella, I want you to go home and stay there. The slaughter of your chickens was a warning to you. Heed it. Go home. Keep away from me. And above all, keep away from Dodie Wyatt and Flynn Hudson. Ella, are you listening to me?"

No, she wasn't listening.

She wasn't breathing.

She wasn't thinking.

All she could hear was this—*Keep away from me*. The words were gnawing at her. *Keep away from me.*

Don't you know that when I am away from you, I die?

"Don't look like that, Ella."

She hooked two fingers between the buttons of his shirt, finding the warmth of his flesh.

"Why can't I stay with you? You're a policeman, I'd be safe."

His hand closed over her wrist. "Oh, Ella, it's precisely because I am a policeman that you must get away from me. Listen now." He held her wrist tight. "Sir Harry Oakes was shot four times behind his left ear. We believe he was killed somewhere else, because there was blood all over the stairs and doorknobs, as well as the fact that the dried blood showed a flow from his ear up over the bridge of his nose, which indicates that he was moved. If your chickens were killed as a warning, someone could be watching you and getting jumpy when they see you with a policeman."

"No, I—"

"That someone is not playing games here, Ella. This is deadly serious. I don't want you involved."

"I'm already involved."

"Damn the Red Cross. To hell with your blasted fund-raising. If only you hadn't gone there the night Morrell was at Westbourne— with all that gold on show."

"Too late for that."

"But not too late to keep you safe."

"What about the wallet and coins in Flynn Hudson's room? Don't they give you any clues?"

He gripped her hand. "You say Hudson is American Mafia, so get it into your head that the odds are that he probably committed both murders and that it's his lot who killed your chickens."

Ella clamped her fingers on his shirt and couldn't let go.

Chapter 49

Dodie

Dodie was loitering in a shop doorway. It sold handbags. That was as much as she noticed. The point was that it stood next to the Bay Street entrance to Harold Christie's real-estate office and she had already spotted a handful of men in seersucker suits trying to make themselves invisible in various shop doorways and across the street. One was wearing a green plastic eyeshade as if he'd just stepped away from his newspaper's typewriter and forgotten to take it off.

As the hours passed, several of them drifted together and huddled into small groups, reporters from all parts of the world, hillocks of cigarette butts emerging at their feet. The street was busy and a man with a camera and a hard nasal accent took over a piece of her doorway. He told her he was from Boston, but she didn't listen to his chatter, because already she'd heard the click of the door that bore the brass plaque that declared MR. H CHRISTIE. REALTOR. The back entrance through the alleyway was also well covered by newspapermen, so Dodie guessed he would head for a car right outside his door on the wide main street. And she guessed right.

It was over fast. Two big Bahamians shouldered a path to a waiting car, its motor running, while reporters pushed and shoved each other worse than feeding sharks, shouting questions to the small crumpled figure, thrusting microphones under his nose.

"Did you see anything that night, Mr. Christie?"

"Why didn't you smell the fire?"

"What was your relationship with Sir Harry?"

"Look this way."

Cameras clicked.

Dodie slipped under the arm of one of the big bodyguards and called out, "I need to talk to you about Portman Cay, Mr. Christie."

He halted on the pavement, glanced at her, then plunged into the rear of his car. He wound down a window a crack, muttered something to one of the other bodyguards, and before she could open her mouth, Dodie found herself being tumbled into the back of the car alongside Christie.

"Sit down," he said. No trace of charm today.

As the car pulled away she didn't waste words. "Thank you for your time, Mr. Christie. Flynn Hudson is in jail. He has been framed for the murder of Mr. Morrell."

"What the hell has that got to do with me? I have my own worries right now, as you can see."

He rubbed a hand across his creased face, roughing up his sandy eyebrows, but didn't manage to remove the look of nervousness and distress that hovered under his irritated manner. Was it the natural reaction of a man who has found his friend murdered in bed? Or something more? Dodie wanted to peel off his bald pate and take a look inside.

"It is a coincidence," she pointed out, "that just after turning up in your office asking awkward questions, Flynn Hudson is locked up in a prison cell." The car was slowing down. Her time was running out. "Did you get someone to make that phone call to the police, Mr. Christie? You and your Mafia friends from Prohibition days? Was Flynn Hudson becoming too much of an irritant?"

Christie sat very still in his corner. "Be careful what you say, young woman."

She was trying to provoke him, to tempt him into an indiscretion, but he kept a tight hold on his temper.

"I did no such thing," he stated. "And I will call my lawyer if you go around saying I did." He took a moment to light himself a cigarette, and when he had sent a stream of smoke swirling through the car, he asked, "What is this about Portman Cay?"

She trod carefully this time. "You handled the sale of that land."

"Where did you hear that?"

"It doesn't matter. Is it true?"

He nodded. "Yes, it is. It's no secret."

"The vendor is a Mr. Michael Ryan, the purchaser a Mr. Alan Leggaty."

The car halted. They were outside a bank. Dodie could sense Christie's wariness.

"Are you Mr. Alan Leggaty, by any chance?"

It was a shot in the dark, but she hit the bull's-eye. He tossed his cigarette out of the window and turned back to glare at her.

"It was you, wasn't it?" he snapped. "You and Hudson trespassing on the land up at Portman Cay."

"Land that you are planning to use for—"

"—for nothing, Miss Wyatt. I think you've said enough."

"That's it, isn't it, Mr. Christie? Flynn Hudson was asking too many questions, so he was set up as Morrell's murderer. But whoever set him up possessed the wallet and the gold coins. Only the killer would have those."

His eyes flickered but didn't look away.

"It's possible, I suppose," he said coldly. "Or he could be guilty as charged."

"Is that person you, Mr. Christie?"

His mouth stretched wide into a grimace and it took Dodie a minute to recognize it as a smile of sorts. "No, it's not." He glanced at the glass partition between them and the driver, and she had the impression he would have said more had they been totally alone.

"I'm telling you this much—Sir Harry Oakes and Freddie de

Marigny hated each other's guts. Oakes couldn't forgive the greasy foreigner for cradle-snatching his daughter. Marigny was in the area of Westbourne between midnight and one o'clock, and he, above everyone, had a motive for murder—his father-in-law's money. So don't come to me with tales of mobsters and land deals. This is a straightforward matter of family feuding."

"That's what everyone seems to want us to believe."

"And where does Morrell fit into this? He got in the way of someone. Stabbed by a prostitute or by your friend Hudson when they'd had too much to drink. You mark my words, that's what will come out in the trial."

There was a firestorm going on behind his eyes. "I suggest, Miss Wyatt, that you go see that nice shiny new lawyer of yours and tell him what you've told me and see just how long he can keep you out of jail." He jutted his head toward her, for all the world like an angry tortoise. "Now get the hell out of my car."

*　*　*

"Dodie, child, you sure are stirrin' things up."

"That's right, Mama Keel, I sure am." They were standing outside the purple door of Flynn's lodgings, the afternoon sun taking bites out of the shadows and leaving the street as parched and dusty as one of the lizards that skulked in the gutters. "I'm poking sticks in nests and seeing what bites."

Mama gave a grunt of disapproval and spat out a stream of green ganja juice onto the dirt. She had the aches in her head today.

"If I don't, Mama, they'll hang him for sure."

"Then you and me better make this work."

Dodie knocked on the door and waited. There was no answer, yet music drifted under the door.

Mama Keel nodded to herself. "You got a white man's knock."

Mama Keel lifted her hand and tapped a rhythmic tattoo on the wood in time to the beat, and seconds later the music ceased and the door swung open. Behind it the landlord was standing in just a pair of vivid green shorts and a vest. In his arms slept an infant with dusky mixed-blood skin and gingery curls.

Dodie smiled. "Good day. Remember me?"

"Yes."

Still one for monosyllables, it seemed. Dodie had hoped it would be easier this time.

"I've brought my friend Mama Keel with me. May we come in and have a word with you?

His eyes skipped from Dodie and settled on Mama. Mama said nothing. Just stood on his doorstep under his inspection. She was a good head taller than he was. After a moment, he hitched the child up in his arms, gave a nod, and retreated into the dark hallway of the house. Dodie let Mama lead the way and together they entered, though Dodie's eyes instantly took to the stairs that led up to Flynn's room. The landlord's wife joined them with arms folded over her plentiful bosom and the four of them were jammed into the small space between the stove and the log basket.

"Please, help me," Dodie said. "Mr. Hudson will be hanged if you don't admit to the police that someone else came here, someone who put the wallet in the mattress." She fought to keep any anger out of her voice. "I know the person must have threatened you."

They continued to regard her with scowls on their faces.

"I understand how terrifying that can be, but Mr. Hudson is innocent. Please. You can't wish him to die for a crime he didn't—"

Mama Keel placed a warm hand on Dodie's knee.

"My friend here is upset," Mama said smoothly. "Her man is in trouble, and that ain't good. She's here askin' for help because we know you're decent folk." A calmness radiated from her as she reached down into the straw basket at her side, drew out three bottles of local beer, and opened a small battered tin which released the smell of ganja weed into the room.

"Dodie, girl," Mama smiled affectionately, "why don't you slip outside and let me and these folks have a quiet chat?"

This wasn't what Dodie expected, but she trusted Mama. With a nod she rose from her seat and left the room. Outside in the dim hallway the ache in her chest sharpened and her feet took to the stairs with quick silent steps.

His door was locked. So someone else had moved in. She wanted to shout out that he wasn't dead yet, that this was still Flynn's room. He would be back. Her fingers touched the handle one last time before she hurried back downstairs. Instead of going outside to wait in the shadeless street, she drifted to the back of the gloomy hall but jerked to a halt when she saw Flynn's jacket. It was lying in a cardboard box shoved among the jumble of objects in the space under the stairs.

She lifted up the box. It had an official Bahamas Police Department stamp on one end. Inside it she let her fingers riffle through Flynn's shirts, a jumper, trousers, a towel. Nothing of significance. No gun, no letters, nothing other than clothes. The police had kept the rest. She leaned back against the wall, eyes closed, and slowly slid to the floor, holding the box tight to her chest. She bent forward so that her face was buried in his jacket and she breathed him in until she could feel him inside herself.

※   ※   ※

The Arcadia Hotel was packed. Olive Quinn was frantic but smiling broadly. The world's media men needed somewhere to stay and the Arcadia welcomed its fair share of them with open arms. Dodie was working flat out, as tea on the crowded terrace was much in demand. She almost didn't see Ella arrive.

Ella was looking thin. Dodie was shocked by the way her clothes hung loose on her and her blue eyes had retreated deep into their sockets. Dodie moved quickly to Ella's table and rested her notepad on its surface, as though waiting for her customer to choose her order.

"Are you all right, Ella?"

"Yes, thank you."

"Would you like something to eat?"

Ella shook her head but she bent over the menu. "Dan won't see me anymore. He says it's too dangerous for me." Her voice sounded raw.

Dodie gently touched her shoulder. "It shows he cares for you."

"You don't understand. I can't not see him . . ." She stopped as she looked up at Dodie's face. "Of course you understand, don't you, you're going through the same."

Dodie didn't want to talk about that. "What did Detective Calder say about Morrell and Sir Harry?"

Ella put down the menu. "That the murder investigation into Sir Harry's death is being deliberately botched. The evidence destroyed. Key men moved out of reach. He thinks there's a conspiracy to cover up the truth."

"Who is in this conspiracy?" Dodie picked up her pad and pretended to scribble something down.

"He doesn't know for sure."

"So what's his guess?"

Ella tipped her hat forward to cover her face. "Take your pick—there's so much going on. So many secrets. Dan thinks it's the duke."

"What?"

"Only someone that high up could order the removal of top men."

"Oh, Ella! I spoke to Christie today. He said that everyone knows there was bad blood between Sir Harry and his son-in-law. That's the story he's pushing to anyone who will swallow it. A family feud." She glanced around but Miss Olive was not in sight, so just for a moment she sat down in the chair next to Ella's, their heads close. "Christie and the duke are the two most powerful men on the island now. They must be the ones manipulating decisions and decreeing what the press hears."

"The reporters will ask awkward questions, you know they will."

"That's why Flynn was framed. For asking too many questions that someone didn't like."

"But, Dodie, that's what you and I are doing now." Ella ran a hand down her cheek and seemed surprised to find its edges so sharp. "Stirring things up. I worry about you. Dan is right, it could be dangerous. I am protected by being the wife of Reginald Sanford, but you . . ." She hesitated and lowered her voice. "You are vulnerable."

The two women looked at each other, the friendship between them weaving into complex knots.

"Taking a well-earned rest, Miss Wyatt?"

The sarcasm in Olive Quinn's voice was finely honed. Dodie jumped to her feet.

"I'm sorry, Miss Olive, I was—"

"Olive dear, don't be a tyrant. I asked Dodie to sit with me. There is something I needed to discuss with her."

"Finished now, I hope. We are busy."

"Very nearly. Just one more minute."

Reluctantly Olive Quinn withdrew, but not without a quizzical glance at Ella.

Dodie bent her head down to Ella's level. "Ella, it seems that one of the keys to it all is the Portman Cay land deal. It connects everything—Johnnie Morrell, Sir Harry, and Christie. That's what Flynn walked into without knowing."

One of the customers raised a polite hand to summon Dodie to her table.

"I have to go," she said. "Be careful."

Ella's smile was grateful. "I'll arrange to see Hector Latcham tomorrow. He's Christie's lawyer as well and so might know something about Portman Cay."

"Be discreet."

Ella actually laughed. "I eat discretion for breakfast."

"I'll bring you some tea."

"What about you?"

"I have another appointment tomorrow to visit the prison before I start work."

"Ah." Ella grimaced. "Good luck."

"Thank you."

As Dodie walked away, she wondered why the one thing that no one talked about was the gold. But by the time she brought the tea tray to the table, Ella was gone.

Chapter 50

Ella

"Reggie."

Ella was standing in the dark on the balcony of their bedroom. Mosquitoes whined around her ears and somewhere in the distance the deep bass rumble of the ocean could be heard as it crooned to itself. Ella had never been a keen swimmer and now felt her limbs too weak to contemplate such a thing. She tried to remember when she had last eaten something, but couldn't.

Reggie materialized at her elbow, as though he'd been just waiting for the sound of her voice.

"Reggie, I've been hearing whispers. Is it true that the duke is moving large sums of money around?"

"I say, Ella, old thing. That's frightfully indiscreet of you. Not like your usual self at all."

Ella turned away and rested her elbow on the balcony ledge. The silence between them was filled by the cicadas and the dull refrain of the tree frogs.

"But then," Reggie said in the kind of conciliatory voice he was good at, "you haven't been quite your usual self recently." He paused. "Have you?"

"These murders are upsetting."

"Of course."

That was all. Neither could find anything more to say, so after a wait that only emphasized the vacant air between them, Reggie removed himself from the balcony and went inside.

"Help me, Reggie," she whispered. "Please, please, help me." Her head dropped on to her hands and she shivered.

*   *   *

It was just after eight o'clock in the morning when Ella drove past Dan's house the first time. Cars were parked in drives, shutters stood open, there was an atmosphere of purpose and activity in the street that was foreign to her. The houses weren't dozing peacefully in the afternoon sun, as they had been before. She felt a stranger. Unwelcome. When she drove past the house in her Rover for the third time, she caught sight of Dan at the upstairs window. He was wearing a shirt and tie, and must have just stepped out of a shower because his hair looked wet and sleek. Neither waved.

A thin streak of pain traveled up from Ella's chest to her throat and she looked down at her cream chiffon blouse expecting to see blood on it. There was none, of course.

Of course.

She turned the car back toward East Bay Street and headed in the direction of Hector's office for her appointment with him, the image of Dan with his wet hair branded on her mind.

Don't you know that when I am not with you, I die?

*   *   *

"Hector, how kind of you to see me."

"My dear Ella, I can think of no better way to start my day." Hector Latcham kissed her cheek, guided her to a comfortable chair, and summoned coffee for his guest. "Now how can I help you?"

"I need to find out a bit about Portman Cay."

"Portman Cay?" Hector repeated, frowning as he tried to place the name.

"I believe you did the legal work on it when it was sold recently. For Harold Christie."

"Ah yes, I did indeed." He tapped his forehead with a self-deprecating laugh. "So many transactions in there that sometimes they get put in the wrong files." He sipped his coffee and regarded her thoughtfully over the rim of the delicate porcelain cup. "But what's your interest in it, Ella? Not your usual preoccupation." He offered her a cigarette from an ebony box and lit one for her with a flourish.

"To be honest, Hector, my curiosity has been roused by a rumor I've heard about Portman Cay."

He crossed his legs, and it occurred to Ella how fit he looked for a man of his age, somewhere around fortyish. It reminded her of Dan.

"As you're a lawyer, Hector, I know I can trust you. I've been hearing about big money deals. What's going on out there?"

"Don't worry your head about it, my dear."

"I asked Reggie."

"Did you indeed? What did Reggie say?"

"He told me I'd best keep my nose out of it too."

"Good advice."

Ella drew on her cigarette tetchily. "I'm not so sure. Portman Cay seems to tie in somehow with the deaths of Morrell and Sir Harry."

"Really? I would be careful, Ella. That could be a dangerous thing to say."

"What can you tell me about the place? What's so special?"

"Nothing much, to be honest. It's just a bay like any other but bigger—the usual sand, sea, and a small forest of pine trees. Very pretty actually."

Ella sighed. "Another brick wall, it seems. Yet there is definitely a connection somewhere and I intend to find it." Abruptly she stubbed out her cigarette and stood up. "I think I'll drive out there and take a look myself."

Hector rose to his feet and smiled fondly. "That sounds like a good idea. But look at you, my dear Ella. You look as if you'd blow away in the first wind. I can't have you dashing around to strange places on your own. Let me drive you."

"Hector, you are an angel."

Chapter 51

Flynn

As soon as the key turned in the lock, Flynn knew it was her.

Dodie entered the cell half a step behind his lawyer, Parfury, and brought a lightness with her. It changed the way the air hung, drab and sour, between the four stark walls. She was wearing her little black Arcadia dress, the one he loved on her with the white cuffs at the elbows, and her hair was tied back demurely with a white ribbon. She strode toward him in the cell with a smile that said there was no place on earth she would rather be.

"Hello, Flynn."

He didn't respond, but neither did he stop looking at her.

"Good morning, Mr. Hudson," the lawyer said.

"Morning, Parfury."

"Miss Wyatt requested a visit."

"I told you I didn't want any more visits from Miss Wyatt."

"She said it was urgent."

"Do lawyers in Nassau take no note of their clients' wishes?"

"Of course, but . . ." The lawyer laughed self-consciously. "That young lady is hard to say no to when she sets her mind to something."

Flynn had not taken his eyes from Dodie's face. "What is it, Dodie? What's wrong?"

She sat down on the edge of the bed and patted the spot beside her, inviting him to join her. He almost didn't. He tried not to. But his legs took him over to her and his body elbowed out the air next to her and claimed the space as its own.

"What's happened?" he asked quickly.

"I've spoken to Ella Sanford." She glanced at Parfury, who was still standing by the door, regarding her with professional interest, clearly intending to listen to her every word. She swiveled round on the bed so that her back was turned to the lawyer, blocking him out. "She told me things."

"What things?"

"The investigation into Sir Harry's murder"—she spoke softly—"is being deliberately sabotaged, evidence destroyed, and this could only come from the top."

"That's one hell of an accusation." He checked whether Parfury had heard. Hard to tell. Flynn was eager to ask for details but thought better of it, and hid his frustration with a shrug. "And the fall guys are me and Marigny."

"I had a few minutes with Christie. He looks terrible. Going to pieces. Threatening me with lawyers."

"Better lawyers than goons."

She smiled. He wanted to take hold of her shoulders and shake her till she recognized the danger she was in, till she was a nervous young woman again, the way she had been when he first watched her patrolling the shallows of her beach before . . .

Before this. Before him.

She saw something of his thoughts, because her eyes grew fierce and she leaned her face toward him, daring him. But she continued speaking as if nothing else was going on.

"We don't know whether they're protecting themselves or protecting the island. And no one is mentioning anything about gold."

"I bet they're not. They are all wondering which one has it."

"I've been thinking about those gold coins found in your jacket." She glanced over her shoulder at Parfury, unaware that her tied-back hair flew so close to Flynn's mouth as she did so, that he could have caught it between his teeth. He smelled the scent of the sea on it. "Mr. Parfury," she said briskly, "have you come up with any information? What are the police saying about them?"

"They are napoleons. French coins from years ago."

"You see," she said as she swung back to Flynn. "They match. Where did they come from?"

Flynn refused to discuss it. He wanted her to forget all about gold and wallets.

When he didn't respond, she said, "It's obvious that Morrell must have had more gold coins on him, which the killer stole and then used them to frame you." She put out a hand and tentatively touched his sleeve. "Do you agree?"

He looked down at her pale pink fingernails on his arm but said nothing.

"Also," she said, undaunted by his silence, "I went to your landlord again."

"No, Dodie. Stay away from him."

"I went with Mama Keel this time."

Oh, she was clever. If anyone was going to loosen their tongues, it would be Mama Keel.

"So?" he asked.

"They're thinking about it." She rolled her eyes with impatience. "So don't give up hope."

"Stop it, Dodie."

Her fingers curled around his cuff.

"I can't," she whispered.

"You must."

"No."

"I don't want you hurt."

"I am already hurt. Because you're in here."

He wanted to touch her face, to taste her skin one more time.

"Don't worry," she said. "Though Christie may be threatening me, it's only with his lawyer. He told me to go to Hector Latcham and—"

Flynn's hand seized her arm. He shook it hard. "Why? Why the hell would you go to Hector Latcham? Keep away from him."

"Hector Latcham?"

"Yes." The word snapped out of him.

"Why? He's *your* lawyer."

"Like hell he is. Parfury is—"

"I work for Mr. Latcham, sir," Parfury said mildly over by the door.

Flynn's heart shut down. His skin grew cold. After all he'd done to protect her, he'd not allowed for this, not this . . .

"Flynn?"

He was on his feet and standing right in front of Parfury. "Give me two minutes," he said urgently. He saw the lawyer glance warily at his clenched fists. "Two minutes. That's all. Let me have two minutes alone with her."

"No, I can't, it's against the rules."

"Then break the goddamn rules. Two minutes."

"No, Mr. Hudson, I . . ." But something Parfury saw in him made him change his mind. He gave a quick rap on the door and made his exit. "Two minutes," he muttered. "I'm counting."

The moment the door swung shut, Flynn pulled Dodie to her feet and spoke fast. "Don't go near Hector Latcham. You hear me? He's dangerous."

"But he was helpful. He is Ella Sanford's friend and so is being kind to—"

Flynn gripped her shoulders. "Remember I told you that the mobsters had another guy on this island, my contact here. Named Spencer?"

Her lips opened, their color drained away.

"His real name is Hector Latcham. He's the one who hired thugs to beat you up. So don't tell me that mob lawyer is helpful and kind. Don't . . ."

Without warning he pulled her against his chest, so hard that her chin nearly cracked a rib. "Dodie, you must swear to me you won't go near him again. I didn't tell you his name before because I figured it meant you wouldn't go near him. I was trying to keep you safe."

She stood still and silent in his arms, but he could feel her heartbeat. Out of control. Quietly she started to talk.

"Flynn, this means you won't get out of here. Not with Hector Latcham overseeing your case at the trial. I'll arrange a different lawyer immediately, I can't . . ." The words seemed to swell in her throat. "I can't . . . bear to think that—"

"Don't, Dodie."

She lifted her face and he kissed her mouth. He had only seconds left. "Promise me you won't go near him."

"I promise, but . . ." Suddenly she pulled back from him, eyes huge. "Ella!"

"Ella Sanford? What about her?"

"She was meeting him today to ask him all about Portman Cay."

Before he could argue, she was out of his arms and hammering on the door. "Let me out!"

Chapter 52

Ella

Hector parked up on the road and they walked down together through the shade of the trees. The gleaming white beach burst out at them with blinding brilliance when they emerged, a perfect horseshoe of shimmering sand that curled away in both directions. Beyond, a sea and sky of such fierce turquoise was clamped tightly around it that for one odd moment Ella had a feeling that there was no escape.

"What do you think?"

"It's certainly beautiful," Ella commented.

Hector was pressing a hand flat on top of his smooth brown hair as if he were suffering a headache, but his eyes were bright and his movements alert. He reminded Ella of one of the sandpipers that stalked the water's edge, never still.

"I need to know more about the person who bought this beach," Ella said. "Dodie Wyatt told me it was someone called Mr. Alan Leggaty."

"Did she indeed?"

"Do you know him? You must have drawn up the contract."

"I didn't meet Mr. Leggaty personally."

"Isn't that odd?"

"Not really. I have minions for that."

Something was wrong. Ella didn't know what, but she could feel it. Perhaps Hector was regretting giving up so much time to bring her out here, because certainly his mind seemed to be else-where. They were walking a stretch of the beach close to the surf where the sand was firm and Ella carried her shoes in her hand, letting the breeze snatch away the images in her head of the mass grave at the bottom of her garden. But she couldn't stop a shiver when she thought of Dan.

"Are you all right, Ella?"

"Yes." She looked at the man beside her, solid, dependable Hector whose passion was yacht racing and whose only vice seemed to be a tendency to bore his wife, Tilly, with boat talk too much. "No, Hector," Ella said truthfully, "to be honest I'm not all right." She came to a halt on the warm sand and looked up into his face. "I'm frightened."

His cheeks were red. The sun? Or the headache? Strangely he didn't look startled by her admission.

"Frightened? My poor Ella, tell me why."

She shook her head. "No, I can't . . ."

On the empty beach he took her hand between his. "Yes, you can tell me. I'm your friend, Ella. I'm here to help."

So she told him. About the chickens. About her worries that someone could be watching her.

"Why would anyone be watching you?" he asked, and she heard the understandable ripple of amusement in his tone.

"Because I saw something that I wasn't meant to see."

"And what was that?"

She almost didn't tell him. Almost. But his concern felt so real and he wasn't the kind of man to scoff.

"I saw a hoard of gold in Sir Harry's house. The night Morrell was there, the man who was—"

A strange noise came from him. Partway between a cough and a groan. "A hoard of gold? Are you sure?"

"Of course I'm sure. I called there that night collecting for the Red Cross and it was on the table."

She told him about the coin that Dodie had brought to her and that she had believed it was a warning from Morrell to beware of Sir Harry. But now she wasn't so sure.

"They both saw the gold and now they're both dead." Slowly she raked her foot through the sand. "What do you think, Hector? Should I be frightened or am I just being foolish? You're a lawyer, you know about these things. I don't want to worry Reggie. Give me advice, because I haven't told the police yet, not formally."

"Haven't you?"

Hector was staring out to sea, where the waves were rolling in with soft murmurs.

"Have you told anyone you think the murders are connected with the sale of this tract of land?"

"No."

"Good," he said, and it seemed to be aimed more at the waves than at her.

Ella frowned. Again that feeling that something wasn't quite right. She followed his line of sight and noticed a yacht anchored about a mile offshore, flickering like a white seabird in the sunlight. She lifted her hand to shade her eyes.

"Hector, is that *Storm Cloud*?"

He nodded.

"What's she doing here?" Ella asked.

"I sail her to this bay sometimes. When I want some peace and quiet." *Storm Cloud* was Hector's new boat. "I keep a tender in an inlet among those rocks over there. A guard watches over things some days."

"I didn't know."

"Morrell is dead, Ella. So is Sir Harry. Why don't you leave it to the police? That's my advice to you. Don't get involved."

"Like Dodie Wyatt has done, you mean? No, Hector, it's too late for that." Ella started to walk up the slope of the beach. "Let's go back. I've seen enough."

But she hadn't gone more than a few paces when Hector said with deliberate emphasis, "When Miss Wyatt found Morrell dying, she claims he didn't have any gold with him. Not even the ivory box it came in."

Ella's foot halted. Her breath stopped. All she could hear was the silence as she turned back to face Hector. He was smiling sadly at her.

"What ivory box, Hector? I've not mentioned any kind of box."

"Come out to my boat, Ella. It's a good day for a sail, there's a stiff breeze out there."

Hector's words sounded ridiculously calm and reasonable. But her heart was thundering in her chest. Could she be mistaken? Surely a man who was her friend, whose wife was her closest friend, could not be saying what she thought he was saying, could not mean what she thought he was meaning.

"You know I'm a rotten sailor, Hector," she called over her shoulder. "Let's head on home now. It's too hot out—"

"Ella!"

That one word told her what she didn't want to know.

She turned to face Hector. He was pointing a gun at her.

Chapter 53

Dodie

Dodie raced through the streets of Nassau. She dodged across roads, tore around corners, ducked under parasols, wove through the crowds ambling along the hot streets, a scream of fury lodged in her throat.

Hector Latcham.

He had smiled at her.

He had promised her help.

He had called her *my dear young lady*.

And all the time he was laughing. Because he'd burned down her house. Had her beaten to a pulp.

Hector Latcham.

The name was branded on her skin in bruises. What kind of man was he? One who destroyed people at will. One who hid behind a wall of smiles, passing unnoticed among his colonial herd.

She ran onto Bay Street. With its friendly pastel face. Its canopied walkways. Its elegant shops. Her heart was pounding as she sped over the pavement, aware that above her, above the shops, above the street, above the law, rose the offices. Where lies were told. Deals were struck. Fates were sealed.

Hector Latcham. The name gleamed innocently on the brass plaque on the door. She rang the bell to his office.

Be there, Ella. Please. Be there.

*   *   *

"So where is she?"

"I don't know, Miss Wyatt."

"Where did he take her?"

"I don't know, Miss Wyatt."

"You must know something."

"I'm sorry I can't help."

"When did they leave?"

"Well over an hour ago, I think. But Mr. Latcham didn't mention where they were going."

"Did he say when he'd be back?"

"No, he didn't. Look, Miss Wyatt, is it really so urgent that you can't wait until—"

"Yes. It's urgent. Yes. It's very very urgent. Please, think. Did either of them mention Portman Cay?"

"No, not that I heard. But . . ."

"What?"

"Well, just as they were walking out of the office, I heard Mrs. Sanford laugh and say she wasn't wearing shoes that were right for the beach."

"Thank you. Thank you."

Chapter 54

Ella

"Hector! What are you doing?"

"I warned you, Ella, not to get involved."

He approached her over the sand. Even a bad shot couldn't miss from there. Ella forced herself to look away from the blunt business end of the gun and to look at the face of the man who intended to kill her.

"Hector, have you gone crazy?"

But it wasn't Hector's eyes that looked back at her. They were the cold eyes of someone she didn't know. His pupils were dark pinpoints of anger and his mouth was twisted in a grimace.

"Why did you force me into this, Ella? You fool, there was no need for it. If you'd kept out of everything and let me deal with your interfering friend, Miss Wyatt, and her Yankee troublemaker, there'd have been none of this."

He nudged the gun toward her and she backed off a pace. The trees were close but not close enough. If she made a run for it he'd put a bullet in her back, she didn't doubt it for a second.

"The chickens were my warning?" she asked.

"Of course."

"And you expected me to lie down and keep my mouth shut? To do nothing?" She was advancing on him now, a pulse pumping at her throat.

A bullet hit the sand in front of her feet. It shattered the silence of the bay and sent a flock of gulls wheeling up into the air with a clatter of wings.

"No further." The gun pointed at her chest.

"Or what? You'll kill me? You're going to do that anyway. Like you killed Morrell, I presume. And Sir Harry too? Or was that Christie who . . . ?"

She saw his eyes narrow a fraction and knew he was about to pull the trigger.

"Why, Hector? What's this about? Tell me that much, at least."

"What do you think it's about, Ella? Money. Everything is always about money." He gave her a crooked half smile. "Or love."

The way he said the word "love." It had claw marks on it.

"You know about me and . . . ?"

"Detective Sergeant Calder? Of course I know. I've had you followed."

Her mouth was dry and words were stumbling on her lips but she tried to talk to him the way she would talk to the old Hector.

"Don't do this, Hector. Don't make things worse for yourself. I am your friend and you know that Reggie and I will do all we can to help you."

"Nice try, Ella. But don't waste your breath. You would tighten the noose around my neck yourself, let's not fool ourselves." He was sweating. "Now get down on your knees and say your prayers."

Ella didn't move. "Sir Harry was right. Gold has rotted your soul."

"Like your lover is rotting yours." He sneered and stiffened himself to pull the trigger. His mouth tensed and his eyes were no more than slits. She felt a flicker of satisfaction that he was not finding it easy.

"No!" a voice bellowed behind her. A great roar of sound charged down on to the beach from the trees and a shadow plunged toward her, racing over the sand. "No! Throw down the gun. Now!"

Hector froze for the split second Ella needed to swing round and see Dan coming toward her like a bull. The sight of him, the sound of him, the sheer physical presence of him on the beach wrenched all fear for herself out of her.

"Dan, don't, he'll kill—"

The gun fired. The sound of the shot ripped through her. Then she saw Dan's knees buckle, heard a strange whistle of thin sound escape from his lungs, felt the vibration under her feet as the full weight of him hit the sand.

Ella couldn't scream. Couldn't find any air to breathe. She threw herself on her knees beside him and clutched her hand over the hole in his shirt, as if she could push the blood back inside his chest.

"Dan!"

She saw his eyes glaze over. Witnessed the life seep out of him into the grains of sand beneath and only then did she start to scream. The blow to her head, when it came, was a relief.

Chapter 55

Dodie

Dodie stole a bicycle. It was old and hand-painted canary yellow, leaning against the wall of the cathedral, but she didn't even hesitate. The instant she saw it, she took it.

She pedaled fast. But the five-mile ride out of town to Portman Cay felt more like fifty, because each minute seemed like an hour while her mind filled with images of the danger Ella was in. The road was hot and parched, pockmarked with holes, and Dodie had to squint against the glare as the morning sun climbed above the tall pines. An occasional cart or car rumbled toward her, kicking up dust, and she took it as a good sign. No dead bodies on the roadside up ahead. No panic.

If she hadn't told Ella about Portman Cay.

What then?

What had she done?

*   *   *

No.

Not this.

Not another death. Through the web of trees Dodie saw the body, a dark smear on the white sand, saw the gulls, and ran screaming at them down the slope, arms whirling with rage. The birds abandoned their prize at the last possible moment, screeching up into the skies, and Dodie hurled an impotent handful of sand after them.

No. Not this.

A moan rose out of her as she dropped to her knees beside the big policeman and flapped her hands over the black ball of flies that whirred and hummed, crawling on the wound under his shirt. A great wave of sorrow hit her square in the chest. It knocked the breath out of her. She cradled his heavy hand between hers, as if she could bring warmth back into it and persuade blood to flow through its veins once more. Tears seeped from her.

She couldn't believe that Hector Latcham was responsible for this. It was unthinkable. Yet even as a tremor shuddered through her, she thought the unthinkable.

Ella? Where was she?

She tore off the scarf tying back her hair and carefully bound it around the face of Detective Calder to keep it safe from the scavenging gulls. She had to move quickly. She examined the footprints in the sand, but they told her little because the tide and the wind had been at work. She checked that the beach and the rock pools held no other surprises, then scoured the undergrowth under the trees, poking it with sticks, disturbing lizards and a nest of hutias.

She found nothing. She stood wiping sweat from her eyes and stared up and down the beach. "Ella, where are you?"

A breeze rippled the gleaming surface of the waves, sending darts of sunlight to dazzle her eyes. It was a world that dozed as peacefully as the cormorants on the rocks.

"You're here, Ella, I know you are. His car is still parked up on the road." A big black Buick, a lawyer's car, had been tucked away in the shade.

That was when she saw the boat. She had been too absorbed by the beach and the lifeless body of Detective Calder, too focused on what was under her feet, but now she swore at herself and tore off her Arcadia dress.

*   *   *

The yacht loomed up above her, as white as a wedding cake. With silent strokes Dodie circled it, noting the tender tied alongside, and lifted herself out of the water onto the ladder.

A wave slapped the hull of the boat, making it rock, and she rolled over the side, crouching on the deck. Just to her right she could see the entrance to a companionway. Dodie wasn't used to boats but she knew enough to remember that you descended a companionway ladder backward and that seemed a bad idea. A very bad idea. Whatever was waiting down below would get first crack at her before she could turn. Her breath came fast and shallow.

Flynn. Help me.

She tried to think like him. To move in that alert way he had and to make no sound. She edged up to the companionway and listened. Silence and heat drifted up to her.

What if she was wrong?

But the tender was tethered to the boat and that meant someone had to be on board. A sudden noise started up below and startled her, the mechanical sound of pumping. If Hector was busy with something, now was the time to climb down. Instantly she slid down the companionway ladder, her pulse pounding, and was hit by the heat and the gloom. Hatches closed. No air. She'd stepped into a narrow saloon of varnished teak and brass with a long thin table and fixed padded benches on each side of it. Slumped on one of them and facing Dodie was a woman.

"Ella?"

The corn-colored head shot up. Huge bleak eyes stared at her.

"Dodie! No, leave quickly. Don't . . ." Her head was shaking back and forth as Dodie moved toward the table.

Just as Dodie registered with shock the handcuffs that chained Ella to a brass rail behind her, a tarpaulin descended over her own head. Strong arms forced her to the floor. She kicked. Screamed. Fought for air. But it wasn't enough.

*   *   *

The world came back to Dodie in pieces. Blood in her mouth. A pain in her chest. The metallic click of a lighter. A swaying motion that was not just in her head. A hand hot on her cheek.

"You bastard, you've suffocated her." It was Ella.

"She'll come round." Hector Latcham's voice.

"Let her go, I beg you, Hector. Just leave her somewhere on the beach. She hasn't seen you yet, so doesn't know anything."

He said nothing, but must have shaken his head because Ella burst out with sudden anger. "Haven't you killed enough? Are you dead inside? Don't you care that . . . ?"

Dodie opened her eyes.

"Ah, Miss Wyatt, I see you are with us again."

Slowly Dodie raised her head. It felt as if a jackhammer was at work in it. She tried to brush her wet hair from its sprawl over her face but her hand wouldn't come, and she jerked around to find her right wrist handcuffed to Ella's left wrist. Worse was that they were both attached to a brass rail behind them at shoulder level.

"You bastard! You murderer!"

"Enough of that, Miss Wyatt. No good yelling. We're in the middle of the ocean."

"Just let us go."

"Now, why would I do that? You are proving too dangerous. I should have had my boys finish you off before, but I didn't want to draw attention to you. It would have had even our sleepy police asking awkward questions if you had turned up dead right after Morrell did. But nice of you to drop in to see us." He was standing back against the wooden wall opposite, his gray eyes inspecting her coldly. "Interesting dress code."

She was almost naked. It hadn't seemed to matter till then, but now her skin flushed uncomfortably.

"Give her something, Hector!" Ella had somehow found her diplomat's wife voice.

With a shrug he unlatched a drawer next to him and threw Dodie a flowered beach sarong that must have belonged to his wife. "Here, you might as well be decent when they find you dead."

Dodie draped it over herself and with Ella's help tied the knot.

"Why don't you just shoot us and get it over with?" Ella demanded bitterly.

"Ah, my dear Ella, I really hate to shoot a woman."

"Easier to dump us at sea. Is that the plan?"

"Something like that. Or leave you here on the boat to die of thirst."

"What about Tilly? How can you do this to her? She'll find out, you know she will. She'll discover what you've done to Dan and to us and report you to—"

"Detective Calder, I admit, is more of a problem." Hector glared at Ella as if she were to blame for that. "The police don't like to lose one of their own."

"God damn you to hell for this."

"There's no such thing as hell, Miss Wyatt. Only this world and what we have in it. I was just doing a deal to make a lot of money. That's all. Nothing wrong with that. Then came the all-hail Sir Harry Oakes." Hector's face stiffened as he said the name. "He believed that this island was his fiefdom and he should decide what did or didn't go on here."

"Hector," Ella said, "no normal person kills a man for spoiling a deal." Her voice was husky from the tears she'd shed for Dan. "Let Dodie go, please." Her face was looking gaunt and desolate.

"Tell us," Dodie said, "what happened?"

He was never going to let them go, she knew that. But if she could keep him talking, the more time that passed, the more she could gather the parts of her head together and come up with ideas.

Hector pushed himself off the wall and lit a cigarette. "Christie and I have a good deal going. We are buying Portman Cay from Oakes and developing it into a center of luxury hotels and a casino for tourists after the war. This war has widened ordinary people's horizons like never before and they're going to want more. It can't fail. Of course the mob wanted to be in on it. They're paying for the development but we have to put up money too. Big money."

"What about the no-gambling laws?"

Hector gave Dodie a sly smile. "The duke is in on it. He'll make sure the law is changed. That bastard Oakes loaned us millions. He backed us to the hilt till we were both in over our heads and then he pulled the bloody rug from under us."

"What?"

"He called in the loans. I'd have gone bankrupt, Christie too, and we all know the one thing you don't do is owe the mob money, if you want to keep out of a concrete grave." He wiped sweat from his neck. It was very hot down in the small claustrophobic space.

Dodie asked for a drink.

"No."

"Ella needs one. She's not looking good."

He regarded her coldly. "It doesn't matter."

"Please." She was hoping to get a drinking glass in her hand. Not much of a weapon, but something.

"No. Don't ask again."

For a moment there was a tense silence broken only by the wind whining through the rigging.

"That's where Morrell came in, isn't it?" Dodie said. "To deal with Sir Harry."

"Damn right it is. He was supposed to *persuade* Oakes. Morrell was a mobster, he knew a hundred different methods of persuasion—backed up by your sharp young friend who is now first in line for the hangman's noose." He slammed a fist down on the table. "It fell apart. Because Oakes bought Morrell off with his gold."

"So you killed Morrell and Oakes." The words tasted sour in Dodie's mouth.

Hector started to laugh, a thin lifeless sound that made Ella drop her face into her hand.

"Don't look so horrified, Miss Wyatt. I'm not the only one with his hands dirty. Your American friend—"

"He has a name," Dodie said angrily.

"Well, do you know that your Mr. Hudson went over to the Gregory Sewing Factory before he was arrested and put Stan Gregory in hospital?" He smiled with grim satisfaction. "Ah, I see you didn't. I rather thought you might have got him to do it for you."

Flynn. Oh, Flynn.

"He will see you hang before he does," she hissed.

Dodie didn't see it coming, the sudden explosion of rage that transfused Hector's face, turning his narrow cheeks purple. He stepped forward and lashed out at her, a slap with the full weight of his arm behind it. Her head snapped back and her eyes rolled in their sockets. She sprang to her feet, making a lunge at him, but he had stepped quickly away and she was anchored to the brass railing by the handcuffs.

"Listen to me, you bitch," he shouted at her. "I don't intend to swing for those murders. Or for yours."

He bounded up the steps and was gone.

Chapter 56

Flynn

Each step was agony. Because each step should be taking him to Dodie's side, but instead it was wasted in the narrow channel that ran along the center of his cell. Flynn paced it, hour after hour, mile after mile. Willing Dodie to return to him before the sky grew dark.

She didn't listen.

He could see it in her eyes when he told her to stay away from Hector Latcham. She was saying yes, when what she meant was no. He knew it when she ran for the door, he knew that the first place she would go was to Hector Latcham, to protect her friend Ella Sanford. He paced out the hours, cursing himself, cursing Morrell.

Cursing Hector Latcham.

He thought of the *obeah* curse he had wished on Hector. The hairbrush. The fine strands of brown hair from Hector's head, and the power of Mama Keel's magic. Could it destroy him? He grimaced at his own foolishness, but it was all he had left now.

That one small bead of hope.

*   *   *

"Out!"

Flynn was under the window, watching the day drain out of the sky. The lights in his cell were so bright and so relentless that his eyes had to fight to focus on the subtle changes of color outside that told him the passing of time.

"Out!"

Flynn regarded the prison warden with distaste. "What now?"

"You're free to go."

"Is this a joke?"

"No, man. You can walk out of here."

Flynn headed straight for the door. "A free man?"

"Yes. Collect your belongings, sign the form, and get out of here." He was grinning, a big white-toothed grin.

"What happened? Why now?"

"Ah, it was your landlord. He thinks he made a big mistake."

Flynn was running down the corridor. *Thank you, Mama Keel. I owe you.*

*   *   *

Where was she?

Too late now for her to be at Portman Cay.

Hector's office? It would be shut for the night.

Hector's house?

He remembered the dark-haired wife asleep in the bed. She was probably at the house right now, waiting with her martini for her husband to finish his drinks in some bar with the Bay Street Boys. A normal day. No, she wasn't likely to help him.

Who then?

Ella Sanford.

*   *   *

"Mrs. Sanford ain't here."

The maid in her white uniform was staring at Flynn with wide, worried eyes, her hands fretting at each other.

"Do you know where she is?" he asked.

"No, sir, I surely don't."

"Do you have any idea where she went?"

"I wish I did. She left real early this mornin'."

"Have you seen Miss Wyatt today?"

"That young girl who came here before? No, sir, I ain't." She clutched at the flimsy straw of hope. "You think they just out havin' fun together somewhere, is that it?"

"No," he said as the image of Hector Latcham's cold eyes rose in his mind. "I don't think they're having fun."

Chapter 57

Dodie

Their mouths were parched. The heat was intense. The constant motion of the boat under her set Dodie's teeth on edge as it dipped and rolled with the waves. Only now that the light had begun to dwindle did she accept that Hector was not coming back. He was doing what he said he would—leaving them there to die on the boat.

Ella wasn't good. There was a tightness to her face, and her hand was clenched in distress as if only just holding on by a thin thread of willpower. Her eyes looked bruised and had sunk deep in her thin face. Dodie tried to keep her talking but Ella had succumbed to the sounds in her own head and had no room for any voices except Dan Calder's.

All during the long hot hours of the day spent in the belly of the boat, Dodie had worked to escape, but it was hopeless. Their wrists were bloodied and pestered by fat hungry flies. The handcuffs were looped around the brass rail that bordered a shelf behind them, and however hard she pulled and pushed, twisted and tugged, it refused to come adrift from the teak wall. Her efforts were tearing their wrists to shreds, though Ella never uttered a whimper.

Only once did she murmur, "Give up, Dodie. There's no point."

"There is, Ella. It's our only way out of here."

Ella had let a faint smile spill out of her. "They are Dan's handcuffs. They were in his pocket. It's ironic that he died trying to save me but his own handcuffs will kill me." She was rocking back and forth on the bench. "Don't you think?"

But Dodie was stern with her. "Concentrate on getting out."

"I'm frightened of living, Dodie. Not of dying. I've never had to live with this kind of loss because I've never felt this kind of love before. I am not strong like you." She brushed her fingers regretfully over Dodie's bloody wrist. "I'm sorry, Dodie."

"Don't, Ella. You are stronger than you think. We have to get out of here. I am not going to die here. Not in a stinking boat. Not while Flynn is still drawing breath."

"Dodie," Ella murmured as she laid her head down on the table, "you deserve better."

※　　※　　※

There was the sound of footsteps on deck. Dodie jerked awake. How long had she slept?

Minutes only. It was still light enough to see. The boat was rolling more under a rising wind and she could feel it pulling on its anchor. She nudged Ella.

"He's back."

Ella blinked but her eyes were dull as a figure clattered noisily down the ladder rungs and stumbled into the gloomy room with an oath.

"Tilly!" Ella exclaimed.

Dodie stared in disbelief. Relief swept through her and her fingers jittered with the sudden release of nerves.

"Thank God," Ella whispered.

Dodie stood, her right arm in a spasm of fatigue. "Mrs. Latcham, your husband has imprisoned us here and . . ."

Only then did she realize Tilly was drunk. She was weaving sideways as she walked, holding on to the wall.

"Darlings," Tilly said as she eased herself onto the bench opposite them, "how absolutely vile. You look terrible."

Dodie sat down again to be on the same level as Tilly, but she could sense this was not right. Tilly was too brittle, too accepting of their plight. She should have screamed in horror and rushed to the toolbox.

"Mrs. Latcham." Dodie spoke clearly and slowly. "Please fetch a chisel or a hammer from—"

"I've come to tell you something."

Now Ella was aware of the oddness about her. "Tilly, please, this is serious."

"So is this."

"What is it, Mrs. Latcham? Tell us quickly. Mrs. Sanford needs attention."

"I came to tell you, Dodie"—Tilly's words were thick but her eyes were focused hard on Dodie's—"that your friend Mr. Morrell should not have been so damn stupid that night in our car. If he hadn't refused to tell me where he'd emptied the gold from the wretched ivory box he was carrying, I wouldn't have had to stab him."

"What? Tilly, no!"

"Hector recognized what the ivory box was and I persuaded Morrell into our car, but when he was so uncooperative about everything, I had to threaten him with a knife and . . . well, we struggled and . . . that was it."

"My God, Tilly," Ella gasped, "you must go to the police at once, tell them the truth. That it was an accident."

Dodie put a hand on Ella. "Can't you see? That's what this is all about for Hector Latcham? Not just the land deal. It's about protecting his wife."

The boat creaked and lurched as the wind turned suddenly. Darkness in the islands fell fast and Dodie was certain that Tilly would want to leave quickly before the seas grew too rough for the rowboat.

"Mrs. Latcham." Dodie strove to keep her voice calm and reasonable. "Ella is right. You must go to the police. You can't let

Flynn Hudson hang for a crime you committed. You have to tell them."

"My dear Miss Wyatt, why on earth would I do that?"

This woman wants me to die.

The realization sent a shiver of revulsion through her and she glanced at Ella to see if she realized it too, but saw no signs.

"So why," Dodie asked, "did you save me so dramatically from kidnap in the car in Nassau if . . . ?" She halted. Instinctively she drew back from the table, farther away from the lawyer's wife, as if she were contagious. "Of course, I should have realized. You set it up in the first place, didn't you, so that you could come riding in to save me."

The scarlet slash of a mouth smiled, pleased with itself. "Cunning, wasn't it? I hoped you would confide in me and tell me what dirty little secrets you know about where the gold is." She shrugged. "It almost worked." She popped open her leather bag, removed a cigarette case, and lit a Dunhill for herself. The hand that held the lighter was rock steady. She exhaled a plume of smoke that hung from the beams overhead like old cobwebs in the stagnant air.

"The foolish man. He should have cooperated."

Dodie did not want to hear Morrell called a foolish man.

Tilly shook her head with frustration. "He'd buried the coins somewhere on Sir Harry's estate, but he wouldn't reveal where."

Dodie pictured the big bear of a man, Johnnie Morrell, bargaining desperately for his life, with a knife doing the arguing for the Latchams. It made her want to seize this pampered woman by the throat.

"That is why," Tilly confided in a sudden rush of intimacy, "Sir Harry caught us digging in his grounds the other night and everything turned nasty."

Ella stared at her, aghast. "You? Are you saying you are the one who shot Sir Harry?"

"Oh, Ella, it wasn't meant to happen."

"Tilly!"

"Well, the bloody man was going to hand us over to the police and I had to stop him. Poor old Hector had the devil's own job covering it all up in that ghastly storm, what with Christie there as well. And he even scattered those stupid feathers on the body, for heaven's sake."

A low visceral moan issued from Ella and she rose menacingly to her feet.

"It was you. All this was because of you. You're the reason Dan is dead on that beach out there. You. Not Hector."

"How was I to know the stupid detective would get in the way, darling? That's why I've come all the way out here to see you. I wanted to explain. I didn't intend for him to die." She pulled a face at Ella. "Anyway we've been good friends, you and I, and I wanted to say good-bye."

"You are not my friend."

"Darling, don't be so rude. Hector was right. He told me not to come, but I insisted. He was even willing to row me out, but I wouldn't let him. This moment is between just you and me, darling." She blew a kiss to Ella.

Ella tried to seize Tilly, one-handed across the table, but despite the drink inside her, Tilly was faster. She withdrew a tiny pearl-handled pistol from her bag and flashed it in Ella's face.

"My darling girl, don't make me."

Dodie leaped to her feet. "Mrs. Latcham, it'll be dark soon. Fetch the tools immediately, please. We need to get out of here. Or do you have the key to the cuffs?"

Beside her, Ella was shaking with fury.

"No, I don't have the key, I'm afraid. Such a shame. But I think I'll give the tools a miss too." She looked from Ella's white face to Dodie's, then at the fading light. Beneath them the boat rocked warningly. "I shall say good-bye to you, dear ladies."

It was the work of a moment for Dodie. A quick smack with her free hand on the side of the gun. Tilly was not expecting it from Dodie, her eyes were watching Ella. Dodie had been calm and respectful, no threat, no smacker of guns, but Tilly was wrong. The pistol flew out of her hand onto the table, where Ella seized it in her right hand and aimed it straight at Tilly.

For ten seconds neither moved. But neither of them would back down. Then Tilly threw herself forward, hands reaching for the pistol.

"Give me the gun!"

Ella pulled the trigger. The noise of the shot exploded in the small space and gulls shrieked outside as they rose in alarm from their roosts on the yacht's sleek deck. Tilly whimpered. A small sound. Nothing more. Blood oozed out in a dark burgundy stain across the stomach of her pale crepe dress and Tilly stared at it with surprise.

"Mrs. Latcham, listen to me." Dodie spoke loudly to gain her attention. "We'll help you. But you have to get something to free us."

But Tilly continued to frown, bemused at the stain on her dress, then with a jerk she set herself in motion and staggered up the companionway ladder. Minutes later they heard the slap of oars on the water.

The wind was rising.

*   *   *

Dodie held the gun steady. She released her breath and pulled the trigger. The varnished teak of the boat's wall splintered and the end of the brass rail broke away, so that they could slide the handcuffs down it and off the end.

"Freedom!" Dodie said, and shook the burning muscles of her arm. "Of a kind, anyway."

They were still attached to each other. It was dark inside the boat now, so she couldn't see Ella's expression clearly, but she had sensed a deadness in her ever since she'd turned the gun on the woman who had been her friend.

"Let's get out of here," Dodie urged.

"Do you think she'll be all right?"

"Of course she will. She'll get to the hospital and they'll patch her up. She was all right enough to row a boat, so it can't be so bad." But she heard Ella's murmur of doubt and it echoed what lay hidden behind her own words. They had both seen Tilly's face when the bullet hit her.

"Now," Dodie said firmly, "let's go. Before they come back."

* * *

"I can't."

"You can, Ella."

It was dark on deck. The vast stretch of blackness below them pitched and rolled as the ocean wheeled around the boat and rumbled underneath them. They could hear its boom and smell its salty breath. Out on deck the air was sharp and sweet after the heat below, but the moon had not yet risen and the stars were no more than faint pinpricks in the immense sweep of darkness above them.

"I'll help you," Dodie promised.

She had searched the deck for life belts but found none. She counted to three. They jumped.

Chapter 58

Ella

Ella panicked the moment her head plunged underwater.

Her arms and legs spun out in all directions, forcing her down, and she was dragging Dodie down with her. Her mind splintered. Which way was up? She had no idea.

Her eyes were wide open yet she was blind, totally blind. A wall of nothingness. Terror gripped her and her heart thundered in her chest. Not like this. She didn't want to die like this with someone hauling on her arm, pulling her down to the depths where fish would eat out her tongue.

No. She kicked hard against it. Tried to breathe and felt water flood into her lungs. The shock of it made her go limp and she didn't resist when she felt herself tugged down farther because she realized this was the end. But she had it all upside down. This way was upward and her head shot above water and air burst into her lungs, making her cough and retch as a hand held her chin above the waves.

"Dodie!"

"I'm here. You're all right. Keep calm."

"I almost drowned you."

"Just remember what I told you."

What had she told her? Ella had no idea. She was kicking with her legs to keep afloat, but already her muscles were tiring. She tried to suck in air but a wave smacked her in the face.

"Relax." Dodie was at her side, though she could see no more than the outline of a dim head shape against the black waters. "Let me do the work."

Things came back to Ella. Spiking into her mind. *We'll try swimming one-handed together*, and *I'll tow you*, and always *Relax. Don't tense up. The waves won't be big.*

But they *were* big. Massive rolling monsters that lifted her like a cork and flung her forward, tumbling her over and dragging her back again. But she started to swim. Dodie was as good as her word, pulling her onward over the swell of the waves, keeping her clear of the crests when they broke. Easy smooth strokes.

It was possible. For the first time it seemed possible they might reach the shore. But the swimming seemed to go on so long, as if they had somehow gotten lost, and it occurred to Ella to wonder whether Dodie had gotten it wrong in the darkness. Was she swimming out to sea instead of inland? Ella could feel her body growing colder. Her mind growing cloudy. The great black weight of night was heavy on her shoulders, pressing down on her, but Dodie calmly flipped them both on their backs so that she could support Ella's head on her chest while she kicked with her legs.

But an idea started to fix itself in Ella's mind. If she could reach down to the bottom, put her feet on the soft white sand far below, she would find a door she could open that would lead her to Dan. The idea grew so strong inside her head that she twisted herself so that she was upright in the water, closed her eyes, and felt her body drop like a stone. The black water enfolded her and this time she welcomed it.

Her arm dragged above her as she descended, then a foot suddenly kicked the side of her head and a hand yanked her under her arm. Again she was forced to the surface coughing foam from her lungs, with waves barreling down on top of her. But beside her Dodie was screaming. It took her a moment to realize it wasn't at her. It was at a light flickering on and off in the blackness.

* * *

He held her. By the light of the flashlight Ella knelt weakly on the sand and watched Flynn Hudson hold Dodie as if he would stop breathing if he let her go. The pair didn't speak, just rested their dark heads together and let their hands touch, their skins reconnect. He released her with reluctance only when she stopped shaking.

Flynn carried Ella on his back up through the trees to a car that was parked on the road. No one mentioned that the car was Dan's or that the keys to it must have come from Dan's pocket.

"I'll telephone the police," Flynn said with a close look at Ella on the backseat.

He'd wrapped her in his jacket and Dodie sat next to her, chafing her hands. Flynn had opened the handcuffs in seconds with a set of picks in his pocket and Ella was shocked to find she missed the cuffs when they were gone. She felt disconnected. Cut adrift. Out on the black waves again, but this time on her own. Each part of her hurt in a way she'd never known was possible as grief clawed its way through every vein, leaving dead white shreds behind.

Ella didn't close her eyes.

The headlights of Dan's car were cutting bright yellow holes in the blackness of the outside world and she wanted to crawl into one to him.

Chapter 59

Dodie

The car swerved to a halt.

"What is it?" Dodie asked instantly.

"Something back there. Under the trees."

Flynn threw the car into reverse and shot backward to a spot where there was a gap between two banks of trees. It was another car. Its parking lights were on but no headlamps.

"Wait here," he said, and opened his door.

"I'm coming." She checked on Ella on the rear seat, then slipped out of the car.

"Stay, Dodie," Flynn said. "You're wet and cold."

But she tucked her arm tight under his and was glad when he didn't argue further. The wind was high, whipping the palm fronds into a frenzy and carrying with it a strong tang of the ocean. She could taste the salt on her tongue and feel the staghorn ferns lick around her ankles as she approached the big black Buick.

"Stop right there!"

It was Hector Latcham's voice. But it sounded as if someone had a wire around his throat. Flynn immediately stepped in front of Dodie, but over his shoulder she could see the car no more than six feet away. Their own car's headlights picked it out of the surrounding night, strange shadows writhing across its bonnet as the wind lashed the tree branches. But on the ground with his legs stretched out in front of him sat Hector, leaning back against the running board of his car. On his lap lay Tilly.

"Stay away or I'll shoot."

Dodie locked a hand around Flynn's arm. "Leave him," she whispered.

But Flynn couldn't let it go. He had too much history with this man. On the drive from Portman Cay she had given him a quick account of what had happened on the boat and she had felt his anger in the car.

When would this end?

In the strange yellow light, Hector looked sick. His usual neatness was gone, his hair raked by the wind, his skin the color of tallow, and his pale blue shirt streaked with what looked like purple stains. In his hand sat a gun.

"What now?" Flynn demanded, his gaze on the inert figure of Tilly. "What are you doing here?"

Hector's arm was curled around his wife, supporting her against his chest, his chin tucked against the dark waves of her hair. She looked like a tired doll, because there was a slackness to her limbs that turned Dodie's stomach. His jacket was draped over her middle and tears were running down his cheeks.

"She's dead," he said.

"Mr. Latcham, I . . ." Dodie tried to step forward but Flynn didn't let her move. "I'm sorry," she said, "but she brought it on herself."

He nodded, heedlessly, everything about him a pale travesty of the ruthless man who had threatened her earlier that morning and left them to die on the boat.

"Tilly insisted," he said, "on going out to see you both on the yacht. I tried to stop her but . . . She was too drunk to be behind a wheel, so I drove her to Portman Cay but she refused to let me row her out. I begged her. I warned her. But she wanted to face Ella on her own. She was angry about the death of the policeman and we had a quarrel." His voice broke and he tenderly kissed his wife's head.

"Mr. Latcham, we'll go and telephone for an ambulance immediately."

"She loved him, you know."

The yellow bubble of light distorted Hector's thin face, so that he looked like a wraith, already separated from life, a part of the shadows behind.

"Loved who?"

"She's always loved him." The wind snatched at his words. "Ever since the day she first met him."

"Who? Sir Harry Oakes?"

He uttered a raw bellow of laughter that sent a scattering of wings through the trees. "No, the Duke of Windsor, of course, he's the one she loved. He bewitched her, you know, with his blue eyes and his infantile smile and the smell of his blue blood. She couldn't bear to see him unhappy. That's why she hated that Wallis woman and Sir Harry. Their affair was killing the duke."

Dodie felt Flynn tense. "Your wife shot Sir Harry because of his affair?" he said in a low voice. "Not because of the gold?"

"Ah, Hudson, it was both."

Hector raised the gun and Flynn threw Dodie to the ground, but there was no need. Hector placed the gun barrel in his own mouth and pulled the trigger.

Chapter 60

Ella

"There is too much light." Ella shut her eyes.

"You need light, Miss Ella. You is in the dark too much these days. Ain't you feelin' better none?"

But she closed the blinds halfway and the slats of sunlight settled around Ella's feet, while Emerald waited patiently with her hands on her hips for a reply. She wasn't going to let Ella get away with another of her silences.

"You gonna lose the use of that tongue of yours soon if you don't use it, Miss Ella." She had just placed a cup of tea in front of her and a slice of walnut cake fit for an elephant. "Now you eat up."

Ella was tired of people being patient with her. That's not what she wanted. Dan had never been patient, he had always been ready to push back at her when she'd tested where his limits lay.

"Thank you, Emerald."

Emerald took the dismissal, but with ill grace.

* * *

"Ella, lovely to see you down for breakfast again."

Reggie beamed at her and she saw his eyes carefully scan her face, looking for signs.

"I'll always be here for breakfast, Reggie. You know that."

She smiled at him across the table, laid out with his favorite Fortnum & Mason marmalade from London and white Egyptian linen napery, exactly as he liked it. She wanted to make him happy in the ways she could. There were so many ways now in which she couldn't. That's why she was wearing the gold gate bracelet with the sapphire.

"Good."

His tone with her these days was resolutely cheerful. Sometimes she heard herself copying it and that made her want to cry, but she didn't because he had been wonderful. He had dealt with everything. Cars and bodies had been removed and discreet funerals carried out without scandal. The police were kept at arm's length, such is the power of a diplomat's word. Ella had told him everything—without any mention of Dan. She had left that part out. Reggie knew she had left it out but never asked, and in return she didn't go to Dan's funeral, which had nearly killed her. When she complained that Freddie de Marigny was being held in jail for a crime he didn't commit, he had patted her shoulder and promised that the injustice would be dealt with when it came to his trial. She believed him implicitly.

"Toast?"

One word. One simple question. A husband offering his wife food. But they both knew it was more. Ella lifted her gaze to the garden lawn spread out behind him, to the abundance of oleanders and zinnias and the cascade of scarlet bougainvillea, and she knew that to say no to the toast would be unforgivable.

"Yes, please, Reggie."

"You're looking lovely today, my dear."

It was so untrue, it made her blush. In the mirror she could see ten years etched into her face that had not been there before the day on the boat.

Reggie passed her the toast rack.

"Enjoy it, Ella."

"Thank you." With her eyes still on the toast, she added, "I'll make you as close to happy as I can, Reggie."

"Thank you, my dearest Ella. You always do."

So polite it hurt.

Chapter 61

Dodie

"The gold, Dodie."

Flynn squatted down and placed a square box at her feet. It was an old Huntley & Palmers biscuit tin with a picture of the Derby horse race on the lid and a speckling of rust like a ginger snowstorm in one corner.

Dodie stared, appalled. "Take it away."

"Don't you want to look?"

"No, I don't."

Nevertheless he removed the lid. Inside lay the stuff men's dreams are made of and Dodie wanted to turn and run away but couldn't. She stared down at the coins that Sir Harry Oakes had given to Morrell to buy him off, at the burst of light that dazzled the eye and beguiled the heart.

"I found it exactly where the Latchams said on Oakes's estate, buried where only a guy like Morrell would think to bury such treasure."

"Where?"

"Under the pond." Flynn smiled. "The same as Oakes's gold mine lies under Kirkland Lake."

Dodie laughed at that.

"Morrell was smart," Flynn said.

He lifted a coin between his fingers and offered it up to her, but she wouldn't touch it, so he dropped it in his pocket and replaced the tin lid over the rest. They were in Mama Keel's yard. The sun was baking the earth as hard as concrete and a handful of barefoot boys in shorts were kicking a ragged football around.

Flynn looked up at Dodie from where he was crouched on the ground and eyed her carefully. "Do you want this gold, Dodie?"

"No, Flynn. It's blood money."

He patted the tin. "Yes, it's that all right."

"Are you going to give it to the police?" she asked.

His eyes widened with amusement. "Sure as hell I'm not."

"To Sir Harry's family?"

"Those guys have more than enough already."

She paused. "Are you going to keep it?"

He frowned, as if thinking hard about it, but he was teasing her. He tipped his head sideways toward where Mama Keel was hanging out washing on a rope line. "I know someone," he said under his breath, "who will know how to use it." He nodded. "Sir Harry would like that."

They walked down to the beach, where they ambled through the shallows of the surf together, the sky an endless arc of gleaming blue above them. Dodie didn't hurry to ask the question on her tongue because she wanted this moment to stretch into the future. She fixed it in her mind as one she would hold on to. The feel of the warm skin of his arm around her waist and the sight of his long pale feet swimming like lazy fish beneath the waves.

But she could sense the vibration in the air, like thunder out at sea, and she knew what was coming. Out of the western sky roared a formation of B-24 Liberators. Seven of the great monsters were climbing up from Oakes Field and droning overhead, young men with their hearts tight as they set off to patrol the Atlantic. Each plane boasted the United States Army Air Force roundel, a dark blue circle around a white star, and she saw Flynn's eyes while he watched them. There was no need to ask her question. She already knew the answer.

"You'll be leaving."

He turned to her, surprised, and then smiled when he recognized what was in her eyes. "You see too much, Dodie." He laughed. "You see what's in me before I see it myself."

She stood in front of him, the waves meandering around their ankles, and looked him full in the face, loving each feature of it. Every rise and fall of it constantly revealed more to her of the person inside.

"The Bahamas has stamped its mark on you," she said, and kissed the light golden tan that colored his cheek. "Our sun has got to work on you so you won't forget us in a hurry."

"No, you're the one who has got to work on me, Dodie."

He didn't smile as he said it and he didn't say, *I won't forget you in a hurry*. But he took both her hands solemnly in his and Dodie knew the words she dreaded to hear were going to spill out into the bright sunlit morning.

"I'm leaving."

It was said. The day crashed to a halt.

"Sir Harry Oakes and Johnnie Morrell were my friends, Dodie. More than friends, they became like fathers to me—for good or for bad—and it was because of those guys that I stayed linked to the mob. I don't have a damaged lung from tuberculosis. That certificate was forged by the mob's doctor to keep me out of the forces. But now"—he looked up at the airplanes still in formation but no more than small birds in the distance now—"all that has changed. I want a different life."

"You're going to sign up."

"Yes."

"To the army?"

"The Army Air Force."

Twenty thousand feet of nothingness between him and the ground.

"You'll be good at it, Flynn."

"Even the mob thinks twice before getting mixed up with the

military, so I will be safe there, but I'm taking my mother's sur-
name just in case."

"What is it?"

"O'Hara."

"Flynn O'Hara. That's good. I like it."

"I'm glad you like it, because I'm coming back to get you used
to it, Miss Wyatt, you and your bewitching island."

Dodie felt her day start up again and she looked around her at
the silvery beach, at the lazy palm trees, the effortless blue of the
sea and sky, at all that she had here on this side of the sun. She
wanted to share it with him.

"Too many people have been killed, Flynn. In Nassau. In
Europe. In places we've never heard of on the far side of the world.
Death changes us, it takes away parts of us that we can never get
back."

She thought of Ella and the deep gulley at the back of her eyes
where her sorrow lay buried. She was busier than ever with her
Red Cross work and had invited Dodie to join her at it in her spare
hours, but there was a look about her these days, as though she
had left too much of herself at Portman Cay.

And now Flynn was taking to the skies, where airplanes were
shot down in flames every day and death became the thief that
stalked young men's lives.

"Dodie," Flynn said, and cradled her chin in his hand, "You
mean too much to me to take away a part of you. I'll never do that,
I promise."

"Good, Flynn O'Hara. I'll hold you to that."

AUTHOR'S NOTE

A Story of Greed and Gold

The reason that I felt drawn to set a story in the beautiful Bahamas was not just because I fancied a glamorous research trip! It was because of a car. Not any old car, of course. It was a glorious, monstrous, coffin-nosed Cord automobile produced in America in 1936.

More than twenty years ago my husband owned one of these magnificent cars and through the Auburn-Cord-Duisenberg Car Club he met an author called James Leasor who also owned a Cord and who wrote action-packed crime novels. But James Leasor had also published a nonfiction book about a strange real-life crime that interested him, and out of politeness I read it. It was called *Who Killed Sir Harry Oakes?*

Immediately I was hooked. The book examined the unsolved mystery of how and why one of the richest men in the world was brutally murdered in Nassau in the Bahamas. The corpse was partially burned and scattered with feathers. This murder was committed in 1943 while the Duke of Windsor was governor of the Bahamas, and the investigation that followed did nothing but muddy the waters. Suspicions and allegations were flung in all directions in the full glare of the spotlight of the world's press attention. It became a cause célèbre, knocking war news off the front pages.

It was an extraordinary story, far more bizarre than any fictional tale, and it remained with me for years to come, hovering in the shadows at the back of my mind. To my surprise, when the time came to start plotting a new book last year, the questions about this mysterious unsolved murder elbowed their way to the forefront of my mind and I became excited at the prospect of examining it further. I wanted to dig deeper, compelled to find out more about what had precipitated the tragic event on the paradise island of New Providence.

During the course of months of research I discovered that it was a fascinating whirlwind of mystery and murder. Of glamour and beauty. Of secrets and corruption. And above all else, it was a story of greed and gold. I was powerless to resist it. I hope you will be too.

Around these events I wove a passionate love story, and I must point out that, although a number of the events and people whose names you will recognize are included in my story, it is a work of fiction.

DISCUSSION QUESTIONS

1. At the beginning of the novel, Dodie and Ella are presented as complete opposites in character and social status. However, when Flynn is arrested, Ella says to Dodie, "Perhaps I see something in you that's in myself." By the end, Ella seems to have embraced this wildness inside her, but Dodie is the one who saves them from the boat. What do you think this says about Ella's true character? Could she ever be as strong and "wild" as Dodie?

2. The island presents a unique setting for the story, as it is both a paradise and an escape, and also in the midst of political turmoil. How do you think this environment impacts the behavior of the characters?

3. Across the island, there is tension between the white people and the black Bahamians. Emerald is an interesting character as she has her foot in both camps: She works for Ella and Reggie and seems to have a respectful bond with them, but she is also a Bahamian. When push comes to shove, where do you think Emerald's loyalties truly lie?

4. Dodie considers herself "unclean" because of her past, but Flynn physically and emotionally cleanses her after she is attacked. Ella on the other hand likes that Dan can see her dirty and muddy after their picnic together. In what ways are these relationships similar and in what ways are they different?

5. In Ella's final scene, she is at the breakfast table with Reggie. Do you think she will ever be happy in her marriage, after her affair with Dan? Do you think she feels any regret for her unfaithfulness?

6. Throughout the novel, Tilly presents herself as a self-assured, good friend to Ella. But when Dodie speaks with her, she catches a "glimpse of a loneliness that tugged at something in her." Do you

pity Tilly at all? What about Hector, who goes to extreme lengths to protect his wife?

7. At various points throughout the novel, love is equated with gold, and Hector says that "Everything is always about money . . . or love." We are led to believe throughout the novel that the killings are all in pursuit of gold, but that doesn't turn out to be the case. Do you think the decisions people make out of financial greed are similar to the irrational decisions people make when they are in love?

8. Throughout the novel, Reggie is described as a good and decent man. At the end of the novel, he seems clearly to have forgiven Ella for her infidelity, even though they don't speak of it. Do you respect Reggie for this decision? Why or why not?

9. About Morrell, Dodie thinks, "She didn't want his shoes or clothes or his filthy gold coins, all inanimate leavings, all objects that meant nothing and possessed no trace of him." Later, Ella says that "As the wife of an MP she would be able to do something positive, influence his policies. She could leave a dent in the world that said *Ella Sanford was here*." Do you think that Dodie and Ella have made their mark on the world by the end of the novel?

10. When we first see Ella, she is helping Reggie with his cuff links while wearing an evening gown, seemingly happy with her lifestyle. By the end of the novel, she has thrown herself into an affair with Dan, and has become more outspoken in her search for the truth about what happened to Morrell. Is there one particular moment, or character, in the story who you think first sparks this change in Ella?

11. Dodie calls Morrell a "killer" in front of Flynn, which naturally would extend to Flynn as well. Yet, Dodie has relatively few reservations about Flynn and dives headfirst into a relationship with him. Why do you think she is so trusting of this man?

12. What purpose does Mama Keel's character serve in the story? What does her presence say about the island, its culture, and its people?

13. Why do you think Dodie and Ella are so protective of each other? Is it simply because they are both women, or are there other reasons that they form such a strong bond?